The Girl Who Played with Fate

Daniel Basil Lyle

LylePublishing

Sulphur, Oklahoma

The Girl Who Played with Fate

ISBN 978-0-9794101-5-4

Published by LylePublishing
505 W. 12th Street, Sulphur, OK 73086
(www.LylePublishing.com)

Printed by CreateSpace, an Amazon.com company. Available from Amazon.com and other retail outlets. The book is also available as an ebook on Kindle and other devices.

LCED10292018

DISCLAIMER and FORWARD

Although this book draws heavily from experiences of the author, all characters are fictitious. Any resemblance to real persons, living or dead, is purely coincidental. Although a real Hildegard von Bingen existed in history, the character depicted in this book is different, loosely based upon her known history, as are other related figures from the 12th Century. This entire book is a sequel to *"The Girl with the Turtle Tattoo,"* beginning where that first book left off.

Chapter 1

<u>RESET</u>

Do you sometimes wish

That you could start over again?

When an ugly mess is too much to bear

Devastating consequences already happened

Considered decisions you thought were right

Learning too late they were bad mistakes

Choosing the wrong exit off the highway

Taking the road to doom instead of home

"Zigging" when you should have "zagged"

A tortured web of irrevocable decisions

From which you'd like, somehow, to flee

Impossible now to disentangle or disavow...

If only you could take that hard-won insight

Back again, to the very beginning!

The Luminary Chronicles, 1:57-69

Sally knew that Earth was doomed.

And it was her fault.

Yes, she was fully aware that the sun would run out of nuclear fuel and become a "red giant" in about five billion years. It would swell so large that all its planets would be incinerated. Long before that happened, however, the Earth's surface would get so hot that life would cease. Earth would be uninhabitable in a mere 2.8 billion years.

Yet Sally also knew, without a doubt, that the sun would *not* destroy Earth billions of years in the future—but in just a few short decades.

She knew this because she had already witnessed a *massive solar super-storm* unexpectedly erupting on the sun's surface. Gigantic waves of nuclear plasma were thrown into space. Those vast maelstroms stripped the Earth of its atmosphere, melted the continents, and boiled the oceans.

And the extinction of humanity happened due to events *she* helped set in motion.

Fortunately, an alien race sympathetic to her plight had sent her back in time.

They'd given her a second chance.

She was determined to find a way to save Earth—even if it meant sacrificing her own life.

And now she was back to the beginning of her insane previous adventure, starting all over again...

"Is that a turtle?" he asked, peering down at her exposed left wrist.

Sally absently glanced at the man. Usually the unending progression of customers didn't make an impression on her. There were so many customers in a day that they blurred together in her mind. But he sounded...jarringly familiar. Yet she didn't recognize him. Who was he?

"Excuse me?"

She was expertly sliding items through the scanner. It was just another uneventful day working at her service job, dutifully checking out groceries and goods at the local Megamart. She kept herself mentally engaged by refining formulae in her mind that underpinned computer algorithmic evolutionary subsets. So it took a moment for her to shift her mental perspective and realize what was happening.

A chill ran down her spine.

Her attention riveted on the customer.

A strange thought jumped into her head.

It's all happening again!

Startled, she rapidly blinked her eyes, focusing on the man standing there leaning on the check-writing stand. He had longish hair held together with a rubber band in a pigtail at the back of his head. He had a neatly trimmed full beard. He wore a vest and dress pants. He looked like a professor. Certainly he was an Elite Citizen. Only

Elite men were allowed to grow beards. She automatically knew to give him extra politeness and deference.

"Your tattoo..." he patiently repeated. "Is it a turtle or maybe a little green sea serpent?"

"Yes, it's a baby turtle," she gulped, trying to get her swirling thoughts under control.

The bearded customer continued to admire her tattoo as he leaned there on the check-writing shelf, just a couple feet away from her. To Sally he looked to be hanging on too tightly. He looked unsteady, as if he were dizzy.

If I've never seen this man before, how are things "repeating"?

It didn't make any sense. But her feeling of *déjà vu* grew stronger. In addition she felt dizzy. Was she somehow linked to this person? But how could that be? Though greatly confused she resolutely kept at her job, sliding the items through the scanner. She kept her feet planted firmly beneath her.

It wouldn't do for her to topple over from vertigo. At the least, she'd draw unwanted attention from her supervisors, who were ever vigilant for the State.

"It's really cute," he grinned at her. He stood poised to hand her another of his carrying-bags.

It's nice of him to bring his own bags instead of cluttering up the environment with our disposable plastic ones—she thought to herself, trying to ignore the spinning merry-go-round that was now whirling around her.

Then everything snapped back to normal.

Relieved, she handed the filled bag to him as he gave her an empty one. He set the filled bag in his shopping cart.

"Thanks," Sally replied, continuing to expertly slip his items past the scanner and then into his second waiting bag. "I treated myself to it the other day."

She felt peculiar warmth on her wrist.

Am I imagining things, or is my turtle tattoo glowing?

The little tattoo indeed gleamed with bright greens, rich browns, and deep blacks. It looked alive, ready to jump off of her wrist.

And now it was so bright it was actually *shining!*

She ground her teeth, fighting against the pain.

It's got to be my imagination. The stress of my illegal religious activities must be getting to me. I've got to keep it together.

"It's real? I thought it might be one of those stick-on ones," the man calmly continued. "I've never seen a real tattoo that bright!"

Something huge was trying to take over her mind.

The store blurred around her and she raggedly sucked in her breath. She vividly saw HER DEAD MOTHER OPENING HER EYES AND SMILING... A GIANT LONG-NECKED DINOSAUR STOMPING TOWARD HER... DEEP CRATERS SEEN FROM THE SURFACE OF THE MOON, and A BURNING EARTH PITIFULLY GLOWING IN EMPTY OUTER SPACE...

What's happening to me?

The bizarre images seemed to compete with each other. It was like looking into a gypsy's crystal ball, where vivid scenes appear only to be instantly erased or eclipsed by others.

Am I going crazy?—she grimaced, closing her eyes tightly.

Opening her eyes she felt the colliding PAST successfully merge into her new PRESENT.

And she started to *remember*...

It felt like her brain was sliced in two—then mushed back together. Sorting out two different conflicting memory-sets was more than a gigantic puzzle, it was a titanic battle!

"It's brand new, that's why," she managed to raggedly continue as the mental battle raged in her brain. "That's when the colors are brightest. It will fade with time."

Even now the glow seemed to be fading.

She paused in her work behind the counter to push the sleeve of her ocean-blue sweater upward on her left arm to just below her shoulder. Other wonderful creatures were briefly revealed: a creepy *black spider* with white specks, a flapping red and yellow *parrot*, and a coiled blue *snake* embracing a blooming pink rose.

She wore a red blouse under her blue sweater, plus a work apron that went down to her knees. A name badge on her chest proclaimed her name in big black letters: "*SALLY*."

"Wow, those are also amazing!" he said, sounding truly impressed. "I wish I could do stuff like that. You're very clever to make your body into a work of art. I'm very impressed."

"I'm sure you're also quite talented..."

"Nope," he sighed, "I'm a total failure. But I still try to do my duty. You just gotta 'keep on keeping on,' right? We can't all be wildly successful."

"Success is how you define it, isn't it?"

He paused. She could see the "gears" turning in his mind. Before, it was just polite small talk as he got his groceries checked out. But now she'd caught his attention.

Why on earth did she say that? She was no slacker herself in terms of professional success, but it sounded like she was questioning him. An Elite could have her fired from her service job, barred from professional circles, and even thrown in jail. Come to think of it, had she seen him at one of her yearly professional conferences?

"And how do *you* define success?" he asked.

"It depends," she cautiously replied.

"On what?"

"Well, first of all, the particular endeavor I'm pursuing."

"Like your tattoos?"

"I have others..."

"I'd like to see them."

"Sorry, they're private," she snapped at him. The hidden tattoos were on her back and thighs. If anyone saw them, she'd definitely be jailed as a subversive. They were both religious and macabre. They invisibly proclaimed her carefully hidden rebellious nature. But she'd better soften her harsh reply to the Elite: "I guess that's kind of sad, huh? The best of our lives are often unseen, unappreciated by others, don't you think?"

It wasn't just her bizarre tattoos—it was also her Animist religious beliefs and actions. If they were revealed she'd be put on trial for illegal, subversive activities. Or she'd be summarily sent to the rare earth mines in Africa. That was a horror she hoped to never experience!

"That's an astute observation."

What? The Elite is answering me back.

She felt embolden by his encouraging tone, so rare in her society.

"I suppose. Does that surprise you?"

"Frankly, yes it does. I apologize. I guess I thought you were just a pretty face doing a routine job. Obviously you're much more."

"Thanks."

Momentarily flustered, she ducked her head. She wasn't used to Elites paying her attention. Within her scientific discipline she was well regarded. But it was an esoteric field not known to most of high society. And her assigned service job was beneath contempt to most Elites.

"I appreciate Art in every form. I don't ink my own body, too afraid of needles. But I admire it in others."

She nodded shyly as she pushed the sleeve of her sweater back down, placing the last of his items into his opened bag.

She knew she was attractive. At five-foot-five-inches, lean and trim, in her early twenties, she easily fit into her slim blue jeans. She often got admiring looks and compliments. Usually she just let them slide past. Talking with this middle-aged, longish-haired, bearded Elite, however...she felt that things were uniquely different.

That feeling of close familiarity returned. And with it came a sense of almost panicked *urgency.* Just who was this guy?

Then, suddenly, it all came *flooding* back to her! Despite his regal appearance, he wasn't an Elite at all. He wasn't from this society a t all. In fact, he wasn't even from this world!

"Something wrong?" he frowned at her, seemingly concerned by her wide-eyed stare.

"N-no," she stammered, "just getting your total calculated. The register's hanging up. We've been having some trouble with the computer program. It'll just take a minute," she lamely finished.

She knew him.

He wasn't an Elite.

He was her boyfriend from an alternate Dimension!

His name was *Dave*—Dr. David King. Yes, he was indeed a failed scientist, a societal nobody on his world. But just minutes before he'd been unknowingly transported here from his world!

Presently on *his* Earth he was an instructor at a small college. And after work, to the side of his regular teaching job, he puttered away in his small house's garage in Edmond, Oklahoma. Using ancient surplus research equipment he was trying to make discredited *cold fusion* work. And he was on the verge of perfecting the most *dangerous* invention in the history of mankind!

Overnight he would go from being a "nobody" to the most famous scientist on Earth...and *then* the most *in*famous!

This was a man with the power to *destroy the human species*, in both of the human Dimensions.

But no more! It didn't have to be that way. With her future knowledge she could alter the timeline!

I can do it. I can save the world. It'll only take a few small changes. It'll be so easy...

But new Visions suddenly appeared around her, even more terrifying than the previous ones: A DYING NUN LOOKING UP IN AWE AT THE STARS, A TOWERING RED OBELISK, A HANDSOME YOUNG MAN NAILED TO A CROSS, A DESOLATE LANDSCAPE DOTTED WITH ACTIVE VOLCANOES, A CHILD-LIKE BLOND-HAIRED ROBOT CRYING, A SPACESHIP ON A TAIL OF FIRE RISING UP INTO THE SKY, and A MASSIVE LAYERED ROCK HURTLING THOUGH SPACE STRAIGHT AT THE HEART OF A DEFENSELESS PLANET!

She closed her eyes, blocking off the horrific apparitions. She had no doubt what she'd just witnessed. They weren't hallucinations. What she'd just seen was a *deadly new future*...also caused by her!

And opening her eyes she saw her *partner in crime* standing casually right there beside her.

Maybe...not so easy—she mentally groaned.

Was she a pawn of fate? Or could she *change herself* to alter the new future she'd just glimpsed?

The path forward was not clear. The end result was unknown. But the warning was unmistakable: *screw up and everything you hold dear will be destroyed!*

"So how much do I owe you?"

Startled, she focused again on the bearded man. He didn't recognize her. He didn't know what had happened in the past/future to them! He didn't remember any of it. She was the only one who knew the future.

The weight of her task was crushingly heavy, unless—could she possibly reenlist Dave in her task?

Just a few small alterations...I've got to believe it's possible. I can cheat fate, especially if I have his help! We did it before. We can do it again!

It was time for her life to radically change. But it would take courage. It would require determination and sacrifice. She'd have to upend everything that went before. She'd have to throw her newly resurrected comfortable life into turmoil. But she didn't want this heavy burden. She wanted to run home and hide in her studio apartment, wrapping herself up in her all-engrossing mathematical work. She wanted to forget the terrifying glimpses into a new, terrible future. Tears began welling up in her eyes. She had to get a grip on herself!

Every word I say, every action I take from now on, is critical.

"Your total is nineteen, even," she managed to whisper.

He reached into his back pocket, pulled out his billfold, and handed her a folded bill.

She looked at it carefully then resolutely handed it back to him.

"Something wrong?" he asked, puzzled.

"No, nothing's wrong," she answered, forcing a smile onto trembling lips, trying not to sob. "This is my treat."

"What?"

It was her first major alteration to the timeline. It would change everything. Simply not accepting that "funny money" from the other Dimension would cut short a whole chain of catastrophic events!

She reached down into the personal space beneath the counter, lifted out her brown leather shoulder bag, undid its large metal latch, and pulled out a wallet. Then she resolutely placed the proper amount of "real" money in the till.

Closing the register, she took off her apron and signaled to the floor manager that she was shutting down her lane.

"But...what are you...?" Dave began, confused but obviously intrigued.

For a moment she stared at him.

"Do you like my eyes?" she now playfully grinned at him.

She knew he did. She knew he was intrigued by her presence. She knew that he'd yet again be her happy boyfriend.

"They're green like your turtle tattoo...quite beautiful. In fact, I think that *you* are beautiful!"

She reflexively snorted at his lame "come-on"—but then hurriedly stated: "Well then, if that's so—there's only one thing to do."

"Oh, what's that?"

"I'm going to church with you and your Mom. And afterward we're going to have a long talk."

"About what?" he grinned back at her.

"About everything!"

Sally saw his friendly grin slowly fade, replaced by a puzzled squint.

He moved back a step.

"I...don't get your meaning," he replied, seemingly perplexed by this unexpected turn of events. Sally could see that his playful remarks had evoked a response he'd obviously not expected. So he was "set back on his heels"! Well, that was understandable.

Sally knew that from his perspective she was a girl he'd never seen before. And here she was making bizarre declarations concerning both him and his Mom.

"Please don't be scared, Dave," she tried to reassure him as she finished hastily shutting down her register. "I know this is strange to you. I'm only just wrapping my own mind around what's happening. I'm asking you to trust me. I'll explain it all—after we get out of this store and back to your world."

His puzzled squint turned into a deep frown.

"*My* world? What? And just how do you know my name, or that I'm taking my mom to church this morning?"

She ignored his flustered questions. The two of them had to get out of the store. The ephemeral transit portal to his world might evaporate at any moment!

"Oh—I almost forgot...wait here a moment, Dave," she ordered, suddenly remembering critical items she needed. "There's a couple things I've got to get. It'll just take me a second!" she said as she suddenly *ran* back into the shopping area of the large store, her dangling shoulder bag bouncing against her leg.

This time around I'm going to do it right!

"What the bloody hell?" Dave whispered to himself, left standing there with his cart.

This was indeed a confusing turn of events. His mind always worked slowly, particularly when confronted with unexpected events. As a strong introvert he needed time to process what was happening.

Ok, then. What's the deal here? Let's figure this out...

Well, the checkout girl was, indeed, rather cute, just like her little turtle tattoo. And apparently she had some sort of romantic interest in him. But...he was significantly older than she. Surely she must have a similarly tattooed, big-muscled, young, hormone-dripping biker boyfriend. Likely said boyfriend would happily come and beat Dave to a pulp for just flirting with his girlfriend at the checkout stand. So her aggressive interest in him just didn't feel right.

But then again, in addition to being pretty, the young lady sounded uncommonly intelligent. Perhaps she was attracted to his (obviously) distinguished, professor-like, brainy handsomeness?

Despite his self-flattering fantasy his common sense kicked in.

Uhm, I'm actually not all that handsome...but maybe I'm somewhat smart concerning exotic aspects of nuclear interactions?

True enough, but she didn't know any of that.

Oh, I think I know what's really going on here—he sighed to himself in resignation.

There was a much more plausible explanation here than "love at first sight."

He pulled out his cellphone from his top pocket and dialed up his mother. Normally he hated carrying the cellphone around with him, too accessible to everyone else's beck and call. But he was glad he'd brought it along with him today.

"Hello?" a quavering voice answered.

"Hi, Mom," he began...

"Is there a problem, Davey? You hardly ever call me before you arrive!"

"No, Mom," he replied, trying to move to the side with his cart so as to not block the exit lane from departing people. "Say, do you happen to know a young lady here in Sulphur named Sally? In fact, did you *tell her* to talk to me when I did my grocery run here at...?"

"What?"

"I'm at the grocery store and..."

"Did you pick up my Ensure?"

"Yes, Mom, I did. I've got it right here."

"Is it Butter Pecan?"

Oh, hell. It was strawberry. He could never remember the right stuff that she liked.

"Uh...well..."

"It's no problem, Davey," her tinny voice came out of the small speaker. "I love those milkshake things. But I know it's *you* that likes the strawberry ones, so that's fine. Today I might even eat one of your cupcakes! And who's this Sally person?"

"Uhm, you mean you didn't...? Well, she's just a girl I met that..."

"You've got a girlfriend? Praise the Lord! You say she's a local girl?"

"I guess. She says she knows you and..."

"Oh, I know lots of people. I can't keep them all straight. Maybe she's one of the teenagers from church. I just call them 'sweetie' and..."

"Ok, Mom," he said, cutting her off. If he let her prattle on he'd be standing there for an hour. "I gotta go. See you in a few minutes."

"But..."

He stuck the cellphone back in his shirt pocket.

Ok, then. If he wasn't actively "set up" by his Mom—who nagged him every time she could about not being married making her more grandkids—then maybe the girl *was* from church. She certainly wasn't a teenager. He'd never seen her there, at least not that he recalled. But then again he didn't pay much attention to the membership. Reluctantly taking his sick Mother to church on Sunday mornings, he just wanted to get in and out as quick as possible.

Impatiently, he looked around for the girl. Where was she? In fact, even if she was from church *why* in the world would she mess around with *him?*

As his confused mind methodically sorted things out cold reality set in.

There's no logical reason why a cute young girl would be romantically interested in a middle aged dude like me—no matter how distinguished.

Chillingly, he realized he didn't know a thing about this girl. In fact, the more he thought about it, it sounded like she had an *agenda*—and he was part of it!

Maybe I should just get the hell out of here...

Yep, just grab his bags and get away from that weird girl. She seemed giddy, even deranged. Her "thoughtfulness" could just as easily be cunning predation. She could be dangerous! There he was just making polite conversation commenting on her cute little tattoo and she "came on" to him like he was a long-lost family member. This had all the earmarks of a *scam* in the making.

"Hmmm—I think I better dodge this bullet," he reasonably concluded, lifting his bags out of the cart.

There was *no* way he was going to have anything more to do with that spooky girl. And he certainly wasn't going to expose his sick, dying Mother to a possible psychopath or even con artist.

After all, "caution is the better part of valor." He'd always been a cautious person and wasn't about to stop now. Definitely, his best course was to just walk away.

As he left the store he breathed a sigh of relief. No telling what might have happened if he'd "hooked up" with that weird chick.

Sally glanced over the tops of the racks and displays not far from the checkout stations. She saw that Dave was quickly walking away.

Oh no! He's not staying like I ordered him. I can't let him leave without me! How will I cross over into his Dimension if he gets away?—the panicked thoughts zipped through her head as she grabbed up a box of blond L'Orelay Women's Hair Coloring plus five pill cartons—all that was on the shelf—of *Optimmune* "vitamins"...hastily stuffing them all into her shoulder bag.

"Wait!" she called out to Dave as she raced after him.

"Just a minute there, Miss Smith," a uniformed Keeper ordered, standing near the door. He was a young oriental gentleman that Sally knew casually from her years working in the store. She vaguely recalled that his first name was Paul.

"No time, Paul!" Sally gasped, seeing Dave exiting the main doors.

"Did you pay for those?" he demanded, moving into her path, even drawing out his gun!

What's he doing? Why's he pulling his gun on me? Whatever, I can't let him stop me!

In a near-panic she swung her heavy shoulder bag with its jagged metal latch *hard* into the left side of his face.

He dropped like a stone, groaning, spasmodically clutching at the slashed left side of his face with both hands, his gun falling from his hands...

—which Sally managed to snatch in midair. She stuffed it into her already-bulging shoulder bag as she breathlessly caught up with Dave.

She plastered herself against his back in a tight bear hug!

Wow. This is just like before, but at the end. Some things are definitely repeating themselves! I hope...

"What?" he gasped, thrown off balance, "What are you...?"

In the soft morning light of the parking lot outside the entrance to the store, they both *dropped* together two feet downward, tumbling onto hard pavement!

"Jesus Christ..." Dave groaned from beneath her. She was staring straight down into his face. "Are you crazy? You knocked me over! What the hell is wrong with you? Get off of me!"

She hastily rolled to the side, popping up to her feet. Then with her free hand she yanked him up, all the while looking around for pursuing store guards...

There were none.

"We *did* it!" she grinned, looking around excitedly.

A few customers approaching the store looked startled, as if she and Dave had just appeared out of thin air.

"*Wahoo!*" Sally shouted out in glee, dancing around with her arms held high. "We're here—and the bubs...I mean *cars*...are all so *pretty!*"

Her long red hair flew around her head as she spun about. Her blue sleeves flopped up to her shoulders, revealing the tattoos on her left arm. She knew she probably looked to Dave like a *maniac* bizarrely rejoicing at the styles and colors of cars in an ordinary parking lot.

But she couldn't help it. It was just so incredible to be back in Dave's parallel Dimension!

Here there were no haughty Elites, no brutal Keepers, no all-controlling Empire, no rigid social castes, no beaten-down slaves, and no limits.

Here she could be anything she wanted.

"Look, lady," he cautioned her, still tightly clutching his two bags of grocery store purchases as he slowly backed away from her, "I don't know what your game is and I don't care. Please leave me alone—or I'll call the police!"

She stopped dead in her dance, lowered her arms, and looked at him soberly.

"Oh...of course," she apologized. "I'm so sorry, Dave. It's been a shock to me as well. I'm still trying to adjust. It must be a hundred times as weird for you without your future memories in place. I can at least remember what happened to us before when..."

"*Look*, Lady!" he shouted at her, having now arrived at his big yellow Chevy Cavalier. He was hastily unlocking the door. "I've never seen you before in my life! If you think that something happened between us in the past then you've just got the wrong person. And if you're trying to pull a 'con' job on me then I'm not interested. I have neither the time nor money to indulge your evil expectations. So please go away."

"But Dave, you have to..." she pleaded with him, advancing a step.

"I meant what I said!" he angrily barked at her. "Back off and leave me and my mother alone! If you try to approach me or my Mom I swear I'll call the police. Look, I don't want to cause you any trouble. Just stop whatever you're trying to pull here—and we'll each go our separate ways. No harm done. Ok?"

She blinked in confusion as he tossed his grocery bags into the backseat of the car. How could everything be going so wrong? He was supposed to be madly in love with her. In the prior timeline it was *him* pursuing *her!*

By the Great Spirit, he was supposed to be her devoted boyfriend!

Alright then, I can still get things back on track...

She resolutely stepped up close to him. Simultaneously she reached into her shoulder bag and pulled out the store guard's *black gun.*

Jamming her shoulder bag forward she prevented the car door from closing. Dave was trapped between the door and the car, half-in and half-out.

"What are you...?" Dave gasped.

—as with her index finger she flicked over the top safety cap, glancing down to make sure that the gun was set at its lowest, one-star setting.

Shoving the gun's barrel solidly into his side, she coldly ordered him: "I'm coming with you, Dave. Either you do *exactly* what I say or I'm going to *shoot* you!"

Dave looked down in disbelief at the black gun—then incongruously broke out laughing.

"Hah, hah, hah!" he snickered, grinning at her. "We're at a major shopping center with surveillance cameras watching us from every angle in front of dozens of witnesses. And you're going to *shoot* me? Lady, if you're serious and not just joking around—then you need some heavy-duty psychological therapy! Now get out of my personal space and let me get on my..."

She pulled the trigger.

CRACKLING ELECTRICITY danced over his entire body as he convulsed in-place before crumpling into the driver's seat, slumped across the steering wheel.

The car's horn began to blare.

"Well, you're right, Dave. We certainly don't need to draw more attention," she grated as she roughly pushed him away from the steering wheel, stopping the horn.

His face banged into the edge of the car's dashboard.

She saw blood dribbling from his mashed nose. Served him right! How dare Dave yell at her?

"You were *never* that nice to me," she angrily asserted as—with a glance around to make sure others weren't watching—she roughly shoved the unconscious Dave completely over into the passenger seat. She tossed her own shoulder bag into the backseat along with his grocery bags. Then she slid into the driver's seat.

"Now, let's see if I can remember how to drive one of these complex 'cars'..." she scowled. She quickly searched Dave's pants pockets for a keyring, found it, and then tried various keys in the ignition.

"Ah, here we go," she grinned as the motor caught and the car *lurched* forward before stalling out.

Luckily there wasn't another car parked in front of them.

"What?" she blinked rapidly, confused. This hadn't happened with her duplicate mother's car in Dave's Dimension, nor the black van holding the cold-fusion Device. She'd quickly learned how to drive both. "Hmmm...maybe there's a car manual...perhaps in the glove compartment? Ah...here it is," she muttered to herself as she pulled it out across the top of Dave's slumped body.

"What a stupid idea!" she snorted, reading the section on how to work the "clutch." "Why would you put such a clunky thing in your vehicle when you could have automatic transmission?" she accused the unconscious Dave. "But, I guess I have to remember this is a backward, primitive society. People here are free to do all sorts of stupid things," she resolutely reminded herself as she restarted the car. In a series of jerky movements she managed to work the clutch well enough to exit the parking lot onto the nearby street.

"Now where was it we turned to get to Dave's Mom's house before...oh, yes, there it is..."

It was at the stop light at 12th street, turning south in the direction of the National Park.

"Wow, this sure brings back memories, doesn't it, Dave?" she smirked at his crumpled body. "It was *you* holding a gun on *me!* You were kidnapping *me* against *my* will! So I guess turnabout is fair play, huh?"

He didn't answer.

"Oh, don't worry," she snorted, concentrating on her erratic driving. "At least no one's trying to destroy our car with laser beams, like before. You should be happy I'm being so nice to you!"

He just moaned.

Well, she'd win him over later. For now, she was in control. And it felt good.

Dave woke up with his entire body aching. He felt like he'd just finished running a marathon.

He was on the living room couch in his mother's house. Blearily he looked over at a wall covered with old familiar pictures of his

Mother, his deceased Dad, his sister Catherine and himself. They all seemed so innocent.

And just why was he sleeping on the couch?

Groggily, he heard his Mother sitting at the dining room table happily chatting away with someone.

Christot!—he yelped to himself, *it's that psycho-chick!*

He leapt up off the couch, staggered getting his balance, and then *ran* into the dining room...

—where *the girl with the turtle tattoo* was sitting on his right at the table. His Mom was behind the table facing him. Then that checkout clerk...*Sally*...fixed him with an icy stare and made a small back-and-forth "no" gesture with her head. Then she raised the *gun* hidden in her left pants pocket up a notch up so that Dave could see its handle!

On the floor at her feet was her leather shoulder bag, bulging from poking-up pill containers.

"Oh, there you are you sleepyhead," Jean King widely grinned, her smile seeming to split her bald head horizontally. She looked like a carved Halloween pumpkin as she sat there bundled up in an old, orange robe.

"I've been having such a *nice* talk with your girlfriend, Linda," Jean happily continued. "Where on earth did you find her? And wasn't it lucky she was there when you fell asleep at the wheel? Oh, you might have had a serious accident if she hadn't reached over and steered the car over to the curb. I hope your nose doesn't hurt too much. We cleaned up most of the clotted blood. And I do *so* appreciate you coming on Sunday mornings from Edmond to take me to church, Davey. But it is *such* a long drive for you to come to Sulphur on that crowded freeway—and you have to get up so early. I don't want you falling asleep and..."

He struggled to contain his rage. He couldn't just pounce on the girl. She had a gun. With a twitch of her finger she could kill either him or his mother!

"It was a...*freak*...occurrence, Mom," he interrupted her monologue, "One that I doubt will *ever* happen again!" he angrily glowered at the red-haired, green-eyed, tattooed girl. "And didn't I see a different name on your name tag at the grocery store, 'Linda'?"

She grinned back in a friendly way at him, though her cold green eyes told a different story.

Dave was flustered, confused, and terrified. The girl with the turtle tattoo was clearly deranged. And not only was she kidnapping *him*, she was now in his mom's house! He'd best not make any sudden moves against her least she lash out at his mother.

"I...uhm...borrowed that from a friend. I forgot to bring my real name tag from home. And yes, your—accident—will never happen again if you are *very* careful!" the red-haired girl glared back at him. She pointedly fingered the just-visible black handle of the gun protruding from her pocket.

"Oh, I'm just so glad that you are alright, Davey," his Mom sighed, apparently trying to resolve the tension. "Come sit with us. We have time before we have to leave to go to church. We're not going to make Bible Class, of course, since you were late in arriving. That's alright, though, I'm just happy you got here ok. But the Worship Service doesn't start for forty-five minutes yet. We've plenty of time to visit before I need to put my 'hair' on. Now come and tell me what happened out on the road as you were driving over from the grocery store with Linda."

"Yes, Dave," Sally now beamed at him, prettily dimpling her cheeks, "*Do* sit and tell us *exactly* what happened."

"And please have one of the nice cupcakes you brought with you from the store," Jean cheerfully added. "Linda and I have already eaten several of them. I put the rest in the refrigerator. But we left one out for you."

Dave winced as he painful lowered himself into a chair next to the girl. His face hurt. His nose felt like it was broken. And his entire body ached from when that crazy girl tackled him to the pavement. In addition, he was trembling uncontrollably. He felt like he'd been electrocuted! And—did that crazy bitch *shoot* him? Yes, she shot him with that gun as he tried to get away from her. It must be a stun-gun! But he'd never heard of one that powerful looking like a regular gun.

His mind was racing in circles.

And cheerfully sitting between him and "Linda" on the other side of the table, oblivious to the danger of the situation, was his innocent mother.

He knew he had to be *very* careful in what he did and said.

"Well," Dave said between clenched teeth while reaching shakily for the lone cupcake, "as to my 'falling asleep'...it felt more like being hit with a *Taser!*"

"Oh my!" his Mom gasped with deep concern. "Do you think you were having a heart attack? Should we take you to the emergency room? You know that our small hospital here in Sulphur has a very nice emergency room. Of course it takes forever for someone to see you there unless you're an actual real emergency—like you're dying with all your blood pouring out or something. But it's such a blessing to have that level of care so close by ..."

"—I'm fine, Mom," he cut her off, now holding the chocolate cupcake tensely in one hand. He could barely grip it as his fingers were trembling so hard. "I guess it's better than being shot with a bullet," he snidely finished, glaring at Sally.

"What is a 'Taser'?" Sally politely asked.

"It's a gun that fires out *barbs* that stick into you while attached to wires that carry a large *voltage* into your body!" Dave shouted, half-rising angrily from his chair.

His mother recoiled, clearly shocked at his outburst.

"Well that sounds just brutal," Sally calmly replied, "cluck-clucking" with her tongue, her eyes narrowing as she also half-rose from her chair. "But it sounds quite *ineffective* having to rely on *darts* sticking into the targeted person!" she pointedly concluded.

"It's...very painful," he growled at her, "whether it's from darts or from some sort of *super* stun-gun held right against a person by a sadistic maniac!"

"Well, painful or not," she "huffed" back, "why not just *distally* induce such a charge?"

"Because that *isn't* possible!" he shouted again at her, seething.

Jean King seemed bemused by all the yelling, uncertain of how to respond.

"Says you..." Sally mildly replied.

"—who happens to be a *Ph.D. Physicist!*" he angrily glowered at her. "There are things that the Laws of Nature allow and things that *aren't* allowed!"

"Like what?" Sally grinned, apparently enjoying the verbal dueling.

"Oh, you young people," Jean laughed, firmly interrupting them, apparently thinking they were just joking with each other. "Now just sit back down, the both of you. It's so fascinating to have two prestigious scientists sitting at my living room table—my own brilliant son and his girlfriend mathematician, arguing over *science*. My, but you are both so *passionate* about it!"

"What?" Dave sputtered, reluctantly lowering himself back down into his chair, still clutching the uneaten cupcake. "She's not a scientist. She's just a checkout clerk at the grocery store. And besides that, she's also a..."

"A *what*, Dave?" Sally scowled at him as she also slowly sank back down into her seat. Her left hand stayed near her pants pocket as if she were an old-west gunslinger.

He struggled to say something biting but not incendiary.

"...a...very...*enigmatic*...person," he weakly concluded, slumping fully back into his seat, grimacing as his body was wracked with another round of intense pinpricks.

"—and so smart!" his mother cheerfully added. "Why, Davey, she even gave me some brand new vitamins. I've already taken one and I feel like a million dollars on top of my new vigor. I feel like I could even walk to church today instead of your having to drive me there then push me inside on my squeaky wheelchair."

Oh no! That crazy girl gave Jean some pills? It must be drugs. Is that her game? Is she trying to addict some new users? Is she a drug dealer?

"Just what did you give to my mother?" Dave coldly questioned Sally/Linda. "Don't you think she's suffered enough?"

"Oh, Davey, don't be upset," Jean tried to soothe him. "I know you don't think much of my vitamin-mineral-herbal supplements, but these new ones..."

"—are just the same as your other ones, *placebos*," he snapped back at her. "If they make you *think* that you're better, then fine. But they *won't* cure your cancer, Mom. And if this girl is trying to sell you a miracle cure, then she's just *lying* to you."

Jean frowned back at him.

"Is that any way to talk to your girlfriend?"

"She's not my girlfriend! She's just...someone that I'm...taking to church for..."

His voice trailed off.

Sally/Linda glared at him.

"Oh, Davey," Jean sternly admonished him. "Linda hasn't tried to sell me a thing. We were just visiting. I was explaining why I look like a plucked chicken—my hair fallen out from all that terrible chemotherapy—and she mentioned some new vitamins she'd purchased for herself. So she kindly volunteered to give me some. She gave them to me for free. *Look!*"

She dramatically held up a plastic freezer bag containing maybe thirty large white pills. Jean loved to seal everything in plastic zip-lock bags. In fact, filled or loose baggies were all over the kitchen—lying on the table, the kitchen countertops, and shelves.

"Mom, those pills could be anything," Dave protested, reaching for the plastic bag, which Jean promptly yanked back away from him.

"No, Davey," she firmly stated, for the first time *frowning* at him. "You insisted I had to go through that awful course of chemo and radiation therapy. I did those hideous treatments to please you. But doing so was contingent on my continuing taking my vitamins, minerals, and herbal supplements. Linda says that these new 'Optimmune' natural supplements are very helpful to debilitated people. So I am going to take them just as she directed me. I'm taking one pill per day for a month, whether you like it or not. So *there!*"

"Just be sure to keep taking them for a month," Linda gently cautioned her. "Otherwise the positive effects may not continue."

"Oh, I will," Jean firmly nodded. "It is so nice of you to be concerned for me, dear. Maybe that attitude could rub off on my grouchy son, huh?"

So that was it. This was just too much. The psycho-pill-pusher was trying to put a wedge between him and his own mother. This girl was a *monster!* He had to find some way to stop her.

But first he had to reassure his mother.

"I *am* concerned about you," Dave protested while considering if he should launch himself across the table at that dangerous girl. But his every little movement was still very painful and difficult. He decided against a frontal attack. He'd have to outwit her. "I just want you to have therapy that actually works. I know it's hard, but the doctors are doing what's best. They've slowed the growth of your tumors, Mom, and..."

"—slowed but not stopped," she shrugged. Her emaciated shoulders poked up pitifully through her robe. "Those terrible drugs and radiation only make me feel miserable. What's really kept me going—dealing with this stupid metastasized breast cancer thing—is my supplements. They do more from me than all the poisons that the doctors make me take. In fact, I've been meaning to talk to you about that, Davey. And since you get so angry at me when I tell you things you don't like, it's very nice to have Linda here as my backup. You can't go totally off the deep end while your girlfriend is sitting right here at the table with us. I don't like it when you yell at me."

"I *don't* yell at you!" he yelled at her.

Sally shook her head, sadly.

"And I'm *not* her boyfriend!" he angrily concluded.

Then, reacting to his mother's shocked expression at his outburst he turned his glare on a still-disapproving Linda. Defensively he tried to explain his harsh words..."She's—just someone that was interested in...uhm...in going to church! Yes, that's it. The preacher always says...that we should just jump on people out of the blue and tell them what Jesus has done for us, right? And then we're supposed to drag them to hear his boring sermons at church, correct? Well...ok...so I happened to mention Jesus to her at the grocery store—and she just wanted to come with us. That's it! She's just a lady from the grocery store who I'm taking with us to church."

His Mom still had a puzzled look on her face. He knew he needed to add more to his story. It would hurt to say it, but it was necessary.

"And then I dozed off and maybe got banged a bit when we stopped at the curb. So I'm a bit confused. Sorry if I've been short-tempered. I apologize...really....I do. And...ah hell...what's it matter, anyway? What does anything matter? Take the damn 'vitamins' if you want."

He knew it was a lame explanation. But it was the best he could come up with. He hoped that his mother's strong faith would embrace the religious result without complaint, enough not to set-off the insane woman sitting two feet from her with a hidden gun.

"Oh, that's much better," Jean now smiled warmly, reaching over and patting Sally's small right hand with her own desiccated, spotted one. "Of course I accept your apology, Davey. Linda said she was your girlfriend, so I figured you had a long-time sweetheart who you were finally revealing to me—to make me happy in my final days. Then we got chatting about me and my ailments. Learning she was a fellow fan of dietary supplements, I immediately liked her. But I'm also happy to find out that some of the teachings from the Word of God rubbed off on you, Davey—even though you hardly go to church anymore except to escort me there on Sunday mornings," she mock-pouted.

This "Linda" was clever—he had to give her that. But, again, what was her real game? Surely he and his mom were small-potatoes, hardly worth the effort she was making to kidnap and lie to them. She was tricking them into doing what...to take vitamins and go to church?

This still didn't make any sense.

What did she really want?

"Yes, yes," he insincerely agreed. It was time to change the topic, to let Linda make some mistake. "But what's this 'disturbing' news you wanted to talk to me about? Maybe we should ask Linda to *step outside* if it's something that just you and I should speak about privately?" he pointedly insisted.

"Oh, Davey," Jean laughed, reaching over with a thin hand to touch him lightly on his arm. "I've already told her all about it. She agrees with me—thinks it's a good idea. In fact, that's the main reason why she gave me the new vitamins."

Oh, great. How long had he been knocked out? Had they pulled out ancient albums and gone through his naked baby pictures?

"Mom, how is it that a *stranger* hears confidential news before I do? No offense...*Linda!*" he glared at the hidden-gun-toting, pleasantly smiling girl beside him.

Wow. She sure had green eyes. They looked very *scary*—like those of a cat waiting to pounce on a mouse.

"Oh, I've already told it to my doctor, the gay young man that does my nails at the salon, the other ladies at my weekly in-house woman's bible study, the postman, the delivery boy, the plumber, our next-door neighbors, Catherine, and..."

"—apparently everybody except me!" Dave exclaimed, dropping the now-forgotten cupcake in frustration as he grabbed his beard and mustache with both his hands. "Do I have to *tear my hair out* to get you to pay attention to me?" he exclaimed, now moving both his hands up to the longish brown hair on the top of his head.

"Oh, Davey," she laughed at him. "Don't be so melodramatic. You know full well that's the opposite of what normally happens. *I'm* the one that *you* hardly ever pay attention to. And, yes, I know I must get pretty boring to listen to as I ramble on and on. But you 'tune me out' whenever I try to say *anything!* So...maybe," she choked out as she started to tear-up, "I won't tell you this at all. So *there!*"

She abruptly stood up, grabbed the bag of white pills, and marched off into the kitchen.

The girl continued to look at him sadly, again shaking her head.

Damn girl! What did she know? She hadn't lived her whole life with that irritating woman!

Then Jean returned to the dining room table with her arms crossed. She was clearly struggling to get herself back under control. She had plastered a cheery smile upon her grotesquely-bald head.

"I'm going to go and put on my hair," she formally stated, starting for the hallway leading to her bedroom and private bathroom. "Linda, the spare bathroom is in the garage if you need to comb your own hair for church. Davey can show you where it is."

Then Jean was gone, leaving Dave staring angrily at the girl—who just as defiantly stared back at him.

Dave resolutely sat where he was, glowering at 'Linda', the last cupcake sitting on the table between them.

"You going to eat that?" she asked.

"No," he replied peevishly.

"Good," she snapped snidely, reaching with her right hand for it...

—a tempting target for Dave to reach out and grab?

—as, simultaneously, she moved her left hand above the tabletop, still firmly grasping the big black gun. It was pointed directly at him.

"And if you want to get 'conked'-out again," she coldly warned him around a mouthful of the iced cupcake, "then just make a wrong move."

God, I should have eaten that cupcake—he groaned to himself as his stomach growled.

"I need to pee," he quietly said, squirming uncomfortably in his chair. "Whatever you did to me with your Taser-gun loosened up every valve in my body!"

"Then march ahead, Sonny-boy," she ordered him, standing up from the table while munching down the last of the cupcake, still pointing the gun straight at him.

"It's out in the garage."

"I know—so no funny moves."

Damn girl! She seemed to know his every thought. Was she a mind-reader?

But he knew she'd make a mistake. Then he'd get the upper hand, call the police, and be rid of her once and for all.

Damn psycho-bitch!

As Dave turned to walk to the garage door, Sally grabbed one of the freezer bags to take with her.

Dave pushed open the door to the garage with Sally kept right behind him. She had the barrel of the gun jammed firmly into his back.

Jean's old grey sedan filled up most of the garage.

"Does your Mom's car have automatic transmission?" she absently asked. "And why on earth do you have a 'clutch' in your car? That thing is a *pain!*"

He swung open the door of the small bathroom at the back of the garage, stepping inside.

"Yes my Mom's car *does* have automatic transmission—and it just so happens that I *like* using a clutch," he growled at her. "So are you going to watch me use my 'stick drive' or can I close the door?"

"If you're thinking about the cellphone in your shirt pocket to call your Keepers with, I already took that out when you were unconscious," she mildly replied, taking hold of the edge of the door and closing it behind him. "I'm keeping it safe with me, right here in my jeans pocket."

She heard him angrily "snapping" the inner lock closed. Obviously he had hoped to use the "bathroom" ruse to call his "police." Hah! She'd shown *him* who was the smartest.

"Well...do you need to use the bathroom after me?" he resignedly said from inside as she heard him "tinkling" into the toilet. "Don't you need to...comb your hair...or something?"

Obviously he was emphasizing Jean's comment, hoping that might also give him the chance to escape.

"While you were sleeping off your 'Taser' experience, your Mother kindly allowed me to use her private bathroom," Sally replied. She unscrewed the top from one of the pill containers then shook its contents into the plastic freezer bag she'd brought from the kitchen. "And my fluffy mop of red hair is just fine as it is for your little church thing. I hear from Jean the church service is casual dress."

"Not true! It's Sunday-morning *wear-a-suit* time."

"Whatever..."

The folded insert inside the box fell out and she snatched it up...

—just as a bunch of the pills fell "clattering" onto the floor.

"Oh, nuts!" she said, trying to balance all her things at once while trying not to drop the gun as well.

She snatched the wayward pills up, popping them back into the plastic baggie.

On a notepad taken from her shoulder bag, she scribbled a hasty note and inserted it into the transparent plastic bag along with the pills.

"*What* do you want from us?" Dave exclaimed in exasperation from behind the closed door as Sally heard the toilet flushing.

"Just what I said," she angrily replied. In emphasis she *banged* once with her clenched right fist on a panel of the closed door. "We're going to have a good long talk—after I take care of your mother. It's a long story. I know you'll need time to properly digest everything. Plus you're going to have a lot of questions about..."

"Don't you touch my Mother!" he retorted through the door.

"I'm not going to hurt her," she angrily replied. "Don't be stupid, Dave. I like her. I always have liked her. In fact, that's why I'm here with you in this house instead of immediately lecturing your tied-up ass in an abandoned toilet off at the back of the Park."

Ah, that brought back bad memories of the prior timeline...except it was *she* tied up while *he* tried to convince her that he was from another Dimension.

He was silent, apparently perplexed by her reply.

"So why not lecture me now?"

"As I said," she slowly repeated, speaking as if to a dense little child, "I like your mother. It's almost time for her to go do her Church thing. She's not getting there unless you take her. So we're together taking her to Church before we have our extended talk. Understand?"

"Don't you hurt my Mom!"

"Did you not hear a word I just said?"

"You're kidnapping both me and her!"

She sighed deeply, just about at her wits end with this pig-headed version of Dave.

"I wish her only the best, even though you seem determined to make her life miserable."

"Stop talking like you know me," he snapped back through the closed door. "You don't know anything about me. Nobody does!"

"I wish," she muttered in frustration.

"Let me wash my hands in peace."

He was proving to be even more of a pain in this timeline than he'd been in the last. Yes, it'd been only toward the last that she began to understand his good qualities. Unfortunately it seemed to take an awful long time for those "good" qualities to emerge. And it was even worse now. He was severely handicapped in the social graces. No wonder he had such a hard time getting support for his research efforts.

But, back to her mission...*small* changes with *big* effects!

As she heard the water in the sink running, she quickly tiptoed out of the garage. She slid the plastic bag with the pills under the small pile of other plastic baggies on the tabletop. Then she hurried back to stand outside the still-closed bathroom door in the garage.

She'd made sure to close the door from the garage to the house so that their words wouldn't be heard by Jean inside.

He was sure taking a long time washing his hands. Was he preparing to try something? Was he going to burst out waving a plunger at her?

"I'm trying to help your mother to..." Sally began.

"—by giving her poison?" Dave interrupted from inside the bathroom. She heard water splashing. Apparently he was taking the chance to wash his bloodied face. Maybe he wasn't stalling after all.

"It's not poison! If you'd just listen..."

"What kind of con are you pulling?" he continued to interrogate her from the safety of the bathroom. "Are you trying to rob us? If so, I don't have any money. I'm just a low-level college instructor who barely makes enough to pay my utilities month-to-month. I can't even afford to do decent high-school-level experiments."

She realized that this Dave just wasn't the same person she'd dealt with in the previous timeline. He was subtly different. He was angrier and louder. His bitterness seemed deeper. She realized she was fast losing him. She had to find a way to regain his trust.

"I know all about you, Dave," she said, trying to speak reasonably and calmly. "You're a lot more important than you apparently think. In fact, I know all about the so-called 'cold-fusion' research that you're doing in your garage at your house. I'm actually trying to help you as well as your mother. I know what's happening now doesn't make any sense to you—but once we have a chance to talk at length then..."

"What—you're going to get me funding? *That's* what I need! And how do you know about my pitiful attempts at research, anyway? I've only published a few trivial papers recently in obscure journals that..."

"It's *dangerous*, Dave," she interrupted him through the door, ignoring his question. "In fact, your jerry-rigged garage setup is building up to an explosion! When you get home you've got to immediately shut down your present run—then *keep* it off, forever."

"That's absolutely ridiculous," he coldly replied as he unlocked the door from within, starting to step back out into the garage.

She backed up a couple steps in case he lunged at her.

"Is that why you're after me?" he continued from inside the bathroom. "Are you a *terrorist* thinking I can provide you with a new weapon? My little experiment at its most potent could only warm a cup of tea, if that. You've made a big mistake targeting me. I've got nothing of value to you."

"I know a lot more about your experiment than you think," she angrily retorted. "What you're doing in your garage is far more dangerous than you can imagine. It may even kill you! Besides, it's a waste of your time. It'll never work as you intend."

"It'll work!"

"No, it won't," she asserted as she stood there with her gun pointed at the still-closed door. "Why not just live your life and have some fun? Find a cute young student of yours to date. There are lots of them who'd swoon over a relatively young, single 'professor' being interested in them. For God's sake go get married like everybody else, Dave. Make babies!"

He stepped out of the bathroom obviously relieved to have his filled bladder emptied, blood washed off his face, and beard combed out. But he looked even angrier than before.

"I'm much too selfish to become some woman's ready sperm-donor and in-house baby-sitter," he snorted at her in defiance. "And as to my present experiment, your accusations are totally unfounded. I'm not doing anything that's dangerous. But even if it never works, I'm still having fun trying. I don't know how you know what I'm doing and I don't care. You're wasting your time on me. I repeat— you've targeted the wrong person!"

"Not in the slightest," she glared at him. "Both you and your experiment are *very* dangerous. You've *got* to listen to me, Dave."

"While you're pointing at gun at me?"

"Would you listen otherwise?"

"Why not try me? Just put the gun away and then we can talk as long as you wish."

It was a tempting offer, but she knew he wasn't serious. He'd bolt the first chance he had, carrying his mother away on his shoulder if he had to.

"You look like a smart girl. Why don't you use your God-damned brains?" he persisted.

Ah...that tore it. She was a smart "girl", was she?

"Don't do anything stupid, Dave."

She kept the gun leveled on him, her eyes grimly narrowed, fixing him with a smoldering glare. She backed up beside the old car, allowing him to step in front of her toward the closed door leading back into the house.

He paused, turned to face her, and made an obvious effort to sound "reasonable."

"Look, 'Linda'—if that is your name—if you'll just leave us alone then we'll call it even. Ok? My offer I made previously still stands. Maybe you read somewhere about my research and you sincerely think that it's some sort of a new superweapon, but it isn't! I'm puttering-about with something nobody in the scientific world takes seriously. I repeat: you're *wasting* your time on me! You should take your fancy stun-gun and go terrorize someone else who's worth your effort."

She grimaced at him, her gun still firmly held in her hand, pointed directly at him.

"I *said* I'm going to church with you and your Mom—and that's just what's going to happen!" she coldly instructed him. "And I'll be right next to you all the time, my gun held in my pocket—aimed through the fabric straight at you. So *don't* try any funny business! Do you understand me?"

He growled under his breath.

"What kind of a stupid criminal are you anyway?" he indignantly replied, turning to face the door into the house. "Can't you just go rob a bank? What is it you have against me and my relatives?"

"We have a *history!*"

"—one of which I am totally *unaware!*" he shot back at her.

"One which you will *learn*, whether you want to or not," she angrily insisted. "Open the door and walk into the house."

He did as ordered, with her right behind him. Inside she saw Jean in the kitchen finishing drinking a glass of water.

She was wearing a long-haired, glossy-*red* wig.

It clashed garishly with her plain brown pants suit.

"How do I look?" Jean giggled, putting down the empty glass and preening for them.

Dave was aghast, speechless.

"You look spectacular!" Sally complimented her.

"Oh, I just put this on to be silly," Jean grinned, pulling off the garish wig and swapping it for a short-haired grey one.

Now she looked proper and respectful.

"You're certainly cheerful enough today," Sally heard Dave sigh as he stood there beside her, apparently resigned to his fate. Her gun was concealed back inside her pocket, but ready to pull out if needed.

"So, are we ready to go?" Jean beamed at them happily. "You know—now that I've my appetite back—I think that was the most delicious glass of water I've ever drunk. I took another of Linda's wonderful vitamins. The first one made me feel so perky I figured I'd *really* be ready for church with a second one."

"You took a *second* one?" Sally frowned, now not as flippant as she'd been before with Dave. "But...I said you were to take just *one* per day."

"It's only a super-vitamin pill, right?" Jean grinned, smacking her lips.

"Yes..."

"Then let's go get preached at," Dave sighed beside Sally. "I'll get your wheelchair, Mom," he said as he started to open the closet to get out the collapsible contraption...

"Don't need it!" Jean happily answered while doing a little "jig" across the room.

"Mom!" Dave cautioned her. "Please be careful. You *can't* be feeling *that* good."

"But I am!" His mother happily exclaimed, clapping her hands together loudly. "Let's go learn more about God. *Yay!* Hallelujah, *praise* the Lord!"

Sally saw Dave's mouth drop open at his mother's antics. He was speechless. Sally knew Dave was in shock at the present course of events. But Sally also knew that unless she made the right moves, world-destroying catastrophes loomed.

Yet Sally was particularly concerned about Jean.

Sally's initial euphoria at escaping the terrible events of the prior timeline was fading. In the rush of the moment she'd been careless, even reckless. She should have cautioned Jean more strongly against taking more than one pill per day. But everything had happened too fast. In her eagerness to help Jean Sally neglected to make the main point strongly enough. But perhaps it would still be alright?

Just because this sequence of events was a "do-over" didn't mean that the same terrible things had to happen as previously, did it?

Sally had a deep foreboding.

If the present events were any predictor, things certainly weren't going to be the same as before. They were going to be far *worse!*

She had to be more cautious, make better decisions.

After all, the fate of not just Dave's Mother but all humanity hung in the balance.

"Well, I'm sure it's going to be a great Church service," Sally lamely agreed.

As they walked out of the front door to Dave's yellow Cavalier, Sally desperately hung onto her dwindling hope. The present escalating disaster could be fixed. She was certain that with her detailed future knowledge she could "right the ship." Despite bland church sermons, the *Day of Judgment* really was fast descending upon humanity! But she also knew a hidden truth. To prevent Divine Judgment from destroying Earth all she had to do was convince Dave to give up his crazy experiments.

That shouldn't be so hard. After all, he wasn't having any success. He was ready to give up. If he had a suitable *diversion* then he'd forget all about his failed experiments.

So...if it must be...then she *would* become his enticing, sexy, diversionary girlfriend. But that assumed the stubborn fool would let her.

Yet the idea of seducing him now filled her with *disgust*. Whereas in the previous timeline she'd learned to tolerate then genuinely love Dave, now that seemed impossible. He was definitely a different person than before, angrier and darker. And like many strongly introverted mathematicians she'd never been good at pretense, subterfuge, or diplomacy. Her engrained introversion was clashing ever more strongly with his! To get into Dave's pants after what had happened between them to-date, she'd have to be the greatest actress of all time.

Yes, Earth was definitely doomed.

Chapter 2

CROSSROADS

If only the path were straight

No ups, downs, twists, or turns

Always a single way forward

No confusion or ambiguity

What's right is invariably right

And what's wrong is always wrong

And what's in the middle doesn't exist...

There's never a doubt which way to go

Unless, of course, you're forced to awaken

And open your eyes to scrambled life.

The Luminary Chronicles, 2:24-28

Pastor Cliff Davis stood at the entrance to the church building greeting the late arrivals. It was almost time for the worship service to start.

"Ah, my favorite 'delinquent' member," he heartily greeted Dave, sticking out a chubby hand.

Cliff was the preacher for the small congregation. He'd been there for a long time. He was white-haired, paunchy, and relentlessly jolly.

"Hi Cliff," Dave sighed, reluctantly taking the offered hand.

"And who is *this* young lady, your *sister?*" Cliff jovially greeted Jean, who looked much better with her neatly-coiffed grey wig in place on her head. Her pale skin was livened up with carefully-applied makeup. She wore a distinguished-looking, brown, women's pant suit. She carried a pearl-inset white purse.

Jean laughed at the compliment.

"Oh, Cliff, you teaser," she smiled at him. "I want you to meet a *true* young lady with a mind to know more about Jesus—*Linda Powers*, Dave's new girlfriend."

"I'm *not* her boyfriend," Dave muttered.

"Oh, Dave is such a kidder," Sally grinned at Cliff as she pressed her gun held under her blue sweater even more-firmly into the small of Dave's back. "It's nice to meet you, Pastor."

"Oh, we're not formal here. Please call me 'Cliff.'"

"Yes, Cliff. It's a pleasure to visit your congregation. I'm looking forward to your service."

"So you are interested in learning more about Jesus?" Cliff tentatively asked.

"You bet," she grinned widely. "And I'd sure like to have that small pocket New Testament you've got in your inside suit pocket if you don't mind? I really want to read more of his teachings."

"Uh...what?" he said, puzzled.

"I, uhm, saw the bulge there?" she grinned up at him, realizing she'd revealed her alternate timeline knowledge.

"Oh, right."

She used her big, twinkling green eyes to beguile him, forcing him to reach into his suit and hesitantly pull out the small black book and hand it to her.

She gratefully took it with her right hand, slipping it inside her pants pocket.

"And I assume your business card is also inside, just in case I have any questions that I need to phone you on?" she sweetly asked.

"Actually that's true, also," he nodded. "But how did you know?"

"I shall read it with pleasure," she grinned widely at him, avoiding his question.

She was taming him, making him play into her objectives. It wasn't hard. All she had to do was let the previous timeline's words spill from her mouth.

They were engrained into her memory. Appropriate or not, they were on the tip of her tongue.

But she knew the preacher wouldn't be suspicious of anyone sincerely seeking to "know Jesus better."

"You haven't read the New Testament before?" he frowned, again perplexed.

That's ok. She just had to convince him.

"Oh, I mean, *Dave* is going to explain it to me," she hastily explained. "He's *such* a good friend to me. And yes, of course, I've read *some* of it—but not in detail. In particular, I'm fascinated by what the Bible teaches of the Judgment Day. Do you know about this topic?"

Now she was getting somewhere. She'd use this event not just to help Jean, but to learn more about the immediate looming catastrophe.

"Well, of course. Jesus taught his disciples about his 'second coming' when all mankind would stand before God and be judged! It's a very profound topic. And if you'd like, I'd be happy to set up a home study with both you and..."

"I sure hope you touch on that in your sermon today. Gotta get to our seats," she cheerfully nodded to him as she shoved Dave onward.

He grimaced as the gun's nozzle poked hard into his back.

"Act normal," she harshly whispered into his ear.

"I am!" he angrily whispered back. "I'm always groaning in this place."

"Why?" she asked, truly curious as to his dislike for the church services.

"It's boring, unproductive, and hypocritical," he whispered as he followed behind his Mom to her favorite pew.

"I think maybe it's *you* that is boring and unproductive and hypercritical," she insisted, keeping the gun hard-pressed into his side as he slid into the pew beside his mother.

"You're a real *pain*, do you know that?" he whispered at her.

"At least I don't disrespect the Great Spirit," she spat at him, immediately regretting her assertion.

Indeed, it was the *Wrath of God* that would destroy the entire human race just a few decades in the future. Perhaps she *did* hate the God of Dave's world. But then this Christian "God" seemed so loving and kind. How could such a wonderful, supportive Deity—willing even to give up His own Son as the Ultimate Sacrifice for mankind— so cavalierly destroy His own Creation? Perhaps her request to Cliff would give her some clues. Maybe he'd insert key points concerning Armageddon into his sermon. She only vaguely recalled the sermon from the first time she'd heard it, disoriented by being "rescued" from her Dimension by Dave. This time she'd listen more closely.

Still keeping her gun firmly jammed into Dave's side, she prepared her mind to focus on everything that happened in the church service.

She had to figure out what the real "God" was up to. In her world, religion was actively suppressed, particularly for Citizens. Despite that—driven by an intense curiosity to understand the nature of personal reality—she covertly attended a small sect of Animists, who recognized spiritual essence in everything. They saw a "soul" not just in humans but even in animals, objects, and the forces of nature. Together, this Essence revealed aspects of the Great Spirit. The Spirit bespoke that which lay beyond our limited physical senses. But that primitive concept was different from there being a thoughtful, plotting Supreme Intelligence, as taught by the banned Great Religions. Sally's encounter with the topic of "Jesus"—through her prior future association with Dave and his Mother—had been her first direct exposure to the concept of an intelligent, personally-engaged "God." But how could such a "loving" God then cavalierly destroy His own creation? What was this Supreme Entity—whether Jehovah or Great Spirit—really thinking?

Yes, upon the Mind of God rested the fate of the world. Sally knew, without a doubt, that *God's Terrible Judgment* awaited mankind not just spiritually, or philosophically, but in actuality—and in just a few decades.

And if subjected to that intense scrutiny, mankind would miserably *fail*.

It wasn't some vague religious doctrine. It was a sobering reality.

"Welcome, everyone, to today's service," one of the Elders began from the pulpit.

Dave tried to come up with a plan.

As the Elder droned on with announcements, Dave glowered at his "girlfriend" jammed up against his side. He was not impressed by Sally's seemingly intense interest in the service. Her actions were beyond bizarre. In fact, they were inexplicable. She kidnapped him then tricked his Mother into taking her pills. What was she up to? And what was her sudden interest in Judgment Day all about? That damn Turtle Tattoo on the inside wrist of her left hand summed her up quite well: cute and pretty on the outside while paper-thin with blood on the inside.

Dave knew he had to contact the police—or this crazy girl with her electrical gun was going to do something terrible.

And then she did exactly that...

"Sing!" Sally ordered him, jamming the gun into his ribs, as the song leader began leading the first song. She lustily joined in, singing a strong but sweet alto.

The song was *The Old Rugged Cross*.

To Dave it was just a glorification of the brutal execution of a pesky trouble-maker centuries ago. He didn't see it as a "praise" song to a Savior, but a sad excuse for people putting-up with senseless suffering!

"I don't sing," Dave petulantly replied, pursing his lips tightly together.

It wasn't just a matter of talent, but of being ornery. When he finally walked away from his mother's denomination, he'd left it all behind—including singing Gospel songs.

"Oh, Davey," Jean leaned into him from the other side, whispering into his ear. "Linda's right. You have a beautiful tenor voice. Come on, for me. Let's sing together!"

He was hemmed in from both sides, "check-mated" as it were.

Growling under his breath, Dave took a song book from the rack on the back of the pew in front of him, turned to the indicated page, and began quietly singing tenor or bass, whichever contributed best to the overall harmony.

Reluctantly, he realized that he enjoyed singing with the two women—harmonizing with the thoughtful, smooth alto from Sally on his right and the happy, thin soprano of his Mom on his left. It had been a long time since he'd sung the Old Gospel Hymns...not having done such since he'd been a child.

Perhaps the service wouldn't be so boring after all?

He was wrong.

The sermon by Cliff was about Jesus' last days—his agonized final words to his closest disciples at the Last Supper, his betrayal in the Garden of Gethsemane, his trial, his brutal whipping, and finally his hideous death upon the Cross of Calvary. At the last, Dave seemed to "tack-on" a short supposedly uplifting message of the risen Christ who would return to usher in a new age for the righteous. Apparently that was in response to Linda's urging to explain the horrors of the "End-of-Days."

But Dave had heard it all before thousands of times, said in the same way, arriving at the same doctrinal conclusions. It was as deadly boring to him as ever.

Sally, on the other hand, seemed fascinated.

As the preacher again, in protracted conclusion, solemnly intoned the last words of Jesus upon the cross..."*Forgive them Father—they know not what they do!*" and "*It is finished...*" Dave noted tears trickling down Sally's cheeks.

She didn't even brush them away.

Dave was perplexed. Either she was a great actress, or was genuinely touched by the story of Jesus.

But if that was true, why did she still hold that gun under her sweater firmly jammed into his ribs?

He decided that she was a great, but totally insane, actress.

Afterward, the three of them sat at a table at the local Italian restaurant, "Alessio's."

It was one of his mother's favorite sit-down eateries, specializing in Italian food. She loved pasta dishes, at least before the chemotherapy destroyed her appetite. Today, though, she seemed unexpectedly hungry.

Dave was amazed at her appetite.

"Oh, it's all so delicious," Jean enthused, savoring her Fettuccine Alfredo. The dish consisted of hot noodles covered with butter sauce and Parmesan cheese. Over the top was a sprinkling of golden shrimp. She was busily stuffing it all into her mouth.

*At least it's stopped her from rambling on and on—*Dave thought to himself.

"It is very nice of you to take us out to lunch," Sally smiled at Dave, nibbling on a forkful of Lasagna. She held the fork in her right hand. Her left hand was still concealed beneath her sweater.

"Did I have a choice?" he asked, wary of the concealed gun she was still aiming at him.

"Oh, you're so funny," she smiled brightly at him.

Actually, her bright green eyes were quite spectacular. If she weren't such a psycho-bitch, Dave might even be attracted to her.

As it was, she was very, very *dangerous*.

"So what now?" Dave asked, nervously pushing Ravioli around on his plate.

"Now we start talking," Sally grimly replied, her smile gone. She put down her fork and leaned toward him, her eyes narrowing.

"About what?" Dave grimaced.

"About your...God," she flatly stated.

"Oh, Linda," Jean grinned widely, between mouthfuls of noodles. "I'm so pleased you are genuinely interested in moving closer to God. My boy here has done the exact opposite. I don't know why. I don't think he knows either. But maybe with your help he could..."

"—*yes*, Mrs. King," Sally smiled at her, "I'm happy to help him. But *I* need help first. I have questions. Can *you* help *me* with answers to my questions?"

Jean also put down her fork. Unlike Sally's and Dave's plates, nothing much was left on hers. She'd voraciously cleaned it all up.

"Oh, dear," Jean shrugged, "I'm sure Brother Davis would do a much better job of answering your questions, Linda. But I'm happy to try. I have been around for a while, don't you know. I've seen many things in my lifetime. So I guess I can give you practical answers. Cliff, however, knows the theology much better."

"What I'm mostly interested in, Mrs. King," Sally sincerely stated, "is practical answers. So I'm very pleased to have you here instead of your Pastor. I can talk to him later if I need further explanations. For now I'm very interested in your take on these matters."

"Oh, Dear, just call me Jean, won't you?"

"If you wish...Jean," Sally replied shyly.

They stopped talking as the waitress came by to clear away their plates. Jean had insisted on ordering deserts up-front, saying that she was famished. So their deserts were now being brought out.

"*This* is what you wanted to talk to me about?" Dave warily asked. "You went to all this trouble just to talk to me about God? What's *wrong* with you, anyhow?"

She was a criminal. She was some sort of terrorist. And now she was a religious fanatic? *Really?*

She was crazy!

"Well, Davey," his mother "huffed" at him, "What is more important than God? I, for one, am delighted that this smart young lady went to all the trouble to talk with you at the grocery store and then come with us to church. It's been a real pleasure having her along with us. You should apologize to her."

Dave sighed deeply before reluctantly relenting.

"Alright," he spoke through clenched teeth. "I'm sorry I sounded—ungrateful...*Linda*."

"That's better," Jean primly nodded. "Oh, aren't they just marvelous!" she exclaimed as the deserts arrived.

Jean had ordered a *Tiramisu*. It was a stacked dessert with layers of pudding, crumbs, and cinnamon—with shaved chocolate liberally sprinkled on top. Jean attacked it with her spoon, luxuriating in its exquisite sweetness.

"It's good to see you with your appetite back," Dave sincerely stated, picking at his own cherry cheesecake.

Sally had several types of Cannoli on her desert plate, each with a different filling. She, like Jean, had an expression of shear ecstasy on her face as she ate crispy exteriors filled with creamy cheese or chocolate or jams.

"It's so nice to see that both of you are enjoying your desserts," Dave said sarcastically, shaking his head in bewilderment.

"We've nothing like this in my world," Sally sighed contentedly, licking her lips after scarfing the last fragment of the final Cannoli.

"What?" Jean said, tilting her head to the side in puzzlement.

"Oh, I mean...in the places I usually go. You know, like 'McDonna's' and 'Hamburger Queen' and 'Piece-of-stuff.' And the other fast-food places," she finished weakly, her voice trailing off.

"Right," Dave frowned. What was wrong with this chick? It was like she was from another world, trying to remember unfamiliar fast-food signs.

"Anyway, it's all great," Sally lamely concluded.

"Well...even the cheese cake is good, I've got to admit," Dave reluctantly agreed.

At least there wasn't any other excuse left for his mother to be there. He could drop her off at home and then be alone with this "Linda." Then he'd have a much better chance to catch the attention of the police or just run away!

"And since your tummy is happy, Davey—this sounds like a good time to tell you why *I* feel so good," Jean firmly stated, gently placing the spoon she'd been eating with to the side of her empty dessert plate.

"You said you felt much better after taking that pill that Linda gave to you. I'm sure it's just a placebo effect, but I'm happy for you."

"Yes I did," she nodded firmly, the gray wig shifting slightly out of position on her skull, giving her an odd lopsided look. "And yes, it did give me a boost. But the main reason I'm able to eat solid food—not just that syrupy Ensure diet—is that I *stopped* my chemotherapy and radiation treatments! I'm *not* going back to those oncologists in Ada. They meant well but they're torturers. My doctor here will do just fine to give me whatever medication I really need. I refuse to spend my last few months or weeks miserable. There, I've said it."

Dave stared at her for a moment in disbelief, hoping he'd misheard her.

"But...Mom...that means...?"

"It means I'm going to pass onward maybe a few days or weeks sooner than otherwise," she shrugged. "So what? Catherine will confirm everything to you. Your sister was with me at my last visit in Ada a week ago when my oncologist said that there was nothing more they could do for me except slow the growth of the tumors. The cancer is throughout my body now—in my liver, my intestines, my spinal cord, and even in my brain. With continued poisoning of my body, making me sick as a dog, I'll be gone in a few months. Getting off those miserable treatments I'll still be gone in a few months—but enjoying my life nearly up to the last. So I choose to eat Fettuccine. What's so wrong with that?"

Dave momentarily forgot that a crazy girl was sitting next to him with a gun aimed at his ribs.

"But...Mom..." he choked on his words. "I don't want you to..."

"Oh, the good Lord has given to each of us only this one single moment that we occupy right now," she cheerfully declared. "Our future is in His Hands. If we trust in God, then the little pains that happen to us will just fade away into insignificance."

Dave saw Linda looking askance at Jean, seemingly deeply pondering her words.

"But Mrs. King," Sally hesitantly asked, "Why does your loving, concerned God let us suffer in this way at all? Does He get pleasure from our pain?"

Jean shrugged.

"The ways of God are beyond the minds of us little humans," Jean gravely replied. "But we do know that '*all things work together for good to those who love God and are called according to His purpose.*'"

"Is that in the New Testament?" Sally politely asked.

"Yes, it is in Romans 8:28," Jean proudly answered. "It's one of the few verses in the Bible that I have memorized."

"But what does it mean?" Sally eagerly asked. "Will God take away the pain from his own special people?"

"Not likely..." Dave grunted.

"Davey!" Jean admonished him. "Even *Jesus* had to suffer terrible things—God's own Son! If our Christ had to go through agony to be pleasing to His Father, how can I or anyone else expect to have things easy in this life? It's not when everything is going along sweet and smooth that our Faith is proven. It's when we have to *suffer* for the Lord."

"Mom, those are just *excuses*," Dave angrily asserted, feeing his face turning red from barely-contained rage. "That skewed logic is for when your God *fails* to answer your prayers."

Jean frowned, looking down at the tabletop.

"Why would people have to make excuses?" Sally innocently asked, now looking at Dave. "Oh...I see," she nodded, seemingly realizing what Dave was saying. "You think that God does not exist at all—that He's just a figment of people's minds to make death easier to confront?"

"Yes!" Dave emphatically barked. "That's exactly right! Now you understand the truth about 'religion', Linda. God will *not* save us. We have to save *ourselves!* That is why I've insisted that my Mother take advantage of the very best medical treatment that science has discovered to-date."

Jean shrugged.

Dave knew he had already argued with her over this point numbers of times in the past, to no avail. He wasn't about to change her mind. Her conclusion weren't based on science. They were based on a "Faith" that went beyond science, or so she claimed.

"But *you* are wrong about one thing," Sally soberly said in a low voice, her wide green eyes peering earnestly into Dave's.

"What's that?" he suspiciously asked.

"I don't know if what you call 'God' cares about us, watches over us, or is happy when we suffer," she whispered. "But He *does* exist. I know that for a fact."

"Oh, you are such a dear," Jean said, leaning over to kiss Sally lightly on her cheek.

"And just how do you know that?" Dave contemptuously replied.

"I've seen his handiwork," She choked, as if remembering some awful spectacle.

Dave narrowed his eyes, seeing real fear in her eyes. Again he was puzzled as to whether she was a great actress or a totally psychotic nut-case!

He was getting a cold feeling in his gut. There wasn't a choice to make. She was *both!* She was the worst possible criminal-terrorist: a *religious fanatic!* No wonder she was so intense. Religious nut-cases don't respond to logic. They've "short-circuited" the real world. They "know" their path and take it regardless of whether it makes sense or not, or what terrible things they're "called" to do, or how many innocent people they have to "sacrifice."

"What sort of 'handiwork'?" he suspiciously asked.

"Oh...just the *End of the World*—Judgment Day!" she gulped, her eyes stretched wide.

"You're...saying...you've 'seen' for yourself—the end of the world?" Dave very slowly and precisely asked.

Her wide green eyes narrowed.

"I saw the entire planet Earth engulfed in flames, everything dying, the atmosphere stripped away, the oceans boiling—leaving behind a burnt-out husk," she whispered, barely audible to Dave.

"Oh Linda, that's awful!" Jean gasped. "You had a Vision? Did God reveal this to you?"

"Yes," Sally slowly nodded "It's an awful 'vision', wouldn't you say? But—according to part of what the Preacher said this morning—the Bible confirms this, right?   He said that Jesus predicted this would happen. And didn't the Pastor also say that this is in the last book of the Bible, a book called 'Revelation'?"

"Yes, it is," Jean stated, smiling. "But the message doesn't stop there. Evil gets destroyed, yes—but the righteous are *saved*. Jesus takes his people to a New Earth. God *rewards* his true believers even as the evil people are thrown down to hell!"

"That's just a myth," Dave frowned.

"No, Davey," Jean insisted. "And it's not only at the End Times. It's also when things are at their worst. I know from my own experience—just as Linda knows from hers. When I feel the most despondent I feel His Presence. He lifts me up. He gives me strength. I realize that everything we experience and have to suffer through is just a test. The pain isn't there to drive us down but to *grow* our spirits!"

"Oh, Mom," Dave sighed, shaking his head in sad denial.

"If God were to hand us 'heaven on earth'—where we were just mindless robots with no free will, all of us bowing in unison—where's the joy in that?" Jean continued, undaunted. "The real joy in life comes from *struggle* against fierce opponents. And what is there any stronger or more awful than death? All earthly things pass away, don't they? Our spiritual courage isn't certified in peace, but forged in war. *Significance* isn't from merely existing, but in *rising above* the inevitable negatives. *This* is the message of Jesus!"

"That's very beautiful," Sally quietly added.

"Thank you, Linda," Jean nodded in gratitude for her support. "And that's what Faith is—finding Meaning where others lose hope. And that's what I choose to do, Davey. I choose Faith and Hope over fear and death. Is that so wrong?"

Dave sat wordless, without a ready response. He was stunned by the brilliance of Jean's sincere statement. It didn't change his mind about religion, but it changed his mind about his mother.

Maybe she wasn't as simplistic and dumb as he'd always thought?

Her words weren't a speech. They weren't a sermon. She wasn't spouting a philosophical argument. It wasn't a rigid church doctrine. It was a sincere expression of defiance in the face of certain defeat.

"Wow," Linda nodded appreciatively. "That was even better than Brother Davis' sermon today, which was itself quite interesting. *You* should be a preacher, Mrs. King."

"Oh, my," Jean ducked her head, embarrassed. "I just say what I think, is all. It's..."

Suddenly, her face twisted in pain.

"Oh, *my!*" she now gasped, swallowing hard. "I feel dizzy. Maybe you should pay the bill, Dave, and take me home—I've got to lie down."

"Sure, Mom," he said, waving a hand at the waitress. He handed her three twenty dollar bills. "Keep the change, please," he said as he rose, reaching over to help his Mom up. "We'll go straight home and..."

"No, you won't!" Dave heard Linda say, her voice low and hard.

"What?"

"We're going straight to your local hospital's emergency room," she ordered him, shoving the gun again into Dave's ribs from beneath her sweater.

"B-but," Dave stammered, confused. "It's just her being weak from her condition. It frequently happens to us that..."

"We're going to your hospital—now!"

"Oh, that's not necessary," Jean grinned weakly, "It's just this wonderful but unusual exertion, like Davey said. I'm not quite up to it yet. I've probably just got indigestion from the delicious solid food I've been scarfing. A good nap will do me just..."

Her eyes slid shut as she slumped downward, still mumbling about just needing to go home.

"Oh, my God!" the waitress gasped. "Should we call an ambulance?"

"It'll be faster in my car," Dave said, lifting up his Mother's limp body in his arms.

She was surprisingly light. The months of cancer therapy had indeed taken a big toll upon her. This was the first time in weeks she'd had a decent meal.   She couldn't weigh much more than ninety pounds.

He ran for the car.

"I'll drive," Sally said, grabbing Dave's keyring out of his hand as she yanked open the door.

It was only a few blocks to the hospital.

By the time they arrived—after a few fits and jerks from Sally still poorly applying the clutch—Jean had regained consciousness.

Dave reached out before Sally could react and *grabbed* the keys away from her!

"You are a *terrible* driver," he said as he stuffed the keys into his pocket and lifted his mother up in his arms.

"Oh—no need to fuss over me," Jean protested as she groggily looked around. "It's just the blood rushing from my head down to my tummy to digest all that wonderful food. I don't need to see a doctor. I'm fine...just a bit woozy is all."

Dave looked at Sally in concern, now not knowing what to do.

"Bring her along," Sally briskly ordered him, stepping out of the driver's door. "She's *not* fine. She needs expert medical care. I made the mistake the first time underestimating her body's reaction.   I won't do that again.   The first time she almost died.   Now, with prompt care, she'll just be sick for a few days."

"What?" Dave said, totally confused by the girl's cryptic words. He was carrying his Mother. As they rapidly approached the sliding glass doors to the emergency room of the hospital Jean continued weakly protesting.

"What do you mean 'before'?" he snapped at Sally.

"No time to explain, Dave," Sally said as they hurried through the metal detector arc that surrounded the entrance doors, where a guard sat at a desk to the side.

Dave was too upset to react to the fact that the metal detector had failed to register Sally's hidden gun.

In a panic, he approached the Admissions Desk carrying his limp mother.

"Nurse!" Sally barked before Dave could say anything— pointing at him carrying his mother. "This woman needs to go to your ICU immediately!"

"What's wrong with her?" the stern-faced nurse calmly replied—dressed in a white uniform, sitting unruffled behind the admissions desk.

"We were eating lunch and she collapsed!" Dave urgently explained, gently setting Jean down in a chair in the immediately-adjacent waiting area.

The nurse hurried around the desk, felt at Jean's forehead, and looked into her eyes.

"What's her name?"

"Jean King," Dave replied.

"Jean, can you hear me?" the nurse sharply spoke to her.

"Yes...I'm ok...just need to go home...get some rest is all," Jean grinned weakly, opening her eyes. "My son...and his girlfriend...are just overly protective..." she said as her voice drifted off again and her eyes closed.

"Well, it doesn't seem to be a stroke or a heart attack," the nurse said, moving back behind her desk. "We'll have a doctor look at her when one becomes available. He may want her to be admitted for observation overnight. But that's for him to decide. So if you'll please fill out these forms?"

The nurse started to hand Dave a sheet of papers on a clipboard.

Ok, then. He needed to do paperwork. That would keep his mind occupied. They'd just wait for a doctor to check out his Mom. Surely it couldn't be as bad as Linda thought—just indigestion was all.

"No!" Sally yelled at the nurse, knocking the clipboard aside to "clatter" onto the floor.

The nurse looked at Sally with a shocked expression on her face, which instantly became the stern demeanor of an emergency room professional who'd seen it all.

"Miss, please take a seat," she ordered Sally. "We'll get to your friend as soon as we can and..."

"This is an emergency!" Sally shouted at her. "You must admit this woman *now!*"

"Ma'am, we've got about thirty other 'emergencies' waiting their turn also," the nurse reasonably insisted. Dave realized that the nurse was probably pressing a button behind her desk to summon hospital security. Great! This would scare off Linda! She'd go running away and he could explain to the police that...

"Does *this* look like I'm kidding with you?" Sally yelled ominously—now that all the personnel and waiting patients were looking at her curiously—as she pulled out the *black gun* from under her sweater and pointed it directly at the nurse!

"Linda, what are you...?" Dave gasped, still standing next to his mom who was now slumped-over in her chair, her eyes tightly closed.

Linda was going stark, raving mad! Dave was suddenly scared not just for him and his mother—but for everyone else present in the hospital.

Linda was a lunatic!

"Miss, *put down* that gun!" a guard ordered her as he ran up, starting to draw his own weapon...

Sally glanced down at her gun, flicked the power up to two stars, and abruptly swung her arm to aim it at the emergency room's entrance's sliding glass doors...

BLAM!

The shot echoed through the large admittance area as the glass panels *SHATTERED*, spraying the people inside and those approaching from outside in shards of half-melted glass!

The guard staggered back from the blast then slumped to the floor, knocked out by the shock-wave.

Everyone still conscious froze in place.

"*You*—are you a Doctor?" Sally gestured with her gun at a man in a long white smock who was crouched-down carrying a clipboard.

"Y-yes," the man stammered.

"Then get over here!" she yelled loudly at him, her gun trained directly on him.

She flicked the setting back to one star.

His eyes stretched wide in fear, he hesitantly did as directed.

"Examine that woman in the chair!" Sally again yelled at him.

He went over to Jean, checked her pulse, and lifted up her eyelids.

"She's going into cardiac arrest," he said, his professional training snapping into place. "Get a gurney over here! *Code Blue!*"

As the attending personnel scrambled to obey, Dave stepped over beside Sally, who was now lowering her gun.

"How...did you know?" he asked in bewilderment.

"*Listen* to me, Dave," she urgently said, drawing his higher head down to her level with her right hand, speaking directly into his ear so that the other people around couldn't hear. Her words were fast and intense: "She's going to get very sick. But with the proper emergency care which she's getting now, she will recover. She's going to be fine, in fact—*better* than fine. What's going on now is a surge of her immune system that's attacking and destroying the huge volume of cancer cells scattered throughout her body. That process is throwing massive amounts of debris and toxins into her bloodstream, clogging and shutting-down her organs. She'll probably need kidney dialysis. Your sister, Catherine, will want to 'pull the plug' on her when she's at her worst—since your sister has medical power of attorney, according to Jean's Living Will—but don't let your sister do it! Stall for time. And then, once your mother recovers and is out of the hospital, make sure that she keeps taking the Optimmune 'vitamins' that I gave her—twenty-eight more of them, one per day, for a whole month. They're in a plastic baggy on the kitchen countertop next to the refrigerator. If she doesn't take them all, one per day, she may regress. Do you understand what I've said?"

"No, I don't! How is it that you know...?"

"It doesn't matter, Dave. Just do what I said!"

"But...it's *you* that *poisoned* her," her barked at her.

"No, I didn't," she protested. "It's a new medical treatment—similar to the ones of which you're so fond," she insisted, punching him lightly for emphasis on his chest. "Remember what you were said in the restaurant? I'm a...rogue agent from a pharmaceutical company. Yes, that's right. I said it! This is a new experimental therapy. It's dangerous for cancer patients who are as advanced as your mother, so the company wanted to bury it, too much liability. But I stole it...and it will likely totally *cure* her if you just do what I said."

He looked at her in disbelief.

"That's ridiculous," he bitterly replied, shaking his head in denial as those around him rushed to get out of the emergency acceptance area, away from the both of them. "You've done nothing but try to order me around since I ran into you this morning. If what you're saying is really true—then why didn't you tell me earlier?"

"And you'd have believed me?" she laughed. "You'd have turned me over to the police, like you're still going to try to do, wouldn't you?"

"But...you're dangerous! My mother is dying because of you. You *poisoned* her. You're waving a *gun* around, for God's sake!"

"*Phagghhh*," she spat at him in disgust, taking a step back from him. "You're just as dumb as I remember. But for the sake of your mother, have a little Faith—just a little bit of Faith. Ok?"

Impulsively, she grabbed him in a tight hug and *kissed* him smack on his lips.

"When I next contact you," she whispered in his ear as she still hugged him tight, "you'll believe me."

He jerked away from her, turning to accompany the gurney with his mother's motionless body on top of it—as it and the accompanying medical personnel wheeled rapidly away.

Despite the drama of the situation, he grinned to himself.

In the hug from that insane bitch, he'd managed to slip his cell-phone out of her jeans pocket.

Hah! He showed *her*.

"*Drop* that gun!" a voice yelled at Sally as she, in response, lurched to the side and *SLAMMED* the gun back into another approaching guard's forehead!

He dropped like a stone, unconscious, blood gushing from a gash on his head.

"Don't anyone try to follow me!" she shouted as she swung her outstretched arm firmly holding the black gun around in a half-circle, stopping the other advancing guards in their tracks.

She slowly eased herself backward out of the shattered sliding doors...then *ran* for Dave's bright yellow Cavalier.

She had Dave's keyring, having grabbed it back from out of his pants pocket when she hugged and kissed him.

Hah! Try to keep her from his precious car, would he? She sure showed *him*.

She jumped into the car, put in the key, and turned on the motor...

—causing the car to *jump* forward, *crashing* into another car in front of it, denting the fronts of both cars, before stalling out!

"God damned clutch!" she yelled, slamming her fist onto the dashboard.

She looked out the side window to see the guards again running out of the hospital, almost upon her—with their guns drawn!

She opened the door and fired at them.

Covered with *crackling electricity*, they fell onto the pavement, convulsing...

—as she just managed to get the Cavalier into gear, back it away from the smashed car in front of her, and lurch away.

The car jerked fitfully as she managed with difficulty to get it out of the parking lot.

Turning onto Broadway, she headed out of town, in the direction of the freeway.

She was on the run.

Her Quest to change future history and save humanity couldn't have gotten off to a worse start.

She'd been certain that Dave would be her ally, helping her change the timeline for the better. Sure, he'd need some convincing. She knew she'd have to explain everything in detail before bringing him around to her side.

But she never once thought he'd be her enemy!

She was on her own now, *abandoned* by those that should have loved her the most.

She had never felt so alone.

Chapter 3

ABANDONMENT

It's so very sad

When those you trust are gone

Leaving you to handle everything

Without warning or explanation

Just vanished, departed, run away

Leaving behind just an unoccupied space

Where you expected to find sanctuary

That once you were happy to call home

Bright, comforting, and warm

Now but a dark, scary, cold place

Devolved into a dreary, empty cave...

The Luminary Chronicles, 3:123-125

"I don't know who she is," Dave protested. "I never saw her before this morning..."

"So you say, but..."

"—when I just briefly talked with her at the grocery store," Dave wearily repeated yet again for the third time. "She was checking out my groceries. I admired her tattoos."

"And yet according to the supervisor and other workers at the store, she never worked there."

This was news to Dave.

"Never worked there?   But she was checking out my stuff this morning. She said her name was 'Linda Powers' and..."

"—they have no employees of that name."

"What?"

"They also say they have no employees of her description."

"But...she has those tattoos on her arms—they're unmistakable."

"No one with tattoos such as you describe works there."

"No turtle tattoos on wrists?"

"None."

"But...how is that possible?"

"The security cameras did record you walking to your car with her," the officer admitted. "But before that, there's no record that this...'Linda'...ever existed."

Dave gaped at him with his mouth hanging open.

"Maybe you'd better come with us to the station," the police Detective insisted, taking Dave's arm roughly in his own big hand, then starting to lift Dave out of the chair in which he was nervously sitting.

"Why?" Dave gasped, shrinking away from the officer, shrugging off his big hand. "I haven't done anything. I have to stay here with my Mother. She's very sick! I've already told you everything that I know, damn it!"

The man was large and strong, with a square face, steely-blue eyes, sporting a neatly trimmed black mustache, and short-cropped black hair. He was just one of many uniformed officers crowded into the small examination room along with Dave.

"Witnesses claim you said that woman *poisoned* your mother," another officer, a blond lady with two stars on the epaulets of her uniform, stated.

"I've already explained that," Dave shrugged, petulantly ducking his head down.

He knew what would happen if he admitted that Linda gave his mother a pill. They'd go to his house, find the baggy with the remaining pills, and take them away.

Just on the off-chance that the crazy psycho-bitch was telling the truth that she was a rogue pharmaceutical agent with a new miracle treatment for cancer, Dave intended to not let those pills slip out of his possession.

"Explain it again," she insisted.

"Like I told you, it was Linda's crazy *language* poisoning my mother's mind against me," Dave said, wearily putting a hand to his forehead as he sat at a desk in a small hospital room adjacent to the Intensive Care Unit where his mother was being worked on by the Doctors.

The room felt much too warm.

He was sweating profusely.

"What sort of language?" the lady officer probed.

"She made me take her to church with us," Dave grimaced. "I've already told you this. She was some sort of religious nut. She wanted my Mother to stop her chemotherapy and radiation treatments, despite my wishes. She kept talking about the end of the world—everything getting burned up. Somehow she knew that I come here to Sulphur on Sunday mornings to take my mother to Church and she was using us to make some sort of crazy point. What that point was—I don't know!"

"So where'd she get that exotic energy-gun of hers?" the Detective continued interrogated Dave, now looming over the table with his big hands flat on its surface.

"I've got no idea," Dave weakly protested. "The first I knew of it she shocked me with it at my car in the grocery store's parking lot."

"Yes, she almost electrocuted four of the hospital's security personnel," the big man nodded as he continued to grill Dave. "And yet it wasn't a Taser or anything like a Taser. The glass panels in the entrance to the emergency room weren't shattered from a bullet—they were ripped apart and melted, as if from some high-energy discharge. That's not an ordinary gun. Plus, it didn't register on the metal detector at the hospital's emergency room entrance. How do you explain this, Dr. King?"

"I've got no idea," Dave repeated impatiently. "It must be some new type of gun. I don't know about guns. I'm not a gun person. Perhaps it was some new terrorist weapon?"

"Hmmmm..." the officer grimly nodded. "Maybe you're onto something there, Dr. King? A terrorist gun, you say?"

"I've read that they want plastic guns to get them through security so that..."

"And did *you* help her get that gun, Dr. King?" the man relentlessly continued the questioning. "We see from your publically-available publication record that you are a scientist. In fact, you're a renegade researcher engaged in high-energy physics research. Did you, in fact, *make* that gun and give it to her? Is she, perhaps, your *accomplice* who got mad at you concerning your mother? Did you, indeed, have a fight here at the hospital—and are now trying to cover up your relationship with her?"

"Accomplice?" Dave gasped, peering wide-eyed around at the room of very serious law officers. "I'm not a terrorist. I was kidnapped by *her*, for Christ's sake. *I'm* the victim here!"

"But you've written about your distain for the rest of the scientific community, in opinion-pieces in the local newspapers," the blond lady calmly inserted, stepping up close to the table. "Isn't that correct?"

"The funding agencies are too conservative," Dave quickly tried to explain. "There are lots of other relatively-young scientists like me who agree. It's too hard to get funding for unconventional projects."

"You mean like your 'cold-fusion' research—which colleagues of yours say that you do in your *garage* at your house?" she coldly continued.

"It's more like a hobby," he shook his head. "I've given up serious research. I'm just a small-town college instructor now. I teach introductory physics to nursing-major students, for God's sake. I'm *not* a 'radical' in any shape or form!"

"*Where* did she go, Dr. King?" the big man insisted, leaning even closer. "She took your car, didn't she? You had to give her the keys to do so, right?"

The man was leaning so close Dave could smell his breath. He had apparently not bothered to brush his teeth since consuming tacos earlier.

"She stole it. She grabbed my keys out of my pocket. I had no idea she'd taken my keys to..."

"Where did she go?" the man insisted, his face just inches away from Dave's.

"I don't know!" Dave yelled at him. "I've got to get back with my mother, who's..."

"She's in good hands," the burly man stated, cutting him off. He again grabbed Dave by his arm, yanking him up out of the chair. "The hospital personnel here are top-notch. Your sister is with her. So you don't have to worry about your mother's care. You'd be much better off just concentrating on answering our questions."

"Cat is here? But..." Dave swallowed hard, remembering the confusing but explicit warnings that Linda whispered to him.

"Yes, your sister is at her bedside," the man repeated. "So, as I said, you don't need to be here right now. What *we* are going to do is take a short trip to the station where we can interrogate you more properly and thoroughly. You can come willingly or in cuffs."

"But..."

"*I'll* take it from here," a deep, gruff voice intruded.

All eyes turned to the doorway.

A burly man in a suit stood in the doorway, wearing dark glasses, sporting crew cut short blond hair. Another even heftier fellow, also wearing dark glasses, stood behind him.

The first man held up a badge.

"FBI, gentlemen and lady," he announced as he pushed through the crowd. "We're taking over this case."

"But it's our jurisdiction and..." the officer holding Dave by the arm peevishly protested.

"Please leave the room," the FBI man cut him off. Then he sat solidly on a back-turned chair facing Dave.

One by one—grumbling about Federal overreach—the other officials filed out.

The accompanying, silent FBI agent closed the door behind them and stood in front of it, obscuring the view of those outside of what was happening inside.

Dave knew he was in *big* trouble.

He *cringed*...

"Don't be upset, Dr. King," the man at the table said in a soothing, deep voice. "I'm Agent Anderson. Arthur Anderson. You may call me Arthur."

"Uh...ok...'Arthur'..."

"This is my card," he said, handing Dave a plain business card with just his name and phone number on it. "I know you are not a terrorist. Those other officers were just grasping at straws. They need to prove they deserve their salaries. I, on the other hand, take a wider view. I know that the woman who kidnapped you wasn't what she claimed to be. But she's also not a run-of-the-mill terrorist. Instead, she is something far more dangerous. Can I get your promise to phone me if she tries to contact you?"

Dave looked at the card then slipped it into his top shirt pocket behind his cellphone.

"Uh...sure, I guess."

"I also know that you need to be with your mother right now, since your Sister's presence is a serious issue for you," Agent Anderson blandly continued. "Later on, we'll talk more. Is that ok with you?"

"I suppose..."

"Then I wish your mother the best," he said, standing up and pushing his chair back under the table.

"Thanks..."

"And don't worry about the police out there. I'll tell them to concentrate on pursuing and capturing the *Girl with the Turtle Tattoo*. Like you said, you were just an innocent victim, right?"

Time slowed for Dave.

He was acutely aware of the uniformed officers milling outside. He heard the "clicks" and "clanks" of gurneys rolling past in the hallway. He glimpsed beyond Agent Anderson many white uniforms of hospital workers hurrying past. He smelled the omnipresent odor of disinfecting hospital chlorine—and he looked straight into the lenses of Agent Anderson's black eyeglasses looming above him at the table.

He was scared.

He wanted to run out of this place, get a cab, and go home to Edmond. Above all, he wanted to escape those black eyeglasses that seemed to be drilling into his mind.

But his mother needed him.

"I'm...just...an innocent victim," Dave repeated, ducking his head, not meeting Anderson's inscrutable gaze.

"You're sure that you're not holding anything back from me?" the Agent gently asked in a soft voice. Dave suspected he was being mocked, but couldn't be sure.

So Dave lifted his head and shook it firmly in the negative.

"Good," Agent Anderson nodded. "Then please don't feel that you're alone in this, Dr. King. If you need me, I'm just a phone call away. Remember, Dr. King—I'm on your side."

With those cryptic words, the FBI Agent abruptly stood up and walked to the door. As he and his fellow Agent departed, Dave felt a wave of relief and gratitude.

He knew he should be very afraid of getting mixed up with that man. Something about Agent Anderson was very unnerving. But at least the Agent wasn't hauling Dave away to prison.

But now there was the immediate medical situation to deal with.

"Mom...?" Dave whispered, weakly arising and going out in search of where they'd put her.

The hospital workers outside directed him to ICU—the Intensive Care Unit.

Entering the small ward he was met by Catherine.

She looked terrible, her short blond hair stuck up in disarray. She had no makeup on her face. Her eyes, deep-set in her somewhat chubby face, were red from crying.

He grabbed her in a tight hug.

"Mom's gone," she sobbed. "There's only a shell of her left. You can see for yourself."

He fearfully walked toward the sliding doors she indicated, afraid of what he was about to see. The tops of the doors were entirely made of glass, as were the doorways to the other two alcoves spaced evenly around the central nurses' station. Since it was intensive care, there was no privacy. The hovering doctors and nurses had a continuous, complete view of all the patients. And through the windows he saw his mother.

Cat was right.

"Mom?" he said, his voice catching, as he walked past the doors which "shushed" to the sides, into the room filled with *blinking, beeping* machines...in the middle of which lay the shrunken body of his once-vital mother.

Only her head and one hand were showing. The skin of her face hung slack, grayish, her eyes closed but puffed-out. Tubes ran into her mouth, her nose, and directly into her neck via a tracheotomy. Electrodes were pasted to her bald skull. Under a thin covering, her chest rose rhythmically up and down...up and down...up and down...

"She's only breathing because of pulmonary assist," a white-coated, female doctor quietly stated, placing a comforting hand on

Dave's shoulder. "I'm afraid your mother has multiple organ failure. Her liver has shut down. Her kidneys are gone. Her heart is beating irregularly. She's in a deep coma. Her lungs are failing. We have her on pulmonary assist and dialysis. That's what's keeping her alive. I'm afraid there's little hope for recovery. I'm so sorry."

Dave slumped into a chair set to the side of the bed.

"I...I've got to...process...all of this," he gulped.

"Of course, I understand," the polite doctor nodded. "If you have any questions just ask one of the nurses to contact me. My name is Dr. Joan Mathews."

"Thanks, Doctor," Dave nodded gratefully, just now focusing on the kind face of the physician. She wore a white doctor's gown over blue scrubs. She had the ubiquitous stethoscope draped around her neck. She was a dark skinned woman with short-cropped black hair.

Cat came tentatively into the room, placing her chubby hands on Dave's shoulders.

Beside them, the machines were quietly beeping, clicking, and sucking.

"It's time that we let her go," Cat quietly stated. "She gave me her Durable Power of Attorney, so I'm legally responsible. I'm the one she wanted to make her healthcare decisions if it came to this. I don't have to get your approval for this, Davey—but it'd be easier if you agreed."

"So...you want to pull the plug," he raggedly sighed, "whether I agree or not?"

"It's my decision. She wanted it this way."

"Why?"

"She knew you were too...scientific," she sadly informed him, her hands still on his shoulders. "She knew you'd try everything to save her even if there was no chance. And she didn't want to go through that nor put us through the needless pain and expense of a hopeless quest. She knew I was the level-headed one of her two children. She knew I'd do what needed to be done."

"But Cat..." he choked up, tears dripping down his cheeks.

"Yes it is hard for me too," she softly nodded, her hands gripping his shoulders firmly. "But it's what she wanted. You know she never wanted to be kept alive by machines."

"But if there's a chance for recovery, then...?"

"Doctor Joan says there isn't."

"She said 'little' chance, not 'zero'!" he snapped at her.

"Dave," she sighed, "even if she was to come out of her coma—to what would she return? She has end-stage metastized breast cancer! It's all throughout her body. She didn't want to suffer like this. It's better to just let her slip away. After going off her chemo and radiation therapy last week she had several good days. How was she with you at church and lunch today?"

"She was cheerful—happy, even."

"You see?" Cat comforted him, looking over at the shriveled remains of their mother being kept alive on the hospital bed by the surrounding machines. "Isn't that the way we'd want her to experience her last conscious days on this earth?"

"I suppose..." he gulped, wiping the tears away from his eyes.

Cat made perfect sense. But...that crazy girl with the turtle tattoo...it seemed impossible...but he was grasping at straws!

"Yah...I can see that," he nodded. "But...I still need to make sure—make a couple phone calls first. Is that ok? There are some doctors I know that can advise me on..."

"I've already made my decision," she cut him off.

"Come on, Cat," he pleaded, looking up into her sad blue eyes. "Give me a little time, ok?"

"There's no point, Dave," she sadly stated. "I don't see any sense in delaying the inevitable. It will be better for both Mom and us to just do what has to be done."

Behind Cat, Dave saw Dr. Joan walking back into the room accompanied by a nurse and a couple security guards. Clearly, they were prepared to deal with Dave if he got violent.

"Cat!" he exclaimed, suddenly standing up abruptly and shoving a pointed finger into her face.

Startled, she lurched backward...

—as both of the security guards started forward...

"What about *God?*" he exclaimed, moving forward another step, holding up his right hand palm-out as a "stop" signal to the guards.

"God?" Cat said, puzzled...

Unsure of what to do, the guards hung back.

"Of course, God!" Dave desperately continued, trying to find a "hook" that would pull his stubborn sister back from the brink of exercising her legal authority.

"But you don't believe in God," she frowned at him.

"But *Mom* does," Dave said, pointing now at the comatose face on the bed. "Surely she'd want for God's Power to be given a chance to work in her life—particularly as she lies at death's door."

"Well..." Cat reluctantly admitted, "I guess so—but just what are you proposing?"

"Simple," Dave said, laying a hand now on Cat's shoulder. "Just let Cliff come and pray for her."

"That's all?"

"It's what Mom would have wanted," he said, trying to sound reasonable.

"I suppose..."

"Did someone mention my name?"

It was Jean's Pastor, Brother Davis. Dave had hoped it would take a while to contact him and have him show up—but here he was!

Dave was flustered but had to play the hand he was dealt.

"I'm so sorry to hear about..." Cliff began.

"And just what are *you* doing here?" Dave belligerently began before catching himself. Dave had just requested for him to be here. He couldn't just kick Cliff out on his fat ass!

"I already called him," Catherine stated, looking soberly into Dave's eyes. "I also figured Mother would like to have him here when we stopped the machines and freed her to move onward in her spiritual journey. So, yes, I'm sure he is indeed quite willing to say a final prayer on her behalf."

"Yes, I am indeed happy to call down the Blessings of the Lord upon all of you in this sad situation for..." the Pastor dutifully began.

"So you *don't* really believe in God, then?" Dave angrily accused Cliff, stepping up to him and pocking a finger into his ample gut.

"What?" he responded, his eyes widening.

"So it really *is* all just an *act*, isn't it?" Dave relentlessly continued his verbal assault. "You stand up there and preach God as being this all-mighty, loving Deity—and when the worst actually happens all you can do is ask for 'blessings'?"

"But..."

"Why not ask God for a real, *true* miracle, Cliff?" Dave angrily demanded. "Put God to the test! See if He's really there. See if He's really as powerful as you claim He is. Ask God to *cure* my mother, Cliff. Why not? If you really believe that he is all-loving and all-powerful—then why don't you ask Him for a *real* miracle?"

Cliff was obviously struggling to maintain his professional calm. But he was well-acquainted with Dave's angry rejection of God's Authority—and Dave's history.

"If this is about your Father's passing, then..."

"Damn right it is," Dave bitterly asserted, his face twisting in anger.

"Perhaps you'd better come with us," one of the guards said, stepping resolutely forward toward Dave.

"No, gentlemen," Cliff turned to them, raising his fat hands in a calming fashion. "I am this family's Pastor. This is a very painful situation. I don't blame Dave for being upset. I assure you he is no threat to anyone. He is quite educated and just needs to have his intellectual doubts satisfied, that's all. Why don't you and the rest of your personnel just go about your other business? We will call you when it is time or if there's any real problem."

Doctor Joan glanced at the nurse and guards, silently assenting to Cliff's suggestion.

"We'll be right outside if you need us, Sir," the same guard said as the group reluctantly left the room.

"You see, David?" Cliff gently smiled in a calming, professionally-benevolent fashion. "There's no need to get overly upset. As to your concerns about God's Power—I of course will pray for God to cure her if that's what you want. I usually place it all in God's Hands—asking Him to do what He deems best. I trust in God. It is not for us to dictate to Him or try to give Him orders. But He does tell us in the Holy Bible to lay our concerns before Him, so..."

"Then do it!" Dave curtly interrupted him.

"As you wish," Cliff said, reaching out a hand to Dave and a hand to Catherine.

Cringing, Dave took hold of Cliff's mushy, soft hand.

"Now, let us bow our heads, close our eyes, and pray together," Cliff solemnly intoned as he launched into a standard prayer saying the predictably-"right" things.

Dave bowed his head but did not close his eyes.

He indeed remembered vividly the same thing happening with his father. He was only ten years old. His father went hunting with friends in the woods. One of the other men—seeing what he thought was the movement of a deer in the trees—accidently shot his father in the head.

His father lingered in the hospital for a week in a coma, mortally wounded.

The local congregation, led by a younger Cliff, gathered in Dave's parent's home. One by one, each of the men led a prayer asking for God to heal Dave's father. They continued praying late into the night.

The next morning, Dave's father was dead.

Dave never forgave the congregation, the men gathered at his home, Brother Davis, or God. When it mattered to Dave the most, God wasn't there. Either God rejected their request—or simply didn't exist!

Either way, Dave was finished with God.

As soon as he was away from home—on his own at college and out from under his mother's influence—he quit going to church, except when he had to be there in support of his ailing mother.

But now that he had to stall for time, he was going to use every bit of his hard-won knowledge of Cliff's theology against him.

"...Amen!" Cliff concluded.

The "clicks" and "beeps" of the machines connected to the body on the bed continued unchanged.

The corpse-like figure on the bed didn't move.

"Thank you, Brother Davis," Cat said, taking her hand away from his. Dave gladly did the same.

"Now that we have asked for God's blessings," she continued, "it's time for us to do what Mother requested. I'll go call back the..."

"So you *don't* believe in God?" Dave indignantly asked her.

Cliff's normally-congenial expression turned hard.

"David, we just prayed to the Lord..."

"—and asked Him for nothing except for some sort of generic 'blessings'!" he angrily retorted. "*I* said to ask God for a *Miracle!* I said to ask God to *cure* my mother! Did you do that?"

"Well, not in those exact words, but..."

"Do I have to do this damn prayer *myself?*" Dave loudly yelled at the man. He saw that heads out in the central nurse's station were turning to their room. "I doubt God puts much stock in my requests. Aren't you supposed to be our resident 'holy man'? Are you *afraid* to ask God for anything except to do 'His Will'? Why can't you ask for a *Miracle*, Cliff? Is it because you know he *won't* do it or *can't* do it— just like with my father years ago?"

On the bed, Dave noticed yellow phlegm being sucked from a tube in his mother's nose. He felt an urge to vomit—but forced the bile down and continued.

"Davey...we were all upset about Father—but that's in the past and..." Cat tearfully tried to get Dave to agree to what she clearly felt had to be done.

"No!" he stubbornly stated, "plopping" himself down into the chair at the bedside. "I'm not dwelling in the past, Cat. I'm right here sitting beside my Mother. And I'm giving your God, Cliff, *one more* chance. Say a *real* prayer this time!" Dave loudly yelled at him. "Tell God we request that he get my mother out of that hospital bed. Ask God to *cure* my mother from her attack and also her metastized breast cancer!"

Cliff glanced with concern at Cat, who resignedly shrugged.

The preacher bowed his head, closed his eyes, and reluctantly intoned what he obviously considered a very improper prayer: "Dear God in Heaven, we come before you again. If it be your Will, please raise this woman out of her sickbed. Fix her malfunctioning organs. Cure her cancer. We know you have the Power to do all things. We humbly ask for this Miracle to occur. Bless the hands of the doctors who are caring for her. Let their efforts be completely successful. We ask for this in Jesus' blessed name. Amen!"

He lifted his head and looked at Dave.

"Ok?" he said.

"Much better," Dave nodded.

They all looked at the bloated body on the bed. It neither spoke nor moved.

"Then I think it's time that we called back the doctor..." Cat weakly tried to continue.

"And not let God have any time to do His work?" Dave mildly interjected.

"Well...mother is not getting up out of her bed and..."

"Brother Davis qualified his request by asking that the Doctor's methods be successful—didn't you, Cliff?"

"Well...yes..."

"So then his 'miracle' request wasn't for instantaneous results, was it?"

Cliff shrugged his rounded shoulders.

"Alright, Davey," Cat sighed resignedly, "you win. We'll let God have time to work His Will. But you also will have to do your part."

"What do you mean?"

"For once in your life, you are going to have to stick by your decisions. You can't just force things on others and then walk away. You will sit here with Mom until you agree with us that it's time to let her go. If you run away to your pet snakes in Edmond, then I'll have complete discretion to decide if God's answer is 'yes' or 'no', agreed?"

Dave knew this was going to be even harder than what he'd gone through with his Father's death. He hoped he was doing the right thing, not just prolonging his mother's suffering.

"Agreed," he whispered, settling back in his seat, and resolutely crossing his arms over his chest.

"Then I'll be in the cafeteria getting some lunch," Cat stated as she turned away, "but I'll be back."

Dave watched her depart with Cliff.

He turned his gaze back to the hospital bed.

One of Jean's hands lay motionless on the sheets.

It was swollen to twice its normal size. It was black with numerous broken blood vessels on its surface.

Dave placed his own hand on it.

It was cold. It felt like the hand of a corpse.

"Don't worry, Mom," he whispered to her. "I'll give God—and that crazy psycho-bitch tattooed girl—a chance."

He withdrew his hand and pulled out his cellphone.

He hit the number for George Johnson.

After a few rings George picked up.

"Dave, what's happening?"

"Hey, George, I'm at the hospital with my mother, and..." Dave began.

"Oh my, I hope it's not serious!"

"I'm afraid it is," Dave sighed. "Could you check in on my critters this evening? I'm not going to be home tonight, probably not for several days in fact."

George was a tenured Professor at the small local two-year college where Dave had a job in Edmond. George shared a love for reptiles with Dave—although being married, George wasn't allowed by his wife to have any of his own in his house.

But George was happy to stop by and make sure that Dave's reptiles were fed and watered whenever Dave had to go out of town.

"Sure! No problem. Have you called up the college? They'll have to find replacements for your classes tomorrow."

"Right...at the very least I'll leave them a message," Dave agreed, having completely forgotten that he had classes to teach the first thing in the morning.

But that would all have to wait.

For once, he was sticking by his mother.

Catherine would see that he could be trusted.

Sally was hiding in the Rock Creek camping grounds nestled in the Chickasaw National Recreation Area—the "Park."

She was sitting on a toilet in a closed restroom facility, her leather bag lying on the stone floor beside her. It was the only place to sit in the isolated, small building. Everything was very peaceful and quiet. No campers were near because it was in the back end of the forested encampment grounds, in a rope-off area that was rarely used.

She'd driven Dave's bright yellow Chevy Cavalier along the main street of Sulphur headed out of town towards I-35.

Then, at the edge of town, she'd darted onto a side street and driven to the park's fence. Finding a gap in the fence, she'd driven the car into the forest itself, found a gully, driven the car into it, and then covered it with shrubs and branches.

By foot she'd stealthily crept through the underbrush, crossed Rock Creek at a narrow point where up-thrust boulders gave footing, and reached the closed toilet facility—avoiding any campsites along the way. Forcing open a locked door, she'd hidden herself within.

It was the same place Dave took her after kidnapping her from the Megamart in the previous timeline.

She'd been there all afternoon. Now the light outside that came in through a high small window was fading. She was getting hungry and thirsty.

"Time to go," she resolutely told herself.

It didn't take long for her to slink through the gathering darkness out to the main park road, then onto West 12th Street leading out of the Park into town. Just a few blocks up 12th Street was Jean King's home.

She fumbled with Dave's keyring until she found a properly-sized key.

Yep! It opened his Mom's back door quite nicely.

Inside, she found it just as they'd left it when they'd departed for church earlier.

"Good...they're still looking for me out on the highways," she sighed.

She was exhausted, sweaty, and dirty from creeping through the woods. She knew she should get some sleep now that it was nighttime. But who knew if the police would suddenly arrive to search the place, or Dave might return?

But she had to do something about her appearance.

In Jean's closet toward the back she found some women's-style trench overcoats. One of them was stylishly belted, extended down to her knees, with an attached large hood—and colored grey, perfect for blending in.

Great! She could hide herself in that quite nicely.

But her hair...?

"I don't want to cut it," she told herself, looking at her image in a mirror in the bathroom. "But since I was so clever as to remember what happened before...heh!"

She stripped naked, pausing to admire the many large tattoos covering most of her body, before jumping into the shower along with her bottle of blond hair dye. She congratulated herself on snagging that plus the pills from her Dimension in her hasty exit from the Megamart.

It took a while for the bleach to work, but instead of long red-brown hair she was now a dirty blond.

"Hah!" she smiled as she admired her new image in the mirror. "I look radically different now. As long as I'm careful, I can go anywhere."

Putting her clothes back on, she felt refreshed. Her clothes were still dirty, but her body was clean.

"Now for something to eat..."

In the kitchen she found little to consume. Beside the few cupcakes left, the only other edible thing was six cans of strawberry "Ensure" that Dave had purchased that morning. Poor Mrs. King apparently had lived on the stuff before briefly regaining her appetite.

"Hmmm....not so bad," she said as she swigged down a bottle. "It's like a strawberry milkshake."

If only Mrs. King had not taken that extra pill.

Sally knew that it was too much. The printed instructions explicitly forbad taking more than one pill at a time. But, of course, Sally had taken the pills out of their official boxes, retaining the instructions. The boxes and instructions would have given away the origin of the pills—as being not from this world! But there was nothing Sally could do after-the-fact. She wished Mrs. King the best, hoping she would survive the massive dose of interactive retrovirals that she had inadvertently self-administered to herself. Even in a healthy person, that amount of radical reprogramming of the DNA of her immune system would be a shock. But in a very sick person with a huge load of cancerous cells...?

Sally shuddered, munching down the remaining cupcakes before grabbing the five remaining bottles of Ensure, stuffing them into her already-filled shoulder bag, and...

Wait!

What about the extra pills she'd left?

Yes, there beside the refrigerator on the counter sat the clear plastic baggy with the remaining pills for Jean. That is, if she survived the initial dosage...

And there, hidden away under the pile of empty bags on the dining room table, was the other baggy.

"Should I take that with me or leave it?" Sally mused.

She knew she probably wouldn't need it. She still had three more filled pill boxes. That would be enough.

"Just in case Dave gets my message," Sally said to herself, "I'll leave the extra pouch I put there."

She went into the garage where Jean's old grey sedan was sitting, found another key on Dave's keyring that fit the car, and opened the driver's side door.

She tossed her bag plus the hooded trench coat into the back seat.

Sliding into the driver's seat she tried various keys in the ignition. One fit. It took a few times for the engine to "catch" but it seemed to run ok.

"Automatic transmission!" she nodded gratefully. "I'm on my way to Ada, Oklahoma. Hah!"

She left the car in park, got out, quietly opened the big garage door from within, drove the car out, closed the big door behind her, and took off down the street headed for Ada.

"*Snake!*" she nodded to herself in satisfaction.

She knew exactly where she was going.

She was headed for the tattoo parlor where she—and her presumed duplicate in this world—originally got her turtle tattoo inked by the artist known as "Snake."

She knew he wasn't an ordinary tattoo artist.

Indeed, he was a disguised member of an *alien species* that sent her back in time!

Now she needed his help to survive in this place—and then to *change* the timeline to prevent the impending destruction of the world!

For the first time since that morning she felt in control. She had a plan. It was good feeling.

It only took an hour for her to get to Ada, driving cautiously below the speed limits on back-roads so as not to attract attention.

It was pitch black when she arrived. There was no moon. Most of the streetlamps on the mostly-abandoned East end of Main Street were out. She had trouble remembering exactly where the parlor was located along Main Street in the dark. She'd always gone there during daytime. But finally, she saw it.

Driving into an alley behind the parlor she parked.

Since the night was chilly, Sally slipped on Jean's trench coat over her blue sweater. She flipped the hood up over her head. Not wanting to leave anything of value out in the alleyway, she slung her bag up onto her shoulder.

Then, breaking in a back door to the parlor, she found...*nothing!*

Inside, it was totally empty.

There was only dust and cobwebs.

Using a flashlight that she'd found in the trunk of Jean's old car, she searched the place, careful to not let her light shine out the front windows and attract attention.

It was like the place had never been a tattoo parlor at all!

"What's going on?" she gasped, confused.

In her own world, she'd just gotten her turtle tattoo inked there only last week!

Suddenly she gasped in pain, pushing up the sleeve of the trench coat and underlying sweater of her left arm.

The turtle tattoo on her wrist was *glowing!*

And yet, as she backed up in pain, it dimmed...

It was *pushing* her somewhere!

She kept backing in whatever direction that caused the white-hot, glowing tattoo to dim.

She stumbled out of the back of the empty parlor and along the deserted alleyway.

Two blocks away, the tattoo went completely dark.

Crickets chirped in the night.

Using her flashlight, she read an old sign above a doorway leading into the back of a building.

It said: "*Main Street Theater.*"

But wasn't that closed? Yes, it had been closed for a number of years. This was in the mostly abandoned part of the old Main street section of town. Only a few restaurants and specialty shops operated in this area of the town. Most businesses had years before migrated out to the strip malls and big box stores on the edge of town. The little movie theater hadn't been used in many years.

But still, her tattoo had led her to it.

So she'd better investigate...

She easily jimmied open the old door. She closed it securely behind her, making sure it was again firmly locked.

Inside, cautiously moving forward—seeing only by the dim light of her flashlight—she was surprised to see a large hallway with many entrances along it. Presumably the wide, arched doors led to small movie-viewing rooms off to each side?

"It sure didn't look this big from outside," she said to herself.

Each small viewing-room on its outer wall had an ancient, faded poster in a holder advertising the last movie that had been shown there.

The first poster she came up on said: "THE PARTY AT THE END OF THE WORLD!"

It depicted the earth being torn apart while a gaggle of people stood off to the side cheering.

In smaller letters near the bottom of the poster it also said: "*Don't be left behind!*"

And in yet smaller letters, the credits said: "*Starring Linda Powers and David King!*"

"What?" she gasped. "How can that be? This movie was shown years ago—and neither Dave nor I are actors...are we?"

A deep sense of foreboding unsettled her already jangled nerves.

Clutching her flashlight firmly, she cautiously entered the dark archway.

Dave was startled awake by a *loud ringing* in his ears!

"Ok, ok, I'm getting up," he coughed, blinking his eyes, thinking his alarm clock was ringing...

But it was the heart monitor beside the bed in which his mother lay. It was right behind where Dave sat on his chair, having dozed off.

"Code Blue, Code Blue!" a nurse yelled, sweeping into the room.

"You've got to leave *now!*" Doctor Joan ordered him, right behind the nurse. Joan grabbed him by his arm and shoved him toward the door. Other personnel were pouring into the room, making it hard for Dave to leave.

"But what's...?" he gulped.

"*Leave!*" she ordered him, thrusting him bodily out against the incoming tide of emergency personnel.

"What's happening?" Catherine worriedly asked as she ran up, pulling him safely off to the side.

"I don't know," he said, still trying groggily to awaken. "I guess I dozed off and then..."

His voice trailed off as they stood anxiously off to the side, hearing the sounds of barked, muffled orders from inside the room, mixed with the wailing of a heart alert-monitor.

Then everything went silent.

Doctor Joan emerged from the room, shaking her head sadly.

"Doctor...?" Catherine tentatively asked.

"I'm sorry," the Doctor said, "she's gone."

"What?" Dave asked, not sure that he'd heard her right. "Gone where?"

"Your mother is dead," the Doctor grimly stated. "Her heart stopped for good. We did our best to get it started again, but there was nothing we could do. Her circulatory system just collapsed."

"But...that can't be true...she was supposed to...that psycho-bitch assured me," Dave whispered as his words became more incoherent and muffled. He slowly sank to the floor, ending up crumpled in a sobbing heap.

"*...body taken to the morgue...refrigerated until you can contact a funeral home for transport...necessary paperwork...death certificate...*" Dave vaguely heard the instructions being given to Cat by the considerate female doctor.

"I've got to go," Dave said, surging up to his feet and stumbling for the exit of the Intensive Care Unit.

"Davey..." Cat called-out from behind.

"I'll call you," he choked back at her, quickly walking away.

It was as if the world—without warning—had abruptly ended.

Yet as he walked out of the hospital's front entrance doors—glass intact and in place, unlike that of the emergency room entrance—he saw that the sky above him was blue and the just-emerging morning sun's yellow light was bright.

How could nature be so peaceful when it had just savaged his poor mother?

Nothing made sense.

In one short day his whole world had been turned upside down.

Chapter 4

PERPLEXION

It's nice to know

What's right and what's wrong

Which way is good and which is bad

All of the Answers to all of the Questions

And what is the Truth and what's a damn lie

When you must retreat and when you should fight

How to set a course that's always straight

And shoot true with AIM unerring

Knowing with certitude your Path

Before God scrambles everything...

And has the last laugh.

The Luminary Chronicles, 4:38-40

Sally stepped through the dark doorway into *eye-squinting BRIGHTNESS!*

She reached up and pulled her hood lower, trying to shade her eyes...

"Help me, help me!" she heard an anguished cry at her feet.

Looking down, Sally saw a little girl with big brown eyes pitifully staring up at her—her small hand stretched upwards and *grasping!*

She was dressed in a curious little jump-suit that seemed to be made out of aluminum foil.

She was lying on a pavement composed of a white ceramic-like substance.

"What's wrong?" Sally said, reaching down to grab the little girl's thin hand.

Looking up to where the little girl was staring, Sally saw the problem.

The sky was the wrong color.

Instead of a peaceful bright blue it was an angry *orange-red!*

And it was *roiling...*

What was happening? Was she somehow inside the movie? Was this some kind of advanced holo-projection? But she wasn't wearing 3D glasses—and this vision was all around her.

Well, at least there were other customers here. The little girl at Sally's feet was real enough.

"I want Mommy," the little girl said as Sally lifted her up. "We were running...fell *smack*...hurt leg...couldn't walk...the others kept going—Mommy didn't hear calling!" she sobbed.

"Sure, sure," Sally comforted the kid, hoisting her up so the little girl could put her small arms around Sally's neck. "I'll carry you. Where are they? Which way did they go?"

The little girl pointed in the direction behind Sally.

Sally turned, expecting to see the doorway leading back into the theater-proper.

But behind her was only the wide expanse of the empty, white ceramic street—leading a couple blocks away to a *large, blue, half-dome.*

Sally paused, taking in her surroundings.

All around her was a vast, futuristic city. High sweeping spirals took the place of rectangular skyscrapers. Swaying skyways ran from spiral to spiral above Sally. The weird buildings were all constructed out of multi-colored crystal. The city looked very...relaxed! Indeed, it had its own soothing beauty—if not for that evilly pulsating sky looming above.

And it was *hot!*

Her hood was shielding Sally from the blazing light pulsating down from above, but not from the stifling, thick air.

She was starting to sweat as she now rapidly strode toward the blue dome. There weren't any vehicles on the street. And the little girl in her arms was heavy. Inside her thick trench coat Sally was getting hot.

"My babe!" a spiky-haired woman called out, rushing out of a suddenly-appeared round doorway in the blue dome, snatching the little girl out of Sally's arms.

"Mommy!" the little girl cried. "This nice lady picked up me."

"Oh, thanks to you!" the woman said, hugging the little girl close. "Thought you with Father! He thought me! Thought I lost you... came back to find. Oh, Glory you safe!"

She grabbed Sally by her arm.

"We've inside to go. First wave almost topside! Isn't it Glory?"

Greatly puzzled by the strange happenings, Sally let herself be dragged through the round opening which smoothly winked-out behind her.

The woman with the little girl slumped to the side, panting from her exertions, obviously happy to escape the outside furnace. The metallic-looking dress she wore glittered without crinkling. It was a very strange fabric.

Inside the dome it was much cooler. Sally breathed a sigh of relief, gratefully slipping the hood back off of her head.

"Priestess?" the woman with the little girl gasped, looking in awe at Sally. "Why hair change? Ahhhh! You show End Time when *everything* changes!"

Others were coming up to them from the crowd of people crammed into the large blue dome, also gaping at Sally as she cringed back against the cool blue wall...

—as high above them, clearly visible through the protecting transparent dome, Sally could see *tongues of fire* spitting-down from the sky.

"*Ahhhh! Ahhhh! Ahhhh!*" the whole crowd of people suddenly shouted in unison, ritualistically craning their heads upward at the extended cosmic flames.

Then they all held up their hands as if in supplication.

"*Clean us up! Clean us up! Clean us up!*" they chanted together...

—as a blistering wave of what looked like *volcanic lava* "thudded" down on top of the dome, making the entire structure *shudder*...before slipping off to the side.

With a growing terror in her heart, Sally knew exactly what was happening.

It was *Judgment Day!*

Word of Sally's presence was quickly spreading through the thousands of people jammed into the protecting dome...

—as they turned towards Sally and began chanting in deafening unison: "POWERS! POWERS! POWERS! POWERS!"

In confusion, Sally cringed back against the blue dome's inner surface.

"What—is happening here?" Sally marveled.

Then she noticed what stood at the center of the huge circular chamber. A *hundred-foot tall painted marble statue* of a green-eyed, red-haired woman towered up into the air. The woman chiseled in stone was wearing a white pants suit. On top of that was depicted a jacket with a pushed back hood. And the regal woman on her feet had *white tennis shoes*. One of her arms reached outward. In an opened hand she held a pile of big white pills.

Oh, my goodness—Sally gasped to herself. *That's me! Except for my blond hair, it's my spitting image. But why would I be wearing tennis shoes? This makes no sense. Is this "movie" truly real? Or is this just some sort of induced hallucination?*

Then the crowd went silent, dropping in unison to their knees. As one they all *bowed* to Sally.

"No worries, Priestess," the little girl's mother said, having recovered her breath and now standing proudly at Sally's side. She respectfully lowered her head as she continued. "Temple is intact. *Blue Force* protects us. Thank you, coming to be with us—saving my daughter and us. How blessed we to have you from the Sisters with us as world is washed clean, purified, and we are *changed*. You will lead us in out-go—taken up together! New World awaits us. Finally, End Time is here. How Glory, with us you share. *We love you, Priestess!*"

The chant was picked up by the still-bowed crowd who thundered back: "WE LOVE YOU! WE LOVE YOU! WE LOVE YOU!"

Totally confused, Sally looked out of the transparent dome as the delicate city spirals slowly sagged, visibly *melting*...

—as the thousands packed into the dome now respectfully stood up from the floor. They silently and obediently awaited Sally's next words.

"Holy Priestess!" the woman with the little girl at Sally's side addressed her in a shrill voice which everyone in the dome could hear.

"Give us Blessing. *Prepare* our minds and bodies with your Affirmation!"

Sally shook her head in distress—her green eyes stretched wide, her mound of blond-colored hair flopping limply.

They were expecting something from her. She had to help them, somehow.

They needed direction.

"Even if your...force field...protects you—you can't live in a place where there's no atmosphere or solid land," Sally gasped in horror at what was transpiring. "This is awful—you must *leave* this place!"

Apparently mistaking Sally's words of warning for spiritual affirmation, the vast audience together *CHEERED!*

—as in raging religious ecstasy, the crowd started *dancing* in unison while their world literally *dissolved* around them!

They were chanting again in roaring unison: "POWERS! POWERS! POWERS! POWERS!"

But it wasn't so cool inside anymore.

Even the black ceramic flooring beneath Sally's feet was heating up.

Sally grabbed the mother of the little girl, clutching the woman tightly while shouting into her ear above the loud chanting of the crowd: "What *year* is this?"

Outside, a *sizzling-ROAR* was getting louder and louder—like a giant piece of bacon cooking and sputtering in a city-sized frying pan.

"Year?" the woman blankly replied, her black spikes of hair on her skull starting to wilt in the ever-increasing heat.

"What is today's *date*?" Sally screamed again into the woman's ear.

"Year is 3123," the woman laughed, caught up in the excitement of the crowd. "Is it not Glory, Priestess? It is just as our Holy Mother Linda Powers predicted long ago. It is the Rupturing! God is cleaning us. God will take us, the Faithful, to Him."

She pulled away from the stunned Sally, vanishing with the now-cheering little girl who was pumping her little fist up into the blisteringly hot air in glee—vanishing into the midst of the packed, likewise-cheering mob.

"Oh, Lord," Sally gasped. "If this is real, I'm more than a *thousand years* in the future."

She turned around, trying to get away from the rapturously shouting crowds—their exultations now fading as the heat inexorably increased within the Dome while they were not yet "taken"—their shouts of ecstasy now turning to screams of pain and fear.

"I might as well cook quickly," Sally gasped to herself, hardly able to breathe in the scorching air of the now-trembling Dome, feeling along the vibrating blue wall—its force field obviously laboring to maintain itself—trying to find the exit back onto the flaming streets of the burning city...

—and *fell* through the opening to sprawl upon a dusty floor.

For a moment Sally didn't realize what happened, thinking she was hallucinating a cool retreat in the moment of her incineration.

But, no, she was definitely back in the central hallway of the closed, dark theater.

She *sneezed* from the dust stirred up on the floor.

And it was gloriously *cold!*

"Oh...my," Sally whispered, rolling onto her back to look up at the faded poster on the wall, illuminated by the dim light of her likewise-fallen flashlight.

"That was...a *hell*...of a movie," she gasped, reaching out a shaking hand to retrieve the flashlight, flipping it off to preserve its battery.

Exhausted, still lying on her back, her head pillowed with the bunched-up hood behind her neck—she drifted off to sleep, wrapped up in delicious coolness.

Dave realized that he had no car.

That stupid girl with the turtle tattoo!—he thought to himself, standing there alone in the parking lot of the hospital, shaking his head in dismay. He placed his hands in exasperation upon his hips, pondering what to do next.

She kidnaps me, poisons my mother to death, and then steals my car leaving me stranded. If I ever see her again I'll strangle her with my own two hands!

It felt good to release his rage, even if it was just internal muttering.

On impulse, he looked upward at the sky and *howled!*

Some people walking into the hospital looked back at him in alarm.

He ignored them, resolutely setting his shoulders as he starting trudging down the road.

It wasn't that far back to his Mom's house. This was a small town. You could get anywhere in five minutes—in a car, that is. On foot it'd take him a good hour of walking to get to his Mom's house and see if her old car still ran.

He felt in his pocket for his keys...

Damn, stupid girl with the turtle tattoo!—he groaned again to himself, remembering. That bitch took his keys! Now how would he get into his Mom's house? How would he start up her car? *Au-uuggghhh!*

Well, he'd find a way.

And walking did give him time to think...

Who the hell is she, anyway?

Why could no one in the grocery store identify her?

What sort of weird gun does she have?

Why is she interested in me? I'm nobody. I thought that terrorists went for big targets, not nobodies!

And why would she want to murder my mother—and do so in such a bizarre way...with a poisoned vitamin pill?

Then the thought thudded onto him like a ton of bricks: his mother was dead.

His vision began blurring from pain at his loss.

He knew in his gut that it should not have happened. Something was wrong with the world. She was supposed to recover, not die!

"I can't think about it," he sternly ordered himself. "I've just got to get back to Edmond, get back to my own house, and figure things out from there. That's my goal. Step-by-step is what I've got to focus on. One step at a time...one step at a time," he repeated as he wearily slogged along the sidewalk, still puzzling on the unanswered Questions swirling around that awful girl.

—when he tripped on a wide crack and fell flat on his face on the concrete!

He heard a sickening "crunch".

"Damn it!" he moaned, feeling at his bruised nose. No blood. Lucky he didn't break anything... did he?

"Oh...hell," he groaned, feeling in his front shirt pocket to discover the "crunching" sound came from his cellphone being smashed!

"God damned girl with the turtle tattoo!" he shouted. Lucky no one was nearby. They'd have thought *he* was crazy!

Dropping the shattered remains of the cellphone into a trash can beside the road he kept on walking—furiously steaming and mumbling to himself.

Finally, he trudged down 12th street and stood in front of his Mom's house. Well, now it was Cat's. Jean made out a will a couple years back when she first got sick, leaving everything to Dave's sister. Jean figured that Catherine with a family and kids needed the house, or what money would come from its sale, more than her strange, *snake*-raising bachelor son. Well, that was perfectly fine with Dave. Cat did need it more than him.

After all, he had a good teaching job, which he'd kept for ten years now, with no other dependents other than his small zoo of pet reptiles. True, he barely made it month to month on his paycheck, like anyone else. But even though he wasn't yet "tenured", his lecturing was a steady job. The Junior College would always need someone to torture—that is "teach"—uninterested, bored kids with introductory science courses.

Walking to the rear of the house, he reached into his back pocket for his wallet to get a credit card to jigger the lock...

"God *damned* Girl with the Turtle Tattoo!" he *screamed* up into the sky, shaking his fists above his head in anger!

Then he sat in exasperation on the concrete steps at the back door.

She also stole my wallet!

It must have been when she "smacked" him at the hospital with her juicy red lips...

—grabbing his wallet out of his pants at the same time that she snatched his keys!

He stood up, took his shirt off, resolutely wrapped his hand in it, and SMASHED his hand through the small window that was set-into the back door.

"Ouch," he grimaced, seeing blood spurting out where glass shards had pierced through his hand's wrappings, staining his shirt-sleeve.

"Well, that certainly didn't work as well as it always does in the movies," he sighed, knocking out the remaining shards before reaching gingerly inside to unlock the door.

Inside, he located Band-Aids for his pierced hand. He got a fresh shirt from the old stored boxes of clothes from his Dad. Then he went into the kitchen to get something to eat for breakfast. He remembered that there should still be some cupcakes left...but damn it, they were gone! Maybe he was misremembering that his mom put some leftovers into the refrigerator? Well, at least there was the strawberry Ensures that he'd purchased the day before.

But they were also missing.

"Oh...no...I don't believe it," he moaned, a terrible thought occurring to him.

He ran over to the door that led from the house directly into the garage, jerked it opened, and looked in disbelief into the *empty* garage.

"That *God*-damned *Girl with the Turtle Tattoo!*" he screamed at the top of his lungs, tears of rage running down his cheeks.

She'd stolen his mother's old car.

The police weren't happy to see him again. But he didn't care. He just wanted them to catch that thieving murderer!

They came right away when he called 911 to report the theft. At least they looked grateful that they had a new lead on the terrorist lady. They'd gotten nowhere trying to locate his yellow Cavalier anywhere on the roads leading out of town. The highway patrol saw a few of them on the freeway, but none with the license number registered to him.

Now they knew what she'd done.

They appeared to have a grudging admiration for the woman terrorist—who'd doubled back to change vehicles so she could now travel in a previously unidentified old sedan.

"So, how are you going to get home to Edmond, Sir?" a polite young officer asked him.

Dave sat, dejected, at the dining room table.

"Don't know," he muttered, "thudding" his forehead down on the tabletop in front of him.

"Well, I'd suggest a taxi cab," the crew-cut young man kindly said. "It's not too late yet. There are probably a number of them out there still working the evening rush hour."

Yes, the questions and searching of the house for clues by the police had taken most of the day. But now it was evening. The detectives had finished their fingerprints dustings, taken whatever looked useful, and were gone. Just the friendly cop was left.

Dave suddenly remembered his Mother's emergency-stash of cash. He was sure that Cat wouldn't begrudge him taking it. As soon as he got new credit cards and debit cards made up, he'd pay the emergency money back. His mother always kept several hundred dollars or so in small bills hidden at the bottom of her sock drawer.

"Good idea," Dave thanked the officer. "I still have some cash so I'll be ok."

"If you're sure?" the man said, going out the front door. "We've taken prints and everything so we won't be back this way unless there's some other need."

"No, thanks a lot. I'll be ok," Dave gratefully assured him as the last remaining officer walked out to his patrol car.

Dave went into his mother's room and found the cash just as he'd remembered it.

"Thanks, Mom," he whispered into the empty room. "You always did your best to look after me even if I didn't appreciate it. And here you are still looking after me."

He fought back tears. There'd be plenty of time for that later. It wouldn't be long until the funeral.

"Wait—I totally forgot!" he gasped.

He ran out to the front door to see if the officer was still there.

But the officer was gone.

Those God-damned poisoned "vitamins"! There was no reason to keep those pills a secret anymore. They *hadn't* cured his mother of her cancer—they'd *killed* her.

Where was it that the murdering monster-girl said the rest of the pills were? Oh yes, in a plastic baggy sitting beside the refrigerator.

There they were...

The police had ignored the pills, apparently thinking they were inconsequential—along with similar other items his mother had scattered around.

"You killed my mother," Dave growled, picking up the baggy with a trembling hand.

The large white, elongated pills rolled around in the bag. He was tempted to just flush them down the kitchen drain and be rid of them.

But he set the bag back down on the dining room table. Then he sat in a chair, staring at the pills angrily. He'd phone the police again. That's what he'd do. They'd come and gather up the evidence.

As he started to get up from the table he noticed something under the pile of empty plastic baggies on the table. It was a *second* bag of the same white pills, this time with a note in it.

What the hell?

He pulled out the bag, opened it, and read the note.

It said: *"Dave, here is another month's worth of Optimmune. It's not for your mother. One month is sufficient for her to not regress. This additional bag is for a friend of hers whose name is Samantha Smith. She also has cancer. She lives in Ada. She's a personal friend of mine as well as your mother's. I don't know her address. Please get this to her and ask her to take one pill per day for a month. She should go to the hospital if she feels sick. Thanks!"*

Christ, that fiend wanted Dave to poison yet another poor woman!

In a fit of rage, he took both bags of pills, walked outside the backdoor to the big bin filled with a week's worth of garbage—and unceremoniously dumped the contents of the plastic bags into the trash.

There! Evidence or not, they were *gone*.

It was his one act of defiance against that insane terrorist religious-nut girl.

He walked back into the house, locked the back door behind him, and went over the landline phone to locate a cab company willing to haul him two hours to Edmond.

"Yellow cab" didn't mind at all as long as he had two hundred dollars cash.

Yes, he did. Indeed, that was about all the cash he had. But it was enough to get him back home to Edmond.

Waiting for the cab to arrive, Dave decided to check the doors of the house to make sure they were all locked. He didn't know how long it'd be before he or Cat returned. He didn't want anyone to walk in and mess things up. With his mother deceased, Cat would want to sell the house as soon as possible. So Dave was careful to leave it secured.

But in the garage he noticed a slip of paper on the floor.

Picking it up, he saw it was a several-time-folded official *pillbox insert.*

Back sitting at the dining room table, he started idly scanning through it.

"Jesus Christ!" he gasped to himself. "It says never to give more than one pill per day—*'dangerous side effects, including death'*!"

He sat stunned for a minute, considering.

Then he quickly searched the printed text for one more item...

"Ah, there it is!" he exclaimed in wonderment.

It said: *"Approved for sale by the Food and Drug Administration."*

How could that be?

He'd never heard of such a medication—an *"overlapping retroviral DNA-reprogramming immune system maximizer"*! And it was supposedly sold over-the-counter, not by prescription?

What the hell?

He went back to the phone and called up the cab company, canceling the ride.

It was going to take him some time to dig through all that trash out in the bin in order to retrieve each and every pill. And then he was going to read carefully through the fine print of that impossible insert, word by word.

If this really was some new miracle-medication—complete with a mock-up of what an approved insert would read—then it wasn't only a treatment for a specific terrible disease but an entirely new modality likely worth *billions* of dollars!

Dave didn't care about the money. But he did care about those suffering from incurable diseases, like his mother. If, when taken properly, this "retroviral-mediated immune-system rebalancing" would cure those people—it'd be worth all the pain he'd suffered from that ding-bat girl.

In fact, come to think of it—could "Linda" be a criminal, terrorist, religious fanatic *and* a renegade pharmaceutical company employee all at once?

Perhaps she told him the truth.

If this medication was really what it claimed to be—and Linda was on the run threatening to reveal it to the world—then powerful forces were after her and anyone else aligned with her.

It was a matter of *big money*.

Chapter 5

<u>MONEY</u>

"Oh Lord, won't you
Buy me a Mercedes Benz
My friends all drive Porsches
And I must make amends…"
Janis Joplin was a star
A rock-and-roll phenomenon
Brilliant in poetry and song
Dead at the age of twenty-seven
Her artistry and earnings cut short
Too much alcohol and heroin…
The Luminary Chronicles, 5:68-72

Sally woke up groggy, aching, shivering, conflicted, and hungry.

It wasn't so pleasant sleeping passed-out on the hard floor of an abandoned, dusty theater.

Then again, it beat being incinerated at the end of the world.

For a while after awakening she just lay there, staring up at the paint-flecking ceiling. Several large cobwebs stretched from side to side in the hallway. Daylight was now filtering in from the dust-covered windows at the front of the theater. She could hear cars going past on Main Street outside. It was Monday, a work day. Occasionally, Sally heard muffled voices on the street as people walked past.

A *thousand* years in the future—she marveled to herself. Yes, it was still the end of the world, but pushed off to a "safe" distance.

When she was sent into the past by the aliens to have a "do-over", Judgment Day was only ten years off. Somehow her actions would push off God's destruction of humanity by a thousand years!

How would she do this?

Ah, of course—she nodded to herself.

She didn't have to dream something up. She'd just *seen* how to change the future. The ending of the "movie" was horrific, but the "take home message" was beyond fantastic.

I'm going to start a new religion!—she thought to herself, amazed. She recalled that towering statue of herself, plus all the loving devotees. Dark Energy generation still existed in that future, but seemed well-controlled and carefully restricted. *And now that I know my course of action, I bet I can do even better. Maybe I can prevent Judgment Day entirely from happening!*

Yet...she knew that starting a new religion was a huge undertaking. It couldn't happen in her Dimension. She'd be stopped dead by the State. It could only happen here, in Dave's permissive world. Was this why she'd been prompted to latch onto Dave and enter his "United States of America"?

But her exhilaration was cut short by a sober thought.

This wasn't just stopping Dave's research. This was founding a whole new social movement. Destruction is easy. Building from scratch a brand new elaborate system is incredibly hard!

"How in the world can I accomplish such a giant undertaking?" she whispered to herself.

And why was she being so quiet? There was no one else around. She was safe for the moment, hidden away in the closed-down movie theater.

Ah, she knew the answer. It was obvious.

"All it takes to be successful at any big movement—whether commercial, political, or religious—is *money*...lots and lots of money," she spoke aloud. "And I've just the means to do it!"

She reached out a hand and patted the leather shoulder bag affectionately, which was lying beside her in the dust. In it were her *pills*. Despite the drastic side effects on uninitiated recipients, they could work real miracles. There were large pharmaceutical companies that routinely paid a billion dollars to bring just one "breakthrough" medication to market for a single, well-defined medical condition.

And Optimmune was a medication that could effectively treat *multiple* diseases. In Dave's Dimension the pill was a goldmine.

"First, though, I've got to have food," she admonished herself as she sat up. She retrieved her shoulder bag and pulled out one of the remaining bottles of Ensure.

"No," she said, reluctantly placing the small bottle of syrupy drink back into her shoulder bag. "I need real food, *solid* food."

It was then that she smelled a strong odor of *breakfast* being cooked. It caused her mouth to start watering. There must be *restaurant* nearby.

Her stomach was *growling* in anticipation.

She levered herself to her feet, gathered up her fallen stuff, and slipped the grey hood up over her head.

"I'm no terrorist," she laughed as she departed by the back door of the theater into the alleyway. "I'm 'little *grey* riding-hood.' Hah!"

Then, more soberly, she whispered to herself as she walked down the alleyway... "But what will I pay with? They'll think that my real money from my Dimension is just counterfeit 'play' money?"

She smiled, reaching into her back pocket.

She held up the money she'd taken from Dave's wallet. Pictures of strange-but-acceptable people stared back at her: *Washington, Lincoln, Hamilton,* and *Jackson—*whoever *they* were?

"I'm *rich!*" she said, dancing around in a little circle. "Maybe it's not the billions I truly need—but rich enough in this Dimension's strange money to buy me a big, delicious breakfast."

Maybe things were finally looking up for her.

Dave was riding high. Things were finally looking up for him!

The police phoned him at his Mother's house as he sat studying that inexplicable Insert. They'd found his car. A hiker in the woods near the Park reported seeing it in a gully, covered by branches. FBI agents quickly searched it, lifted fingerprints from the steering wheel, found nothing else of value in it, and authorized turning it back over to him.

Oh, they'd also found his wallet sitting there on the front seat. The money in the wallet was missing, but his driver's license, credit cards, and other contents were still there.

That was a relief not to have to deal with reporting stolen cards and getting new ones.

The front of the car was banged up. *That damn terrorist bitch couldn't drive a simple clutch!*—he groaned to himself. His car would need some body work, but at least it still ran fine.

Now he was in it, leisurely cruising up highway 1-West towards Ada.

It'd taken only a quick phone call to the operator to find the phone number of Samantha Smith in Ada. There was only one such name in the directory for the city. She answered right away.

Yes, she said she knew Jean from their treatments at the cancer center. And yes, she was so sorry to hear about Jean's passing. And, of course, she was happy for Dave to come by on his way back to Edmond to drop off a gift that Jean had wanted to give her.

He was going to give her the pills.

It was obvious from her short conversation with Dave that the lady was dying. She sounded terrible over the phone, gasping out her words.

Maybe if she took the required dosage instead of accidently doubling it, then...?

It was the least Dave could do for his mother.

Perhaps, in memory of his mother, another cancer-stricken person might yet live.

Sally walked into the restaurant with her head ducked low, the hood safely obscuring her face.

It was indeed near the closed theater, on the first side-street: *"Georgia's Happy Home Kitchen."* Not to attract any undue attention, Sally walked to the end of the alley and back up the street to enter at its front.

It had a big bright sign hung high outside proudly proclaiming its name. Big picture windows adorned the front. Sally could see a large blackboard inside along the left wall spelling out the day's specials.

She paused in the doorway, surveying the interior. The walls were lined with shelves sporting old pots, knick-knacks, and pictures of dogs and cats. The lighting was a soft yellowish glow. And smacking her in the face like a ton of bricks was the enticing smells of breakfast: *fresh-baked oven bread, sizzling pork-products,* and *cooling pies,* causing her to salivate in anticipation!

Yummy!

"Hi, honey," a middle-aged waitress called out to her in a casual and friendly way. "Sit wherever you want. We'll be by with a menu in a jiffy."

"Thanks," Sally replied, happily moving to a booth at the back of the restaurant where she'd draw the least attention.

She set her shoulder bag to the side in the booth while keeping its strap in the crook of her elbow. What it contained was too precious to let out of her grasp.

The place was two-thirds filled. There was an array of tables, booths, and an elongated bar. People were quietly visiting with each other, happily shoveling in eggs, bacon, and sausage—and laughing.

Several waiters and waitresses bustled about.

"Morning," a petite young waitress wearing a white apron politely greeted Sally, handing her a menu. "What would you like to drink?"

Sally took the menu, laid it flat onto the table, and looked up past her hood into *deep green eyes!* The pretty young girl also had longish, red hair.

Startled, Sally had no words—then, lowering her voice to sound more masculine—she said: "Uhm...just water, please."

"Ok, then," the girl brightly answered. "Be back with that in a sec'. I'll take your order whenever you're ready."

"Thanks...uh...nice tattoo," Sally hastily added, peering from under her hood in amazement at a *bright green turtle tattoo* on the inside wrist of the waitress' left arm!

The girl smiled prettily, pausing. "Thanks, I just got it recently."

There wasn't any doubt. The waitress had on a short-sleeved shirt. The other tattoos on her left arm were *exact duplicates* of what was hidden under Sally's trench overcoat!

The waitress was *herself!*

This couldn't be a coincidence. The implications were staggering.

"If you don't mind my asking, where did you get it? I've got some myself and..."

"Oh, my boyfriend did it for me," she shrugged, chewing noisily on bubblegum. "He does nice work."

"Does he work at a tattoo parlor?"

"No, he's a freelancer. I can fix you up with him if you'd like."

"I'd appreciate getting his phone number."

"Happy to do so—remind me before you leave," she said as she went to a dispenser for ice and water. She returned briefly with the glass before moving on to another table.

Sally gratefully took a long drink from the glass—while her eyes were fixated on her *identical twin!*

—as a slender young man carrying a load of clean plates walked up and gave the cute waitress a peck on her cheek.

"How's my girl doin'?" he said as he walked on past.

She giggled, continuing to take an order from the patrons at the next table...

Snake! It was *Snake!* It was the boyfriend of the "Sally" of this Dimension—the disguised alien that sent her back in time!

He was wearing an apron, a meshwork on his head holding his long black hair into a tight bun. A cigarette dangled from his thin lips. He sported a scraggly goatee. On his bare arms there were numerous tattoos of every color and shape. On the left side of his face a black tattoo of a cobra crept from his forehead to his throat.

"*Ouch!*" Sally winced as a sharp pain hit her wrist which sported her own turtle tattoo...

—as simultaneously the young red-haired waitress gasped, dropping a tray of dirty dishes to the floor with a clatter, grabbing at her own left wrist where her green turtle tattoo was also *glowing!*

—as the glass picture windows EXPLODED INWARD and a pickup truck *SMASHED* through the front wall into the restaurant!

Patrons screamed as they were tossed to the side or crushed beneath its wheels.

"Bill! Help!" the middle-aged waitress screamed.

"What the hell?" a beefy man yelled, running out of the back of the shop waving a bloody butcher's knife...

—as a black-clad, black ski-masked man with a hand gun emerged from the pickup and started *firing* into the dazed crowd!

The beefy man lost the butcher knife, which clattered to the floor. He dived behind the bar, now emerging with a shotgun in his hands...

BLAM!—the sound of the shotgun being fired briefly deafened Sally as she now lay on the floor, broken glass and plaster covering her body, still clutching her shoulder bag.

She saw the window of the pickup truck *shatter* from the shotgun blast!

Bang! Bang!—the pistol in the intruder's hands barked, catching Bill on his shoulder and spinning him around...

—as Sally felt a heavy weight pressing down on her.

It was the prone body of the girl waitress, who appeared to be stunned. She'd been struck by hurtling debris.

Snake grabbed a stool, *flinging* it at the approaching gunman, who disdainfully knocked it to the side with a karate kick.

"You stupid, god-damned *window-smasher!*" Snake shouted as he jumped at the shooter, his thin arms flailing around in the air like a three-dimensional living tattooed painting. But just as quickly he was dropped by a brutal punch to his throat.

Snake fell to the side, clutching his throat, gagging—then jumped right back up with the *butcher knife* poised to slash the shooter...

—who fired one bullet into the young man's head, killing him instantly.

Blood spurted from Snake's skull as his body crumpled to the floor.

The shooter stepped up to Sally who was lying prone with her twin sprawled on top of her, bending over to grab the other girl's hair...

—and Sally *jabbed* the man through the webbed eyeholes of the black ski mask with two stiffened fingers.

The gun dropped and Sally struggled to roll over to grab it as the shooter immediately recovered, *stomping* hard on her outstretched hand!

"Damn it!" Sally yelled, jerking her hand away from the crushing pain, while with her other hand she grabbed a fallen dinner plate and *launched* it at the man's concealed head.

"CLUNK!" went the plate as it smashed into a thousand pieces on the shooter's head...

—who momentarily staggered backward...

—as Sally finally got out from under the girl's body and leapt at the shooter, kicking the man's feet out from beneath him, spinning him around while simultaneously slapping on a *rear naked choke-hold!*

Thank God for the State-mandated self-defense courses she'd taken over the years.

"Call the police!" someone at the front of the restaurant was frantically shouting. "Call 911!"

—when the shooter deftly jerked out of Sally's grasp, leaving behind the black ski mask dangling in her hands as he simultaneously knocked the hood back off of Sally's head.

He froze in place.

"You!" he gasped, stumbling backward, obviously recognizing her. "But...?" he said again, looking in confusion from the blond-headed Sally over to the red-headed waitress on the floor then back again.

It was an elderly oriental man with a jagged scar on his left cheek.

"Paul?" Sally gasped, recognizing him.

Making a decision, the shooter spun away from Sally to grab his gun up from the floor and point it straight at the prone girl's head...

—as Sally simultaneously pulled her own gun out of her still-dangling shoulder bag and *yanked* the trigger...

And the oriental man instantly convulsed, covered in a *cloud of roiling, crackling electricity!*

He screamed in agony.

Then he fell to the floor, unconscious.

Sally stepped up to him, grabbing his gun. For a moment she was confused. The gun looked exactly like a standard-issue Keeper's weapon, but fired solid projectiles? Clearly, Paul didn't want to advertise his being from another Dimension. Whatever, Sally quickly slid the bullet-firing black gun into her shoulder bag. At the rate she was going, she was going to need all the weapons she could get, whether they fired bullets or pure energy.

Outside, she heard the wail of rapidly approaching police cars.

Still holding her own gun at-ready, she backed through the debris to the ragged gap in the front wall where the entrance door had been.

"Sorry about the mess," she giddily apologized to no one in particularly as she turned and darted away down the street.

Damn it! She wasn't going to get any breakfast after all.

Dave pulled into the driveway of the address that Samantha Smith had given him.

He saw an elegantly thin woman hurrying out of the house wearing a polka-dot scarf around her bald head.

She thrust her wrinkled face into his opened side window. A cigarette dangled from her thin lips.

"Are you Dave King?" she curtly asked.

"Yes," he greeted her. "And I assume you are Mrs. Smith?"

"Mind giving me a ride out to my daughter's workplace? I'm just a poor widow lady who can't work because I'm sick. I've got no money for expensive cabs."

"Uhm, sure, I guess," he shrugged. "Perhaps we could talk on the way?"

"I don't drive anymore, young man," she sternly replied, yanking open the passenger door. "I'm too disoriented for that—what with the radiation therapy and all," she said as she slid in beside him, slamming the door shut behind her.

"Do you mind?" she preemptively asked, taking a long draw on her cigarette before exhaling two long streams of white smoke from her pinched nostrils.

"Well, actually..."

"Then let's get going!" she said, not waiting for his answer, taking another long draw on her cigarette.

"What's the problem?" he asked.

"It's on all the news channels," she cryptically replied, as if he should know. "Drive to Main Street. You know how to get there, don't you, young man?"

"Yes, Ma'am, I do," Dave nodded. "My Mom likes to...well...*liked* to go to a restaurant there on Sunday afternoons..." he choked up.

"Which restaurant?"

"It's a Chinese buffet restaurant," he unsteadily replied, getting himself back under control.

"That's not where we're going," the stern woman angrily insisted. "We are going to *Georgia's Happy Home Kitchen*."

"Where's that?"

"It's where my daughter works as a waitress. Get moving, young man. Hurry it up!"

"Uh, sure—I meant the address...?"

"It's two blocks east of your Mom's Chinese place."

She rolled her window completely down and flicked ashes out into the street.

"Ok, then—but what's happening?" he asked.

"I hate taxis!" she said, mushing her lips together into a thin, angry line.

"Uh...ok..."

"And since you were coming, I figured we could kill two birds with one stone. That ok with you?"

"Fine with me, Ma'am," he said, pulling out of the driveway, "but what's the rush?"

"It's that *terrorist girl* everyone's been hunting. She blew the place up! My daughter's been hurt. The police called me. They said to come right away. She was knocked unconscious. But she's awake now. She's been asking for me. She won't talk to the police unless I'm there with her. So the police insisted I've got to come right down! Is that plain enough for you, young man?"

"Say what?" Dave gasped, not keeping up. "A female terrorist, you say?"

"Yes—with a Chinese accomplice," she barked. "She got away. Now they're hunting her. There must be a thousand police and military there. They've got the male terrorist in custody. The female one's still at large. Hurry up! My daughter needs me!"

He drove on through the crowded streets, dumbfounded. As they got closer to East Main the streets got even more congested, with roadblocks in place turning people around.

Dave explained to the officers at the roadblocks who he was chauffeuring. They let him through without delay.

Soon they were at the restaurant.

It looked like a war zone.

The back half of a pickup truck stuck out of the bashed-in front of the restaurant. Police barricades restricted access to the side street. Police patrol cars with flashing red lights were thick on the street. Military personnel in uniforms, carrying rifles, patrolled the sidewalks.

The whole closed-off street bustled with first responder emergency personnel. Several ambulances stood with their lights flashing.

Stretchers with groaning patients on them were being carefully removed from the rubble of the smashed interior of the restaurant.

"Oh, this is terrible, just terrible!" Samantha gasped as they were
directed by uniformed officers to park close to the smashed-in restaurant. "My poor little girl—I must get to her!"

Dave got out of the car then walked around to help Samantha out.
She dropped the stump of her cigarette onto the street, wobbling
weakly.

"I'll help you, Ma'am," a big man in a suit said, taking her thin
arm. He had a square face, steely-blue eyes, sporting a neatly
trimmed mustache, and short-cropped black hair. Dave recognized
him. He was the same police Detective who'd initially interrogated
him at the hospital before that friendly FBI Agent showed up.

"Well, Dr. King—fancy meeting you here," he said to Dave, grinning lopsidedly.

Dave realized that the Detective was expecting him. What was
going on here? Did the police put a bug into his car?

Dave also recognized the blond lady officer that asked him a question at the hospital. Now she was leading Mrs. Smith away.

"Mrs. Smith asked me to drive her here."

"And just why are you here in Ada in the first place?"

"She was a good friend of my Mothers. I was just stopping by on
my way back to Edmond to let her know about my mother's *death!*"

The man paused in his questioning, ducking his head in acknowledgement.

"Yes, I'm sorry to hear of that and..."

"So if you're finished with me maybe I can leave?"

"Come with me, Dr. King," the Detective ordered, briskly turning
to walk toward the entrance, avoiding the largest hunks of broken
glass littering the sidewalk. "We need you to verify something."

Seeing little alternative, Dave reluctantly followed along behind
him.

He glimpsed the interior of the smashed building...

"That's her!" Dave gasped, pointing. "That's Linda Powers!"

Yes, inside, at a still-intact booth to the side of the rubble, sat a
girl with red hair, green eyes, and a turtle tattoo on the inside of her
left wrist.

"That's the God damned *terrorist bitch* that took me hostage yesterday!" Dave excitedly yelled in the Detective's ear, grabbing him by one of his strong arms.

"Are you sure?" the man calmly replied, allowing Dave a better view by moving to one side.

The light was dim inside due to a number of the ceiling bulbs having been broken when the pickup truck smashed inside, but there was no doubt. *It was her! It was the Girl with the Turtle Tattoo!*

"Yes, that's her! But...what's Mrs. Smith doing with her?" Dave paused, perplexed to see the elderly woman wobbling up to the girl, supported by the blond police woman, and then *hugging* the girl around her neck.

"We have the prints we took off the steering wheel before we returned your Cavalier, Dr. King," the Detective mildly stated, his normally-grating voice now soft and somewhat distant.

"So?" Dave said. "That just proves that the girl in there's the same girl that kidnapped me, right?"

"Yes," the man sighed, "*but...*"

"But?"

"But this girl, Sally Smith, was not in Sulphur yesterday. In fact, she's not been there for more than a year."

"What?"

"Yesterday morning she worked a full shift here at this restaurant. Dozens of witnesses attested to her presence," he shrugged.

"But the fingerprints, the tattoos on her arm, her appearance..."

"—yes, all identical to the woman who kidnapped both you and your mother Sunday morning," the man nodded grimly. "By every measure, it's the same woman. But there's *also* no doubt that she *isn't* the woman who kidnapped you and shot up the Sulphur hospital."

Dave shook his head, frowning. What was happening here? Was he going crazy? Was the whole world going crazy? Linda looked just like that woman. Yet this other woman was...who?

—and that name...*Sally*...that was on the nametag of the girl in the grocery store, which she claimed was wrong! The officer had called the woman there sobbing in the busted-up restaurant Sally *Smith*, Samantha Smith's daughter?

Dave coughed from the dusty air, the debris still being stirred up by the many people walking through it.

He noticed a police blanket covering something, over by the booth where this new Sally and her mother sat. Underneath was a puddle of *red*.

"Did...did someone...get...?" Dave gulped, shakily pointing over at the blanket on the floor.

"That's her boyfriend, 'Snake,'" the Inspector explained. "He's a high school dropout, a dishwasher, working here at the restaurant. Apparently, though, he was also a respected local artist. He did a lot of local tattoo work, including a number of the ones on Sally."

"Is he really...?"

"Yes, the oriental male terrorist killed him," the Detective shrugged. "One clean shot to the head. It was a 9mm full-metal-jacket round, from a Glock handgun. But there was another gun in play. Witnesses were very explicit on the 'cloud of electricity' that your Linda Powers used to subdue the shooter. Then she fled the scene."

"You mean," Dave gasped again, "both Linda and this 'Sally' person were there in the store at the same time?"

"Your Linda has apparently dyed her hair blond. The people present at the scene didn't get the connection, of course. But we've got prints off the glass of water she drank from. They're identical to the girl you see at the table. We're also going to try a DNA comparison. There are probably mucous cells left from Linda when she drank, on the top of the glass. It's at the lab being analyzed as we speak."

"Detective, I am totally baffled," Dave shook his head in puzzlement, though he was beginning to suspect the truth—an incredible truth he knew he had to keep hidden. "And, by the way, why would that oriental terrorist kill some ordinary tattoo artist?"

"We don't know yet, Dr. King," the man said, unblinkingly, looking Dave square in his face. "But we want you to help us find out."

"Me?"

"You obviously have a connection with both of these girls—and we want for you to figure out what's going on and let us know."

"But...how?"

A siren from an ambulance went off loudly as it pulled away carrying wounded patients.

The Detective looked at him with an odd expression, half intrigue and half fear.

"Give Sally and her mother a ride back home—get to know them. Chat them up!" he said.

"How could there be any possible explanation to this? It's impossible! There can't be two identical girls who..."

"Perhaps identical twins, separated at birth—or, some sort of sophisticated identity theft with micro-plastic surgery," the Detective suggested. "The fanatical terrorists in today's world will go to no end at blending into their target society. There's obviously something special about this young lady at the booth, something worth the risk of trying to take her place."

"I guess..."

"Then you'll help us."

"But I need to get back to Edmond," Dave lamely protested.

"You don't need to do anything out of the ordinary," the Detective stated, handing him his card. "Just give them a ride back to their house, establish a connection. We'll continue working the case from our end. We've got lots of men scouring the city. That terrorist girl, 'Linda', won't get away. We found and have secured your mother's car so Linda is on foot. We discovered the car in an alley not far from here. Whatever you may find out from casual conversation is just an additional line of investigation for us. We'd really appreciate your cooperation."

The unspoken threat for *not* cooperating was obvious. Yep. He'd be taken into custody and "escorted" to the nearest police station.

Dave looked at the card: *Inspector James R. Kilbourne, Oklahoma City Police Department.*

"Aren't you out of your jurisdiction?" Dave tentatively asked.

"There are a lot of people on this case, more all the time," the man replied. "I'm just the local cop dealing with our Oklahoma people."

"What about that FBI guy that let me go at the hospital?"

"What about him?"

"Should I report to him as well? He gave me a card also."

"Sure, why not?" he shrugged, "The 'more the merrier', eh?"

Dave hesitantly grinned back.

The blond lady officer was leading the now-weeping Sally plus her frail mother through the debris out toward the street.

Dave wasn't looking forward to chauffeuring them back to their house, but knew he had to do as ordered or he'd be in big trouble.

At least this way the police would think he was being useful. Maybe he could slink away and get back to his life when their attention turned elsewhere.

But Sally's mother had been unpleasant enough. Her daughter was likely even worse!

And despite this new girl being undoubtedly a different person from Linda—Dave was scared of her as well.

If her genetics were identical to the terrorist kidnapper, she was likely a formidable person.

Could she somehow be an identical twin?

Maybe he should charge them for his "cab" ride and totally piss them off—so he'd never have to deal with them again?

But, no, they'd probably just toss him out and steal his car.

Where was that psycho-bitch Linda anyway?

He wouldn't feel safe until she was either dead or in jail.

Sally had no idea how to get home.

She was stranded *125 million years* in the past...

Her present predicament began after she escaped the destroyed restaurant. Sally heard police sirens rapidly approaching in the direction of where she'd parked Dave's mother's old sedan, so she ran to the alleyway and back up to the rear of the closed-down movie theater.

It took just a couple seconds to slip the lock again, go inside, close the door so it looked undisturbed, and get safely into the hallway.

Light from the distant front windows was dim, but allowed her to move without turning on the flashlight that was in her leather shoulder bag.

She was safe for the moment, but where to go?

She was a "sitting duck" on the streets outside. Doubtless they were searching all the buildings close to the restaurant.

She glanced at the darkened archway leading into the first movie, *The Party at the End of the World.*

There was *no* way she was going back in there!

But the next poster...?

"Hmmm, '*Casino Royale*'?"

It was a picture about a secret agent called "James Bond" gambling at a sea resort casino.

The faded poster showed a handsome man in a suit holding a gun. He was pursuing a slender girl in a yellow bikini up a beach. It looked exciting and sexy.

At Sally's wrist, she felt the *soothing warmth* of her Turtle Tattoo gently *glowing!*

Outside in the alleyway she heard heavy boots stomping-up to the locked door.

"Oh, hell," she shrugged, stepping through the dark archway, hoping it opened only for her and not to her pursuers...

—and found herself standing on a *vast seashore!*

"Whoa," she grinned. It was spectacularly beautiful. "Maybe I should strip down and go swimming?" she said to herself.

The ocean was a deep blue, stretching to the horizon. Over it hung many fluffy banks of white clouds.

She breathed deeply and instantly recognized the smell. It instantly filled her with apprehension.

She *knew* this powerfully musky, fresh-smelling, invigorating air!

Somehow, she'd been transported back to the *early Cretaceous*—when dinosaurs ruled the earth! Dave and she, in the earlier timeline, were transported there by the cold-fusion, Dark Energy-tapping Device he'd constructed with her help.

But now she was there yet again...how and why?

A brown *reptilian head* slowly rose out of the water on a very long neck. Black eyes stared at her—hungrily!

As she poised to turn and run, another huge dinosaur with brown stripes down its body thundered past her on four massive legs, galloping like a horse into the waves. Its head towered above Sally fully twenty feet up into the air. Its hind legs were massive.

In the breaking waves it *smashed* into the other dinosaur and began *kicking* and *biting* it!

Their piercing SCREECHES and ROARS were so loud they hurt her ears.

"Ok..." Sally said, backing slowly away up the rolling, sandy seashore...

—until she abruptly *bumped* into something!

Whirling around, she saw a smaller version of the thick-thighed beast that was busily fighting out in the surf.

Honk!—the miniature version barked at her, startled.

"Oh...sorry," she said. She stood face-to-face with a baby dinosaur fully as tall as she.

Quite possibly that other beast in the waves had not been ogling Sally for a meal—but the baby behind her. And now the mother was busily and noisily defending her offspring!

The baby tentatively sniffed Sally, snorted, and then ambled away.

"Well...I guess we won't see any 'James Bonds' here running after scantily-clad females," Sally gulped as she ran as fast as she could over the soft sand to the encroaching forest.

Later, safely sequestered high on a forked branch in the limbs of a large tree, Sally swung her legs out over the long drop to the ground and reviewed her predicament.

How the hell was she going to get home? Was she trapped forever in the distant past with man-eating reptiles? But she knew if she was going to survive she had to be thoughtful, take stock of her situation.

First, it was swelteringly hot. The humidity must be up around 100%. She was sweating profusely from her exertions in the hot, moist environment.

She took off her trench coat and sweater, careful to lodge them firmly to the side in the fork of the large branches, along with her shoulder bag.

"Ok, Sally, where are we?" she wearily asked herself.

She looked out over a marshy, wildly overgrown vista. Very tall trees with canopies of leaves up high but not lower, dotted the scene. On the ground were big tangles of ferns. Strange elongated bright red and orange "flowers" dotted the plants below.

Honks, *tweets*, and *snorts* rang out all around her. Strange-looking primitive birds with big heads, long feathers, and reptilian tails flitted through the tops of the trees. Down on the ground, small dinosaurs scampered on either four or two legs.

She thought she caught sight of what looked like some small rat-like creatures running in packs through the dense underbrush.

"Hey! My ancestors!" she giddily laughed. "Hi guys!" she called-down from her high perch. "There's a big Asteroid coming along in about sixty million years. Hang in there! It'll wipe out those nasty top predators chomping on you to let *you* become the nasty top pred-ators. Keep evolving, boys!"

Here and there small pods of the long-necked "thunder thighs" dinosaurs happily foraged, reaching up to the lower branches of the high trees to munch on bushels of tasty leaves.

"Ok...*food*...can't starve myself."

Her stomach was growling from missing that delicious breakfast at the destroyed restaurant, 125 million years in the future!

She reached into her leather shoulder bag and withdrew one of her three remaining bottles of strawberry Ensure.

She guzzled it, thinking it was the best thing she'd ever tasted.

Breeep?

On the next big fork of branches, half-hidden under piled-on leaves, she saw a clutch of hatched eggs. Each one was big enough to fill up her hand. Huh! Some dinosaurs had the same idea to escape up into the trees, laying their eggs up high.

They were folded and flattened. They were leathery and already-hatched. But in the center of the pile one lone baby was caught, struggling to get out of its egg.

Cautiously Sally climbed over to the other fork and gently lifted out the egg that was only partially hatched.

Could she eat the chick inside? "Yum—tastes just like chicken!" she quipped to herself.

But in the crumpled shell she saw a cute little beak pushing out. It did indeed look like the beak of a chicken, just with *tiny sharp teeth* lining its jaws.

"You want out of there?" Sally said, gently peeling back the leath-ery shell.

It hopped out and immediately scrambled into her lap, "chirping" excitedly!

"Ahhhhh...." She giggled, lifting it up in her cupped hands. "He thinks I'm his mommy!"

Unfolded, the chick was twelve inches long from beak to the tip of its tail. And it did indeed look similar to a plucked chicken, though it had no feathers or wings. It had thick legs with three toes on each foot. Each toe had a sharp claw. It also had longish hanging-down arms, with three clawed-fingers on each hand. It was leathery, with a long reptilian tail. And it had a little red crest on the back of its head. Its underbelly and beak were yellowish. Its skin was a drab olive green.

"Breeep! Breeep!" it chirped up at Sally.

"Oh, you're a hungry baby, aren't you?" she grinned, carefully carrying it back over to her own branch-fork and settling it safely into her upright shoulder bag.

Its big black eyes just managed to look out over the top of the bag.

"Breeep?" it asked.

"Ok, ok, kiddo...I know you're probably hungry, just out of the egg, and all," Sally replied. "And I think I'll name you 'Breep'. Heh!"

She looked around for something it might eat. Since it had teeth it was probably an omnivore capable of eating either meat or vegetables.

"Oh, there are some goodies," she said, spying hanging berry-like fruits in a pod. "Might they feed me too?"

If it was edible for humans, she might not immediately starve to death once her Ensure was all gulped down.

Carefully, she inched over a couple of branches to try to reach out and grab onto the dangling red fruit.

WHACK!

"Yikes!" Sally yelped as she was almost knocked from her branch dangling a hundred feet up in the sky!

Now hanging upside-down, she stared up at the sky past the branch and canopy of leaves. There, Sally spied a circling flock of *flying predators!*

One of them—diving down at her—had just barely missed her arm. Instead it nicked her with the tip of its leathery wing.

She saw it swooping back up into the sky, turning for another dive-attack.

"I know those things," she gasped to herself, still desperately clinging upside-down.

They had long flat wings with no feathers—their wingspan stretching fully twenty feet from tip to tip. They lacked tails. They had long sharp beaks with a balancing spike on the back of their heads.

"Those are Pterodactyls..." she gasped to herself. She congratulated herself on remembering them from her evolutionary biology course taken years ago.

"—and they're going to *eat* me!" she yelped, as yet another dive-bombed her, barely missing her head with an opened beak sporting many pointed, knife-like teeth! "And they'll eat you, too!" she exclaimed at the little dinosaur as she saw one of the zooming predators snatch an empty egg from the nearby nest.

Breep ducked his bald head back into the shoulder bag.

Sally scrambled back to the fork where her gear was sitting, grabbed it all up, slung her shoulder bag over her shoulder, and started sliding down the wide tree trunk as fast as she could—as more and more of the *lethal predators* dropped from the sky directly at her!

It seemed to take forever for her to slide down the trunk, though it probably only took a few seconds.

Thumping heavily down onto the ground she pulled out the Keeper's gun and fired it up at the descending swarm.

BLAM! BLAM! BLAM!

Loud *squeals* sounded as the flying lizards scattered from the ascending clouds of crackling electricity.

"Hah! Take that!" she shouted defiantly up at them, shaking the black gun at them.

She aimed again and squeezed the trigger...

Nothing.

"Damnation!" she yelped, looking down at Breep who ducked his head fearfully back into her bag. "I think the charge is drained. It'll take time to regenerate!"

But the swarm above wasn't waiting as—seemingly defiant—they flapped back together and now *dive-bombed* in mass at her!

"Yikes!" she yelled, dashing through the underbrush as fast as she could, darting back and forth, batting-away the *screeching* lizards as they beat their ten-foot long wings in the air *hovering* and *snapping* at her!

She spotted a dark cave in a hill in front of her, sprinted towards it with her shoulder bag, trench coat, and sweater flopping in her arms—just barely evaded the whirling flock as she *dived* into its darkness...

—*thudding* onto the hard floor of the *empty movie theater*, skidding to a stop with her face mashed up against the opposite wall!

"Wasn't at all what I expected," she groaned up at the faded Casino Royale poster.

She didn't like that movie at all.

"Where were all the gambling, money, and sexy guys?" she whimpered.

Bruised and battered, with slashes on one shoulder from razorsharp reptilian Pterodactyl teeth, she gathered up her belongings and wearily walked to the front end of the closed theater.

Peeking through a corner of the front window she saw that it was now night outside.

"Breeeeep?" the chick in her shoulder bag softly chirped at her.

Yikes! He was still there. She now was in possession of a real live baby dinosaur!

Just what she needed.

"Shhhhh!" she cautioned it, gently pushing its head back into the bag. "The police are probably still looking for me. We've got to keep quiet!"

As her eyes adjusted to the dark interior from the bright sunlight she'd experienced moments before in the early Cretaceous—she indeed heard people outside shouting orders, saw flashing red lights, and heard the "chuttering" of a helicopter hovering overhead.

The military was still out there, searching for her. She understood their interest in her—if nothing more than to capture her amazing new weapon.

But it was damn *irritating!*

Here she was trying to save them from extinction—from going the way of the dinosaurs—and they were hunting her like a rabid animal.

"Oh, hell...what should we do now?" she asked the little dinosaur in her shoulder bag.

As previously instructed, though, it kept quiet—safely snuggled-down inside.

Now that her eyes were adjusting to the darkness, she could see many boot marks scuffed-into the thick layer of dust on the floor.

The trails also led into and out of the various screening rooms.

Good! They'd searched the theater already—and since they didn't have on their bodies "magic" Turtle Tattoos they didn't see anything inside except for empty rooms and dust.

That meant that she had time before they came back. They wouldn't stop until they found her, she was grimly certain. And there was no way for her to escape on the streets outside the theater. The place was swarming with police, military, and other government officials.

"This is probably a bad idea," she gulped, "but we're going to have to try another movie."

Little "snorts" sounded from her shoulder bag.

"Yep, you've got it right, Breep," she sighed. "Lights out and it's time to go to sleep. But now is also our best time to try to make our escape—if we can."

She slowly went back down the hallway, using her flashlight to carefully study each of the faded, blurred posters.

"Ah," she nodded to herself, "interesting."

The tattered poster on the wall in front of her said: "*DUPLICI-TY—a cool, sexy caper!*" It stated that the movie starred Julia Roberts and Clive Owen as a pair of corporate operatives caught between two giant, warring pharmaceutical companies—who became romantically involved.

It was just what Sally needed—*if* the trip would equal the promise of the poster. The last one to the "beach" hadn't been so forthcoming.

But her turtle tattoo was again glowing!

"Well, you threw me a curve ball last time, Turtle Tattoo," she sighed. "But I don't see any better poster. I need money—lots and lots of money—and this one seems my best bet."

In the gathering chill of the night, she slipped back into her sweater and trench overcoat. She didn't ask to have the fate of humanity resting on her shoulders, but she was determined to do her best. She wasn't going down without a fight.

Clutching her shoulder bag close to her body—containing her two guns, the Ensure bottles, the pills, and the sleeping baby dinosaur—she resolutely stepped into the dark archway.

Chapter 6

UP FROM THE ASHES

Only crazy people love combat
When defeat is certain and one is mauled
Blood dripping down from multiple wounds
Broken bones crippling one's movement
Just waiting for the final, lethal blow
Ending the misery, pain, and suffering
At that moment to choose to jump up
And continue the brutal punishment
Rather than simply give up and die
Now there's the definition of insanity
A brilliant type of noble madness...
Would that we all could embrace
And cherish the noble Fight.

The Luminary Chronicles, 6:122-125

Sally sobbed all the way back to her Mom's house.

Her mother tried to comfort her, but Sally was inconsolable. She kept moaning about her dear, departed "Snake."

Dave, a lifelong amateur herpetologist, certainly liked snakes. But a dopey guy covered with tattoos—even having a coiled cobra inked across his face—was not his idea of an innocent, friendly, beautiful reptile!

To Dave, this "Snake" was just some local jerk that the cute duplicate of that awful terrorist lady had taken up with.

It was sad that the guy got his head blown off, but perhaps this new Sally was the better off for it.

Dave knew that was a rotten thought and immediately discarded it. Her boyfriend—no matter how peculiar or unworthy—was dead.

Dave wanted to help lessen her grief. He understood the irrational depths of agony when losing someone near to you, no matter how dopey or irritating they might be.

"Uhm...I guess we're here," Dave said as they pulled up in Samantha's driveway. "You know, I've just had similar strange and terrible things happen to me, Sally. So if you want to talk about it I can..."

She let out a "wail" as she dashed out of the car and ran into the house.

"—or not," Dave shrugged. Maybe this new "Sally" was as unpredictable and bizarre as the old one.

He grabbed a white plastic bag out of the backseat, went around and opened the door for Samantha. He supported her arm as she stiffly walked to the now-opened front door of her house.

"Oh, don't mind my daughter," the elderly woman sighed. Her thin shoulders sagged downward dejectedly. "Even when she's happy she's unhappy. Most of her free time outside working at the restaurant she's stuck away in her room playing with her computers. Young people nowadays..." she *cluck-clucked* with her tongue, shaking her head in despair.

They heard the still-sobbing Sally stomp off into her room and SLAM the door shut behind her.

"That's so true, Ma'am," Dave agreed. "I teach college courses. I find that my students are increasingly self-absorbed, isolated, and resentful. It seems to be a cultural trend that..."

"—oh yes," she nodded as she interrupted him. "Jean did say that her son was a college professor. You're a Doctor, aren't you?"

"Well, I'm a scientist-type doctor...Ph.D. in Physics, actually...but in reality I'm just a teacher at a small college," he sighed. "My research career took a nosedive and now I just putter around in my garage trying to..."

"Still, that's impressive, being a college instructor," she tentatively smiled at him. "Come on in. What with the emergency we never got around to why you're visiting me. Let's get at it."

"Thanks, Mrs. Smith."

Dave followed her into the house. She indicated an old armchair in her small living room. He sagged down into it, happy to have a break.

"I'll get us a snack. Then we can talk all you want."

Dave leaned back in an old armchair, looking up at the ceiling. The room smelled like an old person—musty, dusty, and smoky.

She unsteadily walked back in carrying a tray. On it was a loose pile of small, hard cookies.

She set it on a low coffee table.

"And what would you like to drink—maybe a beer?"

"Oh, a glass of water would be fine for..."

"You don't drink beer?"

"Your religious friend Jean didn't raise her children to drink alcoholic beverages," he patiently explained, nibbling delicately on a hard sugar-cookie before eagerly devouring it.

He grabbed several more, chain-popping them into his mouth.

"My, aren't you the cookie-monster?"

"Sorry," he mumbled at her, his mouth full of half-chewed cookies, "I didn't have anything to eat all day."

She stiffly turned and went back to the kitchen, returning with a beer in one hand a glass of tap water in the other.

She settled into another armchair across from him, eyeing him appreciatively as he finished scarfing down the entire platter of cookies.

She lit a fresh cigarette, took a long pull on it, and exhaled slowly through her nostrils as she lifted the opened can of beer to her lips.

"Nicotine and alcohol are the spice of life," she sighed, before taking a long drink out of the can. "They can bring you bliss in an ocean full of crap."

"Maybe so, Ma'am," he gently smiled, wiping his lip free of crumbs. "But I just prefer water and cookies. Those were delicious. Thanks!"

"Do you want more?"

"Oh, no Ma'am," he grinned. "That's already way past the single-meal calorie count I should be consuming to keep myself trim and fit," he laughed, patting his somewhat-protruding belly regretfully. "I'm fighting the middle-aged 'battle of the bulge' and losing."

She laughed also, taking another drag on her cigarette before breaking into a *fit of coughing*.

"You ok, Ma'am?" he asked, concerned.

She got herself under control, settling back in her armchair.

She sighed deeply.

"Well, Dave, I've got a tumor the size of a baseball in my brain from metastasized lung cancer that even radiation therapy can't control anymore. I'm dying. My daughter who grudgingly supports me financially hates me. And now she's going to be even more distant that her little hippy boyfriend got himself killed trying to be a hero. Who knows if her one place of employment will ever open again. So we don't know if we can even pay the rent this month. And my best fellow cancer-fighter friend just croaked off. But besides that I'm perfectly fine!"

Dave sat in compassionate silence, watching her blow clouds of white smoke from her thin nostrils—while trying not to breathe too deeply sitting close to her there in his chair.

"My mother had something she wanted you to have," he quietly stated, reaching for the white plastic bag he had sitting on his lap.

"Oh?"

He held up the clear plastic zip-lock bag holding the thirty white pills.

"These are some sort of new super-vitamins," he explained. "My Mom said that they made her feel much better and..."

"—didn't do her much good, did they?" Jean curtly interjected. She stumped out the stub of her cigarette in an ash tray before immediately lighting another to stick back into her mouth.

Dave looked at her, hurt.

"Oh, I'm sorry," she apologized. "I've always been a bit short with people—and now that I'm almost gone I seem to take perverse pleasure in setting my tongue free to say whatever stupid thing it wants. I liked your mother. She was always cheerful. I don't know how she did it. She was in even worse shape than me."

"Thanks," he nodded to her. "Yes, my Mother was indeed relentlessly cheerful and..."

"But I don't take vitamins, don't believe in them!"

"Well, I'm not trying to force anything on you..."

"—however, since it's from Jean, I don't suppose one of them will hurt me," she shrugged, taking another long drag on her cigarette before proceeding. "I'll try one and see how it makes me feel—how's that?"

"I'm sure my mother would be happy to hear it," he said.

"So that's it? All this exertion and fuss...I'm getting tired out."

"Yes, that's it. I'll be leaving now..." he smiled at her, starting to get up. Then he settled back down, looking at her intently.

"Something more?"

"Yes, one more thing," he said, leaning forward to emphasize his words.

"Yes?"

"If it does indeed make you feel or even get better, my Mom said it's critical to take the entire course of treatment, one pill per day until they're gone. Otherwise, whatever positive effect you experience won't 'stick'. But *only one pill per day*—any more than that and they might be too much for your body to handle."

"Got it—if they help, one pill per day, no more. Take them tell they're gone. I'll give them a try. But no promises, Dave. I'm results-driven. Blind faith don't do much for me. If I feel the same as I do now then they're flushed straight down the drain."

"That's all I ask."

"I live on cigarettes and beer anyway," she shrugged, "so I've lots of room for pills in my shrunken old belly."

She reached over for the plastic bag, took out one of the white pills, and popped it nonchalantly into her withered mouth.

She washed it down with another swing of beer.

"Done and done!" she said, lifting up her thin brows in exclamation. "Hopefully you just gave me a cyanide pill that will hasten my painful exit. Failing that, anything less is acceptable."

He grinned at her. She was a curt-speaking, feisty old lady. Others, including her daughter, were likely greatly offended by her manner. But after a lifetime of putting up with his always-jabbering, relentlessly-cheerful mother he found Samantha Smith refreshing.

"Good," he said, now getting up. He didn't know if giving the old lady the pills was doing her a favor or not. But he had a feeling his mother would be pleased.

"Well, got to get going," he said.

"Do you have a card or something if I need to contact you?"

"Oh, sure," he said, reaching into his wallet for the fancy business cards he'd once made up and rarely had occasion anymore to give out to anyone.

It was blue with a nice picture of him on it, plus telephone number and e-mail address. Under the picture it said: "David Smith, Ph.D." Hardly anyone but an occasional student ever called him by his earned title "Doctor" so it was fun to pretend he was something special instead of an abysmal failure.

"Here you go," he said, handing it to her.

"Thanks for the ride and the vitamins," she said, painfully levering herself up out of her armchair as well. "You'll let me know about the arrangements for your mother? If I can, I'd like to attend the funeral."

"That's nice of you," he acknowledged, heading out the front door. "I don't know yet but I'll call you as soon as I find out."

"Good—and I'd also like you and my girl to get to know each other a bit better," she bluntly stated. "So I'd appreciate *you* attending *her* boyfriend's funeral. Promise me?"

Yes she certainly didn't mince her words. She was right to the point. She was trying to set him up with her daughter!

Dave doubted that the "sour" twin of Linda Powers would think much of *him!*

"Well, I don't know," he hesitantly replied, scrunching his face up. "You see, I have classes to teach and..."

"Make time for it."

He winced. He hated going to funerals, especially for a person he didn't know—and doubly not with relations of the deceased who he also didn't know. He never knew how to act or what to say.

"I'll try if..."

"Don't try. *Do* it!" she ordered him.

"Alright, then," he reluctantly promised. "Tell me when and I'll be there."

"Good," she said, closing the door behind him.

He walked out to his banged-up Cavalier impressed with the woman, wondering what she'd done as a profession before falling ill with cancer. Maybe she was a barroom bouncer!

Naw...probably she was the tough-as-nails head mistress at a school for young women.

Whatever, she was one tough old bitch.

It took a full two hours more until he finally turned into the block where his aging house was located.

The sun was low in the sky. It was Monday afternoon and the thick evening traffic on the freeways had been brutal.

He was exhausted, wanting only to take a quick check of his small "zoo" of reptilian pets and crash upon his bed.

"What the hell?" he said to himself as he drove into the street and had to thread his way between several police cars and fire engines.

Red-coated men were coiling up large water hoses.

He saw his house.

It was entirely *burned to the ground!*

"Jesus Christ..." Dave gasped, not believing his eyes.

He parked his car in an open space on the opposite curb, dazedly stumbling out into the crowd of onlookers.

"Dave, I'm so sorry," a man said, spying him and hurrying up to Dave.

It was Dr. George Johnson, his colleague from the junior college. George was a round-faced, bald, jolly man wearing a blue-striped sweater over his chubby, short body.

"George...what...happened?" Dave gasped, looking in bewilderment at the smoking, black ruin of his house.

"There was an explosion in your garage," George sadly explained. "The fire Chief thinks it was probably a gas line leak. Actually, I was there when it happened. I'd taken some time off from the college and stopped by to do the daily chores for your creatures. I just managed to get them all out. I grabbed a sheet off your bed and bundled the animals into it, tying it off at the top so they couldn't escape. I've got them out in my car. But there was nothing I could do for your house. The fire just consumed everything."

Dave stood blankly staring at his friend for a minute.

Vaguely, he remembered the *warning* that the Girl with the Turtle Tattoo whispered in his ear at the hospital when she'd hugged him!

It came true. Her prediction came true. What did that mean about her other claims?

Then, he numbly asked: "The firemen...they couldn't...?"

"It took a while for them to get here," George sadly explained. "Actually, just as I got your animals out, they came up. It wasn't all that long. Some of your neighbors must have called them. But the fire was just too advanced. They stopped it from spreading to the surrounding houses, but your whole house was engulfed."

"My research...my experiments...my equipment..."

"It's all gone, Dave, I'm sorry," George sincerely said, putting a sympathetic hand on Dave's shoulder. "I tried to call you as soon as it happened, but couldn't get an answer on your cellphone so..."

"It broke," Dave curtly replied. "I thought what happened before to me was bad—but this is a total disaster. This is my life's work. And it's all up in smoke!"

"But maybe it's for the best," George quickly encouraged him. "You weren't getting anywhere, were you? You didn't have any social life outside of puttering around in your garage with your experiments and taking care of your reptiles. I know it's a terrible thing, Dave, but even the blackest cloud can have a silver lining. Maybe now you can just leave it all behind and move on?"

Dave held back sobs.

"What 'silver lining' could there possibly be in this black cloud of smoke?"

"You know our school management has never approved of your wanting to do research," George continued. "We're strictly a teaching college. You've missed many meetings and even classes coming in late after you were working through the night in your garage."

"Oh, Jesus!" Dave exclaimed, "The college! I clean forgot to call them! I was going to leave a message but..."

"Yes, they were up in arms this morning when you didn't show up for your classes," George shook his head regretfully. "As soon as I got there I explained what had happened, your mother in the hospital. They understood, but had to cancel your classes since they couldn't find a substitute at such short notice. But I imagine they'll get over it. How is your mother, anyway?"

"She died."

George sucked in his breath, shocked. "I...I'm so sorry, Dave."

"It was a mercy," Dave said, steeling himself to walk across the street and see if anything was salvageable in the smoking ruin of his house. "The cancer had spread throughout her body. At least this way she didn't have to suffer through the final stages."

"Well, I'll take care of your creatures until you find a new place," George kindly volunteered. "Alice won't like it. But as you know I have large glass bookcases in my study for my books and collectibles. I'll take out the contents and substitute your different groups of creatures. It'll be crowded—nowhere as nice as your beautiful habitats—but with a few hot-rocks, feeding dishes, and water bowls they'll be ok there for the time being."

"You're a good friend, George," Dave said dazedly. "I'll come by tomorrow after I straighten things out with management at school. Then...I don't know...this is all just too much," he gulped, starting to break down.

Then he caught himself, forcing back tears.

Yes, this *was* too much! What the hell was going on here? He didn't believe in conspiracies, but this sure smelled like one.

"Come stay with me for a while, Dave," George gently offered. "You can sleep on a cot in my study with your creatures around you and..."

"You're already doing too much for me, George," Dave said, abruptly waving goodbye. "I'll see you tomorrow at school. I'll stay at a motel tonight. I'd rather be alone, anyway—and thanks for saving my pets."

As Dave walked up to the yellow police-tape that was keeping people away from his ruined home, he recognized one of the people. Standing there in a cluster animatedly talking and gesturing was that FBI guy, *Agent Anderson*.

"So, Dr. King, we meet again," the Agent cheerfully called-out to him, walking away from the cluster of uniformed police to intercept Dave.

"Why are you here at a simple house fire?" Dave bluntly accused him.

"It's not so simple when it involves covert, sophisticated, physics research that's..."

"I applied for grants, my school knows all about it, and it's all completely above-board."

"And was it licensed for residential areas?" Anderson mildly stated, straightening the inscrutably dark glasses on his face.

"It was very low-energy work, the kind any high school student can do for a science fair!"

"The fire started in your garage—that's hardly 'low-energy' work that..."

"My friend George said the firemen think it was a gas line that leaked."

"Perhaps—but maybe it was due to your experiments."

"What do you know of my experiments?"

"After what happened Sunday, we've done extensive background checks on you."

"And?"

"And I, for one—am quite impressed."

"What?"

"You've persisted in a line of research that the rest of the scientific community long ago gave up for dead. You've made significant advances as reported in the few papers you've managed to publish in the past decade. Also, your graduate Professor at Yale speaks highly of you. He says that your approach to interactive matrixes for facilitating the interaction of deuterium atoms is innovative. This isn't 'high school science fair' type of work. It's actually quite sophisticated and unique."

Dave was taken-aback. This government Agent knew a lot about him.

"But then again, it's just the sort of thing that my fellow investigators find alarming, especially in this age of self-radicalized terrorists. They were very suspicious of you back at the hospital. And now *this* happens."

"Am I going to be arrested?" Dave angrily asked.

"They certainly do want to take you in," he smiled in a friendly manner, "if for nothing else than an 'abundance of caution.' But I've convinced them to cut you some slack—let you 'run' and maybe lead us to those involved in a wider conspiracy? Eh?"

Conspiracy...conspiracy...*conspiracy!* There was that word again. And this time an official government Agent was using it. Could it be true?

Dave was silent for a moment, looking at the strange immaculately suited man with the dark eyeglasses. What in the world was he up to? Why was he telling Dave these things? If Dave was truly being "cut-loose" then surely they'd not *tell* him what they were doing?

"Let me run?" he dumbly repeated.

Agent Anderson handed him an envelope.

"If you hurry, you can just catch the flight."

"What?"

"It's a paid ticket for a flight from Oklahoma City out to Newark, New Jersey—leaving in forty-three minutes."

"What the hell?"

"Your prior graduate Professor, hearing of your troubles, just invited you out to his lab for a 'sabbatical.'"

"But...my classes at the local college...?"

"Oh, they're going to fire you tomorrow."

"What?"

"Yep, this is the last straw for them. You've been late and missed too many classes and meetings due to your late-night researching in your garage. Now that you're under scrutiny for possible crimes, they're happily cutting you loose."

"Oh, Christ—then there's no way I can take off to..."

"Not to worry. One of my assistants will stand in for you tomorrow with your administrators, get everything straightened out. She'll get you a nice severance package. You'll find the money in your bank account by the end of the day tomorrow. You'll be good financially for six months, at least."

"You're presuming a lot!"

"Am I?"

"But...there's my burned-down house, insurance adjusters...and what about my mother's funeral—*Snake's* funeral...and...and..."

"It's all happening too fast, isn't it?" the Agent consoled him.

"What *the hell* is going on, anyway?" Dave shouted at him, taking a step backward crumpling the envelope into a wad.

The surrounding crowd of onlookers, police investigators, and firemen all looked over at Dave.

Suddenly adopting a threatening expression, the Agent raised a gun and pointed it directly at Dave!

"You're coming with me!" the Agent loudly yelled back at him, deftly swinging Dave's arm painfully up and around into the small of his back.

"But...?" Dave gasped as the Agent hustled him into a black limousine.

"Play along," Anderson grated into his ear. "Otherwise, the local police will have you behind bars."

Dave ducked his head as he was thrust into the back of the limo. Anderson slid in beside him, waving for the driver to get going.

"It's faster this way, anyway," Anderson happily nodded. "Now we'll definitely get you to the airport on time. And don't worry about your house insurance. My people will take care of that as well."

"But *why* are you doing this?" Dave gasped, leaning back and wearily closing his eyes. "Shouldn't you be hauling me away to military prison—instead of helping me to escape?"

The Agent was silent for a moment as the limo picked up speed.

"I told you before I was on your side," Anderson quietly replied, "and I meant it."

"I can't believe you're helping me from altruistic friendship!"

Anderson nodded thoughtfully, apparently coming to a decision.

"We believe in your work," he confidently stated.

"What?"

"My colleagues and I want to help you continue your work."

"Why?" Dave gasped, incredulous.

"The world is collapsing around us, Dr. King. As a species we are in sad shape: devouring nature, depleting the natural resources, screwing up the atmosphere, and chewing each other to pieces in endless, stupid wars. The only answer is plentiful, clean energy. That's what you are working to achieve, isn't it?"

"Well...sure...but it's not likely to succeed or even..."

"Maybe not, but your lone efforts can easily be nipped in the bud," Anderson replied. "Your best chance of success is getting back together, one more time, with your graduate Professor at Yale University.

We mean to give you that chance. You're not the only scientist we're protecting, mind you. But we have great hopes that you might succeed."

"And just who is 'we'?"

"We're a...consortium...operating to the side of the visible government. We keep a sane, guiding eye on the established scientific organizations and enforcement agencies—doing what we can to protect promising projects from interfering forces."

"Jesus Christ!" Dave gasped as he was swung to the side from a sharp turn of the limo traveling now at a high speed along the highway. "I was right. There *is* a conspiracy!"

"There are indeed powerful forces aligned against you, Dr. King," Anderson softly stated. "The unfortunate events of the last few days have drawn their attention. But you can count on us when you're up against the wall. You have my card, right?"

Dave had it in his wallet.

"I do."

"Good," Anderson said. "Keep it with you. And, oh, here's a new cellphone for you. Now you can call me anytime you need. It also picks up on calls to your old cellphone number. Just try not to smash it like you did your last one. Ok?"

Dave silently accepted a black, slim, cellphone—sliding it into his top shirt pocket.

They drove on in silence for a while before pulling up at the sweeping arch of the *Will Rogers World Airport* passenger drop-off terminal.

As Dave stepped out of the limo, Anderson stuck out his hand.

"I...appreciate...your help," Dave grudgingly admitted, taking the Agent's offered hand.

Anderson's grip was solid and strong.

"Just call if you need help," he said. "Whether you believe it or not, the future of humanity is hanging in the balance. We need you to do your part, Dr. King. *Please* don't disappoint us!"

"I'll...try my best," Dave weakly replied.

Dave gulped, standing there wavering in the evening darkness as the black limo pulled away.

He'd better hurry.

He only had eight minutes to make his flight.

Sally stood at a floor-to-ceiling, full-wall glass window looking *down* over nighttime New York City.

The sight was stunning!

"Wow," she whispered in awe to the baby dinosaur fast asleep in her shoulder bag. "It's not a city from a thousand years in the future, but it's still impressive."

Narrow, vertical steel frames ran up the glass window every six feet or so, but the otherwise-unobstructed view extended along the entire wall.

A dazzling sea of lights swam down below—sprawling and moving as living ribbons on the city streets, climbing up huge skyscrapers, and reflected in the flat waters of the winding Hudson.

"Well—better get to work," Sally happily muttered. She turned away from the spectacular nighttime view to the central, mammoth desk.

On it stood a large display screen plus a computer keyboard.

Sally slid into the comfortable leather chair behind it, knitted her fingers together, turned her hands over, and stretched out her fingers, "cracking" her knuckles.

"So let's just see what the top pharmaceutical company's CEO has on his private computer in his secluded, corner office sitting near the top of the *One World Trade Center*," she chuckled, enjoying the challenge.

As a leading expert in evolved synthetic intelligent programs in her Dimension, Sally had no trouble circumventing the clumsy passwords and encryptions of the "primitive" binary-code computer.

"Hmmmm...." she gloated, bringing up on the screen various spreadsheets, project reports, and personal highly encrypted e-mails. "*Very* interesting, indeed."

The slumbering Breep "snorted" from inside her shoulder bag, which was now carefully deposited on the floor at her feet behind the desk.

"Finally, we are going to *kick some ass!*" she grinned.

Chapter 7

<u>NEGOTIATION</u>

What do you want

When your blood runs cold as ice

All your defenses are melted away

And all your successes turn to failures

Is there anything more pitiful than a ghost

Locked into a dying shell of disregard

"Dead man walking!" not just as a theory

But an apt description of your forward movement

Every step taking you closer to your execution

Just moments in the future to disappear forever

Is "salvation" really worth the price you must pay?

The Luminary Chronicles, 7:38-42

As Dave walked out of the passenger exit at Newark, New Jersey, it was still dark.

He'd caught a few hours of sleep on the flight from Oklahoma City to the East Coast, but it was fitful.

He was dead tired, just hoping to grab a cab to take him to some hotel...

"Dave, my boy!" came a happy shout as Dave saw hurrying up to him a distinguished, white-haired elderly gentleman.

"Professor Volodymyr!" Dave exclaimed as they met in a warm embrace. "I didn't expect for you to have to come out here to pick me up and..."

"No trouble, my boy! From what the FBI agents told me who came to my office, you are involved in very interesting troubles, right? And it gives me one last chance to do actual lab work. Hah! I've kept up with your publications of course, quite innovative. And now there's a hint of effectiveness, eh?"

Victor Volodymyr was a tall man wearing a casual blue cardigan sweater. He was fully a head higher than Dave. A mass of white fuzzy hair drifted around the top of his head. His thin, smooth-shaven face was lined and spotted, betraying advanced age. But his blue eyes sparkled with the excitement of a newborn baby.

"Uhm, what do you mean it's your 'last chance' to work in the lab, Victor?" Dave asked as he was led to a big black van parked in the passenger pickup lane.

"Oh, I'm finally retiring for good," Victor laughed, opening the door for Dave before going around and entering the driver's side of the vehicle. "My lab's been shut for most of this last year. I've no more graduate students or technicians. It's just me guarding the place for whoever takes over next."

"But you're not old enough to retire," Dave marveled, shaking his head in disbelief at his vigor.

"Thank you for the kind compliment," Victor laughed. "But I am a proud ninety-two years old, this very next month. The University's been after me to let someone younger take my slot for decades."

"You'll always be young and vital in my eyes, Professor. I've never seen anyone else with your combination of wisdom and energy."

"Thanks, David. But it does sound old, doesn't it—ninety-two years? Yet I don't feel old at all—at least not where it matters most, in my heart. But...my body *is* letting me down. Do you know that I've had each of my major joints replaced? It's true! I am a 'bionic' man. Hah! I'm literally a walking robot. But the marvels of modern medicine can only keep you going full-speed for so long. That's why I'm finally giving up my laboratory."

"I'm so sorry to hear that," Dave stated sincerely. "Your departure will be a great loss to both the University and to Science."

"Oh, pish-pash," Victor casually brushed-off the compliment. "It's well past time for me to go out and concentrate on enjoying nature at my country house with Ivanna. To tell the truth, I'm getting tired of these science responsibilities. I even renounced my Emeritus status as a past *President of the American Physical Society.* I told them I want to watch the birds come land in the yard. Do you know that I made the birds a feeder, with my own two hands? Yes, David—I started out as a young boy wanting to be a carpenter. And I'm still good at making things. My dear wife, Ivanna, is not as old as me, of course. But she is in her eighties, old enough. It's definitely time for me to finally step away from the responsibilities of academia and research—as addictive as those pursuits are at monopolizing one's time."

"I'll bet few others have equaled your amazing career at Yale," Dave observed.

"Well, my superiors have been very kind to me these last few years in my 'Professor Emeritus' status, as I've wound-down my active research program," Victor casually deflected the praise. "But I see the envious looks directed at my 'palatial' laboratory space. It is definitely time for an eager young man to step into my shoes—someone like *you*, my boy!"

Dave appreciated the compliment but knew it was merely cosmetic. They both were aware that his track record wasn't near good enough even to warrant a submission for a major appointment at such a prestigious institution. Sure, he'd managed to publish a couple of research papers during the last decade. But the person hired to replace Professor Volodymyr at Yale would sport a list of publications as long as your arm, plus have already established, dedicated funding, with a world-class reputation of acclaimed research results.

All Dave had to show was a burnt-out garage of ancient, ruined, WWII surplus equipment.

"You know about the explosion that just destroyed my home in Oklahoma?"

"It was explained to me by the FBI agents," Victor eagerly replied. "It seems that you have an 'anomalous' result. Your surplus-purchased old equipment and feeble feed-through rate of deuterium ions could never generate enough energy to produce such an explosion."

"Yes, that's correct."

"Then how did it happen, my boy?"

"Probably it was just an accident—a gas leak or something."

"Or...?"

"Or I've tapped into something inexplicable."

"—which we're going to try to duplicate," Victor said firmly, deftly steering the large van through the nighttime streets.

"But...how?"

"I'm sure I still have samples of your graduate research material that you produced. It's buried deep in my vault. But we can dig it out."

"And—with that in hand—plus a few modifications I've developed over the years..."

"Plus the miniaturized, state-of-the-art equipment that's sitting unused on my lab benches and..."

"—we can put it back together!" Dave happily agreed, excited.

Then, more soberly, he frowned.

"What is it, my boy?" Victor asked as he deftly steered the big van along the crowded streets.

"And what if it *does* happen again?"

"Then we prove that you are onto something amazing!"

"But we'll have nothing except the same, unexplained phenomenon to..."

"Oh, I've got it!" Victor grinned widely.

"What?"

"We'll make *two* Devices! It won't take much more effort than building one. And if the first one blows up, we'll have the second one to tinker with further."

"Do you think we can, I mean...make two of them?" Dave smiled, amazed finally to be back with someone who cared about his work and had the means to help.

"I *know* we can," Victor said, punching the accelerator hard now that they were onto a major freeway.

Dave settled back, grateful for the confidence exuded by his aging mentor.

But Dave did not share that confidence.

He had an uneasy feeling in the pit of his stomach that maybe he should just return to Edmond, beg for his lecture job back, and give up research entirely.

He didn't want to be a pawn in a game beyond his control.

Sally sat behind the big desk with her feet up on its top, leaning far back in the tilted leather-lined chair.

She was tired but excited.

Ah...it's so good to be a top-executive...heh!—she laughed to herself.

Through the plate glass wall-window she watched the rising sun lighting up the tips of the mighty skyscrapers below.

It was glorious.

She was maybe going to appropriate this office for her continuing work with this pharmaceutical company. It suited her quite well.

She'd spent the entire night hard at work at the computer. She'd researched her strategy, set up an entire new corporation, and transferred the needed funds.

Funny what things you could do with a top executive's computer and his passwords...

Now she just needed the enthusiastic voluntary agreement of the CEO of *Dynapharmaceuticals*, the world's largest and most successful pharmaceutical company. Last year alone, it racked up nearly *sixty billion dollars* in sales! From all indications, the CEO had a great track record and was strongly supported by his board of directors.

"And here he comes now," she grinned.

Not expecting anything out of the ordinary, *Daryl Jenkins* stepped through the thick wooden door into the office. He was focused on shutting the door and locking it securely behind him. Then he walked to the window to look out at the wonderful morning view of the city.

"I also love your view," Sally said from behind his desk.

Whirling around, Daryl gasped out: "Who are you? How'd you get into my office?"

Sally nonchalantly waved her black gun at him, indicating he should come over and sit in the visitor's chair in front of the desk.

Reluctantly, he obeyed.

He was a slight man, dressed in a grey suit with a striped blue tie. He was bald on the top of his head, with short, neatly-trimmed brown hair along each side. He wore plain black-rimmed glasses. He looked like an ordinary, nondescript accountant—not a top executive making fifty million dollars a year in salary alone.

"You're that terrorist that's on the newscasts," he shrewdly observed, narrowing his eyes, recognizing her.

Yes, he was a crafty one. He hadn't risen to his high position by being stupid. Sally knew she'd have to be very careful with him.

"I'm not a terrorist," she simply stated, taking her feet off the top of the desk and leaning towards him. "I have a proposition for you, one that I think you will find very interesting. It's..."

He suddenly bolted for the door, knocking the chair to the side...

—as Sally took careful aim with her black gun and pulled the trigger...

Just about to jerk open the office door, the CEO of Dynapharmaceuticals was enveloped in a *crackling cloud of electricity!*

His nascent scream of agony was abruptly cut off.

Falling limply to the carpeted floor, he lay there sprawled on his face—unconscious.

"It's good you're not a brawny muscle-builder type," she said, grabbing him under his shoulders and easily dragging him back to the chair.

There, she levered him up into a seated position. Then she took strips of sheets that she'd already prepared—torn from the sheets on his hidden-in-the-wall, fold-out, luxurious bed—and firmly tied his arms to the armrests. Then she also tied his legs to the chair legs. Now he was "one" with the chair. Hurray for the executive-chair!

As a finishing touch, she rolled up a length of the sheet to jam between his teeth and tie firmly behind his head. He was gagged.

"Great!" she grinned, going back around to settle again into the comfortable chair behind the desk. "Now, we'll just wait for him to wake up."

"*Breeeep?*"

It was the baby dinosaur, poking his head out of the shoulder bag on the floor behind the desk, ready to get "up and at them" now that the morning sun was starting to shine through the large window.

"I got you some breakfast, my sweet little baby," Sally cheerfully said to him, indicating a plate beside the shoulder bag piled high with a greasy black substance.

Next to it was a bowl of water.

Breep hopped out and began greedily gobbling the black stuff down, taking quick guzzles of water.

"Unnnnggghhhhh...." Daryl groaned as his eyes fluttered open. He struggled for a few seconds before settling back in the chair. His eyes darted furtively around—assessing his situation.

"Yes, you're royally screwed," Sally flatly stated. "Now, you will sit quietly and listen to my proposal. I didn't want to shoot you, but now you realize I mean business. And it wasn't a 'Taser' that shut down your nervous system. It was *this!*" she said, holding up the heavy black gun.

His eyes darted briefly to an unobtrusive camera set into the corner of the large room.

"And if you're looking for your security guards to rush in here to save you, think again," she laughed, swinging the flat screen around on its swivel so he could see what was displayed there.

It showed him working away at his desk, typing, and then having a phone rise out of a recess to make a call.

"Business as usual," she grinned at him. "That's a replay of some security footing from you in here last week, wearing exactly the same clothes as you have on now. Your security guards are seeing this. You're familiar with this dodge, right? I've noticed you've used it yourself to avoid security scrutiny, rather often in fact. I guess that's why you aren't imaginative in choosing your attire, are you? Anyway, no one will detect anything amiss, so you might as well relax and listen."

She set the black gun on the desktop to the side of the computer keyboard.

His eyes narrowed.

"Yes, of course, your secretary," she nodded to him acknowledging his rapid stream of thought. "I've just put your office on 'private' status. She knows not to interfere unless a true emergency comes up. So it's just you and me, Dr. Jenkins."

Now his eyes widened slightly.

"Oh, surprised that I know your academic background? A Ph.D. degree in Biochemistry is impressive for a top executive. If I decide to allow you to speak to me, you may also address *me* as 'doctor'—due to my equivalent higher education degree in mathematics. That, my friend, is to let you know I am your equal. So now you can just focus on listening to what I have to say instead of trying to figure out a way

to dominate or escape. But if you'd rather I leave—I'll just go and visit *Jillian?*"

He actually looked shocked at her suggestion, his eyes briefly
stretched wide.

"So do you agree or not? Shake your head up and down for 'yes'
to hear my proposal—and to the sides for 'no.'"

Jillian was the CEO of *Eligtronics*, a conglomerate that included
the second-largest pharmaceutical company in the world. So she
headed up the main competitor to Dynapharmaceuticals. Jillian's
conglomerate started out as an electronics supply house before
branching into many other businesses, including "block-buster" prescription drugs.

His eyes narrowed back down. Sally saw him processing what
she'd just told him.

Then, slowly, he nodded his head up-and-down.

"Good," she grinned, swinging the flat screen back to her...

—as Breep hopped up on the desk, now smacking his beak together happily, swallowing down the last bunch of his breakfast through
his long reptilian neck.

Jenkin's eyes widened in fear!

Breep looked at the trussed-up man suspiciously.

"Oh, Daryl—do you mind if I'm less formal since we're going to be
good friends and colleagues?—this is 'Breep.' Breep, this is Dr. Jenkins."

The little dinosaur paced back and forth on the desktop on his
hind legs, eyeing the man carefully before settling contentedly down
like a nesting chicken.

Daryl's eyes widened even further. He started again struggling
against his bonds. Clearly he was afraid of Breep.

"Oh, don't be so upset," Sally admonished Jenkins. "Breep is just
a pet I picked up the other day—from 125 million years in the past.
He's a baby dinosaur. He's called a '*Pelecanimimus*'—very rare fossils
of him found in Spain—I looked him up on your computer last night.
Although how 'thunder-thighs' got there, is something for the paleon-
tologists to debate?" she shrugged. "But I'm drifting off-subject," she
said, snapping her attention back to Jenkins.

Daryl wasn't struggling anymore, but he still stared fearfully at the dozing, now-snoring animal in disbelief.

"Yes, this is yet more proof that the extraordinary things I'm claiming are true," she said. "By the way, he just loves those fish-egg things I found in your office refrigerator. What do you call them...'Beluga Caviar'?" she said, picking up an opened jar from the pile behind the desk. "Anyway," she said, setting it back down, "I used up your bottles for Breep's breakfast. I'd like maybe a gallon or so more of it for Breep after we're done here."

Daryl looked angry.

"I *said*...don't be so upset!" she repeated, standing up and walking around to stroke him tenderly on his bald forehead. "You can have some too if you're a good boy."

He again visibly struggled against his constraints. Then he settled back, muttering angrily around his gag.

"Alright, alright," she said, stepping back over to the wide window and looking out at the now well-lit skyscrapers below. "Times a-wasting, I know. So let's get to the business at hand, shall we?"

She turned back to him, holding out a *white pill* in her hand.

She delicately set it right in front of him on the top of his desk.

"This will cure your daughter's fulminant multiple sclerosis medical syndrome," she said.

His eyes blinked rapidly.

"Yes, I know all about Clara," she sadly stated, moving back to "plop" back into the chair behind the desk. "I know that she's in the hospital right now being treated for a severe flare-up. It's autoimmune, of course. Her nervous system throughout her body is being attack by her very own immune system. It's stupid of one's own body to attack itself, don't you think? So wouldn't it be nice if you could just 'reprogram' Clara's entire immune system to function normally?"

He stared intently at the lone white pill sitting there in front of him.

"This pill will do exactly that to Clara's malfunctioning immune system," Sally said. "I know from your private e-mails on your computer that she's declining. She's got dementia and sensory loss. The doctors say her disease will soon result in paralysis, then death. This one little pill will cause a prolonged remission, returning your daughter to being a smart, quick, normal child."

He grimaced around the gag, struggling to speak.

"Ah, you'd like to say something?"

He forcefully nodded his head up-and-down.

"And you won't yell to try to get your voice to carry through the wall to your secretary or outer guards?" she pointedly said.

He shook his head in the negative.

"If you do, I'll have to shoot you again. It was painful, wasn't it?"

He slowly nodded in the affirmative.

"Ok, then," Sally said, hopping up from the chair to come around and unloosen his gag.

He coughed, smacking his lips.

"Sorry about that, Daryl," she shrugged, going back and sitting.

"C-could you...untie m-me?" he sputtered, trying to get his mouth to work properly again.

"Nope!" she said. "First you've got to hear my entire proposition. And then maybe we can proceed in a more business-like manner than captor to prisoner."

"Alright then," he coughed, now talking more normally. "If...what you say is true...then I agree...that could indeed be a blockbuster drug. But...you have to tell me more about..."

"Where I got it? How it was made? Who made it? What are its ingredients? Has it been tested?—stuff like that, right?"

"Yes...of course—I'm not giving my daughter something that might *poison* her!"

"You think I'd poison a little girl?"

"You're a terrorist! You shot up a *hospital*, for God's sake. You killed a poor busboy at a restaurant. And it's rumored that you were also responsible for a woman dying in that hospital from *poison!* I've no idea what else you are capable of doing."

"Wait! She *died?* Are you sure?"

"They're having the funeral this week. It's going to be covered by all the major news networks, and..."

"Damn!" Sally bitterly exclaimed, smashing her fist down upon the desk. Over to the side, the sleeping Breep flinched but didn't waken. "She took two pills the same day! I only gave her one to take. Two of them were just too much for her body to handle."

"So you admit killing a woman with the very same pill that you want me now to give to my daughter?" he bitingly commented.

"Look, I know it sounds bad," she said, getting up and starting to pace back and forth as she talked. "But this is a very powerful medication. And it's not just for curing MS—it's a total reprogramming and rebalancing of a person's immune system. Since many diseases and conditions, including ageing, are related to the immune system—this one medication can help or cure a number of diverse adverse ailments! One of those is cancer. With an optimally-functioning immune system, cancer cells can often be recognized and destroyed."

"You're claiming this is also a cure for cancer?"

"—and heart diseases, muscular diseases, neurological diseases like Alzheimer's, not just overt autoimmune diseases...the list goes on and on."

"Then you've just confirmed your insanity," he coldly stated, "because one medication could never treat all those diverse conditions. What you claim is impossible to..."

"—impossible for your state of medical science in *your* Dimension, but not for mine," she snapped back at him.

There was a moment of stunned silence.

"You're telling me now that you're from...*another Dimension?*" he very carefully addressed her, as if talking to an insane-asylum inmate.

"Yes, I know it's a lot for you to take in at once," she sighed, sitting now on the edge of the big desk and swinging her legs out and back. "But it happens to be true. In my Dimension, citizens of the Empire have their immune systems balanced at birth. The pill sitting on your desk is what we call a 'booster' that citizens take every month or so to stay optimized. For us it's as normal and common as you getting a flu shot once a year—or taking a daily vitamin pill."

He narrowed his eyes, reconsidering her incredible claim.

"If that's true...then why are you here?"

"I've come to you for *money*—lots and lots of it!" she said, leaning close to his now-perspiring face. His bald head looked slick. "This is the quickest way for me to get the money I need. I have a much larger mission to accomplish—one that you are going to help me achieve.

Nothing less than the survival of the entire human species is at stake, both in your Dimension and in mine! And to change the awful fate awaiting Earth I need to make big changes in your global society, quickly. To do that, I require *billions* of dollars. *You* have the money and *I* have revolutionary products that will earn you far more than you pay me."

"Well...I certainly can't fault you for the breadth of your...vision," he said in a strained voice.

"It's not just a crazy delusion," she insisted, standing up again and nervously pacing. "I know it *sounds* completely crazy. But it's *not!*"

"Well...other than a pill that kills people if misapplied...and a strange-looking Taser gun...and a weird looking lizard—what proof do you have? Could you maybe *take* me to this other Dimension of yours?"

"It's not that easy," she said, walking behind him to grab his shoulders with clawed fingers, causing him to tense-up even more. "But maybe I *can* give you something more as proof of my resolve."

"Are you...going to kill me?" he gulped, stiffening further in the chair.

She dangled a white strip of printed paper in front of his face.

"What's that?" he suspiciously asked.

"This is the actual *product insert* for the retroviral complexes that deliver the staged and individualized reprogramming of the immune system's DNA," she triumphantly stated. "It won't give you the details of course—which you'll still need me to provide for you—but there's plenty enough here to convince you that this is indeed a 'miraculous' product from another Dimension."

"Jesus Christ!" he gasped, catching glimpses on the dangled paper of very convincing proper corporate language.

"And it's all yours," she said, stuffing the crumpled paper now into a top pocket of his shirt, to the side of his neat tie.

"Well, that's interesting of course. But still it could be faked," he suspiciously began to interrogate her.

"What's going on here?" a surprised but authoritative female voice demanded.

Sally realized that whoever had secretly entered the room saw her with her arms around the back of the seated CEO—as if they were lovers!

Sally whirled around to see a black-haired, short woman dressed in an expensive-looking suede pantsuit emerging from a *secret hatchway* opening up out of the floor, holding a red cellphone in her hand.

"The privacy shield was on and I tried to phone you but...you're that *terrorist* girl!" the woman gasped, recognizing Sally while realizing that Daryl was not just sitting on a chair but was tied-up.

As the woman dashed for the office door, Sally lunged around Daryl to grab the black gun lying on the desktop...

"Call the police!" the woman yelled as she slipped the lock of the door and snatched it open revealing Sally and the tied-up Daryl to the startled gaze of a male secretary carrying a file...

—as Sally fired her gun, dropping the woman in a cloud of *sizzling electricity*, while simultaneously leaping over to the office door and slamming it back shut!

She clicked-over the deadbolt-type lock, knowing it would only hold back determined guards for a few seconds.

"Hell!" Sally swore, leaping over the moaning woman who still tightly clutched her cellphone, back to the desk and keyboard, frantically typing instructions...

—as with a loud "THUD" heavily-armored protective barriers fell into place across the wall-window! Sally knew that it blocked off not just the window but access behind the outer door, the inner walls, the ceiling and the floor.

"Whew," Sally gasped, sinking back into the chair. "There, that'll give us a few more minutes at least—we're boxed in tight."

"How were you able to trigger the lockdown shields?" Daryl calmly asked, having regained his composure to stare belligerently at her. "Only our security apparatus can..."

"Oh, I'm a very clever 'girl'," she quipped, amused to see that Breep was still snoring with his eyes shut, not diverted from happily digesting the caviar feast inside his rounded little belly.

"But *you* are a *nasty* boy," she continued, pointing an accusing finger at the executive while standing up behind the desk.

He grimaced angrily at her.

Then he looked away to the side.

"My personal life is none of your business," he weakly asserted.

"Oh? And will your Board of Directors agree with you?" she tartly accused him. "So it wasn't just coincidence that you and your *number one competitor* just 'happened' to lease corner office space in the One World Trade Center right on top of each other? And I suppose that the luxury bed folded up in the wall is just for you taking a nap when you work late at night—as you often tend to do? Your wife and kids at home might forgive you, Daryl, but will your shareholders? Maybe it is just an 'innocent' affair—but won't they see you as sleeping...I mean 'conspiring'...with the enemy?"

He didn't say anything, just stared straight ahead.

"I'm certain that your secretary knows about you and Jillian since Ms. McRider ran straight for her—but once the guards and police get here...?"

His normally tanned face was slowly turning white.

"Oh, *I* don't care," she reassured him, dropping with a sigh back into the leather chair behind the desk. "But if the world is to be told she just happened to be here for a long-scheduled meeting with you when I happened to sneak in and overpower the both of you, you'll need my cooperation to make your story stick, right?"

"You can't blackmail me."

"If I *need* to do so, I can and *will!*" she defiantly answered, a bit shrilly. "But, I'd rather not...unless you refuse to cooperate."

Outside the office door, a faint "banging" was now sounding as guards tried to break in.

"Give up!" he demanded, buoyed by the certainly of being quickly rescued. "No one will believe you. You're a wanted terrorist. Everyone will see you as a murder and a liar."

She laughed at him.

"You'll lose your job, your reputation, your family, and your assets—maybe even go to prison for illegal corporate collusion," she acidly threatened him. "They don't have to believe me. They just have to get the hint of impropriety and the many reporters out there will run the story to the ground. Or...?"

"Or...?" he grimly replied.

"Or you can take my little white pill here and give it to your daughter. Don't think you can just have it analyzed and duplicated by your laboratories. It's impossible to reverse-engineer. It's composed of interactive living biofilms. It is controlled by a form of synthetic intelligence of which I'm one of my Dimension's experts. Try to x-ray it, probe it, or sample it in any way and it dissolves into useless goo. Its top secret nature is part of how our government controls its Citizenry. Are you following me?"

He reluctantly nodded.

"And remember that I'm the only one who can direct you how to safely extract and replicate active parts of its structure," she continued, gently scooping up Breep to deposit him safely back into her shoulder bag.

He gave a startled "*gleep*" as he was jerked awake, but otherwise cooperated.

"Also, don't try to double-cross me!" she sternly warned him. "If your daughter doesn't get a full sequence of the pills she'll revert. You'll have her whole and happy for a few weeks and then she'll fade back into her disease. You need me to give her the entire treatment. Once a person starts on this course, they have a form of addiction. Stopping getting the periodic booster pills—whether they're needed daily, monthly, or yearly—causes multiple organ failure and dissolution."

"Then—assuming your pill actually works...?"

"Then you've got *trillions* of dollars of profits to look forward to with your exclusive *monopoly* on this entire, novel technology. No need for patent protection. Like I said, the inherent protections are tamperproof."

"So what do *you* get in return?" he grudgingly asked.

"Ah, good!" she smiled as the banging outside got louder. "We're negotiating."

"Assuming it actually works..." he repeated.

"*One billion dollars* up-front, plus 10% of the profits in perpetuity," she crisply stated, setting the gun on the desk while she slipped into her trench coat then slung the shoulder bag up over one shoulder. She resolutely lifted up the black gun in her left hand.

"That's quite impossible!"

"Already done, Daryl," she crisply stated. "Last night I transferred one billion dollars from your discretionary executive corporate fund into a nonprofit I set up. Now you *really* need proof for your board of directors and your shareholders to justify keeping your job after *your* stunning 'unilateral' decision made from your executive computer with your private passwords and unique bio-identifiers activated."

His composure completely melted. He gasped aloud in shock.

He looked like he was about to start crying.

"Wow! Imagine that!" she continued, shoving the "knife" even deeper. "*You* unilaterally paid *one billion dollars* for an untested new product! And they thought when they hired you that you were a *cautious* CEO. Hah! Did you ever prove them wrong! They didn't know you had such *balls!*"

He groaned like he'd been physically kneed in his groin.

"But that's not all," she seductively whispered in his ear.

"Not...all?" he winced, not knowing what to expect next.

Sally lifted up her left arm holding the gun, aiming it straight at the armored metal shield hiding the wall window...

She felt the Turtle Tattoo warming up on the wrist of her left arm and knew she was making a good decision.

With her index finger she flicked the power level to *three stars*.

"Now close your ears," she futilely warned the trembling, still tied-up Daryl...

—as she depressed the trigger and in an ear-shattering BLAST the *entire wall* blew outward in an *inferno* of blazing hot metal and glass fragments!

An icy burst of air surged in around them.

Yes, Sally thought to herself, *we are indeed very high up in the air in this One World Trade Center building!*

Outside, she saw approaching military helicopters tossed about in the outrushing air erupting from the side of the mammoth skyscraper!

"Don't worry about anyone on the street below!" she shouted into Daryl's ear above the ROAR of the now-whipping wind. "At a setting of three out of five, my gun *incinerates* whatever is close in its path! No debris survives to hurt anyone below. At a setting of *five*—the maximum setting—this one little gun would have destroyed this entire building."

Daryl's chin dropped in astonishment.

"It's yet another completely new-to-your-world technology from my Dimension, Dr. Jenkins," she laughed in his ear. "This is one that I'm going to license to your girlfriend since her conglomerate is better suited to capitalizing on its potential. But you can still be one of its prime players behind the scenes. Convince her of its potential! You see, it sucks energy out of anything that's around—light, molecular movement, wind—and concentrates it. It's fit to use as a power source in your vehicles, houses, planes, cars, or whatever—such that you'll have clean energy available for everybody! It's not going to power starships, mind you—but it'll power the routine needs of planet Earth. There'll be no more need to burn dirty global-warming fossil fuels, or to use radioactive atomic power, or to discover newer and far-more-dangerous energy sources," she cryptically stated.

"But how will I convince her that you will...?"

"I've already downloaded some of its general repair schematics into your computer from its internal artificial-intelligence software," she quickly stated. "It'll be enough for her engineers to start building a prototype. I'll help out with the details, of course. Without those details you'll never get it to work optimally."

"But the feds are going to *capture* you!" he yelled at her against the still-surging icy blasts—the "impossible" destruction of the armored barrier and window having apparently at last convinced him that she was telling him the truth.

"And you've got an *army* of lawyers!" she yelled back in his ear. "Get them onto it. And, yes, once Jillian wakes up, convince her to play along with us. She can't deny what I've just done. She's just as smart as you and even more ruthless. If she still has doubts, there's plenty to convince her in the general schematics I've left in your computer. For this new energy source, it's the same price as for your pills. Get her to prepare the initial payment—another billion dollars—for transfer by the end of the week into my non-profit."

"What's its name?" he asked, his voice growing weaker as he shuddered in the freezing blasts.

"It's the '*Church of Perpetual Health*'—CPH for short," she answered, "a church that doesn't just make empty promises but delivers! You can sell your initial treatment to anyone, but the boosters only go to active members of my new church. We'll make popping your product a religious obligation!"

"But...you're just a young girl. No matter how much money you throw at a new religion...to persist they need a charismatic Founder. Can't you just make your nonprofit not a church but some other charitable organization?"

"It has to be a church. It must persist for many generations. It must carry with it the obligation to accept a set of conditions that only Religions can enforce."

"Then...you must give it to someone else," he gasped, "someone with great charisma or moral authority."

"I have a *Vision!*"

"It's not enough! I know about these things! You have to have the moxie and experience to convince others!"

"I can do it!"

"My Board of Trustees and the general public will see through it!"

"Nonsense!" she yelled back at him. "The bottom line is *money*. With enough money you can accomplish anything! The ongoing profits from the pills and the clean energy source will go into my church. It doesn't require me to be a charismatic Founder. You, I, Jillian, and the rest of your ilk aren't only going to get even more fabulously wealthy as the true Elites of your society—but in the process we're going to change the world for the better! I've already distally set up centers of CPH with hiring instructions and church directions. It's a viable world-wide institution, starting today. So *there!*"

"I still think...your Vision is fatally flawed...lacking a charismatic Founder—but I'll do what I can," he promised, blinking his eyes against icicles starting to form on his thin eyebrows.

Outside the blown-open wall, Sally saw heavily-armed military men dangling on cables from "*chittering*" helicopters that were rapidly nearing the side of the skyscraper.

"I have to escape," she resolutely stated, turning away from Daryl...

"Wait!" he yelled at her. "Take Jillian's cellphone...its calls can't be traced...red button connects directly to my cellphone...got it through a connection at a research University."

"I'll be in touch!" she yelled back, rapping Daryl smartly on his back as she inched across the floor in the icy blasts of wind—grabbing the red cellphone from McRider's trembling hand as she was woozily pushing herself up to her knees—Sally now approaching the still-flopping, opened secret hatchway set into the floor from which McRider had emerged.

"STOP OR WE'LL SHOOT!" she heard a bullhorn from dangling military personnel as they tried to aim rifles at her...

—as she dived into the opening on the floor, hoping that she'd not break her neck on the *armored plating* of the security barrier that had slid beneath it...

If so, it'd be a mighty brief new religion.

Chapter 8

DEATH

"Swing low, sweet chariot
Coming for to carry me home"
Snatch me from the fangs of fate
Hoping that there is a way to escape
Yet fearful that I can't change the trajectory
Of not a welcome-wagon to heaven
But a plunging runaway train
Bound for the bloody bowels of hell...
If only we weren't ruled by Fear and Hate!
It would make dying so much easier.

The Luminary Chronicles, 8:31-34

Sally fell down "splat" face-first onto the dusty floor of the dimly-lit abandoned theater's central hallway.

She saw, with relief, that the cellphone in her hand appeared undamaged. She slipped it securely into her shoulder bag, along with her other treasures.

"Whew!" she gasped, rolling onto her back and looking up at the now comfortably familiar flaking ceiling. "That's a hard landing, but easier than cracking my skull on a metal barrier."

Yes—and better than being killed or captured by the determined anti-terrorist squads in those helicopters.

"You ok, buddy?" she said to Breep who was cowering in her shoulder bag.

"*Breeeep!*" he now answered cheerfully, sticking his chicken-like head out of the bag, waving it about on his long green neck to check out the local environment.

Then he hopped out of the bag and jumped onto her chest.

"*Breep! Breep! Breep!*" he excitedly chirped, hopping off to scamper down the hallway on his strong hind legs.

147

"What's up, boy?" she laughed, getting up to follow him.

He was hopping up and down in front of another of the dark archways leading into a projection room.

Sally reached into her shoulder bag and pulled out her flashlight. She shone it on the faded poster beside the archway.

Its title enticingly asked: "DINOSAURS ON MARS?"

"What the heck?" Sally said, shining her light closer to its faded pictures...

—where she saw a space-suited person in a red sandy canyon digging up fossilized bones of...what looked like the skeleton of an animal similar to Breep!

The subtitle began: "*Documentary of exciting new Mars excavations in Valles Marineris, 2532...*"

"Is this for real?" Sally asked, looking down at the still excitedly-hopping Breep. "That's five hundred years in the future...?"

Squawking loudly, Breep suddenly dashed into the darkened archway!

"Hey, come back!" she yelled, running after him...

—as they both vanished from off the face of the Earth.

"I can't believe this is happening, Victor," Dave said, shivering in the steady wind coming off the North Atlantic Ocean.

He wore a heavy leather jacket. But it still wasn't enough to keep him warm.

"It's marvelous, isn't it, my boy?" Victor grinned widely, his snow-white head of hair swirling in the wind.

"It's all happened so fast," Dave muttered, gripping his arms firmly around his chest.

"Sometimes everything just falls into place," Victor replied.

They stood on the back of a Virginia class *nuclear attack submarine*. They were overseeing the careful loading of their two identical Devices into the ship. Both Devices were securely crated.

"But I didn't want the military to get involved," Dave sighed deeply.

"Oh, nonsense, my boy," Victor cheerfully assured him. "This is the best thing for us. Those FBI agents were very helpful convincing the military to give us a lift out to a secure island. If your 'garage explosion' is replicated, then this is a technology that needs the protection of our entire government."

"Is it 'protection' or exploitation?" Dave asked, uneasily feeling the steel plating under his feet gently moving with the rolling waves.

"Our department at Yale has a long history of receiving funding from the Navy," Victor stated, "particularly from the submarine corps. Compact energy sources are in high demand for them. And if we've finally now got a lead on a nonradioactive source via your persistent pursuit of practical cold fusion—that's even better for them."

"But what if it's a dud?" Dave said urgently into Victor's ear. "This will be just a colossal waste of time and effort. We'll look like idiots."

Victor laughed, shaking his head in denial.

"Just smell that fresh ocean air," Victor grinned, lifting his skinny arms up to the sky. "Isn't it glorious? I'm too old to care if people think I'm an idiot, David. I thought just a couple days ago my life was over—I'd be out feeding hummingbirds at my Vermont retreat for whatever little life remains in me. It's too bad we didn't have time for you to visit out there—it's quite beautiful this time of the year."

"I remember it well from when you held parties out there for your postdocs, techs, and collaborators," Dave smiled. "It was a long drive from the city, but well worth it. Perhaps after this I can visit?"

"Of course! And stay as long as you like," Victor smiled. "We have a spare room out there and Ivanna loves visitors. But for now, I relish this new experience."

"You mean you haven't been on a nuclear submarine headed for an 'undisclosed' test island location before?" Dave teased his friend.

Victor good-naturedly laughed.

"My boy, *this* is what it means to be alive. It doesn't matter if all your novel equipment does is warm up a cup of tea. We'll *learn!* And learning will *more* than be sufficient. Relax, David—this is a fine adventure. Enjoy it!"

Dave did not share Victor's enthusiasm.

Things were indeed moving much too fast.

Spread out before him was the deep blue of the ocean. A tugboat was tethered to the side of the huge submarine. Dave and Victor had just disembarked from the tugboat with the crated twin Devices.

The Captain of the boat looked anxiously down from the top of the conning tower jutting high overhead, just yards above Dave and Victor.

"All secure?" the Captain called down.

"The equipment is loaded, Sir!" another officer called back, standing mere feet away from Dave and Victor.

"Then get our guests aboard. We depart immediately."

Dave took a last look around.

The huge submarine was pointed out towards a couple of long steel bridges, beneath which they were going to travel to get to the open ocean. The sky was overcast. It seemed to Dave that the weather was ominous, casting a pale on testing what Victor and he had frantically cobbled together over the last two days in his lab.

"God be with us," Dave sighed, allowing himself to be directed into the bowels of the monster military machine. He had a feeling that they were headed for deep, *troubled* waters.

And he was in the hands of the military, theirs to do with as they wished.

He felt sick to his stomach, and not just from heading into the depths of the ocean.

Everything was going wrong.

Sally shrank back from a stampeding herd of approaching, huge, *Brontosauruses!*

It was very hot—her trench coat definitely too much for the weather...

"Yikes!" she cried-out as she snatched up Breep and dashed off to the side, away from the thundering herd.

From a safe hill, lying prone peeking over its lip, she watched the mass of long-necked, seventy-five-feet long, sixteen-ton animals stomping past.

What were they trying to escape from so frantically?

"Where are we?" Sally gasped, hugging the panicked Breep close to her. "Better yet, *when* are we? This sure doesn't look like excavations on Mars."

A bright light was growing on the horizon...

Sally looked at it in puzzlement, thinking it was the sun coming up. But the sun was already high up in the sky. And this light was growing bigger and brighter than any sun she'd ever seen!

It was an explosion…

It was a *gigantic* explosion!

Hot, flaming chunks of rocks were starting to fall out of the sky. A pack of T-rex's thundered past the hill, closely followed by a herd of bellowing Triceratops waving their horns up in the air in full-out panic!

—as a *roiling black mass of clouds* poured across the horizon…

"What you doin' in here?" a blue-uniformed lady said, reaching down a hand to help Sally up to her feet. "You lost from the tour?"

Sally cringed as a T-rex came charging up the hill right at her…then passed right *through* her!

Likewise, the rain of flaming chunks of rock—some as big as houses—that were now smashing into Sally, but also passing right through her. Say what?

Breep dived over into Sally's hanging shoulder bag, huddling out of sight for safety.

"I-I guess…I g-got s-separated?" Sally stammered, letting the nice lady lead her off to the side and into a small group of onlookers.

Looking back, Sally saw she'd been inside a big central globe surrounded by glittering light-emitting machines. Outside the globe, groups of people were calmly walking and casually talking.

"Sure reality stark, not?" the tour guide smiled politely.

Sally nodded, noting the name tag on the lady's neat uniform: "*Dinosaur Apocalypse Guide.*"

"So that was a holographic projection?" Sally gulped, looking back at the totally realistic scene of myriad dinosaurs now being engulfed in sweeping clouds of black ash.

"Yucatan Asteroid hit, yes Ma'am," the young lady brightly answered. She had on a blue one-piece uniform made of a shiny plastic-looking material. Her head was clean-shaved except for an inch-wide circle of hair at her forehead. "Started death spiral of the dinosaurs, 65 million years ago. Most dramatic, yes?"

"Yes…very dramatic," Sally gulped, steadying herself. "Uhm…and what year is *this?*"

Sally felt very "bouncy"—as if she'd lost two thirds of her weight. Yes, definitely, she was in a much lower gravity field than on Earth.

"Year?" the guide spoke, not comprehending.

"The date!" Sally barked impatiently. Then, more softly: "I'm...uh...still disoriented from that holographic projection. Could you just help me to...?"

"Oh, no prob—2532, of course. You stable?"

"Yes, yes...I'm...'stable'. Thanks."

Ah. So she was indeed five hundred years in the future. Sally walked quickly away from the friendly guide. No sense in triggering suspicions and getting arrested by the local police.

She was in a huge underground cavern. It apparently was some sort of recreational, cultural exhibit. Other globes featured holographic-interactive displays from other periods in Earth's history.

Off to the sides, Sally saw tunnels leading out to other destinations. Some of them had vehicles taking on passengers. Sally recognized the vehicles. They were similar to the 'bubs' of her world, but larger. Those that were enclosed had clear circular bubbles around the occupants. Others were "open-aired" floaters—with seats on flat platforms.

"Well, maybe we're ok then," Sally whispered to the still-cowering Breep. "Civilization looks good here in the future. Maybe we'll take a quick tour before trying to find a way back to our own time."

She spotted a sign above one tunnel that looked promising: "*Surface Excavations.*"

That was what she wanted. The poster in the theater had 'dinosaur' fossils being dug out of Martian rocks. Whatever that meant had to be important.

She tagged along with a group loading onto a floating platform sitting in that tunnel.

A little shaved-bald boy looked up at her.

"Priestess?" he said, grinning at her.

"Uhm, sure, why not?" she grinned back at him.

Breep poked his beaked head up out of Sally's shoulder bag.

"Huh!" yelped the little boy as he spied the little dinosaur.

Breep yanked his head back in the bag as the little boy's mother looked down in alarm at her son.

Sally just grinned weakly at her.

"Kids..." Sally shrugged.

It was only a short ride up to the surface of Mars. The group disembarked at a platform where they could look through a thick transparent window at space-suited figures crouched around an excavation site. The outside crew was carefully chipping at the rock then brushing away fragments.

Sally saw the high rocky cliffs of *Valles Marineris*. It was an awesome sight. It was similar to being on the floor of Earth's Grand Canyon, but much larger and wider. Versus the one mile depth and up to 18 miles width of the Grand Canyon, Sally remembered from her studies of solar system topography that Valles Marineris on Mars was *four miles* deep and up to *150 miles* wide.

At one point in the past, billions of years ago, primitive life might have existed on Mars before it lost its atmosphere and liquid water.

And now they'd apparently found fossilized evidence of *complex* life—ancient Martian *reptiles*...really?

"Here to see the End of Time?" a cold voice quietly addressed her from behind.

She whirled about to see a slight oriental man in a white uniform. He had close-cropped white hair. He also had an *old scar* meandering down the left side of his face...

"Paul?" she gasped in total surprise.

"Yes—long time since we last met...Sally—or should I say 'Priestess'? You image is still revered by many," the man politely nodded. Then he continued, more grimly: "But you have made a mess of things. We knew you would appear here. I am sorry. But along with the termination of humanity, we must now end *you*."

"No! Wait!" she said, backing off a couple steps as yet more white-uniformed men appeared behind the old oriental man. "At least tell me what is happening. Don't I deserve that?"

He paused, jerking his head upward and to the side.

She looked in that direction—through the transparent window and up at the top of the towering cliffs...

—where the dark sky above was steadily turning a bright *yellow!*

"No!" Sally protested, shaking her head in denial. "Mars was out of the path of the solar super-storm's ejecta! Besides which, that's going to happen 500 years from now—a thousand years in my future!"

Paul shrugged.

"God noticed this pocket of humanity and added it to the 'purge' list," he said sadly. "Along with the solar superstorm destroying Earth, a massive plasma ejectus is also about to encompass Mars. You and the other tourists came at a bad time. A few may survive the initial impact down in the deeply buried city complex, but they'll not last for long."

The white-uniformed men were edging closer, politely directing the other visitors to leave the platform and return to the transport vehicle.

Sally looked backward for possible escape routes, seeing only an airlock mechanism leading out to the virtually airless excavation site.

"But even so, that's 500 years from *now*," Sally again protested, still backing away toward the transparent shield.

"Your actions, Priestess, have accelerated God's Wrath upon mankind," Paul sadly stated. "*Judgment Day* is only 500 years in your future—indeed, right *now!*"

"But how can that be?" Sally cried-out while frantically looking for another way to escape but seeing none. "I've started the Church and provided an energy source to divert scientific inquiry away from the cold fusion path that would have accessed Dark Energy. I'm working to completely *prevent* God from noticing us, not to *accelerate* His Judgment upon us!"

The white-uniformed men were moving ever closer.

"You are failing," the man sadly stated. "And that is why we must now, very regrettably, take drastic action. I am so sorry, Priestess Sally. I wish it could be otherwise. But those are my orders."

"Orders? From who?"

"From someone very close to you."

"*Who?*" she repeated.

"You *are* willing to make the Ultimate Sacrifice in order to save humanity, aren't you?"

"I...I..." she stammered, looking around desperately.

"This was *your* decision, Sally. You knew where you'd be at this date and ordered your execution."

"No! You're wrong!" she angrily said, whipping out her black energy-gun from the shoulder bag with her right hand and pointing it directly at his wrinkled, old face.

He shook his head sadly, though his eyes were narrowed in determination.

"That, dear Sally—is ancient technology," he said as *shimmering blue protective shields* sprang up around each of the white-coated men. "Its energy discharge cannot penetrate our force fields. And we are far superior to your present skill level in hand-to-hand combat techniques. I am so sorry, Sally. But I must insist that you 'accidentally' exit through the airlock onto the surface of Mars *without* a protective suit."

Breep *launched* himself out of Sally's shoulder bag straight at the oriental man!

—going right through the blue shield unimpeded, the little dinosaur grabbed onto Paul's face with his four sets of razor-sharp claws...

—as Paul *screamed*, flailing-about while the dinosaur's twelve claws tore into his eyeballs...

Sally snatched the animal away with her left hand as she dashed past the man, made an "impossible"-on-Earth high leap over the other men, and ran for the transport tunnel.

Behind her Paul was yelling for the others to stop her...

—as she turned a corner, saw the gaping mouth of the now-dark tunnel where the transport vehicle had just departed, *diving into it...*

—"thudding" down, yet again, onto the dusty floor of the abandoned theater's central hallway!

She gasped out a sigh of relief that instantly changed into a *yelp* of fear!

—as right behind her emerged *Paul* with his throng of grim cohorts!

—as Sally leapt to her feet and *dived* for the next archway, barely glimpsing the movie poster which said: "VISION — *from the life of Hildegard von Bingen*"...

—as she simultaneously flicked the setting of her gun to its maximum five stars, and pulled the trigger...

—*incinerating* the entire theater complex behind her in a huge explosion!

The police searching the East Main business district of Ada, Oklahoma were knocked off their feet by the mammoth blast.

Then they hastily retreated to a safe distance as an entire city block was engulfed in a *raging inferno*—burning down any buildings left standing in the vicinity of the vaporized movie theater.

Observing the retreat of the police and the still-expanding fireball from the safety of a circling police helicopter, Agent Anderson nodded resolutely—sad relief on his face.

"It is better this way," he said to his fellow black eyeglass-sporting colleague.

"Better, Sir?" the man asked.

"She's no more trouble to us," he explained. "Even if she survived the explosion, she's trapped in the past. She's got no way back."

"Then Dr. King and Professor Volodymyr will succeed?"

"Yes, they will succeed, my friend—beyond their wildest dreams!" Anderson quietly asserted, his voice trembling with emotion. He watched the still-expanding fireball rising up over the city.

"Hallelujah! *Praise* God!" Anderson's colleague exulted, pumping his fist in glee.

"Yes, my dear friend—'praise God', indeed," Anderson blissfully smiled.

That vile heretic Sally, along with her pagan tattoos, was gone for good.

Time could now resume its smooth, preordained path.

Sally's attempted disruption was cancelled.

Chapter 9

DEFEAT

Every Victory carries seeds of its own demise
From the peak of Success the depths of failure
Trudging down from the exquisite Heights
Back to the mud-hugging flatlands
Wondering if the ecstasy of standing on the peak
Was merely a self-delusion, a fantasy, a beautiful dream
Dimly remembered, heady flight of the imagination
A daring escape from the drudgery of responsibilities
The everyday tasks of making the world go round
For just a moment transcended
Denying our inevitable fall...
In glorious—though too brief—flight!

The Luminary Chronicles, 9:83-86

Dave and Victor stood on the wide, sloping back of the nuclear submarine, peering intensely at the small atoll just barely visible on the far horizon.

"That was *fun!*" Victor grinned.

Despite his wrinkled skin and snow-white hair, Dave thought Victor looked like a little kid with a new toy. Victor's blue eyes were wide and glittering. Dave was afraid Victor might topple over into the ocean he was hopping around so animatedly.

They'd just returned via a custom inflatable transport raft from setting up their self-powered Device on the isolated atoll.

"Are we far enough away?" Dave nervously asked.

"Without a doubt, my boy," Victor enthusiastically stated, shielding his eyes from the whipping wind blowing from their backs. "There's a hundred times the mass of enhanced matrix in your Device as was in your garage. If, somehow, an explosion one hundred times

157

larger occurred here than that which destroyed your house, we'd only feel a small bump at this distance."

Dave grabbed onto a railing that'd been put up around their group, determined not to get "bumped" off into the deep ocean!

"Then are we *close* enough?" Dave laughed, now excited despite his misgivings.

The warm wind whipped through his beard. They were about to restart his experiment. Even if nothing happened, the attempt alone was invigorating.

"Well, you designed the distal control sequences," Victor grinned. "We've got full control up to ten miles away, right?"

"That's the plan," Dave said, glancing at some seagulls hovering above. "And we're only about five miles away right now. All the systems read in the green. We're ready to start feeding the deuterium ions into the reaction chamber. So, whenever you say, it's 'go' time!"

The captain walked over to the two of them. He was a square-faced middle-aged gentleman with short-cropped black hair. He wore a brown, working uniform.

"Are we ready for the test?" he asked.

"We are, indeed, Sir!" Victor enthusiastically replied.

Dave was glad Victor didn't give the Captain a salute. It would have been too much. Dave was happy not to be in the military. Being a "civilian consultant" gave him much more freedom than being tied to arbitrary orders from capricious "superiors."

"Then please give us a countdown."

The military had a variety of equipment trained on the atoll, including sophisticated radiation monitors. The military scientists were lined up on the spine of the huge submarine along with Dave and Victor, eagerly awaiting initiation.

Dave didn't expect that there'd be any detectable radiation at such a distance. His own distally reported monitoring of the reaction chamber would detect any excess of neutrons above background. If he generated enough heat just to boil a pot of water, he'd be deliriously happy. That would mean they'd achieved sustained fusion, where the amount of energy released was more than it took to power up the experiment. He'd join Victor jumping up and down with glee!

"Ok, here we go," Dave said as he noted that the system-monitoring readouts were all up and visible on his laptop computer... "*Ten...nine...eight...*"

He wondered how the crew would react when nothing happened. He'd powered up hundreds of such experiments in the past with little or nothing to show from them except new questions as to why they all dismally failed. Indeed, the one that had supposedly burned down his house had been running for several days before something alleg-edly "happened." Dave was still convinced the explosion came from a gas leak in his garage that was touched off by a spark from his ancient, surplus-purchased equipment.

And how long will they wait here for something to happen?—he thought to himself. In fact, how had Victor convinced the Navy to sponsor this test in the first place? Dave still wasn't sure how Victor got a nuclear submarine to ferry them around at a moment's notice. Victor wouldn't go into the details, other than vaguely cite help from the FBI plus his department's prior association with the Navy. Regardless, Dave was positive that a nuclear submarine couldn't just linger for days on a fool's errand.

"*...four...three...two...*"

Sure is a beautiful day, Dave thought to himself. Vaguely he was aware that the hovering seagulls had vanished. Other than that, eve-rything was peaceful and warm. The submarine must have cruised toward the tropics to find such a nice atoll. Of course the sailors wouldn't tell Dave and Victor their exact location. But regardless of the results of the experiment, he could boast of being taken on a nice tropical vacation...

"*...one...*contact!" Dave loudly exclaimed, punching the key to start the deuterium gas mixture flowing into the reaction chamber...

Nothing.

Nothing at all....

Dave shrugged apologetically to the others...

—as Victor peered intently over Dave's shoulder at the readouts on the laptop.

"There! Neutron spike!" Victor excitedly pointed at the screen...

—as the entire world turned blindingly *WHITE!*

—and a distant ROAR grew closer...

—as *shouts* and *screams* echoed around Dave and he blinked his eyes, trying to see the laptop screen still clutched tightly in his hands...

—as he looked upward, his sight now returning to him, and saw a RISING MUSHROOM CLOUD!

"All hands get below!" the Captain shouted, grabbing Dave by his shoulder and roughly slinging him toward the hatchway leading down into the submarine...

—as Dave, dumbfounded, saw a HUGE TIDAL WAVE racing toward them over the smooth ocean...

He stumbled on the rocking deck, trying to find something to grab onto...

And before he could get into the hatchway leading below, the *entire submarine* was picked up then slammed *upside-down* back into the ocean!

Dave was thrown into the salty waves, floundering, sucked down into the crushing depths by swirling vortices...

—as a strong hand grasped his shirt and dragged him back up to the surface...

Gasping and choking, coughing out salt water, Dave floated on his back being dragged along by a swimming sailor...

—seeing in the sky above him a *roiling kaleidoscope* composed of every color of the rainbow...

—as *searing heat-waves* rolled across him, causing him to duck under the cooler water...

—before being dragged back up the side of the again right-sided, surfaced submarine. He was roughly pulled into a hatch and unceremoniously deposited inside a cool entrance chamber.

"Victor...?" Dave gasped, remembering his friend. He frantically looked around at the drenched, gasping group that was now safely inside the now slanted-downward, diving submarine.

"Right here...my boy," Victor wearily said, sitting with his back to a wall, holding a rag to a bleeding cut on his forehead.

"Are you ok?" Dave said, crawling over next to him.

"Oh yes, no problem," Victor replied. "I was already down the hatch with the Captain before that huge wave hit. I saw you go over the side and feared the worst. How are you?"

"Oh, I'm ok," Dave gasped, still having trouble breathing after having sucked in so much salt water. "A sailor rescued me or I'd be fish bait, for sure."

"Not you, the *laptop*," Victor now joked, grinning widely.

Dave looked down at his hands.

His hands were still tightly clutching his laptop computer!

"Oh, right," Dave grinned, amazed to see that the readouts from the test were still up on the screen.

He admired Victor's "vim and vigor." Something inexplicable had just happened, almost killing everyone, and he was acting like a kid opening Christmas gifts.

Then a terrible thought came into Dave's mind. Victor's grin faded, leaving behind a deep frown. Apparently he was thinking the same as Dave.

"What dosage of radiation did we receive?" Victor now gravely asked.

"Oh...*Christ!*" Dave now swore. "That was a *nuclear explosion*, a big one! *How* is that possible?"

"We'll figure it out later, my boy, if we survive," Victor grimly stated. "The military boys here probably already have the exact readings, but your built-in small radiation monitor should give us the 'take-home' message of how long we have to live, right?"

"Uhm, sure," Dave said, tapping keys to bring up the present values.

"Well, my boy? How long before we die in agonizing pain from severe radiation poisoning?"

"Uhm...well...gamma rays, nothing! Neutrons, nothing! X-rays, nothing! Radionuclides, nothing! But this close, unprotected, we should be dead or dying! These readings don't make any sense at all."

"Most intriguing," Victor mused, leaning his head with relief back against the bulkhead, "most intriguing, indeed! Somehow your experiment released a massive amount of energy, but without any radiation excess. What about the experiment itself, right before the explosion occurred? What do your readings show?"

"I've got it! I see it!" Dave excitedly replied, looking at abruptly-terminated graphs. "At 97 nanoseconds after I started the experiment...there's a neutron flux! And a spike of gamma rays! And the temperature—my God, Victor! When the readings cut out at 453 nanoseconds, the reaction chamber's temperature was near *100,000 degrees Celsius*, and still climbing!"

"It was sustained fusion! It had to be!" Victor whooped. "We did it! We achieved ignition! But...but still, even then, how is what happened possible? How could a relatively few atoms of deuterium fusing produce such a massive explosion?"

"I don't know!" Dave suddenly loudly yelled back at him, causing the rest of the drenched survivors in the small chamber to look at him with concern. "It's impossible! Even if a chain reaction with the hydrogen around the Device happened we'd only have melted down the Device! There's absolutely no way that it could result in..." his voice trailed off, recalling that impossible mushroom cloud looming above them—undeniably there.

Dave tried to get a grip on his surging emotions.

Yes, it was a huge relief to still be alive. Yes, it was incredible that there'd been a nuclear-level release of energy. But that didn't mean he could shout like a maniac. Indeed, he already knew from their brief time on the submarine that the tightly knit crew and military scientists regarded him and Victor as barely-tolerated intruders.

"I've got *so* much to discuss with my colleagues back at Yale!" Victor grinned widely, not disturbed by Dave's shouting. His wrinkly face was alight with excitement.

"I'm afraid not, Professor," said the Captain who was now looming above both Victor and Dave as they soggily sat on the floor leaning back against the wall.

"Uh, come again?" Dave said, bewildered by the Captain's statement.

Dave could feel the floor beneath them tilting further as the sub descended deeper into the ocean.

"Gentlemen, I'm sorry to have to inform you of this, but your second duplicate Device has been confiscated by Military Intelligence. This whole affair is now classified at the highest secrecy levels as a matter of National Security. I'm ordering the both of you to not discuss any aspects of this work with anyone."

"But...how can you...?" Dave frowned, bewildered by the Captain's "orders."

"I'm sorry, Dr. King, but these directives come from the President himself," the Captain flatly stated. "My scientific advisors say you've tapped into a new source of energy, perhaps what you scientists have labelled 'Dark Energy.' They say that you somehow managed to crack open something called 'Sub-space.' We suspected such from the explosion at your garage, but couldn't be sure until the experiment was replicated. We've been monitoring your experiments for quite a while now, Dr. King."

"You've been spying on me?" Dave gasped.

"Just keeping an eye on you and others—under our anti-terrorism authorities," the Captain stated. "It's all perfectly legal. Anyway, we'll be taking it from here. Dr. King, once we return to port you'll be put on the first plane back to Oklahoma. Professor Volodymyr, you will proceed directly to your country estate. You are not to return to the University or discuss this event with any of your colleagues. The President sends his sincere thanks to both of you for your invaluable contributions and continued cooperation."

"What the hell?" Dave yelled again, losing all control at this unimaginable insult. He slid the laptop over to Victor while pushing his water-drenched frame painfully up to his feet. "*I'm* the expert in this technology! It's *my* experiment, my Device! I don't know how it caused such a huge explosion—whether your theory of Subspace and Dark Energy is right or wrong—but I'm the best person to figure out the details! And Victor here is your best bet at getting to the theoretical underpinnings that may allow you to eventually *control* whatever occurred. Right now all you've got is a new kind of massive superweapon. But if we can harness its output—without all the associated radiation that comes with using atomic power—why then..."

"We will bring in experts as needed," the Captain firmly interrupted Dave, reaching down to help Victor get up to his feet. "If we need either of you, we will contact you. But for now this entire matter is Top Secret. That's how it is, whether you agree or not. Please go with your escorts back to your cabins. Oh, and I'll need this for my scientists," he said, smoothly taking the laptop out of Victor's hands.

"You say this is 'Top Secret'?" Dave laughed, allowing himself to be pushed into a narrow corridor by two burly sailors, and calling back over his shoulder to the Captain. "You can't hide a nuclear-type explosion! The news media will be broadcasting this story within the hour!"

He got no answer.

"Oh, my boy," Victor sighed, being roughly pushed right behind Dave along the same corridor. "They'll claim it was just a meteor."

"What?"

"Like the *Chelyabinsk meteor* that exploded June, 2013, over Russia."

"You mean the one that injured more than a thousand people?"

"Yes, just like that," Victor sighed back at Dave. "If it were an actual atomic-bomb event, then there'd be massive radiological contamination. But a kinetic explosion from a meteor would only release heat. That's what any investigating authorities will find at the atoll—only heat. Our equipment certainly was completely incinerated. The world won't even know we were here."

"But...shouldn't we both get...like several Nobel Prizes, at least?"

Victor ruefully laughed.

"I'm very sorry, my boy," he said as he sadly waved goodbye while being thrust into his own small, separate cabin. "I didn't expect this treatment from the Navy—but I should have known better. I'm afraid it's time for me to completely retire and for you to go get yourself some cuddly girlfriend. We're just going to have to forget all of this happened. We've no choice."

Dave heard a door slam shut, locking Victor into his cabin. Then the same happened for him. He had only a bunk, a slide-out writing desktop, a sink, and a toilet to keep him company in the cramped space.

He'd expected this truth in their journey to the atoll, but now was certain. It wasn't just a cramped cabin. It was a jail cell.

"Damn!" Dave spat, banging his head against the wall.

He felt the tilted floor beneath his feet leveling off. They were headed home. The trip had been both a complete success and a terrible disaster.

"'Dark Energy'..." Dave muttered, shaking his head in astonishment. "Could it really be?"

Dave imagined the amazing advances for society that a source of limitless, clean energy could provide.

But, assuming it could be controlled, the military would just turn it into weapons—beamed-energy, laser-guns, and ever-bigger bombs!

But if it was really true that Subspace could be opened up and Dark Energy tapped—then a bomb could easily be built by any capable scientist to *destroy* the *entire* planet!

It was the perfect Doomsday Weapon.

Dave knew he had to find a way to prevent that from happening.

But how?

He had no idea...

Back on a plane from Newark to Oklahoma City, seated comfortably in first-class, Dave scrutinized his cellphone. They'd taken it away before allowing him to go onto the nuclear sub. Then they'd returned it to him.

He'd much rather have his laptop back, but this was better than nothing.

Before considering how to deal with the military, he just stared out the small window. He'd specifically requested a window seat. He liked floating along 30,000 feet in the air, getting the "big view"! Somehow it calmed him to float above it all. It was late in the evening, but there was still enough light to have a spectacular view of what lay beneath them.

They were crossing the Appalachian Mountains. Clouds were drifting through the moderately-high peaks. But then, on the other side of the mountains, they encountered a solid bank of clouds.

On the first-class compartment's monitor screen, the News was playing. He heard a summary about the terrorist "Linda Powers" and her unknown accomplices. The police were still searching for them, but insisted the public need not be alarmed. True, the terrorists had apparently successfully attacked the One World Trade Center, blowing a hole in its side—but the authorities insisted that the global criminals were on the run.

Dave turned his attention back to his cellphone.

There were a number of messages.

Most were spam, but there were several from the school where he'd taught now for years. He was certain they were about his termination. They could wait.

A couple of the messages were from George. He listened to them, which briefly described how his critters were doing. George was doing a great job taking care of Dave's snakes, lizards, and tortoises. They were all safe and snug in his converted glass bookshelves. George was a good friend.

One was from his sister, checking in with him. She still didn't know when their mother's funeral would be held. There were "unspecified problems" that she stated she didn't have time to go into in her message.

And then there was a call from Samantha Smith's landline phone in Ada, recorded just that morning.

Dave hoped she was still alive after having taken one of those "magic" pills from that terrorist girl. If not, then he'd have yet another death on his conscience.

Dave listened to that message carefully...

"Uh...Dr. King...this is Sally Smith. My mother would like you to come to the memorial for my boyfriend, Snake, if you can. She's sick right now and can't call herself. But don't worry, she's getting better. She's taking those new vitamins that your Mother wanted her to have and she says they're really helping her. Anyway, the memorial is tomorrow at noon at Clinton's Funeral Home in Ada. I'd...well, I'd like for you to come too, if you can. I'm kind of interested in what my Mom told me about your research—it sort of overlaps with some things I've been playing with myself that I'd like to get your opinion on them. Anyway, see you tomorrow, if you can make it. If not, don't worry about it."

How did Samantha know about his research? Ah, Dave's mom had probably bragged on him to her. Jean was always looking for a potential girlfriend for him.

He felt a catch in his throat.

So much had happened that he'd almost forgotten that his mother was gone.

He tried to call that number to let them know he'd be there at Snake's memorial—but no one picked up. It didn't seem like Samantha had an answering service. Dave vaguely recalled amongst his mother's jabbering she'd mentioned her friend Samantha who didn't like modern technology, not even owning a cellphone.

Well, Dave didn't blame her. Modern technology was getting more and more difficult for the older generation. And who knew where this "Dark Energy" stuff would lead? It might just as easily destroy the world as save it.

But that was a lot for him to think about. The gentle rocking of the jet plane was very soothing...

—and he was awfully tired.

In a few moments he began dosing off in his seat, drifting into what he hoped would be a mercifully-deep, healing sleep.

It had been a long several days.

Maybe it was actually good for him to go back to playing with snakes—and just turn over his cold fusion experiments to the government. Let them agonize over getting it all to work correctly.

He might even have time, finally, to find a cute, sexy girlfriend after all!

That should have been the fodder for some very interesting dreams.

But all he had were fitful nightmares.

The funeral was both beautiful and pathetic.

Not having anywhere else to go, Dave grabbed a cab home from the airport in Oklahoma City, retrieved his banged-up Cavalier, and then drove straight through the night to Ada. Since it was now getting along towards morning, it wasn't worth the bother and expense of getting a motel room.

So he cruised along Main Street, driving past where the old closed theater had been. He'd heard on the radio while driving that the police now suspected that Linda Powers was responsible for blowing it all to hell! What a weird bitch she was. Dave hoped her inexplicable-duplicate Sally from his Dimension wasn't as bizarre.

Apparently it wasn't certain that Linda Powers died in the explosion. They couldn't locate her body in the incinerated building. But then again, nothing much was left of the building. How had she managed such a big fire? And why did she and her fellow terrorists care about a mostly shut down old business district in a medium sized town? And the authorities had called off the local search. What did *that* mean?

The international search, meanwhile, was still continuing—especially for her accomplice who attacked the One World Trade Center, blowing a hole in its side! A woman much like Linda had kidnapped a pharmaceutical executive there, to what purpose no one seemed to know. But to Dave it all just underlined Linda's claim to be a renegade pharmaceutical representative. Apparently there were also additional renegades out there who sympathized with whatever plot she was planning.

It was all too confusing.

Paradoxically, Dave hoped that Linda Powers had survived the explosion—and was still out there somewhere.

She was incredibly annoying and dangerous, but also fascinatingly unpredictable. Even though she enraged him, she also raised his awareness to a new level. She was an intriguing mystery.

Dave, however, was annoyed at himself for being attracted to such a dangerous woman. After all, she'd killed his mother and almost killed him!

"No more tattooed, weird females for girlfriends!" he sternly warned himself, looking at the blackened remains of the entire block as he slowly drove past—that which just a few days ago held the old theater and restaurant.

Nothing stirred in their flattened, still-smoking remains.

Surely, Linda Powers must be dead—burnt to a crisp.

Arriving at the funeral home a few hours early before the service, he walked in hoping to find a quiet place where he could maybe lean back in a comfortable chair and catch a nap.

But there—sitting all alone in the main chapel—was Samantha's daughter Sally. The room was clearly set-up for a funeral or commemoration, with maybe fifty chairs set in respectfully straight lines in the room. Sally was the only occupant.

On a podium at the front of the room sat one lone white urn. It was engraved with a delicately carved black snake curling around its tapered length several times.

There was no doubt as to what was inside the urn.

There were no flowers or cards—apparently this "Snake" fellow didn't have many friends.

Dave slipped into the seat next to Sally.

"I got your telephone message," he quietly said to her. "I just made it here from my airplane coming from the East Coast, a bit early. I hope I'm not disturbing you?"

She looked at Dave sadly.

It was amazing how much she looked like Linda Powers! But the resemblance was only superficial—her petite size, the fluffy head of red-brown hair, her pert nose, and especially her big green eyes looked exactly like Linda.

But instead of the vivacity of Linda, this Sally was withdrawn and suspicious. She didn't meet Dave's eyes, looking sullenly down at the floor.

She had on a demure, ankle-length blue dress. It had long sleeves with lace at the sleeves, covering up any tattoos on her arms.

"No, you're not bothering me," she quietly replied. "I'm glad you could come, Dr. King. Thanks."

"I was happy to do so—sorry about your loss, of course. And please call me 'Dave.'"

"Ok..."

"So...Snake was your boyfriend?"

She nodded, looking up tearfully at the white urn.

"He was cremated," she simply stated. "He didn't have much money. He didn't have any relatives that I ever knew of. He had a small insurance policy that he left to me. I'm taking care of his affairs, what little there are of them, anyway."

She choked back a sob.

"That must be tough on you."

"It was just so *stupid!*" she tearfully sniffed. "Why did that terrorist guy smash into the restaurant? And who was that girl that I waited on? The police said she looked exactly like me except for having blond hair instead of red. I didn't even get a good look at her. All I noticed was her hoodie. But they almost arrested me because they thought I was her! Or, they thought that the girl with the gun was *me!* How is that even possible?"

"I...don't know," Dave gulped, hesitant to share with Sally his experiences with her inexplicable double.

"And now I'm *scared*...scared all the time!"

"But...why?"

"Didn't you hear?"

"Hear what?"

"That terrorist guy that killed Snake *escaped!*"

"He...escaped?"

"It was on all the news channels! A couple days ago a gang of his fellow terrorists broke him out of a federal prison. Didn't you hear?"

"I was...on a trip."

"The police wanted to put me into protective custody but I refused. I can't be important enough that the terrorists would come after me. That's ridiculous! I was just an innocent bystander in their plot to scare the general public by attacking a random restaurant. At least that's what the police told me."

In the empty, dimly lit room Dave felt a chill go down his spine. That maniac was still out there! He must to be part of Linda Power's gang. Yes, they were both there at the restaurant, likely working in coordination. Now that Linda was dead would her accomplice come after Dave, trying to get revenge?

Jesus, it was too much to process!

"Uh...so where's your Mom?" Dave asked, trying to change the subject while again remembering that he'd given her those suspicious "vitamin" pills which had killed his own mother.

"She's still sick, but doing better," Sally sighed, seemingly also happy to change the subject from dealing with deadly prowling terrorists.

"I'm glad to hear that she's..."

"She's thinking clearer than she has in months," Sally rapidly continued. "She says it's like the tumor in her head is disappearing!"

"I hope that's true."

"And she's stopped smoking! I couldn't believe it. She just stopped! She said she didn't feel the urge anymore. It's like a miracle!"

"That's...amazing," Dave gulped, now more than ever convinced that the "vitamins" were something extraordinary. "But she didn't feel up to coming with you today?"

"Yes, she and Snake never got along," she explained. "I guess she thought I should have a better boyfriend. She always resented him—supposedly reminding her that without her illness I'd be off to college getting married to a boring lawyer or something," Sally shrugged. "Anyway, I told her to get some rest. So I'm here all alone."

Dave knew there had to be more going on here than just random events. Dave knew that somehow this was all connected to his experiments. Too many inexplicable things were happening for it all to be just coincidence.

"If it's any consolation, I've had a pretty bad week myself," Dave admitted weakly. His voice trailed off as he looked for any hint Sally was interested in hearing more. She made no move. But he persisted anyway: "Before that terrorist lady came to your restaurant, she kidnapped me and my mother."

"Yes, I know all of that," she answered. "I heard about it on the news reports. That's one reason I wanted to talk to you more, to see if you had any idea about what was happening. Snake was my...my one real friend...and...and..."

She broke into sobs, burying her face in her hands.

Gingerly, Dave laid his arm over her heaving shoulders.

"Get your hands *off* of me!" she shouted at him, jerking to the side.

"Sorry! Sorry!" he hastily assured her, quickly withdrawing his arm then holding his hands palms-up in an attitude of harmlessness.

"No...no," she choked, getting her tears under control as she settled back into her padded wooden chair. "It's me that's sorry. I just can't stand being touched. I never even let poor Snake touch me except for an occasional kiss. But now he's gone."

Dave was afraid she'd start bawling again.

"But...he was your 'boyfriend'?"

She paused as if considering what to say.

"When I was a little girl," she tentatively replied in a small voice, "my stepfather used to come in late at night and try to touch me," she whispered in a voice Dave could barely hear. "He never actually did anything bad to me, but I got so scared... I've never gotten over it. He's long deceased now, but still haunts me late at night. I guess that's what made me *frigid*. But Snake didn't care. He was a true friend to me—said he'd happily wait for me until hell froze over."

Her voice trailed off and Dave just sat there keeping her company in silence.

"I'm saying too much," Sally whispered again. "I've never told anyone else about my stepdad, not even Snake—but somehow I feel I can trust you. Can I trust you?"

Dave felt an immense wave of sympathy sweep over him as if she were his little sister needing protection.

"I would never knowingly hurt you," Dave reassured her, staring straight ahead at the beautiful urn on its solitary pedestal sitting in its own shaft of yellow light coming from a spotlight set in the ceiling.

Though it contained mere ashes, Dave had a feeling that Snake was kindly watching over both him and Sally.

"Thank you," she said in a small voice.

Though he'd never known this 'Snake' person, Dave felt a strange kinship to him. If there was one thing that Dave had learned over the years of having many snakes as pets, it was total respect. Snakes did not understand kidding or horseplay, as would a cat or dog. To snakes, such behavior was simply hostile. Snakes, however, could sense and respond, in their own way, to gentle respect. Even so-called 'vicious' snakes often tamed down in captivity when handled respectfully and kindly.

To Dave, this Sally person seemed much like one of his easily frightened, vulnerable reptiles. She needed "TLC"—tender loving care, to be handled gently. Apparently her young friend Snake had done this for her. She needed for her personal space to be respected, her boundaries not transgressed. Since Dave felt partially to blame for her boyfriend's untimely demise—due to the crazy Linda terrorist he'd somehow enraged—he could certainly try to do the same for her as had Snake.

"So what was it about my research that you were interested in?" he said, changing the subject to something less delicate.

She perked up.

"My...own interests...relate to your work on catalyzing deuterium ion interactions in palladium matrices."

Dave was stunned.

She was a waitress in a small-town restaurant. How in the world could she have an interest in—let alone her own related work—to his esoteric physics experiments?

But...come to think of it—that likely deceased Linda girl was a checkout clerk at a grocery store, but then claimed to be a pharmaceutical expert?

Intrigued, Dave continued. "How do you know of my work?"

"Well, my mother told me generalities she got from your mother—and I also heard things on various news programs. Plus, I looked online and saw the abstracts to your published papers on low-energy nuclear reactions."

"That's impressive," he said. "And I've been too busy to watch the News much. I didn't know they'd profiled me so completely."

"Oh, you're quite famous—or infamous, rather," she quietly stated, peering at him furtively. "The news reports suggest you had a relationship with that terrorist girl?"

"Nope, not true!" Dave emphatically said, shaking his head firmly in the negative. "I just happened to see her Turtle Tattoo on her wrist at the grocery store and complimented her on it. That's when she for some insane reason decided to kidnap me and my mother. Before that, I never even knew she existed."

"But how could she have the exact same tats that I have?"

He shrugged, shaking his head in bewilderment. "Maybe...she was perhaps following you online? Do you post your tats on Facebook?"

"Actually, I do—not of my naked body, of course, just the visuals of the exposed tattoos," she mused. "I suppose someone else could piece together my body art from my Facebook and other posts."

"If Linda Powers were obsessed with you, then that might explain her similar look."

"Why would she be obsessed with me? I'm a 'nobody'—except, of course, for my body art."

"Well, they are beautiful."

"My tattoos?"

"I don't have any myself—too afraid of needles and permanently inking myself with something I might later want to change—but I admire body art on others. It's living art!"

"I do have some nice ones on me," Sally shyly said. "Snake liked my mix of themes—in fact he inked my best ones, including the Turtle Tattoo on my wrist."

"Your boyfriend was quite remarkable, a true artist," Dave sincerely replied. "I wish I could have known him."

Sally smiled shyly at him.

Slowly she reached across the gap in the chairs and took Dave's hand in her own, giving it a grateful squeeze before hastily turning it loose.

"If it is ok, I'd like to come to your Mother's funeral," she tentatively suggested. "I could drive my mother there so you didn't have to make an extra trip here."

Ok...he hadn't planned on giving Samantha a lift, but that didn't matter. It might be nice to have Sally there. Instead of the whinny clone of Linda he'd expected, she was actually rather nice.

"That's very kind of you, but I don't know when it's going to be—even my sister doesn't know yet, who's handling those matters."

"I heard on the news that the authorities are holding your mother's body in refrigeration, not releasing it to the funeral home in Sulphur. They say she may have been poisoned by that terrorist woman. They want to do an elaborate autopsy but your sister won't allow it. Your sister says that your mother wanted to be buried intact, not pickled or cut-up, to 'reintegrate peacefully' into the earth. So there's a legal fight going on that's..."

"Huh," he interrupted her. "That's crazy! But I'm not surprised," he now sighed deeply. "Both my mother and sister could be a pain sometimes. Now it seems they're together poking my Mom's dead finger into the authority's eye!"

"Good for her," Sally laughed.

Dave grinned at her, feeling suddenly invigorated.

"Well, what *about* my research—and your 'work'—cause them to intersect? We might as well hash it out since we're the only ones here so far."

She grew more serious, straightening up in her chair.

"Well, I've always had a talent for mathematics," she slowly explained. "In fact after high school I was going to go to college to study advanced calculus and computer programming. I even had a scholarship. But then my mother got sick with her lung cancer. She couldn't work...had big medical bills she couldn't pay, even after Medicare payments—so I had to get a job to help her. And the local jobs around here are scarce for just a high school graduate. So I've been working in the restaurant for a few years. The base pay's lousy, but I get good tips."

"That cancer stuff can be rough," Dave sighed, remembering everything he'd gone through with his mother. "Even when you've got help—I had my sister, Cat, to do most of the heavy-lifting—it's still a terrible ordeal for everyone involved. Of course, it's noble to do our part to help our loved ones. We're all going to be old soon, subject to the very same illnesses, so..."

"But do you smoke?" she interrupted him.

He was taken-aback.

"Uhm...no...I never have—never saw the point of it."

"Me neither. But my mother was a chain-smoker, continuing even when she got cancer! Even Snake smoked. He thought it was funny! Why can't people see what's right in front of their noses?" she seriously asked, frowning.

Dave shook his own head sadly, commiserating with her.

"It's got to do with brain chemistry, or so I hear," he sighed. "Some people can start and stop addictive drugs fairly easily. For others, it's next to impossible. I think it has to do with how tightly the nicotine or other drugs bind to receptors in people's brains, or the strength of underlying brain chemical pathways...but my field is physics. Biology isn't my area of primary study. So I don't know a lot about..."

"You know enough," she nodded. "And I totally agree with you. I used to get mad at my mother for smoking all her life while knowing full-well that it might cause her terrible health problems. But then I realized that we all have our hang-ups. None of us are perfect."

"We were *made* imperfect," Dave astutely concluded. "The real one to blame is *God!*" he half-joked.

"You don't believe in personal responsibility?" she seriously asked him.

"Oh, sure," Dave shrugged. "But sometimes I think we put too much blame on each other and ourselves. We are, after all, just collections of cells programmed genetically to behave in specific ways. Our minds don't exist independent of our bodies. Our brains, indeed, are just another organ—a collection of many cells programmed to interact in certain ways producing certain thoughts and responses. So we're much more a product of our genetics than we like to admit."

"So do you see a third arm that conspires with 'Nature' and 'Nurture'?"

"A 'third' arm?"

"Our own conscious brains making emergent choices..." she speculated, her eyes narrowing.

"Oh, yes—to a certain degree," he nodded. "But from what I've read of psychology, our conscious brains are like riders sitting on the back of elephants. The Rider can see further ahead, since he's up high, and can try to steer the Elephant onto the best path—but the big, powerful Elephant has a mind of its own."

"Jonathan Haidt— *'The Happiness Hypothesis: Finding Modern Truth in Ancient Wisdom'*," she nodded knowingly.

"Yes, that's it exactly! So you read modern psychology texts as well as advanced mathematics?"

She tilted her head to the side, shyly.

"I'm very interested in artificial intelligence," she admitted. "But to understand the constraints and facilitators for evolving computer algorithms, you'd need a good understanding of how biological computers—our 'brains'— work. It's amazing how little is known about how our own brains work. Do you know that we still don't even understand the biological details of how memory occurs? It's like you just said, our brains are collections of super-computers interacting with many other super-computers both in parallel and in sequence."

Dave was *very* impressed with this Sally.

"You're very smart," he smiled, but quickly realized that happiness was out-of-place in a funeral home. He stuck a suitably sober look back on his face.

"Yes, that's what my mom keeps telling me," she shrugged. "But I just do what I do. I don't feel particularly smart."

And yet here he was intrigued with her thinking.

"So how does brain chemistry relate to my own stumbles in trying to get room-temperature, sustained 'cold' fusion to work?" he eagerly asked.

"Well..." she hesitantly ventured.

"Come on, now," he encouraged her. "I really want to know."

"I don't have any college, let alone a Doctorate degree like you..."

"Who the hell cares?" Dave sputtered. "College for me was mostly a huge waste of time. It was torture having to memorize and compete on massive amounts of material that had little or no interest to me. It was only when I finally started doing my own research that I actually learned anything. And it sounds to me like you've done exactly the same for yourself, which is far more important than just suffering through a bunch of stupid classes. *I'm* happy to learn from *you!*"

"You remind me a lot of Snake," she shyly smiled at him, before glancing up at the white urn and wiping the smile from her face as well. "He was always looking at me like I was a new species or something—like he was studying me. It annoyed me, but I was flattered at the same time."

"Hey, I'll take the compliment of being a thinker, not just a reactive smart animal. I'm not going to poke inked needles into your skin like Snake did, but I'm sure capable of appreciating your talents."

She seemed to relax, now looking at him with a grateful expression.

"You really want to know about my hobby?"

"Absolutely."

"Well..." she began, "I've been studying and applying my theories every day and night when I wasn't working at the restaurant. There's lots a person can accomplish surreptitiously using the high-speed internet back-channels."

"Such as?"

"Well, once again I probably shouldn't be telling you this? I might be doing things, well, possibly borderline illegal..."

He laughed, too intrigued to censure his reactions. "Tell me! I'm interested. And I promise to be very discrete. Believe me, Sally, I know all about hiding possibly questionable work from the world. Anything you tell me in confidence is strictly between the two of us."

"Well then...I've...hacked into several of the world's fastest super-computers and set up 'hives' of directed-evolution synthetic intelligences."

Dave was flabbergasted.

"That's fantastic!" he said, his eyes stretched wide with amazement. "And what is the purpose you're evolving them to achieve?"

"Be smart."

"Ok...but to accomplish what particular task?"

"Anything."

"*Anything?*"

"Yes, whatever task you need them to do—true independent intelligence! Instead of writing a program from scratch, you'd simply give them general instructions from which *they* would figure out how to accomplish the specific objective."

"But...that's...that's...that's *incredible!*" Dave loudly enthused, clapping his hands together in glee at the idea.

Then, again more quietly—remembering where they were—he urgently asked Sally: "What about directing arrays of billions of nano-lasers to target individual deuterium atoms to nudge together in specific crystalline patterns within a palladium matrix in real time? Could your evolved 'hives' help with something like that?"

"Yep."

"Really?"

"Sure, why not? In fact after reading your journal papers, not just the abstracts—I had the very same idea."

"God *damn* it, Sally! I thought I was done with my research. Maybe not! I've got to tell my friend Victor about this..."

"About what?"

"About this incredibly smart lady, this super-talented amateur scientist, this psychologist-mathematician that just might hold the key to changing an incredibly dangerous weapon into the means to *save* humanity from its own destructive nature!"

She snorted, shaking her head in flattered denial.

"No, no...I'm just a waitress at a restaurant," she mumbled, looking down at the floor.

"Then cook me up a plate of Dark Energy because I'm famished!"

"Huh?"

"Oh...I've got a *lot* to tell you about, Sally!"

"*Harrummmmppphhh,*"—came a polite noise from behind them.

Sally and Dave turned around, startled.

The funeral director was guiding in a couple more mourners. They were a ragged-looking couple, both of whose visible skin was adorned with many colorful tattoos.

"Guess I didn't need these long sleeves after all," Sally whispered to Dave.

"You're funny," he whispered back, quietly snickering. Maybe she wasn't so unlike Linda Powers, but in *good* ways.

Death has a strange way of bringing out both our worst and best.

Suddenly the future did not look so grim to Dave.

There was hope!

After the service, he was going to tell Sally everything!

Damn those stupid Navy censors!

Damn those insane terrorists!

They did *not* hold his future in their hands! And he was *not* going to allow them to define his present and future options.

Dave had never believed in "fate." His life was his own to chart, not a pawn of unseen Forces. The only boundaries Dave could meekly accept were the limitations of his own imagination.

Chapter 10

VISION

Why are you so limited?
Unable to see beyond the end of your nose
When so many incredible sights swirl
Just waiting—begging—to be seen
Gone unnoticed as if they don't exist
When weary, dutiful plodding could explode
Into leaping, jumping, dancing, and prancing
If only you could open up those pretty eyes
Now so dulled by fatigue, pain, and submission
Gathering-in your own array of flowers
Changing a drab desert into a wonderland
Self-developing, empowering, and beautifying...
Would that it could be true!
Well why not?
The Luminary Chronicles, 10:15-19

Sally felt the top of her head *burning...flames* enveloping her grey trench coat and penetrating her skin—as the flesh on her arms started to cook!

She *screamed*, jerking out of searing clothes, running patting at her flaming head heedlessly forward—to *fall* over a cliff, plummet helplessly flailing-about in the air, *crash* through layers of branches and bushes, then SMASH hard down into cold swirling water...

—which, though putting out the fires, dragged her down: struggling, drowning, and fighting to get back to the surface...

—where, sucking breaths in heaving gasps, she floundered, and then splashed weakly toward a dimly glimpsed shoreline.

181

Only half conscious she dragged her savaged body up onto the wide, deep river's edge, collapsing into a shivering heap upon wet mud.

"*Was ist das?*" she heard an excited small child's voice as she desperately blinked trying to clear her sight, blearily making out a dirty urchin looming over her.

"W-what...?" Sally managed to stammer, half-drowned, her head and hands seared, stark naked from the river ripping off her remaining underclothes.

"*Momma! Schnell zu kommen! Ist es ein Dämon!*"

Sally heard pounding feet, saw people in rough-hewn clothes gathering around her as she lay curled up in a fetal position, gasping on the river bank. Then she felt *sharp pikes* poked into her naked body...

—prompting her to surge up to her feet, *scream* and *charge* at them!

They fell back, cowering, shouting "*Lieber Gott hilf uns, hilf uns!*"

Now was her chance to escape the still-gathering mob, but Sally had no strength left...instead falling to her knees in the thick mud, then—with a sigh—onto her face.

She barely felt the gnarled hands grabbing her, dragging her for what seemed a long distance, and then unceremoniously stuffing her into a large woven basket.

"*Sollten wir es töten?... Nein... Nennen Mutter Hildegard... Sie wird wissen was zu tun mit diesem Dämon!*"

Sally's head, hands, and lower arms were in terrible pain from being burned in the fireball inferno. She was shivering from the icy cold of the river and subsequent chill of the day. She was cramped in the rough, closed basket—twisted again into a fetal position. With difficulty she could see though overlapping slats. She realized it was a cage for hauling animals, by the smell probably pigs.

And she realized the people outside were speaking a foreign language. Both the guards and the peasants clustered around her—who were pointing, gawking, and spitting—were speaking in German.

So she must be in Germany...but *when?*

In her Dimension she'd studied for a summer in the French Empire. They were friendly with the English Empire, of which The United States of America was a tightly controlled Province. But the German Empire was a proclaimed enemy. Regardless, part of her language training in the lower grades was in German. Fortunately, she'd elected to take a full four years of German in lower school. It was always good to know the speech of one's greatest enemy, especially when they were scientific and manufacturing geniuses. But that was years ago. She hoped she could remember enough to communicate with these rabid, dangerous peasants.

"Bitte...helfen Sie mir," she managed to croak out...*please, help me.*

"Es spricht...der Dämon spricht!" the people gasped—*it speaks, the demon speaks!*—before backing up a few steps in awe.

"Ich bin kein Dämon," she feebly protested—*I am not a demon.* "Ich bin ein...verlorener Reisenden...ich fiel in den Fluss und verlor meine Kleider," she weakly stated, *I am a lost traveler...I fell in the river and lost my clothes.*

"Sie kam aus der Hölle!" one shouted at her, *you came from hell!* "Sie sind mit dem Feuer der Hölle verbrannt!"—*you are burned with the fire of hell!*

Another taunted her with a now obvious-to-all condemnation: "Sie tragen die Spuren der Satan!" —*you bear the marks of Satan!*

Oh, rats—Sally fuzzily thought to herself. *All my tats are showing!* There for all to see were *snakes*, a lady's face melting into a *skull*, *zombies* fighting, bloody *knives*, and a black *spider*.

In her nakedness her gloriously rebellious, hidden teenager-angst tattoos were starkly revealed to the world. And they were accented by her burned-bald head and raw, reddened arms and hands.

She must indeed look to these ignorant peasants like a monster from the depths of hell.

"Bitte, ich kann sprechen mit einem offiziellen?" she fearfully beseeched the crowd—*please, can I talk to an official?* —as yet more sharp pikes were thrust into the basket, painfully lacerating her sides and back as the crowd got angrier, louder, and bolder!

Sally had no doubt what was about to happen. Trapped in the pig-cage she was about to be stabbed to death by a terrified mob.

But then she heard another, qualitatively different voice.

"Hör auf! Lassen Sie das Mädchen und legte ihre Kleidung auf! Sie is kein Dämon, sondern ein Bote Gottes!" —*stop this! Release that girl and put clothes on her! She is not a demon, but a messenger from God!*

Sally heard the authoritative tones of a commanding female figure, heard the "clomping" of horse hoofs, and glimpsed a figure on the horse's back clad in a long dark-blue robe.

"Danke, danke!"—*thank you, thank you!*...Sally sobbed from pain and relief as the village people rushed to obey the woman, pulling Sally from the small cage and slipping on a rough robe over her burnt skull, covering her entire body.

Sally wobbly stood there—barely able to keep erect—on cut and bleeding bare feet. She looked around in bewilderment. She was in a small village, alongside a wide river, surrounded by thick forest.

Then she spied a door into a thatch-roofed hut and *broke away* from those guiding her to *dash* across a dirt road and *dive* into the dark opening...

—falling down upon a dirt floor in the hut, startling several chickens that'd been huddled there in the dark!

"Clucking" loudly in fear, they scampered over her body and out of the hut.

"What, no return to the movie theater?" Sally moaned, clutching her burnt hands to her chest as she lay prone on the flat floor. "Oh, come on...I need medical attention. I've got to get out of this 'movie' and back to the real world!"

It worked before in the other 'movies'—diving into a dark opening. That' how she returned her the movie theater! But in the light from the opened doorway she held up her arms in front of her eyes and saw something terrible—the tattoos on her left arm and wrist were *obliterated!* They'd been burned off with the skin. The Turtle Tattoo that'd guided her so unerringly in the past was *gone!*

Ah...so that's it...my "return ticket" to the theater in the 21st Century is burned up—she moaned to herself, the awful realization crippling her.

She sagged down into the dirt, quietly crying...

—to be roughly jerked back to her feet, and paraded out to stand in front of the woman on the horse.

Looking up, Sally saw that the woman had on a white hood that covered her shoulders, neck, sides of her face, and her hair. Only the woman's face was showing—a middle aged, stern-looking woman with piercing, unblinking, bright-blue eyes.

"Warum haben sie laufen?" the woman asked, *why did you run?* "Haben Sie bezweifle dass ich die, die Sie gesendet wurden, zu finden war?" —*did you doubt I was the one you were sent to find?*

Sally held up her red, cracked, oozing arms in supplication.

"Ich bin schwer verwundet," Sally said, sensing a potential friend that she'd offended, bowing her head in deference to the regal woman on the horse, *I am gravely wounded.*

The woman on the horse didn't reply, just kept staring at Sally.

Sally knew she was on trial. Either she was a "messenger from God" worthy of being saved, or a deceitful demon from hell.

Whatever age she was in, Sally knew that demons from hell were not held in high regard.

"Ich wurde durch das Feuer meiner Gang verbrannt. Ich suchte Salbe," she continued, *I was burnt by the fire of my passage. I was seeking ointment.*

"Wir haben die Mittel, um Ihre Verbrennungen im Kloster zu behandeln," the woman finally, kindly stated—*we have the means to treat your burns at the monastery.* "Können Sie gehen?"—*can you walk?*

"Ich glaube nicht..." Sally said, wavering back and forth, barely able to stand. *I don't think so...*

The adrenalin and shock was wearing off. She knew she was grievously burned. Without proper medical care she'd likely die of her injuries.

"Legte sie auf ein Pferd!" the woman authoritatively commanded the men following on foot behind her, *Put her on a horse!*

Sally found herself lifted onto the back of a big brown horse. She'd never ridden a horse before. It was a brand new experience, one that distracted her from the fierce pain of her stab wounds and burns. For a moment the exhilarating experience of being on the back of such a powerful animal—bouncing along a rocky path into the forest following behind the blue-robed, white-hooded woman—made

Sally forget that she'd not escaped via the dark opening back to the theater, as she'd done before.

This was definitely the Past. It was a whole new, amazing adventure. "When" and exactly "where" were beside the point. The real point was she could experience something no one else of her time period had done. She'd traveled in Time to another Century! Who knew what she could learn in the "new" world?

*But I'm not in any shape to enjoy this...*she groaned to herself.

She could not trick herself out of contemplating the grim reality facing her. She was stranded somewhere in time, unable to return to her own world.

Oh, Great Spirit, this is even more terrible than my being burned half to-death. Where is my shoulder bag? Where is my little pet dinosaur, Breep? Where'd they go? Did the inferno I unleashed when I set the gun on maximum incinerate them? Or did I drop them in my fiery passage to this place, wherever it is? Whatever, they're gone.

"Bitte!" she called up to the lady riding in front of her own horse, *Please!* "Bitte beantworten eine Frage für mich?"—*Please answer one question for me?*

"Natürlich," the woman called-back, *Of course.*

"Welches Jahr haben wir?" Sally weakly asked, struggling to hold onto the saddle horn and stay on the rocking animal's back now that they were climbing up a trail, *What year is this?*

After a pause, the woman calmly called back: "Es ist das Jahr des Herrn elf und fünfundsechzig," *It is the year of our Lord 1165.*

For a moment Sally was stunned. She was in the 12th Century. This was smack in the middle of the "Dark Ages" following the fall of the Roman Empire in the 5th century and before the Renaissance and Age of Discovery starting in the 15th century. It was in the so-called "middle ages," the Medieval Period. If the history of Dave's world was similar to hers, this a dark period when scientific endeavor died and superstition ruled. It was before the emergence of the modern, industrialized Empires.

She'd been thrown back in time 900 years! But then she recalled recently being millions of years in the past and a thousand years in the future. Actually, this was just a "little" jaunt to an "experienced" time-traveler like her.

Through her pain she managed a small "giggle."

But, without a way to return, this was not some fun little side-trip. This was a *life-sentence* to a dark, dangerous, dismal prison.

"Und woher wissen Sie, dass ich komme?" Sally said, struggling to keep conscious against the sizzling pains now wracking her body— *And how did you know I was coming?*

The hooded woman looked back over her shoulder in surprise. Sally realized that a "messenger from God" should not be asking such a question. But Sally knew if she were to survive she must get her bearings, fast!

"Ich hatte eine Vision," the hooded woman up ahead loudly stated for everyone to hear—*I had a Vision.* "Ich sah das Lebendige Licht in den Himmel."—*I saw the Living Light in the sky.* "Gott hat mich zu dir!"—*God directed me to you!*

Sally realized that her blazing arrival through time had translated into a brilliant flash of light in the medieval sky. She remembered falling off a cliff, tumbling through braking branches and bushes, and then falling again before smashing into the river. The fire she'd generated with her maximum-setting gun blast plus the height of her arrival must have been like a meteor burning up in the sky.

This woman was a religious figure. By an incredible coincidence she was nearby, close enough to come to Sally's rescue. She'd been drawn by the natural phenomenon of Sally's arrival.

Or...had *God* intervened?

Sally did not actually think that the Great Spirit noticed her passage back in time. She knew it was going to take massive tapping-into the underlying fabric of the Universe for the entirety of mankind to come to God's full attention. What was little old Sally to the Supreme Intelligence behind the Creation of the Universe?

But whatever happened, Sally now knew that she was in *deep trouble*. With no way back to her own time, she was trapped in the middle ages! Even in her own Dimension, the middle ages were no fun. Ignorance, incurable diseases, rampant wars, cruel dictatorships, crushing poverty, religious intolerance, social injustice, slavery, subjugation of women, and scientific paranoia had plagued mankind for centuries.

Sally sagged forward over the neck of the big animal beneath her, smelling the mustiness of its thick mane. She felt herself drifting off, lulled by the beast's plodding steps, still wracked by intense pain—but grateful to be alive.

Her last thoughts before falling into a painful, uneasy doze were in German, repeating the woman's cryptic words: *Ich hatte eine Vision...Ich sah das Lebendige Licht in den Himmel...Gott hat mich zu dir!*

Would that it could be so...

Victor sat on a porch swing, idly looking out into the thick Vermont woods surrounding his country retreat.

The sun was just rising, lighting up the upper branches of the trees. The world was awakening.

It was very peaceful...especially since the Professor expected that the entire world might come to an *abrupt end* at any moment!

He just wanted to enjoy it while it lasted.

"Phone for you, dear," Ivanna, his wife, called to him from inside the house.

"I am too lazy to get up," Victor said, breathing deeply of the fresh air, reveling in the lush greenery of the forest, and savoring the tweets of awakening, lustily singing birds. "Take a message. Or, better yet, tell them I'll call back later. Or just lie to them and say that I'm not here. I don't care. I'm finally and completely *retired!* I'm too old to take calls. Tell them I flopped over from a heart attack and..."

She laughed back at him from inside their log-cabin style house.

"Oh, you old fart—come to the phone! It's David. He wants to talk to you."

He perked up.

"David? Why did you not say so? Of course I will talk to the dear boy. Tell him not to hang up! I'll be there as soon as I can get my old bones to move my creaky old body back inside."

He spryly hopped up from the swing and marched inside while Ivanna patiently held the landline phone receiver out to him.

Victor slipped into his comfortable armchair beside the phone stand, speaking eagerly into the receiver: "David! How are you, my boy? Did you make it back to Oklahoma safely?"

There was a pause..."Yes, indeed I did."

"And all is well?"

Another, longer pause occurred. Then... "Victor, I've got to talk to you."

"Yes?"

"In person."

"Oh...yes...private matters...of course," Victor nodded, narrowing his eyes.

There was only so much that they could discuss over the open phone lines. He had no doubt that the military was monitoring his calls, both in and out.

"I have a...new girlfriend...that's interested in studying at Yale. She's very talented," Dave's cautious voice came out of the receiver. "Would you mind if I brought her out to your country estate to discuss with you the present student research opportunities in the science departments at Yale?"

"Oh, not at all!" Victor happily agreed. "I'm out of the game now, of course, but I've still lots of contacts at the University. I'd be happy to advise your girlfriend."

Victor was intrigued. Was Dave finally following his friendly advice? Had he found a girlfriend back in Oklahoma so quickly? Or—was this just a ruse for those monitoring the call, disguising his real intentions?

Either way, Victor was glad to oblige.

"Are you busy now?" Victor heard Dave ask.

"Now?"

"Sally and I took the redeye from Oklahoma City," the voice on the phone calmly stated. "We caught a cab in Newark and we're fifteen minutes out. I didn't call earlier because I didn't want to disturb you in the dead of night and..."

"*Marvelous*, my boy!" Victor happily agreed, "whooping" loudly. He saw he'd startled his poor wife. Then, speaking animatedly into the phone he replied: "You and your girlfriend Sally are just in time for breakfast. I'll tell Ivanna!"

"Thanks so much, Victor..."

"I'll await your arrival in the driveway!"

Ivanna, having heard what he'd said, hurried off to the kitchen to start eggs and bacon sizzling. Victor was happy for the momentary diversion from the grim state of the world. Perhaps he'd yet live to enjoy a delicious cholesterol-heavy breakfast which Ivanna usually restricted him from eating—that she was now making for the guests. Plus he'd have a good conversation with nice young people. *It was just too bad it wouldn't last much longer!*—he thought to himself.

"Oh, well," he sighed, putting the receiver back into its cradle. "At least my young charge has a girlfriend at last...good for him."

"What's that, Dear?" Ivanna called from the kitchen.

"I'm going out to wait for them," he lustily called back. "It's Dave and a girlfriend called 'Sally.'"

"I got all that, Dear," she called back. "You bring them in and I'll have the food ready."

What a gal that Ivanna was. For the millionth time, Victor was glad he'd found her those many years ago. He hoped Dave had found someone of similar grandeur.

A few minutes later, a cab came slowly through the thick trees lining the small dirt road that lead to Victor's secluded house set-off from the main road.

Victor stood waiting. The morning sun was warming up the air. He only had on a light sweater. But he was eager to see his guests, welcome them to his home. It was so nice that they could be together right before the world *ended...*

Sally awoke in great pain, weak, and bewildered.

Where was she?

It was dark. She could hear muffled voices in the distance. A rough-woven blanket lay over her. Under it, she was naked.

She felt bandages on her torso, head, arms, and hands.

She tried to call out for help but only managed a ragged *croak*.

"Versuchen Sie nicht zu sprechen," a voice from the darkness comforted her—*Don't try to talk.*

A light sprang up next to the bed. It was a tall, thick candle on a stand, putting out a pungent aroma.

Next to Sally, sitting on a wood chair, was the white-hooded woman in the dark blue robe. She looked at Sally with a *steely, unnerving STARE!*

It was an arresting stare. It was the arresting stare of a woman with *authority*, who expected others to pay attention.

"Speichern Sie Ihre Stärke. Ich bin froh dass Sie noch nach Ihrem schrecklichen Wunden am Leben sind," the soothing voice continued, *Save your strength. I'm glad you are still alive after your terrible wounds.*

Sally tried to nod in gratitude, but could barely move her head it hurt so much.

"Alle anderen, die ich in ähnlichen schrecklichen Bedingungen gesehen, sind gestorben. Sie müssen über einen bemerkens werten Verfassung," the woman matter-of-factly continued. *All others I've seen in similar terrible conditions have died. You must have a remarkable constitution.*

The woman was correct. It had to be Sally's Optimmune overlapping retroviral systems that permeated her tissues. They didn't stop the terrible damage to her body from the inferno she'd passed through, or the long fall then brutal attack by the peasants. But they did manage to keep her alive through her ordeals. Now, they were helping her heal. But Sally knew her super-boosted immune system could only do so much. She was still very much in danger of dying from massive infections and internal organ damage, especially in a primitive society existing many years before the development of antibiotics and modern medicine.

"Oder, was wahrscheinlicher ist, Gott hat ein Wunder Überleben gearbeitet!" the hooded woman firmly concluded. *Or, more likely, God has worked a Miracle in your survival!*

Sally mustered up her resolve, mentally pushing away the fiery pain that mainly enveloped her head and arms. She breathed deeply, inched backward on the hard pillow behind her, and raised her bandaged head.

She had to know what was happening.

Plus, it was too difficult to keep mentally translating between German and English. So she pulled a mental trick she'd used years ago in language classes: dissolving the thinking and physical speech together into *one single* mental-construct.

It was a mental trick apparently linked to her genius in mathematics. It was a type of mental algebra in which each language became opposite sides of an equation.

Now, though her words came out as German, she thought and reacted to her words and the speech of others as if they were in fluent English.

It wasn't a perfect transition. Until she mastered the language and local dialects the meanings might be blurred. But the process that she'd used numbers of times in the past in language classes and foreign countries would let her get the gist of what was spoken.

"I am better, thanks to your kind help," she managed to croak in a hoarse voice.

"I am so glad," the hooded woman replied.

"And...how may I properly address you?" Sally said, painfully turning her head in the direction of the seated woman.

"I am called *Hildegard von Bingen*. I am the leader, the Magistra, of this Christian Convent. You may call me Mother. And *you* are...?"

"My name is Sally—Sally Smith."

"Is that an English name?"

"Yes, it is."

"So are you from England?"

Sally paused, taking a deep breath. She let her head fall back firmly upon the hard pillow. The fumes from the candle were making her woozy. The wax must contain soothing or healing components. She wasn't thinking straight. She could *not* tell Hildegard that she was from America—a continent that would not be discovered by the Europeans until *three hundred* more years in Hildegard's future!

"I am from...a far land," Sally cautiously answered, looking up at a dark, rocky ceiling above her.

"Oh, how far?"

"Very far indeed, Mother," Sally croaked. Her throat was raw. She needed a drink of water.

As if hearing her thoughts, Hildegard put a mug filled with luke-warm water to Sally's cracked lips. Gratefully, Sally slurped down the entire mug.

"Thank you," Sally sighed, her head clearing a bit.

"Again, how far from here?" Hildegard persisted.

"As far as from here to the moon," Sally sighed, closing her eyes.

"You are from another world?" Hildegard gasped.

Sally's eyes jerked open. This woman was incisive. She was not just an ignorant religious figure from the middle ages. She was a true *thinker*.

Suddenly Sally decided to risk everything. She'd tell this nun the truth. Raising her head slightly from her pillow she continued...

"I am not just from another world," Sally said, her voice raspy and ragged. "I'm from another *time*. I've come from nine hundred years in your future. I've been thrown back in time to your world—why, I'm not sure. Also, I'm from a different time-*line*. In my separate but similar 'dimension' this Jesus Christ person that you worship never existed...or never made a mark on history. But in your world I have learned that he reigns as a spiritual King. I have read some of the writings about him in your New Testament and recognize him as a great spiritual thinker and doer. I absolutely do accept that your God is real, but also distant and cruel. I've seen the End of Time with my own eyes—when God *destroys* both your and my worlds. So in my own little way I am trying to protect humanity from His final Wrath—to push off arrival of the *Day of Judgment!* But now I'm stranded here in your time. Perhaps it is a fitting punishment for my arrogance to think that I could change Fate..."

Her voice trailed off as she began to sob quietly, her scarred face twisted up in pain and utter defeat.

But she realized that crying would gain her no sympathy or ad-vantage from this imperial woman who sat silently by the bed absorb-ing Sally's story.

"So that's the truth," Sally concluded, quickly regaining her com-posure and now defiantly looking over at Hildegard. "I know it sounds impossible, the ravings of an insane person. Plus it's just the 'take-home message' not the details. But I assure you it all really happened. I throw myself on your mercy. Do with me as you will."

Sally leaned her aching burned head back against the pillow, exhausted by her long speech. She awaited Hildegard's response. Sally knew that after her fantastic admission she was likely going to be tossed out as a heretic if not worse.

Hildegard sat in stony silence for several minutes.

Then, in a calm voice, Hildegard asked Sally: "Did God send you to me from this far-distant future?"

Sally could not see Hildegard's hooded face by the dim light of the one, flickering candle. But Sally could feel the intensity of Hildegard's question.

Sally knew that everything rode upon her answer.

"I...don't know," she whispered, truthfully, in reply. "*Something* has been guiding me on my journey. That might be a part of what you call 'God'—I don't know. But, whatever it was that sent me here, it seems that this is indeed my final destination. If there is a purpose to my life, then maybe it is to be here in this place, with you—to learn or to teach, or both. I just don't know."

She groaned from the intense pain of her burns. Things began blurring around her...

"Here, drink this."

Gratefully, Sally took small gulps from a mug of a steamy white liquid held to her lips by Mother Hildegard.

Whatever was in the drink spread a sense of calm throughout her body, driving off the raging pain.

"What...was that?"

"It is an herb I rarely use except to treat extreme pain. Do not expect more of it. Any further usage and you would likely become dependent upon it. And we should only be dependent upon the Love of God. But for the moment it will give you the strength to continue our conversation. Speak truthfully, my child, or you will lose my protection and my medical treatments."

"Yes...I understand...thank you."

Outside, Sally could hear the clomping of the hoofs of horses, men shouting to each other as they worked, and even the sweet chanting of women singing in unison overtly religious themes.

For a couple minutes Hildegard set in silence, motionless. Then she seemed to come to a decision.

"Perhaps you *are* mad," Hildegard mused, her voice so low that Sally could barely hear it. "But I do feel a strange kinship to you. You see, I also was deemed by my peers to be mad. From a young child, I saw wonderful yet horrifying Visions. I did not know if they came from God or Satan. But then I saw *the Light*—the *Living Light!* It was so pure and beautiful I knew it could only come from the Creator Himself. And I heard an order from within the Light: a Voice that told me to *write* what I saw! Many doubted my Visions. Some thought I was making them up. I faced great opposition, especially from the males in the church hierarchy. Then yesterday I again saw the Living Light in the night sky—and raced on my horse with my guards to your rescue."

"I thank you for that..." Sally gasped.

"It is just like all other things in my life," Hildegard shrugged. "I find ways to advance my mission."

"*How* do you do that?" Sally asked, fascinated with this possibly delusional but unquestionably brilliant woman. If she were to die from her injuries, she might as well "go out" learning! This seemed a chance to find out how powerful people accomplished great deeds.

Hildegard seemed quite pleasantly surprised and encouraged by Sally's incisive question.

"I *believed* in my Mission, my 'calling'," the hooded woman carefully replied. "So I wrote letters, I enlisted others to my Cause—and eventually acquired authority even from the Holy Father Himself, Pope Eugenus, to publish books, songs, plays, perform my music, and even to go on my preaching tours! And it is not just words and images that I offer, but tangible deeds. With the help of others, I have founded two monasteries. Here, we heal many who are suffering physical ills, using the diverse herbs and minerals of God's Nature. I then write the results in books and thereby spread abroad the Wisdom of Nature's healing powers."

"But..." Sally gasped, astonished to think that she'd been sent back in time to speak directly with a woman who'd not just built a convent but was much more. Apparently Mother Hildegard was a *writer, composer, artist, musician, philosopher, religious mystic, church executive, diplomat, healer, preacher*, and even in terms of her own time-period a *scientist*.

Sally realized even more profoundly the startling fact that this person, set deep within the repressive Middle Ages, was a *woman*.

In a place and time when women had little or no authority on their own, were subject to the whims of cruel men, and could do nothing on their own—this woman had accomplished amazing things.

"Mother..." Sally respectfully addressed her hostess, "I again ask *how* you accomplished your impressive deeds? How is it that you've become...a Prophetess? What *strategies* did you use?"

Sally felt a tender, strong hand put upon her own heavily-bandaged ones.

"It hasn't been easy," Hildegard replied. "Although I am now an old woman—*sixty-seven* years old, in fact—I continue to face great opposition. But for what I have accomplished, it's been done from a total belief in my mission, from freely admitting that I am but a weak woman only serving as a vessel for Visions from far beyond my own abilities, by building strong personal relationships, by seeking endorsements from the Nobility, by enlisting supporters within the religious hierarchy, and by confronting my enemies when necessary with stark Truth. I've made many mistakes. I've let my emotions take me to places I shouldn't have gone. But I've never ceased to *try!*"

Sally wished she had embraced those concepts nine hundred years in the future.

"You...are indeed...a *strong* woman," Sally emphatically stated.

"No, my 'demonic' friend—I *am*, truthfully, *weak*," Hildegard sighed. "You see, I have been plagued throughout my life with severe bouts of illness—even to the brink of death. But I've always embraced my physical weakness as strength. Indeed, it is only from several crushing episodes where I almost died that my enemies were forced by peer and public pressure to accede to my demands. And it is in my darkest, most bedridden times that the brightest Visions have come to me. Without my sicknesses I would merely be an unknown nun buried in seclusion, without a voice of my own. So I truly am at my strongest when I am at my weakest—as also said the great Apostle Paul in the Bible."

Sally nodded knowingly. This was a woman of great wisdom. She had overcome terrible trials to bring her Vision to life.

"May I stay with you, learn from you?" Sally respectfully and eagerly asked.

"First tell me of your satanic etchings," Hildegard demanded. "I have seen similar patterns on the skin of captured heathens from out of Africa. Our Crusaders have also marked their bodies, but with signs of the church. Your markings, however—are vile, frightful, and heretical! How could I have one such as you, here in this holy assembly? Help me to understand, Sally Smith."

Sally felt the strength draining from her body. The momentary reprise from the incredible pain of her injures was fading away. Along with the lowering analgesic her hope of finding redemption here trapped in the past was fast evaporating. Perhaps she'd not been sent here for final edification, but to be *cast out* for her sins?

She ground her teeth together against the escalating pain, trying to stay mentally alert. She must convince Mother Hildegard she was worth saving!

"Mother, they come from a rebellious youth," Sally struggled to explain. "I lived in a society where our every move was orchestrated by the State. It was only in our own minds and out of the sight of others that we could be free. So I expressed my resentments and creativity in grotesque art safely hidden beneath my outer clothes. I never meant for them to be offensive to other people. The only visible things, sometimes, were on my arms—which had images from the natural world. Indeed, I had a beautiful image of a cute baby turtle on my wrist...that is before it was burned off in the fire of my passage from the future into the past."

"I think I understand," Hildegard said, withdrawing her hand from Sally's arm. "Even now there are people who deliberately afflict their own bodies with crippling devices for self-torture. These are worn beneath the outward robes, directly applied to their bodies, such as barbed chains. Men will even wear them around their groins. Women put them around their bellies. It is an awful practice, one that I abhor and preach against. Yet many persist in this hideous self-mutilation, thinking that they are doing homage and penance to God."

"They serve a *terrible* God," Sally muttered, feeling a growing *hate* of the Deity casually looking to eradicate mankind from the cosmos.

"They are in error," Hildegard firmly corrected Sally. "The *true* God we serve is one of Mercy and Love. There is no need for self-torture with our loving, Almighty Creator."

"And yet your own Christ was tortured by this very same God?"

Hildegard rocked forward in her chair, eagerly engaging in the debate.

"Yes, God indeed did allow Satan to have his day," Hildegard sighed. "But from the Cross came the Resurrection. This is the Story of our Calling—not one of continued torture, but of new life beyond death!"

Sally admired the woman. She was firm in her theology. And yet she did not seem dogmatic. She seemed sincerely interested in exploring beyond the constraints of established orthodoxy—exhibiting a *Divine Curiosity* quite uncharacteristic of her time and place in history.

"So, you must rest," Hildegard firmly stated, abruptly standing up to loom above Sally on her bed. "I caution you to never reveal your body-etchings to the other nuns. You will be a novice and learn our ways. You are under my protection. Under the cloak of our traditional dress only your face and hands will be revealed to others. Fortunately your face is not burned. But your poor cooked hands are hideous. When the bandages on them can be removed you must wear gloves to hide them. Nothing must draw attention to your hidden heretical markings on your back and thighs. Your outward appearance, then—which others both in and out of our order perceive of you—must always be one of humility and deference. You are to be open only with me, in private conversation. Do you agree?"

"Yes, thank you," Sally gasped—the suppressed pain of her many deep burns and cuts now flooding back upon her.

Her vision blurred and the agony of her burns made it difficult to hear Mother Hildegard's next words.

"I believe God *has* sent you to me. He spared your life where any other would have immediately died," Hildegard stated with finality. "And although I do have a few, trusted confidants—none can speak with me of matters outside their experience and upbringing. You bring to me a totally fresh perspective, whether your incredible story is true or not. I value this in you. I pray to God that He will continue to grant you strength so that you will survive your grievous wounds and burns."

"I...will repay...your faith in me," Sally coughed, finding it hard to keep her eyes open.

"I've wrapped and treated your injuries with healing herbs and ointments," Hildegard continued, turning toward the wooden door leading out of the rocky chamber. "I will keep you hidden here in this room, treating you myself, until you hopefully recover. Then and only then may you reveal yourself to the rest of my order—not as a 'time-traveler' mind you, but merely as a foreigner captured to serve on a slave ship going up the Rhine river who fortunately escaped. And of course do not lie. Just do not refute this rumor which will be my honest best 'assumption' as to your origin, spread amongst my people and the townsfolk. Understand?"

"Yes...good cover story," Sally gasped, sinking back on her pillow towards blissful unconsciousness.

"That will explain your strange accent and mannerisms," the hooded woman insisted. "But strive to stay private. Blend in so that none outside the convent even notice your presence. If any should look at you too closely, I assure you that they will not see a fellow visionary like unto me—but, as the peasant villagers assumed, merely a vile *demon!* So please take care, *Sister Smith*...for the sake of both of us, take exquisite care of how others perceive your presence. Your continued sanctuary here will reflect strongly upon me, either positively or negatively."

The door briefly opened then shut firmly behind Hildegard.

Sally was left alone in the dark room with the single smoldering, flickering candle.

It was not *the* "living light"...

But it *was* light!

Sally desperately wanted to escape the terrible pain into unconsciousness, but her hyper-active mind wouldn't let her. She couldn't stop toying with the implications of what she'd heard from Hildegard von Bingen.

She vividly recalled attending the secret meetings of the primitive *Animists* from her own world: the fascination that she felt at spiritual Essence endowing everything with an inalienable vivacity. It wasn't scientific, but it did bring a new perspective upon the struggles of living creatures.

"*'For now we see in a mirror dimly',*" Sally whispered to herself, remembering a verse she'd read out of the little pocketbook New Testament that Jean's preacher, Cliff, had given to her, "*but then face to face. Now I know in part, but then I will know fully just as I also have been fully known!'*"

She shuddered, wracked by feverish convulsions. She groaned from the pain. For now, as her body hopefully healed, she felt safe enough—but for how long? How long could she remain hidden? For how long could she, a "liberated" woman of the 21st century, survive in the superstitious, paternalistic fervor of the Middle Ages?

She was not a religious person in the classical sense, as was Hildegard. She couldn't just fall back on blind faith. At her deepest roots she was a *scientist* who needed credible data. She had to find "cause and effect" to arrive at firm convictions. But now, in addition, she was also a weak, helpless "Novice"...and lucky to be that!

Apparently, Revelations come at a steep price. In order to fully know the Truth, Sally felt a cold fear that—despite Hildegard's kind warning—she would have to bare herself to the entire world...

—which, undoubtedly, would mean her *tortured death!*

Sally, though, was willing to face what had to be. She was ready to defiantly confront her fate.

From the moment that she accepted in her past timeline that alien Snake's alternative to killing Dave, she'd embraced the notion of her own tortured death. If that was the price she must pay to insure the survival of mankind in the face of an uncaring, vengeful God, then so be it! Perhaps the best thing she could do to prevent the excessive tapping-into Dark Energy from drawing the full attention of God...was simply to disappear from future history and die in the past. In that way she'd never contribute the critical evolved artificial intelligence algorithms necessary for reliably and controllably tapping-into Dark Energy! Yes, no artificially intelligent hives would learn to guide the paths of individual deuterium ions. With her gone from future history, Dave's research would be stopped in its tracks. He and his fellow scientists would discover a new energy source too unstable and dangerous to risk working with further.

So in a way, she'd accomplished her task.

Rather than bemoan her fate, Sally knew she should feel grateful. At least she was still alive. But she was tortured by thoughts of what might have been.

After all, she'd been blessed beyond any other mortals to experience what she'd already seen. She'd been to both the far future and the distant past. She'd been to the Moon and Mars. She'd walked with dinosaurs and aliens.

Indeed, Sally—like Hildegard—was *also* a woman of "Vision".

If she was to live out her life here in the past, that was ok. Let come what may! Her future life was over, finished. But now a whole new adventure awaited her. And what was the point of life anyway, to just comfortably exist until one croaked from old age? No, Sally was convinced the true purpose of her life was to *grow* her mind, her heart, her very spirit. She suspected she had much to learn from this extraordinary woman, *Hildegard von Bingen*.

Stranded in the 12th century, Sally felt irrationally comforted as she sank into an uneasy, feverish, pain-wracked stupor.

Chapter 11

PREMATURE TERMINATION

A young man went walking

Seeking his fortune to find

Afraid that his life would be lost

If he stayed in his own place and time

Through the woods, deserts, and seashores

Across high mountains and deep valleys

He looked for a life beyond crushing problems

A palace, a treasure, a mansion, or a kingdom

Making his life possess transcendent Meaning

Certified by the press, the delights, and the vanity

And, finally, acquiring all he'd sought in all its glory

As he sat upon his golden throne ruling all below him

His long white beard flowing down over his purple robe

A silver crown with encrusted jewels on his wrinkled brow

And a diamond-tipped scepter in his shaking hand

He realized that he had lost everything of value

In his heedless pursuit of various Victories

And remembered the distant past of his youth

When all that mattered was to get away

To find a better, fuller life than all the rest

He'd missed the joys of the moment.

The Luminary Chronicles, 11:32-38

Dave saw Victor waving excitedly at him. He waved back through the cab's front window.

Sally sat silently in the back of the cab. Though she'd agreed to this trip, it wasn't as "boyfriend" and "girlfriend." She still kept her distance, even refusing to sit next to him in the cab. Dave knew to treat her respectfully and gently but was peeved at her extreme phobia to close contact.

An arm around her shoulder, or a hug, was strictly forbidden.

It was only after her mother insisted she'd be fine alone for a while that Sally reluctantly agreed to accompany Dave on this hastily arranged journey.

Sally had never been out of Oklahoma, let alone to the East Coast.

Dave knew it must seem strange to her—all these tall, green trees. Oklahoma was mostly rolling shallow hills, shrubs, and low trees.

Dave paid off the cabbie, stepped out to greet Victor with a firm handshake, and then helped Sally out of the back of the car.

As the cab turned around and vanished back along the dirt road into the woods, Dave introduced Sally to Victor.

"Professor Volodymyr, this is Sally Smith—a remarkable young lady."

"Yes—and very pretty!" Victor gallantly bowed to her.

Sally hesitantly nodded back. "I'm very glad to meet you, Professor. A friend of mine—Snake—used to take me out deer hunting in the woods. But your home is in a real forest. It's quite beautiful."

"Why thank you, young lady," Victor grinned at her. "Perhaps I'll have the opportunity to take you hunting. We're big on venison and other game here in Vermont."

"I'd like that," Sally shyly replied. "I'm a dead shot. I've spent a lot of time on the firing range. Outside of my computer work, it's my only active hobby."

"Marvelous!" Victor grinned. "Then we'll go for more difficult game—pheasants and quail."

"You're both making me hungry," Dave smiled.

Indeed, enticing odors of sizzling breakfast foods wafted out the opened front door of the log-cabin home.

"I'll go help with the food," Sally said, carrying her single bag up the steps onto the porch. "I imagine the two of you have a lot to talk about. I'll get back to my real expertise, waiting on tables in a restaurant," she smiled.

"Thanks, Sally, though your expertise is far more than that," Dave gallantly said. He went over to the wide porch swing and wearily sat down as Victor joined him.

"You look tired, my boy," Victor observed.

"I'm exhausted...been up talking with Sally most of the flight here...we've got some schematics worked up...don't know if they'll suffice in getting the Navy to add us back to the project, but the new mechanisms are intriguing."

"Schematics?"

"I think I've figured out the problem to our Device, Victor," Dave said, absently stroking his brown beard with one hand while pulling from his briefcase a pile of papers. "It has to do with the control of the colliding deuterium ions in the matrix. As you know I was using a crude array of micro-lasers, enhanced in our two Devices, but still..."

"—much too slow to optimally control individual ions, right?" Victor broke into Dave's train of thought.

"Well, yes, and..."

"The Navy thinks they've got that figured out," Victor resignedly shrugged.

"They do? How do you know this, Victor? I thought they'd cut you out of the project along with me."

"I have many contacts throughout the physics community, including within the military," Victor glumly stated. "They've kept me up-to-date on what's going on, via secured multiply encrypted Internet communications, of course."

"Well then...?"

"I'm afraid that we don't have much more time," Victor sighed, looking out absently into the rustling trees. "I haven't told Ivanna yet—and don't mean to do so. She's very happy I've finally entirely quit lab work and can be here with her in the woods. I don't want to spoil her happiness."

"Spoil her happiness? What are saying, Victor?"

"They're going to trigger the second Device today, David. They think they've got the massive release controlled with a better micro-array of nano-lasers plus updated software—much as I imagine you've got on your schematics there. It wasn't that difficult to figure out the main problem."

"Then...then we've got nothing to worry about, right?"

A small red bird suddenly swooped down and landed on the porch railing. It let out a series of "trills".

"Oh, how nice," Victor smiled. "It's a Scarlet Tanager!"

Dave admired the red-yellow feathers along the head and belly of the small bird, which sharply contrasted with its black wings.

"But about the Navy's test today that..."

"It'll probably blow up the world, including that little bird. So we best enjoy the beauty of nature, my boy, as in a few minutes or hours *all of us* will be blown to hell!"

Victor reached over to a small closed bag, opened it, and pulled out a handful of birdseed.

He tossed it out onto the ground.

The scarlet bird plus a number of his fellows descended on the scattered seeds, pecking happily.

"Their last meal," Victor sighed. "And I suppose we should go in and eat our last meal as well, then..."

"Victor!" Dave briskly admonished him, putting the schematics back into his briefcase and firmly slamming the lid shut.

The birds scattered, scared.

"What are you saying, 'blowing up the world'?" Dave firmly asked Victor. "I admit that was a spectacular explosion we set off at the atoll, but it wasn't near enough to cause world-wide damage."

"Oh, that was but a taste of..."

"Explain!"

Victor sadly looked up at the sky, his mop of white hair flopping back.

"I've done the calculations, my boy," he quietly stated. "The equations are inescapable. Despite the 'orders' from the President, I'm not isolated here in the woods. My colleagues at Yale agree with what the Navy Captain suggested from his military scientists—the only explanation for the massive energy we unleashed at the Atoll was because we *tore a rip in subspace,* allowing *Dark Energy* to flood through in a highly concentrated form! But it was just a *nanosecond* tear. If that ripping is prolonged even by a few milliseconds—then an exponentially greater amount of concentrated Dark Energy will come flooding out."

"So the Navy, thinking they've got it under control...?"

"—will likely incinerate our entire planet."

"Jesus Christ!" Dave swore. "But, Victor, Sally's got something entirely different. It's not just a better program to control the micro-array. It's a completely *new type* of software that she's developed. It needs a super-computer to handle it, like the Chinese Tianhe-4 running at 100 petaflops per second, but maybe somehow we could..."

"Too late! No time! It's finished! It's over with! The world is doomed!" Victor grandly exclaimed as he deeply inhaled the wafting aroma of cholesterol-rich breakfast. "Even if your new girlfriend has some miracle solution, my boy, the Navy boys would never listen to us. They think they've got it safely figured out all on their own. Besides which, it's quite impossible to provide the control needed even with a super-computer. It's just beyond our present technology. No, I think we should just go enjoy the good food that Ivanna and Sally have waiting for us and not tell the ladies about..."

"I have something that might help," a deep, gravelly voice came from over by the detached garage.

Startled, Victor and Dave looked over to see a dark-suited, black eyeglasses-wearing man calmly walking towards them.

It was Agent Anderson.

He pointed up at the sky.

In the distance, Dave and Victor could now hear the "chittering" of an approaching helicopter.

"If you had the proper interface, could you use Sally's novel software to control the energy flow in your cold fusion Device?" the man asked, walking up onto the porch as Sally and Ivanna rushed out of the house at the sound of the approaching helicopter. He politely held up his FBI badge for their scrutiny.

The helicopter was very near, descending rapidly, the wind from its blades already sending the branches of the nearby trees into rapid oscillation.

A "snow" of blown-off leaves rained down into the yard.

"It's possible," Sally said, having heard the FBI agent's question. "I don't know who you are, but we'd planned on proposing some sort of distal telecommunication with the hives I've up and running at the supercomputer so..."

"Too little, too slow!" the Agent grimly interrupted her. "But I've got something much better. You, I, and Victor must leave right now. Your wife, Victor, could maybe pack us a bag lunch?" he hopefully asked, sniffing at the enticing aromas coming from the opened door of the house.

Her eyes stretched wide in amazement, Ivanna turned around and dashed back into the house. She seemed as startled as the rest at this strange occurrence, but familiar enough with Victor's erratic research jaunts to know when to just go with the flow.

"Well, my boy, is this gentleman a friend of yours?" Victor mildly asked Dave. "If he has a plan to stop the scheduled Navy experiment, I think we best take it."

Dave shook his head warily, uncertainly. "I *think* he's on our side. Agent Anderson, meet Professor Volodymyr. Professor, Arthur Anderson."

The twin-bladed black helicopter descended right in front of the porch, its blades still spinning rapidly.

The wind-blast and ROAR of the blades was blinding and deafening.

"We'd better go!" the Agent said, grabbing Sally's hand and helping her lean forward against the blasting downdraft of the blades.

Victor grabbed the big sack of breakfast goodies Ivanna was handing him, pecked her on her cheek, and dashed after the Agent and Sally, Dave right behind him.

Safely sequestered inside, Dave felt the helicopter leap up off the ground and swoop into the sky.

"*Where* are we going?" Dave yelled at Anderson over the loud noise of the chopper blades.

The FBI agent was happily handing out egg and bacon croissants to the people stuffed into the small space.

"Aberdeen, Maryland!" the Agent yelled back as he stuffed a still-steaming croissant into his mouth.

"What is that?" Sally said, not as loudly as the men but still forcefully. A look of cold determination gleamed in her bright green eyes.

"It's the Army's oldest active test site for new weapons and munitions, my dear!" Victor yelled back into her ear. "It's right on the coast with easy access to the North Atlantic submarine fleet. It's where the military took Dr. King's second, duplicate Device. I assume you know about it?"

"Dave explained it to me! Are we going to try to snatch it?"

"If we can get there in time!" Victor grinned. "Isn't this a grand Adventure?" he enthused, clapping his thin hands together gleefully.

The roar of the blades was quieting as they ramped up to full throttle. They could now speak in normal voices, without having to yell to be heard.

"We can't grab it," Agent Anderson curtly stated around a mouthful of hot croissant. "But maybe you can 'hotwire' it?"

He handed her a slim laptop computer.

"That's my laptop!" Dave gasped. "How did you...?"

"For relative small items, my people are adept at 'relocation'!" Anderson grinned.

Sally grabbed it eagerly, rapidly setting up Internet connections to her hidden hives.

"But they'll never let us get close enough for my laptop to interface with the Device, even if you are FBI," Dave protested, the roar of the blades now growing softer as they got up to cruising level. "They'll just shoot us down before we're in range, won't they?"

Anderson snorted: "If they can see us. But they won't. We've got the latest stealth technology on this baby. Your duplicate Device is sitting by itself near Delph Creek, right on Chesapeake Bay. It's being set up and controlled distally, just as you did at the Atoll. We've got a clear shot to land right on top of it before they even know we're there."

"How long until we arrive?" Victor excitedly asked, now stuffing a loaded croissant sandwich into his mouth.

Dave was amused at his change of attitude. Before he'd been like a mourner watching a funeral march. Now he was a celebrant at a New Orleans funeral parade. Perhaps they were all still going to die, but at least they'd go out with style.

"This baby's small but fast," the Agent grinned. "We clock along at better than 400 mph. We'll be there in less than an hour."

"I can download one of my smartest intelligent programs," Sally said, her wide green eyes focused on her screen as she typed away at blazing speed. "But the operating platform at your cold fusion equipment can't be a standard computer. That'd be like putting a jet engine onto a skateboard."

"You are quite correct, Ms. Smith. Dave's laptop is indeed inadequate. But rest assure you'll have what you need," Anderson grimly replied, licking his lips of the remains of the hot breakfast sandwich. "Don't you worry about the interface. You just get that smart program ready to put in place."

"How did you know we needed you?" Dave asked, suspicious.

The Agent patted Dave's briefcase, reaching into it to pull out a slim, black cellphone.

Dave had forgotten about the cellphone. It was with him all along. Even when he'd met Sally at the funeral home, he had his briefcase with him. The FBI must have heard everything!

"Not to worry, Dr. King," Anderson assured him, slipping the black cellphone back into Dave's briefcase. "Like I told you before, we've got your best interests at heart. We want your work with the Professor to succeed. The Navy's just going to screw it up, or destroy the world, one of the two."

"Probably the later!" Victor barked, sitting beside Dave on a jump seat. "Can't we go any faster?"

"I have my people monitoring the situation on the ground," Anderson stated. "The military is still testing out the control systems. We should get there shortly before they're ready to initiate the reaction."

"What do you mean by 'shortly'?" Dave asked, worried.

"At least fifteen minutes."

"Isn't that cutting it short?" Sally asked, still typing frantically at Dave's laptop. "Why didn't you just sneak in and steal the equipment? Why do you need us?"

"We don't want to stop the test," Anderson's deep voice responded. "We want it to succeed! But it has to be done in a way that the world will recognize and the military can't bury. I assure you if there were any other way to do this, we'd have done it. But it hinges on the three of you doing what needs to be done—with my help, of course."

"And what if we *don't* succeed?" Sally asked, her large green eyes still focused on the computer screen as her fingers flashed across the keyboard. "Do we get a second shot at it?"

"Sadly, no," Anderson said.

"Why not?" Sally insisted.

"Because the world will become another asteroid belt encircling the sun."

"*What?*" Sally gasped.

"We'll all be blown straight to hell," Arthur explained further.

"That's what *I* said!" Victor laughed, seemingly unconcerned.

Dave saw there were definite advantages of living to an elderly age...perspective!

Sally's wounds and superficial burns had healed up nicely.

After all, she was immune-balanced from birth. She still took a booster pill each year, but didn't really need it. If she never got another booster she'd still have a more-capable immune system than any other person on Earth back in the 12th century!

But the top of her head, lower arms, and hands were another matter entirely.

They'd received fourth degree burns. The skin was totally gone, with tissue destruction extending into the muscle and bones. She was lucky she could still move her fingers. But her head, wrists, and hands were now masses of white, cracked scar tissue.

Sally doubted that she'd get regenerative therapy or plastic surgery in the 12th century.

She was hideous—no hair on her head...red claws for hands—truly a "demon" worthy of the name!

But in a nun's habit, wearing white gloves, with only her mostly unscarred face visible to other people, she looked relatively normal.

Sally was grateful that after her terrible trip through the inferno she could still blend in with others. But she resented having to wear the heavy, cloaking garb.

But she never removed her cloaking habit and gloves in the presence of others. All they ever saw was her face.

And it was all because of some ancient writings in the Bible. Religious women, especially nuns, were required to dress "modestly" with "no jewelry" and "their heads covered." What a load of crap! It was all to suppress women and keep them in "their place": meekly obeying men whenever the beasts wanted to have their way with you.

It irritated Sally to no end.

Sally addressed this concern to Hildegard in one of her frequent private audiences with the Magistra...

"Why must we hide ourselves in these ugly shrouds, Mother?" Sally asked, busily engaged in carefully copying one of Hildegard's books, *Liber Vitae Meritorum*, the "Book of the Rewards of Life." Not only was Sally's copying of the manuscript important—since the printing press wouldn't be invented for 300 years—it was exacting and even artistic. Despite her sluggish hands and concealing gloves, Sally was still proficient at copying the lettering and could even reproduce the illustrations. None of the other nuns were good at this job, so it became Sally's niche and main contribution to the work of the convent.

Sally had now been in the 12th century for three years. Through a careful study of Hildegard's books and letters she was gaining real insight into the Magistra's managerial techniques and broader strategies.

For instance, Hildegard was presently engaged in a mediation campaign between the church and the government. She'd just written a letter to the Emperor warning of God's disapproval of the appointment of the "Anti-pope" Callistus III. The antipope was basically a bargaining chip in the present political alliances of Europe, supported versus the true Pope only by a handful of break-away cardinals. As unsavory as it was, political intrigue was part of Church governance— and an aspect of Hildegard's leadership and survival as a Church representative.

"*Tradition*, Sister Sally, plain old Tradition," Hildegard sighed, taking off her headpiece to shake out her long, greying hair. "You are not to tell anyone I said this, mind you. It is heresy to question the dress codes of the Church. Supposedly our Savior Himself set the standards for female attire. Hah! It is merely the fearful dictates of small-minded men intent on making themselves big by legislating the details of others' lives. How is it in your time, nine hundred years in the future?"

Sally shrugged, not taking her eyes off her paper where she was expertly inking each individual letter.

"In my time, many women have control of their own lives, dressing however they and the customs of their society dictate," she said. "But there still persist religious groups that insist women must be subjugated to men, limited in their aspirations, and kept covered from head to toe."

"Does your own religious order require such in your future life?"

Sally snorted. "Formal religion in my Dimension was forbidden for Citizens of the State. But I managed to go to secret meetings of a religion called 'Animists.' I didn't buy everything they were selling, but I did find it interesting. The Animists see things very different from your Catholic Church. For them, spiritual life takes precedence over formal rules. But in your Dimension in the future, even a lot of the minor Christian groups still oppress women, insisting that God wants them to stay second-class spiritual citizens. I find that belief repugnant. People are people, no matter which sexual organs they possessed at birth."

Hildegard sighed, leaning back in the chair in which she was seated, listening to the sounds of workers out in the garden.

"I enjoy your honesty and perspective, Sister Sally," the Magistra smiled. "I get this candor from none else. I am thinking of going on another preaching tour, my fourth and perhaps last. Would you perhaps like to accompany me along with my regular aids? I know you hate Volmar, but I promise to keep the two of you apart."

Sally carefully put her inking pen to the side, looking at Hildegard directly. She'd had little or no opportunity yet to venture beyond the cloistered walls of the convent. This would be a great opportunity to learn more of her new world, the medieval 12th Century. Plus it would be a great chance to see Hildegard in action out among the people. Sally felt very grateful to the Magistra trusting her to be out in the open rather than locked up in the 'prison' of the convent.

"I would be honored, Mother," Sally sincerely answered. "As to Volmar...your faithful male secretary does a good job at transcribing your Visions. I do not hate him. I merely think he is a poor advocate for you. Next to you, he is a poorly talented, 'servant' of a male. I hate it that you must have some ordinary male running interference for your *genius!*"

Hildegard grinned, briefly sticking her tongue out at Sally.

"Don't let him hear you say such," the Magistra admonished Sally. "He is loyal and steady. He is a good friend to me. He has stood by me from the beginning, believing in my gift from God. And, yes, I admit that he is weak and subservient. But I *like* my men that way."

"For a lifelong virgin, you hold great power over men."

"Oh, sexual attraction is a weak power, Sister Sally. After all, I am now seventy years old. Few are privileged to survive to such an old age. If I had to rely on my sexual appeal I would be exiled to the trash heap. Hah! But yes, men *are* afraid of me—for good reason. I understand how political and social power is exercised. Should you ever be burdened with religious governance, Sally, remember what I say: rule from love, not from fear. But do not discount fear! It is better to bring your enemies to you with love. But if love doesn't work, always have a sharp knife ready in your back pocket."

"I envy your astute political talents," Sally humbly mock-bowed to Hildegard.

Then the Magistra stiffened, turning a cold eye upon Sally.

"*Envy is ugly and misshapen!*" she sternly lectured Sally, reciting one of her standard mantras. "*Its bear's paws tear up everything! Its wooden feet walk dead paths! It brings only evil to man!* Love, however, is the greatest power given by God. Repeat this to me, Sister Sally!"

Sally dutifully did as ordered, looking down at the floor humbly—knowing she'd overstepped her limits. The mantra about "envy" was a common one from Hildegard, a fundamental lesson she took joy in imposing upon all her charges. But Sally was learning. After three years now in the convent, she was finally starting to understand the "ropes" of how things worked. She was stumbling less and less often. And the punishments for her missteps were lessening.

"Your penance for your bad words..." Hildegard paused, considering, and then grinning slyly, "Is to sing me a new song!"

Sally snorted, now also grinning widely.

"What, *another* new one?"

"Nobody else dares sing anything different from the ancient, accepted words that we've sung together thousands of times before to the point of utter boredom. You have this uncanny ability to put words together in ways I've never heard before. At times when you sing I almost believe you really are from nine hundred years in the future, instead of some mad escapee from a passing slave ship."

Sally frowned, considering what to sing.

Ah, just the thing—a song she'd heard Dave listening to on the radio while driving in his car. Good thing that she had a near-perfect memory...

"*When I find myself in times of trouble,*" Sally began, sweetly singing the melody she'd heard over the radio, "*Mother Mary comes to me—speaking words of wisdom: 'Let it be'!*"

"That's quite beautiful," Hildegard smiled, the wrinkles in her face smoothing out as she relaxed to the soothing new music. "Please sing more."

"*And in my hour of darkness she is standing right in front of me,*" Sally continued softly singing, "*Speaking words of wisdom, 'let it be'!*"

"Is this your own original tune or from someone in your homeland?"

"It is from a singing group that was very popular across your future Dimension."

"They must have been very religious, beloved by God!"

"Oh, I'm sure they were."

"And what is the name of this Choir?"

"Uhm..." Sally pondered, recalling the name but not daring to share it. "I think...the Silver...*Lights!*"

"Of, what a beautiful name for a singing group!"

"Yes, much better than the 'Beatles'..."

"What's that about insects?"

"Just another of God's lovely but lowly creations," Sally said, struggling not to laugh.

"And what is the chorus of this song?"

"It is very simple," Sally said, "'*Let it be*' is sung four times, then '*whisper words of wisdom*' and a final '*let it be*'."

"Oh, let us together sing this Praise to the blessed Mother Mary, Sister Sally!"

So together, in the year of our Lord 1168, Sally joined Hildegard von Bingen in sweetly singing: "*Let it be, let it be, let it be, let it be— whisper words of wisdom, let it be!*"

Let it be...

Sally was amazed to discover that every ending truly is a new beginning.

She felt a well of hope leap up within her. She was going to accompany Mother Hildegard on a preaching tour in a world where it was unheard of for a woman to preach.

What an amazing thing is *Vision*.

It truly can make the impossible possible...as if Sally were finally being reborn into her new world.

She was learning a lot in her 12th Century exile. Too bad she'd never be able to put it to any use.

Chapter 12

<u>REBIRTH</u>

You must be born again
This the spiritual refrain of the Church
Leaving behind the ugly sins of the Old Man
Embracing again the Innocence of the Baby
Fresh to the world with curious Perspective
The world literally begun, yet again, anew
And we have a chance to start all over
With our prior wise memories intact
Do we cherish this wonderful chance
To totter with developing muscles
Into a brand new, daring Dance
Or just shrug and casually repeat
The mistakes of yesterday...
Are we really so stupid?

The Luminary Chronicles, 12:103-107

"How's the download going?" Agent Anderson asked Sally, as the helicopter swept along—now descended to treetop height—at nearly 400 miles per hour.

Dave tried not to look out the front or side windows.

They were much too low to be traveling at such a speed! One downdraft and they'd be splattered over several city blocks.

Sally punched a key in triumph.

"I've got it!" she exclaimed. "It's not the entire program that's on the supercomputer, of course. But it's enough to repopulate and re-generate itself back into the entire intelligent framework when put into a suitable environment."

"Won't that take a long time, my dear?" Victor absently observed, sitting excitedly in his jump seat intently peering out of the closest window. "Agent Anderson said we'd only have at most fifteen minutes to take control of the duplicate Device. Even if we can get your intelligent program to function in the small computer of the control module, how will it become fully operational in such a short period?"

"This isn't an ordinary computer program," Sally resentfully replied, obviously not happy for her "baby" to be criticized. "It lives on a different timescale than do we. For it, one of our seconds is a year! So in just a few seconds it can easily comprehend and implement our instructions."

"How long will it be until we get there?" Dave asked, getting more and more nervous now that they were fast approaching Aberdeen.

"We're going into full stealth mode now," Anderson answered. He seemed strangely serene. "We're maybe five minutes out from..."

"But they can still detect us visually?" Victor stated, now also looking worried.

"Yes, but no one is looking for us," the Agent calmly replied, reaching up to adjust the dark glasses that covered his eyes. "We'll drop right onto the Device without anyone knowing we're there, at least for a few seconds. My contacts say that the government scientists are monitoring the Device entirely by distal communication. They evacuated the area all around it. There should be no personnel on site."

"Why not just take control with my own interface that's on my laptop?" Dave said. "Once we're near enough we can..."

"They've changed the control interface," Anderson replied, a peculiar smile on his lips. "We'll have to interface physically into the control structure at the source. Otherwise this whole expedition will be futile. And we've got to do it before they realize we're there and send troops to kill us. To them we'll look exactly like renegade terrorists."

Dave was ready to do what needed to be done. If the military succeeded in activating the reaction chamber sequences, the rip in subspace could last long enough to destroy the entire planet.

It would be one hell of an explosion!

Too bad neither he nor anyone else would be around to see it.

"You still haven't told me what I'm going to be transferring my program into," Sally angrily confronted Agent Anderson. "Don't you think it's about time to let me in on the secret?"

He laughed.

"You'll know it when you see it."

"We're over Aberdeen," a call came back from the front of the craft where another of Anderson's dark eyeglasses-sporting colleagues was piloting the craft.

"Get ready to disembark," Anderson warned them.

They hit the ground hard, skidding, almost flipping over before coming to a stop tilted at an angle, the slowing rotor blades still spinning just inches off the ground.

Spilling out of the door, Dave and the others confronted a clearing in the midst of a surrounding forest. A large, square cement slab sat in the middle of the clearing.

"There it is!" Victor happily shouted, pointing to it.

The elevated slab sat beside a wide stream that ran directly into the ocean. Upon the wide slab, bolted firmly into the concrete, was Dave and Victor's bathtub-sized Device.

Seagulls were circling overhead.

"You've got only ten minutes, at the most," Anderson warned them, pulling out a black pistol.

Dave, Sally, Victor, and he ran over to the slab as Anderson's colleague hung back, scanning the horizon for approaching military 'copters.

"They enclosed it!" Victor gasped, running his hands along the square metal encasement. "I don't see any way to get in. We're going to have to snatch the entire thing, my boy, and get the hell out of here!"

"But we can't," Dave groaned. He tried to rock the rectangular Device free, but thick bolts into the cement slab held it solidly. "We've got to find a way to get inside. It's our only chance!"

They could hear a siren starting to wail off in the distance.

"We don't have much time," Sally said, frantically searching with Victor for a panel or access port. "How will we...?"

"Stand back!" Anderson warned them, aiming his black pistol at the casing.

"You'll damage the delicate equipment inside!" Dave protested, starting to push away Anderson's gun, as the Agent *whipped* it around to *knock* Dave backward!

Holding his bleeding forehead in disbelief, Dave found himself sitting in the dirt looking up at Anderson who was twisting the muzzle of the gun *counterclockwise*.

"It narrows the beam," Anderson said. "Remember it!"

Turning, he fired what appeared to be a continuous thin, red, powerful laser beam at the top of the metal casing.

Sputtering and sizzling, the metal evaporated as the top of the casing twisted and pulled to the side.

"Careful, it's hot," Anderson warned Sally as she eagerly reached inside.

"Nice gun you have there," Victor nodded in appreciation to Anderson.

FWIP! FWIP! FWIP!—came the unmistakable sound of bullets slamming into the dirt around them...

"Auuggghhh..." Dave heard Anderson groan.

Anderson, shot in his head, tottered to the side before dropping beside Dave.

Shards of bone from his shattered skull poked up out of a clearly fatal head wound.

Dave gaped at the man, not knowing what to say.

"Here...you're going to...want this," Anderson managed to croak out—blood streaming from the deep wound in the side of his head—as Anderson with a "click" took off his dark eyeglasses and handed them in a shaking hand to Dave.

"What?" Dave said, still stunned from the blow to his own head as he accepted the thick black eyeglasses, slipping them into his shirt pocket as...

Dave saw that Anderson's eyes were *dark, empty pits* around which red blood was dripping: with faint but distinct diamond patterns glittering!

BLAM! BLAM! BLAM!—Dave heard Anderson's colleague firing his own gun, causing massive waves of kinetic energy to SLAM into a rapidly approaching military chopper, *crushing it flat* in midair!

The remnants of the attack 'copter dropped like a stone, crashing into the surrounding forest.

A loud EXPLOSION shook the forest from the site of the wreck.

"Hurry it up!" Anderson's colleague shouted, crouching. "There are many more troops nearly upon us, approaching from the ground!"

Anderson jerked upright, walking hands-out to the slab, blindly feeling for the now-smoking metal casing of the Device.

"I don't see how we can...?" Sally gasped, fumbling at the central control processer that Victor was showing her, trying to find a port to link a cable to from Dave's laptop.

"I've got...what you need...right here," Anderson said as he reached with trembling hands *into* the bloody wound in the side of his own head and *ripped out* what appeared to be a white sponge!

"Unnnggghhhh..." he groaned as he limply dropped it onto the central control processer inside the machine.

He slumped to the concrete slab and rolled off to the side, dead!

—as yet more bullets began *"fwipping"* into the ground and concrete slab.

Victor and Sally watched in astonishment as the wet-looking "sponge" *wriggled* into the central control processor with *white tendrils* leaping out and burying themselves into the rest of the equipment!

"What the hell is that?" Victor gasped.

—as one large tendril emerged, reached up, and blindly tried to connect with the dangling cable from Dave's laptop...

Sally grabbed the moist tendril and stuffed it into the connector at the end of the cable.

"It's something new—maybe a portable biological neural network!" Sally gasped, her big green eyes stretched wide in amazement. "I've imagined such, but never thought it achievable. It's way beyond our current technology!"

Bullets *banged* into the metal casing, causing Sally and Victor to duck back behind it as uniformed military troops emerged from the surrounding woods.

Dave dived over to Anderson's body, snatching up the Agent's gun and pointed it at the attacking troops.

Both he and Anderson's colleague fired a withering stream *of blasting explosions* and *slicing red laser beams*, driving the troops back behind the closest tree trunks before they could return fire!

But snipers had already taken up positions, firing bullets that hit very close to Dave.

Dave's colleague over at the side of the clearing, beside their own crashed helicopter was cut down, crumpling onto the ground.

Only seconds had passed in driving back the troops, but now the Device was emitting a *strange blue light!*

It expanded into a *shimmering sphere* encompassing Dave, Sally, and Victor...

—as Dave saw Andersons dying colleague off at a short distance twist the barrel of his gun completely shut and *toss* it like a grenade towards the again-emerging troops!

"Christ, he's going to kill us all!" Dave gasped, slumping next to Sally and Victor as they both clung to the opened top of the Device. Dave grabbed Sally by her leg to give her additional support...

—as a GIGANTIC YELLOW EXPLOSION expanded from the tossed gun, incinerating everything in its path...

—arriving at the concrete slab just *nanoseconds after the Device vanished!*

Caught up in the Blue Sphere that was now hurtling through a black void, Dave idly wondered how the military would explain the goings-on at Aberdeen... Another terrorist attack? A routine munitions test gone wrong? Or just the "successful" triggering of a new super-weapon?

Regardless, the results could not be what Anderson planned. Anderson was dead. And now he, Victor, and Sally were thrown into limbo, headed to where?

Perhaps they'd actually died in the blast and were now plunging straight to hell.

Dave laughed, amused that his religious *non*-convictions might now be proved false by his own scientific observations.

"What's happening?" Sally gasped above Dave. Dave still had a firm grip on her slender ankle. He realized that the surrounding blue light had sliced through the concrete slab, the inner part of which was traveling along with them safely encased within the blue bubble.

Victor just hung on for dear life, his eyes tightly closed.

—when they WHUMPED down onto something solid, throwing the three of them off to the side like rag dolls, knocking them unconscious.

How long he was knocked out, he didn't know, until...

"What in the world?" Dave heard a quavering female voice gasping in disbelief.

Through a red haze, Dave looked up to see *Ivanna* looming above him with a deer-hunting rifle held loosely in her hands.

Dave absently noted that she was a strikingly good-lucking older woman. Her long grey hair was dyed a bright blond, with just a tinge of grey stylishly left in a lock on her forehead. The skin of her face was smooth and white. She wore a single-piece blue jumpsuit. She was trim and fit. She could have easily passed for a woman in her fifties though she was well into her eighties.

"We've had quite a little adventure," Victor grinned painfully at Dave's side. He levered himself up from where he'd been tossed, tottering over to Ivanna to give her a quick hug.

He carefully took the still-pointed hunting rifle from her rigid hands.

"Where's Sally?" Dave croaked, elbowing himself upward to look around worriedly.

He saw the Device still bolted-into the sliced-out half-globe of concrete, lying tilted upon the ground. The Blue Sphere was still present, but dwindling rapidly. Around them tall green trees spiked up into a deep blue sky. Disturbed birds were flapping angrily amongst the branches.

But Sally was gone.

Sally had now lived for nine years in the 12th Century. It was the year of our Lord 1174.

She was now a full-fledged nun, having finally graduated from her long training period being a mere novice. During that apprentice period she had learned and seen many things. The life of a nun in a convent was not nearly as simple or easy as she might have imagined.

For one thing, Sally had to understand and agree to three sacred vows: the vow of *poverty*, the vow of *chastity*, and the vow of *obedience*. Those were difficult.

Actually, the vow of chastity wasn't so hard for Sally—since Citizens in Sally's English Empire were effectively neutered by their genetic balancing at birth, until counteracted when the State sanctioned an official conception. Private sex was allowed, but wasn't the same priority as it was for the non-neutered lower castes. Plus Sally was so busy doing her assigned service jobs while studying late into the night acquiring higher and higher academic degrees—while attempting her own independent mathematical/computational research—that she had no time and felt no need for ordinary romantic relationships.

The other two vows, though, were very hard for Sally. Poverty in the middle ages meant being *dirt poor!* Even though the nuns under Hildegard's supervision came from the Nobility, theirs was an impoverished existence: sleeping on hard beds, doing all their chores themselves, and eating simple, plain food.

The most difficult vow for Sally, however, was the vow of obedience. Sally had to fight her own constant urge to be independent. Not only would being outspoken raise her already-suspicious profile, it would get her thrown out of the convent. Everyone was expected to obey the Magistra and higher Priests without question. Fortunately, Hildegard often allowed the nuns to express their opinions before she'd make her final decision. But once that decision was made, everyone was expected to fall in line.

Sally had never had any desire to be part of a military organization. But here she discovered that effective Religion is very much like a military organization. Those above you make the decisions, supposedly God-sanctioned. You then obeyed what was passed down to you. If you didn't like it, you were "court-martialed" and then "dishonorably discharged". And as strict and regimented as it was in the convent, Sally knew that outside the gates she'd be torn apart by the "barbarians"—i.e. ignorant peasants.

So she knew to stay in her place.

But working in the garden was peaceful and fun. Going on searches in the woods for natural herbs was fun. However, she and the others didn't venture far into the deep forests around the monastery. It was rumored that *Demons* prowled the dark depths of the forest, waiting to pounce upon anyone who ventured too far! Sally wasn't scared, but had no wish for any so-called "demons" to be further associated with her. She hoped her origin-story was slowly dying out as the years extended onward.

Sally wasn't any good at spinning, weaving, or embroidery—other common jobs in the convent—but studiously continued her job of copying and "illuminating" manuscripts. That was enjoyable but also incredibly boring. It wasn't creative. It was just glorified copying.

Also, Sally chaffed against the regimented schedule of services, readings, chants, and songs. But she learned to do it automatically as a ritualistic habit. She found that during those outwardly obedient times her mind was free to soar to new heights, considering and analyzing the ever-fascinating figure of Hildegard von Bingen, to whom Sally had unprecedented access.

As Hildegard had promised her, Sally got to accompany the Magistra and her companions on a fourth preaching tour. Sally was continually amazed at Hildegard's earnest, compelling lecture style coupled with deep affinity for those in her audience. At dramatic moments, the famous *"Hildegard von Bingen" STARE* entranced her audiences. And versus the boring, plodding sermons of the Priests—who frequently came to Hildegard's convents with the apparent goal of convincing the nuns to believe long-established doctrines which they'd long-ago accepted—Hildegard was always interesting to hear.

She always came well-prepared for her particular audience with fresh observations, compelling stories, and boundless enthusiasm. She always wanted to leave them with something of value that they'd not heard before. This was something Sally had contributed to Hildegard's lecturing style. Sally told her of future-society managerial techniques, such as being "value-added" and "relevant" in presentations. Hildegard eagerly accepted these fresh insights, drinking them in like a sponge, adding them to her existing exuberant but authoritarian style.

Also—versus the academics who Hildegard loved to invite to lecture at the convent—the Magistra never overwhelmed her audience with details, jargon, or arrogant superiority. Instead of standing at a podium, Hildegard often walked among her audience, conversing, answering questions, and inviting discussion. For instance, instead of just lecturing on the abstract topic of "humility", Hildegard *exhibited* humility—respecting the intelligence of even her most ignorant, uneducated, or hostile audience members. In this way she disarmed her enemies and doubters, preparing them to accept different, even new ideas.

Sally noted, however, that Hildegard—coming from a privileged family set-into a Nobleman "high-caste" environment—worried less about educating the peasants and more about impressing the rulers of her society.

When pressed on this point in their private conversations, Hildegard nonchalantly defended her strategy: "Mixing of the social castes will only breed conflict," she claimed. "That is why I only accept Novices from the Nobility, not from the lower castes. We are here to be an oasis of female religious development, not school teachers of the deprived."

Sally knew from her discussion with visitors to the convent that this was not true of other nunneries, many of whom saw a big part of their mission as caring for and uplifting the lower classes.

"I'm not from a Noble family and yet you accepted me," Sally accurately stated. "When I first appeared on your shores, people even thought I was a demon!"

"Oh, but you're a *nice* demon," Hildegard laughed. "And in the world you claim to be from, were you a peasant there?"

Sally thought about that for a moment.

"No...I wasn't," she admitted. "But I certainly wasn't an Elite. I was just a regular Citizen, part of what we called the 'middle class' that was positioned between the rich and the poor..."

"—who lived a comfortable life, had many rights and privileges, and from an early age enjoyed a rich education?" the Magistra triumphantly concluded.

"Well...yes...I suppose," Sally frowned, realizing that she was, perhaps, as much an "elitist" as her much-despised Elites back in her own world.

"Oh, you who think to pull the splinter from the other's eye..." Hildegard smiled, pointing a crooked, liver-spotted finger at one of her own red-veined eyeballs.

"*—first pull the plank from your own eye,*" Sally nodded thoughtfully, finishing the quote from Jesus out of the Bible.

And, yes, Sally carefully considered this deep self-revelation...as time continued marching forward in the 12th Century. Who was she, after all, to think that she could just "form" a whole new religion back in the 21st Century? What monumental arrogance! Not only was she assuming she had "the" Truth—but she'd be disrespecting the centuries-old established Religions as being of lesser-validity or even outright wrong.

Yet, despite the Biblical admonition to humility, Hildegard went on with her preaching tours.

And what was that effort by the Magistra but the very same Arrogance which Sally now recognized in her own self, just packaged differently?

But Hildegard never tried to set up a "new" religion. She, in fact, cultivated the approval of her existing hierarchy, including the Pope. Yet she arrogantly flouted the Traditions and Doctrines of the Church—herself failing to "keep silent" as the scriptures taught that Christian women were supposed to do. But she achieved her unorthodox goals by carefully discovering new, acceptable ways to repackage old thought and reapply dated customs.

Still, though, Hildegard had many enemies.

And those many doubters were starting to focus their ire upon *"Sister Sally"*...

The old stories of Sally's bizarre appearance on the banks of the Rhine River were resurfacing, embellished by gossiping, to make her into the Devil Himself—complete with red leathery skin, horns, and a reptilian forked tail. Instead of just being grotesquely tattooed, she was whispered to host a variety of evil spirits cavorting-about within her body.

Yes, Sally was rumored to be physical proof that this upstart nun, Hildegard, was in league with the Devil. Sally heard these rumors and whispers but kept quiet, not responding in any way. To do so would only amplify the undercurrents.

Those who wanted to discount Hildegard's "visions" now felt they were near to acquiring undeniable evidence proving that Hildegard's radical teachings were not from God, but from Satan.

Sally knew that Hildegard, of course, was aware of this conspiracy—plus the value that her enemies placed on "unmasking" Sally. But the Magistra never allowed outsiders near enough to Sally to have any chance of seeing the horrific tattoos hidden beneath Sally's concealing nun's garb, her "habit." Even Sally's still-scarred hands were kept safely hidden under her ubiquitous white gloves. The flowing robe plus hood—so sanctified by their order, plus the prized isolation of the convent—was a great disguise to keep Hildegard's valued confidant safe.

But now Hildegard's protecting male companion, Volmar the Priest, had just passed away.

Learning the lesson of humility, Sally had found ways to engage the gentle male priest. She was always ready at his side with a cooling glass of water or a helpful hand. Gradually, she'd gained his friendship, even growing to appreciate his quiet virtues.

But now he was dead.

It was a time of great uncertainty.

Hildegard stubbornly promoted her last great masterpiece: *Liber Divinorum Operum*, the "Book of Divine Works." But her heart didn't seem to be in her creative efforts anymore. She was aging rapidly, bedridden even more than usual. Now she was seventy-six years old, ancient for the middle ages. She was clearly winding down.

Sally resolutely encouraged Hildegard to persist. After all, Sally insisted, God gave the Magistra a Gift that was still vibrantly functioning! Hildegard still had Visions. Sally urged her to find an acceptable new male secretary from the Catholic hierarchy who'd assume both the secretarial duties and the critical role of male protector.

Reluctantly, Hildegard agreed.

A new Priest, Father Gottfried, arrived. He didn't have Volmar's unquestioning loyalty, but he did bring a fresh perspective, even toward Sally. He did not see "Sister Sally" as an upstart new addition—as had Volmar—but merely part of the old, accepted crew at the cloistered convent. Sally found she could be more relaxed around him than she had been with Volmar—as long as she kept strictly to her role of a quiet, obedient nun.

But it continually chaffed Sally to be demure, quiet, and submissive. That wasn't her nature. Yet she knew it was absolutely necessary. After all, she still had no desire to be burned alive as a heretic! If her secret got out, the stake was a likely outcome. The Church did not suffer troublemakers lightly. Burning heretics tied to a large stake in the middle of the town square was a widely-accepted punishment. Plus it always drew a large crowd of partying onlookers!

There weren't that many public spectacles in the middle ages. Burning heretics to death in the village square was considered great entertainment.

Sally was determined to avoid that fate at all cost.

So she studied Hildegard even more closely.

She tried to mimic the Magistra's stoic, stern expression—to understand her deep motivations, strategies, and thinking.

But it was obvious to everyone that the Magistra was in failing health and wouldn't be around much longer.

What would happen to Sally when her protector died?

She redoubled her efforts to *remake herself* into the Magistra's venerated image.

It was Sally's only hope for continued survival.

Chapter 13

ROCK MY WORLD

Cry, cry, cry...

And don't wipe your eyes

All of you trying to escape

That looming Fire in the sky

Not wasting the liquid

So precious and pure

Cooling your cheeks

For the very last time

Soothing your pain

As you prepare to die...

Cry, cry, and cry!

The Luminary Chronicles, 13:84-86

Sally awoke in a cool, white, space.

She opened her eyes and tried to think where she was.

But nothing came to mind.

She couldn't remember anything!

Who am I? Where did I come from? What am I doing here? Where is this 'here', anyway?

"Ah, you are awakening, that's good," a pleasant voice sounded above her. Squinting, Sally saw a face leaning above her with yellowish-brown skin, slanted eyes, and long straight black hair.

Vaguely, Sally realized that the person looking down at her was an "oriental" woman—whatever that was!

"Where am I?" Sally groaned, her whole body hurting, feeling like she'd been beat up.

She was now starting vaguely to remember a crash, being thrown from her perch on a mechanical Device, and banging her head on a tree before being snatched away by....

—what?

"Oh, it's more like 'when' are you," the woman smiled, reaching down with a firm arm to help Sally sit up on the edge of the flat surface she'd been lying on.

"Don't be afraid," the woman said, handing Sally a clear glass of water with a small red pill. "This will help with the bruises and your memory loss. I am your friend. My name is Sanako. I am here to help you."

Sally gratefully swallowed the pill, noticing that they were inside a vehicle. She could feel a faint swaying motion. Other oriental-looking women were seated at a control module, facing forward. Behind Sally she could hear other people quietly talking and working. They wore the same identical black uniform.

In front of them was a curved, transparent window out of which she saw *an entire planet* hanging in the blackness of space!

Sanako helped Sally to wobbly stand and face the forward viewing panel.

"Is that...the Earth?" Sally gasped, now making out the continent of Africa surrounded by deep blue oceans. The continent was colored in subtle hues of brown and green, across which drifted white banks of clouds.

"Yes, Sally—you are looking out at your Earth. But this is not your present planet. We are a hundred years in your future...in high orbit."

"In...in the *future?*" Sally gasped, not understanding. "We're in *outer space?*"

"Just watch," Sanako sadly directed her.

"What?" Sally said, straining to see anything different...

Then she saw it.

The green on the vast continent was *browning* and then *blackening!*

Outer space around the Earth began *brightening...*

Instead of a deep black, it began to *glow red!*

"Oh, my God," Sally gasped. "What's happening?"

"Don't worry," Sanako quietly reassured her. "Our energy shield will protect us, for a while."

Sally just sat silently, staring out at Africa in horror.

The white fluffy clouds were abruptly stripped away.

The interior of the continent suddenly began melting—blemished by orange, churning lava lakes!

Around the wide continent the seas were *boiling*, throwing up massive sheets of steam that spread across the surface of the world!

Sally, her mouth hanging open in disbelief, noticed that the thin blue line along the edge of the planet's curved horizon was suddenly *gone!*

A sparkling yellow fog now swept across what remained of Earth's surface, replete with huge sheets of lightning.

And in just a few minutes the crackling fog dissipated...leaving behind a blackened, burnt-out husk where before had floated in the cosmos a beautiful blue pearl.

"No," Sally gasped. "No, it's impossible—it *can't* be happening!"

"It did, it has, it will," Sanako sobbed as well, her high voice trembling.

"The Earth...is destroyed?" Sally gasped again, not believing her own eyes. "How can this be?"

"It's Judgment Day," Sanako quietly stated, so soft that Sally could barely hear her words, "and we were found wanting."

"Judgment Day?" Sally dumbly repeated.

"The end of the world—the end of humanity—the extinction of *Homo sapiens* and all other land animals, the boiling death of most of the sea's animals, reducing life on Earth to a few microorganisms that..."

"What *the hell* are you talking about?" Sally cried-out, reaching forward and grabbing the oriental lady by her shoulders.

Sally shook the woman, hard!

Then she realized what she was doing and jerked her hands back, repulsed by the physical contact with the woman.

"Tell me the truth!" Sally demanded. "What sort of a trick is this?"

"It's neither a trick nor a miracle, not directly anyway."

"Then what is it?"

"It's what astronomers called a 'solar super-storm.' A huge plasma cloud many times the size of Earth impacted Earth's orbit...wave after wave! What you saw was just the first wave that..."

"So on the other side of the planet there may be survivors?"

"Maybe...some...but not for long," she sighed. "Repeated waves throw life on Earth back two or three billion years. Only primitive bacteria and single-celled organisms survive, safe at the bottom of what remains of the seas."

"*God* did this?" Sally rasped in total disbelief.

"Have you never read the Bible, Sally? It clearly states that the Day of Judgment will result in fire destroying Earth."

"But...I...I haven't gone to church...didn't think much of those superstitions that..."

"Do you remember the experiment that you are helping out with, done by Dr. King and Professor Volodymyr?" Sanako coldly urged her.

Sally frowned, wavering back and forth, her memory now flooding back.

"Well, yes...to help Earth not be cooked by global warming from fossil fuels—to get cold fusion to work in a practical way. What could be wrong with that? Surely God, if there is a God, would applaud us as a species for finding a way to preserve our planet?"

"Your experiment isn't what you think," Sanako glumly stated, still watching Earth's blackened surface as it was cooked by yet another colliding gigantic plasma cloud. "Cold fusion will never work as an energy source. But Dr. King's clever matrix plus your intelligent program resulted in making a small tear in subspace, from which Dark Energy pours! His original experiment allowed just a tiny burst of Dark Energy to occur—as a 'bomb' in his garage. And when even slightly prolonged in time, that 'bomb' equals the output of some of your atomic explosions. But with your exquisitely delicate intelligent-program control mechanism, you allowed Dark Energy to be released at a controlled rate. It became a practical energy source, soon powering everything. Indeed, this very craft is powered by Dark Energy. But in my Dimension we used it very sparingly as dictated by our various authoritative Empires. In your world, with your 'democratic' institutions decoupled from your scientific communities, its usage ran rampant."

"I...don't understand...your 'dimension'?"

"We were able to harness Dark Energy in a limited, careful manner that *doesn't* attract the attention of the Creator!"

"Attract the attention...?"

"God has very high standards for his intelligent species throughout the Cosmos," Sanako sighed. "Unfortunately, we don't measure up. As long as we were mostly hidden, we got by. But now—pushing the *'we're here'* button—you've brought upon mankind the Day of Judgment. God *erases* us from the Universe, both in your and my connected Dimensions."

"I find this very hard to believe."

"Then look back out of the window!" Sanako now screamed at Sally. "Do you want for us to land and examine the burnt remains of civilization? If that's what it takes then we will do so. You must be convinced of the reality of what you see! Our fate as a species depends on your subsequent actions."

Shocked before, Sally was doubly-shocked by Sanako's vehement shouting.

Sally weakly slumped down into an open swivel-chair, which instantly molded itself to her buttocks and back.

"I just can't believe this," Sally whispered. "It's too much. Other dimensions, time travel, the Wrath of God—this is a nightmare, or a trick!"

"Turn off the artificial gravity!" Sanako ordered, *yelling* at her crew.

In just a few seconds, Sally felt a strange sensation. It was as if she were getting *lighter!*

And then she floated up off the attached chair into the interior of the craft.

"Oh...my...God," Sally gasped, floundering, feeling a sickness in the pit of her stomach from inner ear canals being disoriented.

She gagged, almost vomiting as she hung suspended, slowly flailing-about.

"Turn it back on!" Sanako loudly ordered.

Sally felt her weight returning, her legs touching down on the floor, wavering woozily as full gravity returned.

She sat back in the chair, silently—staring out at the awful burnt-out husk of a planet hanging so terribly in space where just a few minutes before had been a bright, blue jewel.

"What do you want me to do?" She said in a weak, small voice.

"You must sabotage Dave's experiment," Sanako confidently stated. "And then you must *kill* both him and the Professor. Others might try to replicate the work, but none will succeed. It will push off the Day of Judgment by at least a thousand years. They mean well, the both of them, but they are misguided. They are blinded by their ambition and scientific curiosity. If we brought them here they'd just deny it. And if they believed it, they wouldn't care. They'd think they could figure out a way to escape God. But they can't. They're just viruses inside of bacteria in the guts of ants crawling unnoticed underfoot on a construction site! They don't have the mental capacity to even connect with the Creator, let alone dictate His actions or deceive Him. Dr. King and Professor Volodymyr don't know or don't care about the terrible Evil that they are perpetuating upon not only their own world, but other innocent worlds as well!"

Sanako sank exhausted from her impassioned speech into a swivel chair right beside Sally, covering her face with her hands.

"Then why can't *you* just stop them?" Sally belligerently replied, angered that Sanako was so casually ordering her to do such a monstrous thing. *Kill* them? She might be willing to stop their Device from working—but murder? No! She could *never* do such a horrible thing!

"If we could, we would," Sanako sadly replied, removing her hands from her face to show tears now flowing liberally from her eyes. "But we exist out of time, Sally. We come from a future that doesn't exist anymore. And when we try to intervene it becomes...complicated. Our direct intervention can even makes things *worse*. We only took this drastic action—snatching you out of your timeline into the future—because Judgment Day is fast accelerating its approach to your time. If this keeps up, then there won't be any actions left for any of us to take. We and all of humanity will be snuffed out!"

"Can't you escape beyond this point?" Sally urgently asked, grasping for an alternative. "Can't you go into the far future where the planet's ecology has recovered?"

Sanako bitterly laughed while wiping away her tears, apparently disdainful of her own weakness.

"God has put up a Barrier to our little time-traveling attempts. In all of the doomed, linked Dimensions a *Barrier* prevents us from traveling beyond Judgment Day. The destroyed Earth moves on. We can see it go into the future. But we can't follow it. The human species, Sally, is *doomed*—and only you can save it."

"*I* can't be that important," Sally protested. "I'm just a waitress at a restaurant in Ada Oklahoma who..."

Sanako snorted in disgust, standing up from her chair with her back to Sally, looking out at the charred planet.

"Right—and *I'm* just a Citizen standing in a spaceship," she sneered.

Then, more conciliatory, she turned and laid a hand on Sally's shoulder.

"Certain people have the fortune or misfortune to be in the right place at the right time with the right 'stuff' to become 'fulcrum points' in Time—upon whose shoulders the future depends or turns. Whether you like it or not, Sally, *you* are one of those few people."

Sally sat in silence. The rest of the crew of the craft was also silent, allowing her time to think.

Sally took another look out the front viewing window at the sizzling, blackened Earth.

She now knew what she had to do.

She didn't know how or why, but she knew the fate of humanity rested in her doing the most evil thing she could imagine.

She had to kill Dave and the Professor—*and herself!*

None must remain who knew the secret for accessing Dark Energy and thereby attracting God's full attention.

The next time that the Device was triggered, it wouldn't be the controlled slow release of Dark Energy that the others expected.

It would be an *un*regulated release that *in one blinding flash* would *incinerate* them all!

"Take me back," she whispered. "I'll do it."

The craft slipped into a blue haze which formed in front of them as Sally felt tears rolling down her cheeks.

It wouldn't be the end of the world, just *her* end of *her* world.

But she would know that her short, unassuming life had saved many others. Looking back, she realized she should be grateful.

She'd been blessed with a genius to see beyond the constraints of accepted science and go where none had gone before.

She couldn't let that all be erased. Mankind must endure—even if it meant her own death.

So be it.

The world would not mourn the loss of an unknown waitress from a small city in Oklahoma. But she knew she would die with honor, doing what had to be done no matter how despicable.

Still it would be nice to go back and do it all again, just differently.

Chapter 14

<u>NOSTALGIA</u>

Of all the things of my life

That I could retrieve and hold again

I think the one I'd grab would be Awe

Of discovering a fresh panorama of beauty

Spread out before me like a painting

Bursting with colors and action

Frozen in a moment of time

The emotion of motion

Distilled and pure

Drink it up…

I'll have another, please!

The Luminary Chronicles, 14:33-35

Hildegard von Bingen was dying.

Her fully-gowned, withered body lay upon a bed in the central garden of the monastery.

She'd directed her accolades to place her there where she could look up at the night sky.

Above her, *a million stars* glittered!

Although she could no longer move her body, she could still move her eyes. So she drank in the majesty of God's Universe, eager to be released into its mysterious depths…

It hadn't been a bad life. Yes, there had been great pain and severe loss. But in the end, she gained *God!*

"Come with us!" a harsh voice suddenly ordered Sally. She was kneeling beside the bed of her dying Mother along with the other weeping nuns, Hildegard's closest followers.

"But..." Sally protested, feeling rough hands pulling at her gown, dragging her away! "How dare you interrupt our..."

"—not their vigil, just *yours!*"

She was jerked along a corridor and thrown to the cold stone floor in front of Father Guibert. Vaguely, she glimpsed a number of other robed figures in the room.

Totally bewildered at what was happening, Sally lay in a fully-submissive stance, face-down, arms spread wide, with her gloved hands grasping futilely at the smooth stone floor.

"Father, what is happening?" she gasped, trying to peer upward to see his face.

The year was 1179. The day was the 17th of September. Hildegard was *eighty one* years old. Sally had now been living in the 12th Century for fourteen years.

Father Guibert was Hildegard's latest male secretary, who took over when Father Gottfried died only two years after taking over from the Hildegard's beloved Volmar. Guibert of Gembloux was a stern, intense man who not only corrected the grammar and spelling of Hildegard's Latin, but reworked it considerably—ostensibly to render Hildegard's unsophisticated style more elegant. Hildegard allowed this, though reluctantly, not wishing her Visions to be "corrected" but also wanting them to shine with their full glory. Sally silently observed, however, that Guibert not only enhanced the words, but made them his own.

He was the bane of all creative writers, a jealous editor.

Sally tried to warn Hildegard, but got little for her efforts. The Magistra's health was failing rapidly. She could barely speak. Guibert, however, was quite annoyed when rumors of Sally's defiance reached him. After all, she was a mere nun, and he was a lofty Priest. Plus, he clearly wished for Hildegard to pass the literary "baton" to him—not to be confronted by this lowly attending nun.

"You know full well why you are here," Guibert glared down at her. "With your Protector going to her eternal punishment, your satanic heresy is no longer disguised."

"I have always been faithful to..." Sally tried to protest as her outstretched arms were grasped by two guards and painfully pressed down into the stones.

"That's a lie," Guibert brusquely interrupted her, "revealed to all by what you've hidden away all these years. Guards! Take off her gloves. Show us the demon's red *claws!*"

Though she tried to ball up her fists, her white gloves were jerked off her hands. But the assembled witnesses seemed confused rather than horrified by what they saw.

Sally grinned to herself, looking at her white-skinned, normal hands splayed out there on the floor. They weren't going to entrap her that easily. Over the last few years the cracked scar tissue on her hands had gradually retreated then vanished. The dwindling Optimmune presence in her system was contributing its last dregs to her health!

"You see?" she angrily called upward to the looming Guibert. "I'm not hiding anything! My hands are still tender after the accident years ago that crushed them when I came here and was granted sanctuary. Mother Hildegard cautioned me to wear the cushioning gloves always! But I'm certainly not a..."

"I *know* you are hiding your true nature from us!" Guibert snapped, bending down to grab her left hand and peer at it closely. "You've always kept your coverings tight and closed whenever around me. In fact..."

Shoving the guard on Sally's left side away he jerked the protective sleeve of her gown up into her armpit.

There, visible to all her assembled accusers in the room, were her animal tattoos.

And there on the inside of her left wrist was the *Turtle Tattoo!* Its sly little grin back in the 21st Century was cute. Here, it was a shocking insult to staid religious sentiments.

"Oh, sweet Jesus," Sally whispered to herself, knowing the game was up.

As her body healed from the terrible burns the scar tissue retreated. She had a measure of recovery. The hair on her head did not return. But, as the years went by, the Turtle Tattoo and other lower arm tattoos slowly *reappeared.*

"Do you not all here see the undisputable evidence?" Guibert triumphantly stated, pointing in accusation at the prancing little turtle on her wrist. "It is a sign of Satan, a mark of a *witch*, her *familiar* animal spirit. It guides her reproductions of Hildegard's texts, subtly altering and perverting them. I glimpsed the green of it hidden beneath her glove and sleeve while she pretended to be illuminating manuscripts—but Hildegard would never allow me to draw back her robe. The Mother was protecting the witch. But now the demon's evil is manifested for everyone to see!"

"It's just a little turtle that..." Sally tried to protest before a guard *struck* her on the side of her head, stunning her!

Groggily, Sally saw a richly robed male step out from the shadows. She recognized him. It was Archbishop Christian of Mainz. For the entire last year, Hildegard had been embroiled in a terrible political fight with him. He insisted that the buried body of a so-called excommunicant from the church be exhumed and removed from church property. The Magistra refused, saying it was sin—that the man reconciled to the Church at the time of his death. In retaliation for her disobedience to his direct orders, the Archbishop denied both her and her nuns the rituals of singing their worship and receiving communion. In the Catholic Church that was a terrible punishment. One of the most treasured assets that Hildegard possessed was her music. In her dwindling health, she was devastated by the cruel restrictions, which only hastened her demise.

Only after pressure from other high-ranking officials of the Church, who came to her defense, did the Archbishop finally relent. But his seething anger and resentment against the elderly upstart nun, Hildegard, was known throughout the realm.

Now he had Sally in his grasp.

"It's just some youthful innocent animal images...from when I was on a slave ship!" Sally gasped, her face now mashed into the cold stones by the guards.

"Then let us see how further disrobing you supports your story," the Archbishop coldly stated, stepping closer. "If the testimonies I've acquired from those who first captured you by the Rhine are true, there is damning evidence yet to be revealed!"

"No...please...that is most unseemly," Sally begged, trying to stop them by falling back on engrained church traditions of modesty and female concealment.

But her enemies were not to be deterred.

"In front of God and all the witnesses of this room—*strip* the witch naked!" the Archbishop coldly ordered the guards, who tore and ripped at Sally's habit, first revealing her bare back.

A collective "gasp" went up from the assembled Priests and Nuns.

There on her back, clearly revealed, were the garishly inked pictures of zombies, skulls, bloody knifes, and poisonous snakes.

"She *is* a Demon!" someone in the crowd gasped in horror. "The rumors were true!" another said. And yet others screamed-out: "Our poor Mother has been under her influence these past many years... This is what is killing our dear Mother Hildegard right now... We must save our Mothe!... We must *slay* this beast in our midst!"

Guibert stepped forward as Sally struggled against the strong hands of the guards still keeping her pinned to the floor.

"What must we do?" he obsequiously bowed to the authority of the Archbishop.

The Archbishop of Mainz bowed his own head in mock contemplation.

Everyone went silent, waiting for his august words.

"This vile creature that has subverted the thinking of our 'dear' Hildegard must be *killed!* And if we are quick, doing so may still save the Magistra's eternal soul," the man solemnly declared. "This 'Sister Sally' must be *burned alive* at the stake! Now! Take her out. Destroy this Evil in our midst!"

"No...*please*...no, not that!" Sally pleaded as they jerked her to her feet, wrapped the tattered shreds of her robe back around her back, slapped heavy chains on her hands, knocked her again to the floor, and then dragged her away.

She was overwhelmed by terror and fear. Yet she also felt a perverse relief. Her journey to the 12th Century had been through a self-imposed inferno of fire. She could not endure the thought of being burned alive yet again... But perhaps it was good to have it all finally come to the end.

She didn't like what she'd become. This mild-mannered, passive nun was not her. She *did* have a beast inside of her, raging to be set free!

Self-doubt consumed her. She began to believe the accusations of her accusers. She didn't belong to this place or time. She was a liar, a pretender. She *was* a vile demon, hated by God!

As she bumped along a rough road—having been thrown again into a woven crate intended for the transport of animals, then put on a cart and rolled along toward the village square—Sister Sally heard *sweet singing* in the distance!

Aw, it was so beautiful...

It was the nuns closest to Mother Hildegard, still singing in the night to soothe her spirit as they huddled around her dying body.

Sally felt comforted.

Perhaps she and Hildegard would pass onward together. After all, they were both renegades. Perhaps God would take pity on Sally for the sake of Mother Hildegard?

What a delight that would be.

Victor was clearly happy with what they'd achieved, though pensive now that the moment was upon them.

"We have to do it," Dave said to him, standing at his shoulder.

Victor sighed and put his arm around Ivanna as they stood looking back at his beautiful forest home. They might never see it again.

"We can't stay here," Victor emphatically stated, opening the passenger side door of his big black van and courteously ushering Ivanna inside. "They certainly have surveillance of our attack on Aberdeen. When they find out that there are no fragments of the Device—indeed discover the remains of the scooped-out circle of missing concrete—they'll know that we somehow managed to teleport out from the explosion and are likely still alive. That's when they'll come *here!*"

"But they won't find us," Dave said, climbing into Victor's Polaris Ranger to follow the van. "We'll be long gone."

The Polaris Ranger was an open-air, four-wheel drive, off-road vehicle. It sported thick curved bars that protected the driver and passenger in its front. Fitted onto the front was a Plexiglas windshield. On its back it sported a four-foot-wide open box, now crowded with tightly packed camping gear. The Ranger was military black and green. It was raised up upon thick-treaded wheels. Plus it'd obviously been used a lot, with brown dirt caked into the wheels. It was a *mean*-looking machine!

"Don't go too fast!" Dave called up to Victor, who waved a hand back out of the driver's side window in acknowledgement. The Ranger could hit speeds of 50 mph and up, but it was built to be an off-road vehicle.

They were headed up to the Green Mountain National Forest, to establish a temporary camp near the Somerset Reservoir. Victor told him that he and Ivanna camped there often as Victor and other men went off hunting deer in the thick woods. It was beautiful Vermont country, secluded and primeval. It was just the place to hide out for a day or so.

They'd have time there to do careful tests on the Device before attempting to activate it again. The last time they'd been lucky. Somehow it transported them back to where they'd started in Vermont. Next time, who knew what it might do to them—or where it might send them?

But Sally was gone.

Dave and Victor had searched the woods around his house for hours. There was nothing. It was as if she'd vanished off the face of the Earth. There weren't even footprints leading away from where she'd been thrown when they'd been knocked unconscious by the rough landing of the Device.

Dave was worried that he'd never see her again. Even though Sally could be a pain at times, in the short time he'd interacted with her, he'd "grown accustomed" to her *scowl*. But she wasn't sour and negative all the time, just most of the time. Occasionally she would let loose a little smile onto her lips that could light up a room. And her mind was absolutely brilliant.

He missed her little snort when he'd say something stupid, or that quizzical look she got when she was engaged in a complex mathematical puzzle.

Where did she go? Was she kidnapped—and if so, by whom?

They'd had to use a blowtorch to cut the bolts holding the Device into the half-sphere of concrete. But they'd managed to get it loose and then secure it to the floor of the van with fresh screws.

Dave's laptop, which had fallen into the opened top of the equipment, was still giving good readings on its systems. The cable was still attached into the central control unit of the Device. The equipment components survived the "journey" intact and were giving nominal readings. But the Device refused to obey any typed-in commands. It appeared to be in a dormant state.

And Dave didn't know how to wake it up.

Without Sally there to decipher her "living" program that was now hosted within the dead Agent Anderson's mysterious "brain-sponge", Dave didn't know if they'd ever be able to communicate with the Device.

Perhaps they were just prolonging the inevitable by trying to escape into the wilderness. After all, the U.S. Military had vast resources. As soon as the military personnel discovered that the blast from the FBI's overloaded energy-gun had not disintegrated the Device, satellites would scour Earth's surface searching for them.

But at the moment it was great fun driving the nimble Ranger, particularly when they got to the dirt road leading off the main paved road—and headed into the Green Mountain National Forest. Where the van in front of him struggled, Dave ran loops around them, darting in and out of the trees!

It was thrilling, taking Dave's mind off where Sally could have vanished. But in only an hour and a half they pulled to a stop on a hill overlooking a large body of water.

They got out and stretched, enjoying the early-evening view.

"That's the Reservoir, David," Victor triumphantly proclaimed, gesturing grandly at the meandering lake below them.

"It's beautiful," Dave agreed, while groaning under his breath. The last half hour of the ride had been rough. They'd bounced along on the trail in the woods jarringly. His butt was sore. And he hoped the Device had survived undamaged.

But spread out before him was a stunning panorama, making him momentarily forget the condition of his aching rear end and the much-abused Device. Down below in a wide valley lay the deep blue of a large body of water—stretching out of sight to both Dave's right and left. Towering trees surrounded them. Low mountains arose in the distance. Across the horizon, banks of fluffy white clouds floated in the bright-blue sky. The air was pure and fresh. There was zero smog.

"I just love coming out here," Ivanna smiled, going around to the back of the Ranger to make sure the tent components were still there and hadn't been thrown out by Dave's "stunt" driving.

"You see, my boy?" Victor exulted, taking in a deep breath of the fresh, clean air. "There still exist on our planet untarnished pieces of paradise. We could go there to the water's edge right now and catch trout, salmon, bass, and perch—even Northern pike. Ah, that's some *good* eating."

"But, not today?"

"Yes, of course not today," Victor vigorously nodded. "Today, we have to make camp. Then perhaps tomorrow we return to skewer some fresh meat, eh? I brought fishing poles."

"I would, of course, be honored for you to teach me how to fish," Dave sincerely stated, never having had time for such serene activities before, "—but what about our little world-destroying experiment?"

"Yes, our stubborn Device," Victor nodded again, rubbing his thin, spotted hands together gleefully. "Hop back in, Ivanna and David. Let's get these vehicles to their final destination."

"Is it far?" Dave asked, mindful of his bruised butt.

"Not too far," Victor replied. "We're headed to a small valley a couple miles over to the side, away from the lake. It's totally secluded. No one will be there but us. There isn't even a defined road or path to the site. I discovered it a few years ago in my solitary retreats out here. We will have all the privacy we need to play with the Device to our hearts' content."

Back in the van and Ranger, they carefully rolled off away from the trail, threading the vehicles between towering trees and around large boulders, following a path only known to the Professor.

After a while they started upward, ending at yet another high slope.

"We're almost there!" Victor called back to Dave in his trailing Ranger.

Then they stopped, overlooking a small but pristine valley. Carefully, Victor drove the van over the lip and downward through the thick forest, followed by the smaller Ranger.

After a while they emerged from the trees into a lush meadow.

In the middle of the meadow was a creek sporting crystal-clear, bubbling water. Beside the creek, elevated a bit, was a wide expanse of flattened stones.

"And here is our combined camping ground and experimental platform, my dear David!" the Professor happily exclaimed, having stopped the Ranger and climbed out onto the flattened rocks.

"What is it?" Dave asked as he climbed out of the Ranger to stand beside Victor, intrigued at the flat expanse.

"It's a neat little place that the last ice age carved out especially for us," Victor laughed, squatting down to pat the flattened stone, as Ivanna started expertly unloading and setting up the tent. "A glacier smoothed this out for us. It's very secure. Our little Device will be very stable here. When we're ready tomorrow we can take it out of the van, place it here, and retreat up to the top of the slope before attempting to trigger any functions."

Together, they helped Ivanna finish setting up the single large tent, get a fire going, and heat up a tasty stew that she'd brought along.

By the time they'd finished eating it was night, with a few bugs buzzing around, and a cool wind caressing their cheeks.

Dave felt at peace.

He still wished Sally was there with him to enjoy the wonderful isolation, but he was focused on their task. He was acutely aware they only had a brief time before the military would likely locate them.

They had to get that damn Device working without blowing up the planet! Only then could they turn it over to the military, to the government, to fellow scientists.

"Time to turn in, my boy," Victor grinned by the flames of the dying fire. "I think we've had enough 'adventuring' for one day, right? Grab your sleeping bag and get in here away from the bugs. We've got a lot of work to accomplish tomorrow."

As Ivanna zipped up the netting at the front entrance to the tent, Dave had already crawled into his bag, fully dressed, and was dozing off in his sleeping bag, totally exhausted...

—to be awakened in the dead of the night by an incessant "zzzzzzzzzzz" sound...

"What the hell?" Dave groaned, fumbling at his shirt where the vibration was *thumping* on his chest.

It was the black cellphone that Agent Anderson had given to him. It was so slender he'd forgotten he put it into his pocket. Rats! The military might be using it to track them! But...maybe it was Anderson's colleagues, who actually might be able to *help* Dave, Victor, and Ivanna?

Dave saw by the dim moonlight coming through the netting at the front of the tent that Victor was cuddled with Ivanna in a single, larger sleeping bag on the other side of the tent, snoring loudly.

He didn't want to disturb their rest. Though they pretended they were teenagers, they were both well-advanced in years. Dave knew that the exertion of the prior day had taken a toll on them.

Perhaps if he just answered the phone quietly?

Fearful of who was on the other end, Dave put the phone to his ear as he lay there in his own sleeping bag.

"Yes?" he whispered.

"...where...am...I...?" Dave heard a faint, raspy voice.

"What?" Dave replied. "I can barely hear you."

"...is...is that...Dr. King...?"

"Yes, this is David King," Dave said, irritated and still groggy from being "buzzed" awake in the middle of the night. "Who are you?" he whispered back. "What do you want?"

"...I...want? Uhm...I'm not sure..."

"Then maybe you better call back in the morning!" Dave snapped, getting more and more irritated. "You woke me up. I'm sleeping in the middle of the woods. If you're reporting to someone, tell them that we need help! Anderson is dead. We escaped with the Device— how I don't know. But we're still alive and soon will need extraction to a secure site. Can you..."

"But Agent Anderson *isn't* dead...is he?" said the faint voice, growing stronger.

"He was shot in the head! Then his body was burnt up in the explosion of his colleague's gun! I assure you that Agent Anderson is deceased. Like I said, we need extraction preparation for..."

"But...*I'm*...Arthur Anderson...I think..." the voice whispered introspectively.

Dave looked over at Victor still snoring-away snuggled up with Ivanna in the cool, quiet night.

It *had* to be a prank caller!

"Look, I'm going to hang up," Dave firmly stated.

"I...I'm inside...a physics experiment...I think..." the voice continued.

Dave sat bolt upright, throwing off his sleeping bag.

"You're *inside* the machine?" Dave intensely replied.

Across the tent, Ivanna was stirring, blinking her large eyes, looking over at him curiously...

—as Victor kept on snoring.

"I think...I'm *part* of it..."

"Can you *control* it?" Dave urgently asked the voice in the cellphone, jumping up, unzipping the front of the tent, and running over to the back of the van, opening it up, and slipping in beside the bolted-down Device.

"I...yes...that is my function...I think..."

Dave peered over the sliced-open top of the machine.

Inside, where before there was no visible activity, now there were myriad lights and soft noises of components being *moved*. Fascinated, Dave watched the various parts of the complex Device re-wiring and re-configuring their own selves!

"What—can you *do?*" Dave asked, fascinated.

"What do you *want* me to do?" the voice replied, stronger now. "If you wish, I can take you anywhere you want to travel."

"Anywhere?"

"Just about..."

"Dave, my boy," Victor said, yawning widely, leaning in through the opened back of the van, "Ivanna said something's up?"

Dave grinned at him widely.

"It's Sally's program that's somehow merged with Agent Anderson's personality and memories!" Dave excitedly explained. "It's talking to me over his cellphone. He says he can transport us to wherever we wish! Wait, he's saying more..."

"I can't see!" the disembodied voice continued, now sounding like it was on the verge of panic.

"Well, sure, you're inside of..."

"Do you still have my glasses?"

Dave felt around in his pants pockets—yes, they were there, bent out of shape in his back pocket, but still intact.

"Yes, I've got them!"

"Plug them into the cellphone, please..."

Dave found a small tether on the glasses that pulled out, pushing that end into the USB port on the cellphone.

Dave peered down at the black lenses of the dark glasses.

"You look tired," Arthur said from the phone speaker.

Arthur could see him!

Dave pushed the volume up to the maximum so that Victor and now Ivanna—who'd come up from behind Victor wrapped in a blanket—could hear.

"It's Agent Anderson!" he excitedly stated to both of them. "He's in the machine and communicating with us through the cellphone. He says he can make the machine take us to wherever we want to go!"

"Can you take us to the United Nations?" Victor loudly asked.

"Certainly, Professor Volodymyr," the gravelly voice answered from the cellphone. "Shall I do that now?"

"No, not now," Victor hurriedly cautioned the voice from the cellphone. "We must run tests first. We have to know what you are capable of achieving."

"That would be fine...and now...I'm getting tired myself," the voice said as it grew fainter, "my biological neural net is overtaxed, it seems."

"Yes, rest!" Dave encouraged Arthur. "I'll talk to you more in the morning."

"Goodnight then...and sleep tight...and...'don't let the bed bugs bite'...heh..."

Dave shook his head in amazement. This remnant of the dead Agent was trying to make jokes!

Dave plugged the cellphone into the computer to recharge its battery, shakily crawled back out of the van, and stood there with Victor and the shivering Ivanna.

As one they hugged each other while hopping up and down!

"It's a *miracle!*" Victor grinned widely, throwing up his hands to the star-studded night sky.

"How can that be the dead Agent?" Ivanna marveled, shaking her head from side to side in amazement. "You told me that he was shot and killed!"

"I don't know exactly," Dave marveled, pausing in his jumping to sit on a bolder next to the smoldering embers of the fire.

It was cold. His adrenalin surge was fading. Now Dave felt afraid again, yet strangely hopeful.

"I think we're safe here for a while," Dave sighed. "And now we've got a plan. As soon as we figure out what we've got here..."

"We *announce* it to the world at the United Nations!" Victor crowed, doing a little jig on the flattened rocks. "The military won't be able to suppress it or turn it into a weapon. Concentrated Dark Energy will be available to everyone. It will save the world!"

Dave's excitement dwindled. He had a foreboding that they were embarking on something that was irreversible, something that might *not* be as wonderful as they now imagined.

Ah! That's really foolish—he chided himself. *It's just like you to go beating yourself up now that you're finally on the brink of incredible success.*

He was definitely going to win a Nobel Prize. Hah!

"Maybe we should go back in the tent and get some more sleep. It's still several hours until dawn," Ivanna gently suggested.

Victor yawned widely, "whomping" his arms together over his thin chest in the cold of the night.

"Yes, my dear," he agreed, heading back to the tent. "Are you coming, David?"

"Sure," Dave answered, standing up to follow them.

Out in the night, a wolf howled.

Predators were gathering.

Dave felt a shiver go down his spine, but quickly pushed it away. This was a time to be brave, not cowardly. His only regret was that Sally was not there with them to share this moment of triumph.

Where *was* she, anyway?

Making sure that the three had returned to the tent and fallen back to sleep, Sally finally crept out of the surrounding woods.

She'd heard everything that had just happened in the van.

Sanako and her crew were gone, having dropped Sally off in the woods a couple hours ago. They then retreated back outside of Time, where they were safe from whatever would result from Sally's efforts to alter the present timeline.

Now it was all up to her.

Quietly, she slipped into the back of the van. It was dark inside. But allowing her eyes to adjust Sally could see by the dim light of the cellphone and laptop screens, which were sitting on top of the Device's central control unit. She started typing on the laptop, sending encrypted directives to her artificial intelligence program.

"What are you doing, Sally?" came a soft voice from the cellphone.

"Nothing important, Agent Anderson," she curtly replied, her fingers flashing across the keyboard. "Go back to sleep."

"But you're changing my programming," he protested.

"These are necessary upgrades," she reassured him.

"I see that you are putting constraints on my ability to direct the operation of the mechanisms of this construct," he suspiciously replied.

"Yes I am," she said as she finished the string of commands. "And you are not to tell Dave, Victor, or Ivanna that I've been here and done these things. Do you understand?"

"I can't obey that directive, Sally," Arthur insisted. "The changes you've made will result in the *deaths* of my friends! Also..."

"Then I'm sorry I have to do this," Sally said as she reached a hand into the entrails of the central control module...

"No! *Stop!* You can't...!"

She clenched her inserted hand into a fist that was firmly wrapped-about the squishy "sponge" lodged inside—and in one quick jerk *yanked* it up out of the Device!

Tendrils thrashed madly about in the air as Sally threw the white sponge down onto the van's floorboards and *stomped* on it. Faint pink goo splashed from its mashed remains.

She addressed the destroyed remnants of Agent Anderson...

"When they fully activate the Device it will just explode," Sally grimly stated. "Now it's a bomb barely controlled by my remaining evolved algorithms left in its primitive computer module. Hopefully it'll just kill the occupants of the car without destroying the entire world in the process."

Sally sighed to the still-twitching sponge on the floor. She gingerly gathered up the oozing pad and tossed it out the back of the van. "Otherwise, until the last moment, they'll think that everything's just fine. And then all evidence of this monstrous experiment will be gone forever. Sanako and her crew have already sabotaged the government efforts at duplication. They'll never again get a fizzle, let alone a cataclysmic explosion. Whatever your ultimate agenda was, you've *failed*, Agent Anderson."

She slipped out of the van and back into the woods. It was cold, dark, and lonely as she hiked resolutely away into the depths of the Vermont forest. She had no food, water, proper clothing, or camping gear. Her goal was to just keep on walking and climbing until she collapsed and died. It wasn't a pleasant prospect.

If she had a gun she might have hunted some wild game in order to survive in the woods. She was a dead shot with both handguns and rifles. But she didn't want to survive. She wanted to die. She deserved to die. It was a fitting punishment to her terrible crime.

But she was at peace with what she'd done. No one would ever know that she'd saved the world from the Wrath of God—but *she* knew. She had preserved "the way it was" if only for a few more centuries. Perhaps by then mankind would be wiser...able to look forward as well as backward.

Sally realized that a *Reflective Nostalgia* was a necessary element to an intelligent species' maturity—worthy of her ultimate sacrifice.

"I'm sorry," she whispered, looking back from the peak of the low mountain at the peaceful, moonlit valley below. The black van and tent sat there on the flattened rocks by the stream, as if they would be there forever. But Sally knew the next day, in their place, would be only a smoking crater. "I never thought my creations would offend God. Now, they will rest in peace."

Before being dropped off in the woods Sally had used Sanako's sophisticated communication network to order her evolving intelligent programs hidden in the world's supercomputers to self-destruct. Her creations had dutifully complied with her orders.

Once the Device below detonated, all traces of her genius-level efforts would be gone. It would be as if she'd never lived.

Sally felt tears well up in her eyes. She angrily brushed them away.

Her life hadn't been very long. She'd tried to use her talents for good. But—like many other would-be scientists—"hubris" had taken hold of her. She'd done what she'd done not because of its merits, but because it was fun.

Embracing the mysteries of mathematics had been her version of intimacy. Her brief "romance" at having close friendships—with Snake, Dave, Professor Volodymyr and Ivanna—had all ended in disaster.

She realized she was atoning for her sins.

She turned her back on the doomed small valley and fatalistically hiked onward, all alone in an empty wilderness.

Chapter 15

SACRIFICE

Why give up something you prize
Except to receive something of greater value
A trade, if you would, that's rational and logical
Except when your heart forces you to act unpredictably
Throwing away clinical scales weighing options
No longer concerned with getting or giving
You put into the balance your Spirit
Hoping it is enough to matter
When all is said and done
Capturing tiny fractions
Beyond love or hate
Something deeper
A sparkling Essence
Of an innate self-worth
Infuriating your enemies...
Endearing you to Cosmic Fate.

The Luminary Chronicles, 15:29-35

Sally was roughly tied to a stake. Splinters poked into her back. Random wood was piled up against her legs. The thrown hunks tore the flesh of her feet. Then a burly guard stood in front of her holding a blazing torch.

The peasants of the village were delighted at this unexpected entertainment. Upon hearing that Sister Sally was to be burned at the stake—even though it was in the dead of the night—the occupants of the town came flooding out into the town square. Many carried flaming torches of their own. They'd long hated the "demon" protected by

Mother Hildegard. And while they mourned the impending passage of their beloved Magistra, they celebrated the killing of this "creature."

For them, Sally's punishment was long overdue.

The women of the village had gleefully stripped her stark naked, covering their eyes at her garish tattoos. Then they put Sally into a single-piece, white tunic that extended from her neck to her ankles. Her feet were bare.

Then, as she was led out to the stake, the guards beat her nearly senseless, pummeling her brutally. They didn't rape her since a jeering mob surrounded them, but they came close enough.

Sally felt thoroughly violated, disgraced, and terrified.

And now, in the dark night, surrounded by a seething, angry mob, the guard's flaming torch held just inches from the piled-up wood at her feet—Sally grimly awaited her fate.

Stepping up in front of her to "do the honors" were the officially-robed and unctuous Archbishop of Mainz and Father Guibert.

"Do you, Sister Sally, *admit* and *renounce* your vile heresy?" Archbishop Christian loudly spoke in his best preaching voice to the assembled crowd. "*Recant* and you may yet be spared your terrible punishment—instead you will only be banished from this holy land! We of the Holy Church are not murders. Admit that you are a heretic and you may yet obtain mercy!"

"I...have committed...*no* heresy!" Sally defiantly stated, thrusting her chin upward such that she looked like a battered, red-skinned, bald turtle trying to escape its leathery white shell.

The Archbishop held up his arms, his long, ornate sleeves hanging down from them, and silenced the eager crowd.

He was in his full religious garb. His pointed cap made him look seven feet tall. The flames of the torches glittered off the jewels set into his robe and holy scepter. He was the embodiment of the official State. He accepted an ornate Crucifix from Father Guibert and held it high above his head.

The peasants dropped to their knees, bowing.

"Since you refuse to acknowledge your heresy, Sister Sally, by the power of our Holy Savior I..."

"*Name* my heresy!" Sally shouted at him, interrupting him. "If I am truly the heretic you claim me to be, then you must state it clearly! Otherwise, your superiors will hold this against you. Is that not what you obviously fear? The Magistra's friends in high places will accuse *you!* They will say that in simple revenge against a revered, dying nun you took one of her friends, whom she saved from a prior life of slavery, and *murdered* her. Do you wish for your enemies to use my death against *you? Name* my so-called 'heresy'!"

"You dare to question...?"

Sally thrust her scarred, bald head up even higher in defiance.

"I *dare!*" Sally cried-out to everyone within ear shout. "I am not just a simple woman. Neither is Mother Hildegard. And neither are all the other females of this town. We are *people*, beloved by our God! This is proven by the Mother's many writings from her Visions. Only God could bring such magnificent beauty into her mind. Even our revered Pope himself endorsed her writings and preaching as being from God. And you *men* here—out of petty *jealousy* and *fear* of losing power—can't stand to see God magnified in the words of a 'mere' woman!"

The Archbishop seemed at a loss for words.

The crowd, likewise, was stunned by Sally's defiant language. They'd never heard *anyone* question a Priest—let alone a *woman* do so—and in such defiant terms. Church intrigue by Mother Hildegard and her opponents was far above their lives, unseen. *This*, however, was right in front of their eyes!

And the townspeople far outnumbered the officials and guards...

But the Archbishop quickly regained his composure, sensing the uncertainty of the surrounding crowd, and loudly proclaimed: "God in His Holy Word states that women *must* be *in submission* to me as a representative of the Church, husbands, and all my fellow men. In the Garden of Eden, it was the woman who *sinned* and *tricked* man into..."

Sally rudely interrupted his sermon by loudly *laughing!*

Once again the Archbishop was dumb struck.

"—*and*, my esteemed Archbishop, it was also Saint Paul himself in the Holy Scriptures who instructed the church that *in Jesus Christ all are one*: including the rich and poor, master and slave, high and low castes—*and* men and women alike! This is what God's Word calls us to do. Like *Jesus* appointed the Samaritan Woman at the Well to become a preacher of the Good News, so also God did the same for Mother Hildegard. Now that she passes to her reward, you men are trying to peevishly *thwart* the Will of God!"

The Archbishop looked uncertainly over at Father Guibert, whispering: "Is all that really in the Bible?"

The Archbishop, after all, was just a political appointee with little real knowledge of the scriptures.

Sally, close enough to hear his confused confession of ignorance, replied in a loud voice: "Galatians 3:28...'*There is neither Jew nor Gentile, neither slave nor free, neither male nor female—for you are all one in Christ Jesus!*' And John 4:39...'*Many of the Samaritans from that town believed in Jesus because of the woman's testimony!*' The Samaritan Woman, my esteemed Archbishop, was a prototype for Mother Hildegard, to whom I've been nothing more than a faithful servant!"

The previously jeering crowd was stilled...the Archbishop now dumbfounded and unsure of what to do next—but Guibert took control.

"Look at her hands!" the priest excitedly directed the crowd, pointing.

Indeed, on her wrist, Sally felt the revived Turtle Tattoo starting to *warm*, its bright *glow* readily apparent in the dark night to those in the mob.

"She *is* a demon... *Hell-fire* sprouts from her arms... *Kill* the spawn of Satan!" gasps of outrage surged through the milling crowd.

Recapturing the attention of the crowd, the Archbishop again held high his crucifix, shouting: "For all here in attendance I state the heresy of this woman! For seducing our beloved Mother Hildegard into defying the will of her Superiors, for bringing the Magistra to the precipice of non-repented death, and attempting to incite the females of this crowd to twisted interpretations of the Holy Scripture—I hereby sentence this witch be put to death! *Light* the fire!" he yelled at the guard, hastily stepping back from the piled-up wood.

The guard tossed his torch onto the wood at Sally's feet, as those around her surged backward to be out of range of the imminent inferno.

"I am *not* just a simple woman!" Sally shouted as thick smoke burst up into her face and flames licked at her white garment. "I am a *person!*"

She coughed fitfully, struggling to breathe as the smoke stung her eyes, flames starting to sear her lower body...

Her feet and legs were on fire!

—when *screams* broke out around her!

"It's a demon... It's a *monster*... Help! Help! *Run*... Get away!"

She glimpsed the Archbishop and Guibert frantically racing past her through the stampeding crowd, likewise terrified!

—as Sally felt something *tearing* and *ripping* at the ropes binding her hands behind the stake, freeing them!

She kicked through the burning wood and emerged from the fire, beating-away flames that still swirled about the lower half of her now blackened white gown.

"*Breeeep?*" a squawk sounded in front of her.

She looked straight into the beak-like snout of the now fully-grown dinosaur. He stood six feet high. From his narrow head to the tip of his waving tail he was fully nine feet long.

His three-fingered, clawed hands reached out and rested tenderly on Sally's shoulders. His powerful, ostrich-like legs stamped impatiently into the dirt.

She slipped her arms around his neck and perched up onto his leathery back as he turned and scampered through the screaming crowd out of the village square and into the surrounding dark woods.

She clutched him tightly as she bounced along on his back, gratefully sliding into semi-unconsciousness.

Her last thought was of Mother Hildegard.

Was the Magistra still alive? If so, she surely would have found this unexpected turn of events quite interesting.

Emerging from the tent, yawning, Dave instantly knew that something was wrong.

It wasn't the environment. Everything was beautiful. The creek bubbled along enthusiastically. The air was crisp and fresh. The morning sun was warm.

It was Victor's black van...

"What the heck?" he said, walking stiffly over to the back of the van—where its rear doors hung open!

He knew that he'd closed them last night.

Was it perhaps raccoons or foraging deer?

"Oh, rats," he gasped as he felt his foot "*sploosh*" into something sticky.

Reaching down, he picked up from the flat rocks what looked like a mashed, white *sponge*.

A few tendrils weakly waved up at Dave.

"Jesus Christ!" Dave swore, hopping up into the back of the van, the sponge lying wetly in his hand.

"What's going on, my boy?" Victor yawned as well, emerging from the tent behind Dave.

"Something's been in the van!" Dave called over to him. "The biological interface was ripped out of the central control processor! I found it out lying on the rocks."

"Is it still alive?" Victor asked, quickly running over and following Dave into the back of the van.

Dave was on his knees beside the bathtub-sized Device, leaning over its opened top.

"I think so—but it's badly torn up," Dave said as he gently laid it back on the top of the central control unit. Inside, lights were glowing here and there amongst the connected equipment. White, slimy tendrils were still visible intertwined down into the equipment.

He reattached a water drip-tube that'd been keeping the pad moist from a small reservoir.

"Maybe an animal got in...?" Victor said. He looked at the limp sponge in despair as a few tendrils tried to feebly reconnect with the interior of the Device.

"Let's see if we can communicate with Arthur," Dave said, picking up the still-connected cellphone. He noted that the dark eyeglasses were still connected to the cellphone.

"Arthur, can you hear me? Are you there? Are you awake?"

Nothing.

"Are the Device's components still functioning?" Victor asked.

Dave turned his attention to the attached laptop, checking various readouts, graphs, and charts.

"Everything looks nominal...and..."

"Yes, David?"

"I've got control back!"

"What?"

"It's accepting my direct commands! I think we've got it working again. Whatever Arthur did, he managed to restore full control to us. Maybe that's why he's not talking anymore—there's no more need for verbal communication?"

"But the biological matrix...?"

"Perhaps it was a raccoon or something that got it. The top of the Device is open, easily accessible. I guess I didn't lock the back doors as well as I thought and something nudged them open. But we've got control of the deuterium flow, the matrix oscillations, the micro-array nano-lasers, the flow chamber—everything! Even Sally's intelligent system seems operational, set to guide individual deuterium ions to their optimal positions. I think we're ready to do some preliminary tests and..."

"*Not* before you boys have breakfast," Ivanna called to them from the fire she was starting up. "Catch me a few fish, clean them, and I'll cook them up. I'll add the eggs, sliced potatoes, and carrots that I brought with us. How does that sound?"

"Do we have time?" Dave asked, before suddenly realizing that his stomach was growling angrily at him.

"Oh, me too, my boy," Victor grinned upon hearing Dave's stomach-growls, backing stiffly out of the van. "We can't do good work on empty stomachs. And I always listen to Ivanna. Either that or she comes and knocks some sense into me with a frying pan. Hah! I'll get the fishing poles. The fish aren't as large here as in the lake, but I guarantee they are just as tasty."

It didn't take long for Victor and Dave to walk downstream to a widening which became a deep pool. Through the crystal-clear water they could see medium-sized fish swimming languidly through thick banks of green water plants.

"Do you think the military are looking for us?" Dave asked Victor. They sat on boulders enticing fish towards their baited hooks in the water with little jerks of their lines. Victor was a good teacher and Dave suddenly felt very hungry for crispy fried fish.

"I imagine they are, indeed," Victor sighed, flicking his line expertly up and down. "They'll see my cars are gone at my country retreat. But I suspect they'll think we're fleeing to the city. I've got many colleagues there who would shelter us."

"So we have time?"

"Who knows?" Victor sighed again—then brightened up as he jerked his pole back, snagging a fish trying to escape his hook.

Within a few minutes Victor was proudly holding up a five-pound bass.

Dave had a similar one flopping on the rocks in another couple minutes.

Glowing with pride, the two "hunters" returned to Ivanna at the fire. She had a large frying pan sizzling as she cooked up eggs, potatoes, and carrots in delicious-smelling omelets.

She patiently smiled at her "boys" who triumphantly held up their wet trophies.

"Cleaned?" she mildly asked.

Properly chastened, Victor proceeded to teach Dave the proper techniques for gutting and scaling his catch. They worked to the side of the creek a short distance from the fire.

It was a lot more work than Dave had expected.

"Wow," he gasped, wearily setting his bloody knife to the side. "I'm sorry, Victor, but I think I prefer my meat the way God meant for us to have it—properly packaged from a grocery store!"

Victor snorted, expertly welding his own knife with a flourish to hold up two large, perfectly prepared fish fillets. Each one was a full meal by itself.

Dave held up the tattered remains of his own efforts, hardly meals at all.

"No matter, my boy," Victor heartily observed. "With what Ivanna has prepared, we'll have a feast indeed. You did well for your first try."

Dave grinned.

It was fun camping. He might even do more if the military didn't capture them and throw them into the deepest, darkest, prison.

He was feeling quite jovial—until *bullets* started "whumping" down all around them!

Whisper-quiet *stealth helicopters* were zooming down from the edge of the low mountain looming above.

"Run, David, run!" Victor yelled at him, dropping the meat and stumbling in a random pattern back-and-forth toward the black van, trying to dodge the *thudding* bullets.

"I'll distract them!" Ivanna yelled at Dave and Victor as she dropped her frying pan and ran for the Ranger.

"No, Ivanna!" Victor shouted at her.

But she was already gone, the ORV kicking up a cloud of obscuring dust as she gunned the motor onto the rough path they'd made by the passage of their vehicles coming down from the mountain pass above them.

With Dave safely in the back with the Device, Victor popped the van into gear and spun it around. He headed up the creek, bouncing along beside it, still on the "pavement" of the flattened stones.

"I think we can send out an electromagnetic pulse without fully activating the deuterium sequence!" Dave excitedly called up to Victor, clinging desperately to the top of the screwed-down Device as he frantically typed into the bouncing laptop. "This is what Arthur was going to help us test out before..."

"Better do it quick!" Victor yelled back. "They're almost on top of us! I see commandos coming down ropes from the helicopters. I don't think they're taking any chances with us. They're *shooting* at us! They're not trying to capture us. They want to *kill* us!"

"I've almost got it, Victor!" Dave yelled back. "There's no time for testing, but here goes nothing!"

He clicked the mouse, turning on an energy-production icon and watched the output line zoom up and off the scale of the graph.

"I think it's..." he excitedly started to report.

—when a *shimmering blue sphere* leapt out of the van and swept up across the sky...

—as the helicopters suddenly jerked in midair, sputtered, and came spiraling down into the valley...

—as with a loud *"KABLAM"* the black van and its occupants was *completely incinerated!*

Ivanna drove on, oblivious to what had happened outside the whipping shield of noise and dust kicked up by her ORV.

Her engine had sputtered a few seconds ago, but now ran fine.

It was a sturdy vehicle, for sure.

She was dodging trees and boulders, smashing through undergrowth, bouncing over low ridges, and zooming along gullies—doing everything she could to draw away the attacking soldiers.

She didn't have any idea where she was in the vast forest—just that she had to keep driving as long as she could.

"Watch out!" came a scream from in front of her as she slammed on the brakes and slid to a stop.

Right in front of her was a terrified, hands-up-in-surrender, wide-eyed girl.

It was Sally!

Ivanna jumped out, ran around to the girl, and hugged her tightly.

"Sally, what are you doing out here?" Ivanna breathlessly gasped. "We were so worried about you when you disappeared back at our house! And now...?"

"Where are Dave and the Professor?" Sally asked—obviously just as bewildered by Ivanna's sudden arrival as was the elderly woman at her appearance.

"I don't know," Ivanna worriedly replied, leading Sally back around to the passenger side of the Ranger. "I was trying to lead the soldiers away from them. I heard a loud explosion behind me and..."

Both Ivanna and Sally looked up as they heard helicopter blades descending.

"Don't move!" a barked order came as commandos burst out through the surrounding trees with M16 rifles pointed directly at the two women.

Ivanna put her hands up above her dyed blond hair, now disheveled from her normal impeccably neat appearance. She knew when to run and when to surrender.

But Ivanna saw Sally turn and try to dash away...

—who was savagely knocked to the ground by the heavy butt of a rifle, swung into her forehead! A commando grabbed her arm and twisted it behind her back, jerking her up again to her feet.

Blood ran from a cut on her forehead.

"I've got the woman and another girl," he said, speaking into a communicator at his shoulder.

"What about the two men?" the soldier asked.

"The van they were in disintegrated from the electromagnetic discharge they released at us," Ivanna heard the crackling reply. "They're dead."

Ivanna gasped while Sally beside her grimly *smiled*.

"Check and make doubly sure," came another order over the radio. "Go survey the area. We thought they were dead before and were wrong. I want actual tissue samples on which we can do DNA analysis."

"Yes, Sir!" the commando replied, shoving Sally along with Ivanna towards the opened side of a helicopter which had just landed in the small clearing. "We're headed there now."

Ivanna saw the downdraft from the spinning blades blowing Sally's long reddish hair around in circles.

She allowed herself to be distracted from her deep grief upon hearing her husband and Dave were both dead. She didn't want to believe what she'd heard. She *refused* to believe it!

Instead, she focused on the abrupt reappearance of Sally.

She really is a pretty young girl—Ivanna thought, *under all that hair and blood. It's so sad she got mixed up in this nonsense.*

"What are you going to do with me?" Sally gasped, sitting sullenly beside Ivanna as a soldier handcuffed her. Beside Sally, Ivanna maintained a stoic dignity, staring defiantly straight-ahead.

"We're going to pick your brains," a stern-looking female officer already in the helicopter coldly informed her. "You're going to tell us everything you know."

"Like hell!" Sally sneered at her, blinking through the blood running into both her eyes.

"Oh, you'll cooperate," the woman ominously assured her. "All you terrorists eventually talk. It's that or unending pain."

Ivanna continued sitting in stoic silence.

"Just kill me," Sally dejectedly said as she slumped in her jump seat beside Ivanna. "I've done my job. I'm finished."

"Not until *we* decide you're finished," a stern-looking male officer coldly stated as the commandos piled back into the vehicle.

Ivanna felt the helicopter jump upward into the air, looking with sympathy at the dejected slumped girl in the seat next to her. Then Ivanna was startled by a *wink* that the female officer aimed at Sally.

Sally, in turn, now squinting past the blood flowing past her eyes—seemed to fix her gaze upon the smart-looking, *oriental* female officer.

Ivanna, devastated with worry over what might have happened to Dave and her husband, was nonetheless perplexed.

What was going on here?

What did Sally mean by she'd "done her job"?

Ivanna certainly wasn't a "terrorist", and neither was this sweet young Sally...or was she?

Suddenly—looking at the now-grinning, wild-eyed girl obsessively rocking back-and-forth in the seat beside her—Ivanna wasn't so sure.

Chapter 16

THIS ISN'T VERMONT ANYMORE...

Someday over the rainbow

Blue birds will fly

Just not today

When everything dies...

Your fists clench in terrible pain

And your eyes drip with tears

Wishing that happy endings do exist

Even when the tornado hits you

Hoping it will miss your home

If only by a few inches

Not taking away your dear ones

Sparing your and their lives

Even transporting you to Oz

Where all your dreams are fulfilled

Tragedy turned into opportunities

Which only dare to happen...

In the movies.

The Luminary Chronicles, 16:267-271

"Victor, are you ok?" Dave urgently said. He shook the elderly gentleman gently by his shoulders as he lay sprawled on top of Victor's unmoving body.

They'd been thrown from the van.

It lay smashed off at a distance, lying on its side on top of a thick snow bank.

Victor moaned.

"Maybe I'll be ok," he weakly replied, staring up into Dave's face, "if you'd get off of me, please?"

"Oh, right," Dave gulped, hastily rolling off to the side while trying to see out in the gloom. "Are you hurt?"

"Bruised up, I think," Victor whispered back. "But I don't feel any broken bones."

"I think the windshield burst when we crashed," Dave said, feeling shards of glass scattered over his body. "We were both thrown through it, you from the front and me from the back of the van."

Dave inched himself up to a seating position, leaning back against a wide tree trunk.

"Lucky for us that we went right through the window," Victor groaned again. "I guess it was fortunate we didn't have time to buckle our seatbelts. At least our fall was softened. We seem to have landed in a snowbank."

What, snow? Really? And why was it so gloomy?

Overhead Dave saw...the *moon*.

It was full, shining brightly down upon them.

But it should be bright morning—were they knocked out that long?

A thick layer of leaves in the tree branches lay between them and the moon's light. They were in the forest.

Uh, where are the commandos coming after us?

And it was very cold. Dave found that he was shivering badly. Yes, there was snow on the ground, *lots* of snow. But it wasn't winter. It was springtime!

What the hell is going on here?

"The van's in bad shape," Dave said out loud, vaguely seeing it toppled off to the side, as his eyes started adjusting to the relative darkness.

"So much for our great plan of making some Grand Announcement to the world," Victor coughed, slowly pushing his bruised body up to lean against the large tree trunk, sitting right beside Dave...

—as a loud "honking" and "trumpeting" sounded off in the distance! Elephants? Really? Were they in Africa? If so, how could they be in the tropics with *snow* all around?

"Victor...I don't think we're in Vermont anymore," Dave said to his friend, pointing a shaking arm over beside the van, "at least not in *our* Vermont."

—as a *giant woolly mammoth* curiously nudged at the black van, "thumping" it with its huge, curved tusks! Correlating exactly with Dave's knowledge of the extinct animal, it indeed did sport long, shaggy hair hanging almost to its big flat feet.

"Uhm," Victor mused, putting a shaking finger to his nose in contemplation. "I'm not a biologist...but, correct me if I'm wrong, David—did not those beasts go extinct *ten thousand* years ago?"

"At least," Dave gulped. "But right now one looks like it wants to *crush* our van!"

Indeed, it was angrily ramming the side of the van with its tusks, apparently mistaking it for an uncooperative fellow giant animal.

Then a couple more of the huge animals came strolling into the small clearing, attracted by the first mammoth's curious snufflings and trumpeting.

Suddenly, a small *baby mammoth* went "clomping" right past Dave and Victor!

It gave out a little "bleep" in panic, raising its little trunk high up into the air.

—as behind it came *heavily-fur-clothed "cavemen"* running after the baby with spears held aloft...again right past Dave and Victor!

Fortunately the hunters were so intent on their prey that they apparently didn't see the two men huddled against the wide tree trunk.

With violent "snorts" and "thumps" the herd of mammoths took off into the woods with the primitive human hunting party hard on their heels.

"Well, that was something you don't see every day," Victor weakly laughed, now shivering even more violently than Dave.

"We've got to get the van and get it upright," Dave said, grabbing Victor by his arm and helping him to stand. "If we don't get the engine going and get warmed up inside, we'll freeze to death."

"Right..." Victor said as they both hobbled through the dark woods and clinging snow to the thick snowbank upon which lay the van.

"It's lying at an angle," Victor logically observed. "It won't take much to lever it over onto its wheels. We just need to set up some sort of fulcrum."

Dave spied a large bolder sticking out of the snow to the side of the van, and a suitable downed tree branch.

After much struggling and straining, they just managed to nudge the van back upon its wheels. The top of the van was mashed inward, but still intact. The front window was smashed out. But it looked like most of the rest of the damage to the van was superficial.

"You drive, my boy," Victor said between chattering teeth. "I'm so exhausted I can't see straight."

Inside, they found the Device still solidly bolted-down to the floor.

The engine started ok and Dave cautiously edged the van forward, looking for a place to park for the night that wasn't as exposed as in the clearing.

They inched out of the forest onto the top of a mountain pass. Down below, glittering by the light of the moon was a *gigantic glacier!*

It stretched from beyond the horizon, flowing through the small valley and nearly filling it up to its top. It was a mixture of pure-white fallen snow with blue-glass spikes of ice sticking up here and there like giant spears.

"Ah, so there's our answer," Victor nodded thoughtfully. "We weren't teleported to a new place, as we were when we first activated the Device at Aberdeen. We've been transported into the past!"

"Well, I guess we know for sure where those flat rocks by the creek came from," Dave gulped, agreeing with Victor.

"Yes, the Green Mountains were once much taller," Victor mildly observed. "They were ground down by glaciers across several ice ages in the past, or so I've heard."

"Yep—and now we know by direct observation," Dave sighed, looking at the high peaks around them. "We've definitely been thrown back in time! But—however this happened—we've got to find some shelter. Either more extinct giant Mammoths are going to pick another fight with our vehicle, or those hunting parties of primitive humans will attack us."

"I think I see a cave or depression in the mountain to the left," Victor said. "Do you see it, my boy?"

Dave saw where he was pointing. It was difficult to make out at night. At best, it was an overhang above a shielded spot in the forest right beside the glacier. But it was better than nothing.

"Hang on, Victor," Dave cautioned him. "We've got to drive onto the glacier to get there."

Lucky for them the recent snow gave them a cushion over the sharp ice below.

And just as the sun was coming up, they managed to nudge into a secluded spot next to an overhanging ledge, hidden behind a thick stand of huge trees.

And even better, there was a bank of sloped frozen snow that Dave could nudge the front of the van tightly up against—hiding them better while blocking-off and filling-in their broken front window.

"It's warming up, Victor. We've blocked out the cold night air. The sun will warm the air. We've survived our first night in the Wooly Mammoths' *Pleistocene!*"

"I am glad you know your ancient history well enough to name the Epochs," Victor congratulated him, huddled in the front seat under a blanket that'd been in the back.

"Well, I don't want to become an expert on it," Dave said, now climbing over the back of the seat to start examining the Device. "This pesky thing must have brought us here..."

"—and maybe can get us back home?" Victor cheerfully added.

"We'll see," Dave said glumly as he looked inside the equipment casing. His heart sank on observing the interior of the machine. Where there should have been blinking lights, the components were dark.

The Device was stone cold *dead*.

Sally revived to find the adult *Pelecanimimus* gently nuzzling her shoulder. She was lying slumped against a boulder on a high hill.

She noted that it was still dark. So she hadn't been unconscious for too long. They must be well away from the town. But she could still hear shouts off in the distance.

The townspeople were pursuing her!

Behind her was a sheer cliff looming up into the sky, impossible to climb. Over to her side Sally saw another long drop. Through low overhanging trees and bushes she saw the wide Rhine River. It glistened like a silvery snake, lit by the many stars shining down from above.

Sally realized this was the very spot of their arrival, fourteen years ago. She'd fallen from that high cliff, smashed through the overhanging branches and bushes, then tumbled on down into the river.

It was a terrible fall that should have killed her. Likely the only thing that saved her from crushing internal injuries was residual force from the massive gun-blast, plus her Optimmune cellular enhancements.

And now she'd returned to the "scene of the crime"—likely the *last* scene of this epic "movie"!

The plucky little dinosaur had carried her as far as it could into the hills. It could go no further or higher.

"So, *you* are the 'demon in the woods' that I've been hearing about all the time that I've been here," she laughed, reaching up to gently stroke Breep's neck.

He preened in reply, hopping about excitedly.

Over the last fourteen years in the 12th century, she'd almost forgotten what Breep looked like. He sure wasn't a baby anymore!

He still looked like a plucked chicken, just a really big one.

He was very pretty. He had big black eyes. A small tuft of red feather-like growths stuck up from the back of his head like a "Mohawk" haircut. He had many sharp teeth running along the insides of his beak, visible as his head darted back and forth. The bottom of his arms and legs were bright orange. The rest of him was a deep olive green except for lighter stripes on his back and tail, with bright yellow on the front of his neck.

He'd grown up from a baby to be a very beautiful small dinosaur.

"Well, Breep," Sally sighed, relaxing for a moment as the shouts of the villagers grew ever-closer. "Thanks for getting me out of that fire. I sure didn't want to get burned to death…again! But maybe your rescuing me was for nothing. We can't get up this cliff and I'm too weak to continue running. You're a strong little dinosaur but I don't think even you could carry me much further. I guess the best we can hope for is that when those villagers catches up with us two 'monsters' they'll just stab us in our hearts."

"Breep! Breep! Breep!" the dinosaur repeatedly called-out to her, scratching at the dirt over next to the cliff.

"What's going on, boy?" she said, painfully pushing herself up on her burnt feet to totter over to him.

It was cold there in the nighttime forest. Sally was dressed only in the thin tunic the town ladies had put on her for the execution. Her bare, seared feet hurt terribly. Superficial burns from the fire throbbed all over her body.

She wanted to just give up, but Breep refused.

"*Breep! Breep! Breep!*" he kept calling out to her, his big-eyed head repeatedly darting from the ground then back to her then back to the ground.

He was frantically digging at the dirt with the tough claws on his three-toed feet.

"Something there, boy?" she said, grabbing a fallen branch to start digging herself into the moist ground.

It wasn't too hard to dig a shallow pit. Mostly, she was just humoring Breep. Maybe it was her own grave she was digging...hah! She could just hop into it and save the townspeople the trouble of burying her.

Off in the distance, down the slope of the forested mountain, Sally could distinctly now see—in the dark of the night—multiple *torches* bobbing.

They were definitely tracking her, getting closer and closer. *Burn the monsters! Yay!*

Breep jumped back out of the now-substantial hole and started hopping up-and-down.

"Huh? Find something, boy?" Sally said, reaching into the bottom of the now three-foot-deep pit with her stick to tamp against something *hard*.

She pushed away the remaining soil with her hands and found...

—moldering and damp, but still intact: her *tough leather shoulder bag!*

When she'd fallen off the cliff looming above them, Breep and the bag must have landed right here as she bounced further on down into the river. Breep must have buried the bag. What a clever lizard!

"They went this way! I see the tracks of the demon!" Sally heard a shout from not far away.

The townspeople were almost upon them.

She unzipped the top of the bag and reached inside...to pull out her *black pistol*—which was *blazing hot* to the touch!

"Holy Christ!" she gasped to Breep, who'd backed off a few steps and was now bobbing his head up-and-down. "It's been in the ground *sucking in energy* for the last fourteen years! With the charge it's built up I bet I could level this forest, kill the stupid villagers trying to catch us, and destroy their entire town!" she laughed, brandishing the glowing gun up in the air.

But...then she'd be a mass murderer.

Sure, they were stupid peasants cruelly enjoying the hunt, intent on killing her and her pet dinosaur. But they were also abysmally ignorant, blindly attacking what they couldn't understand. Also, they'd been programmed by their religious leaders to hate so-called "heretics." Plus they just plain didn't know any better. How could they? To them an extinct dinosaur wasn't an evolutionary curiosity, but a frightful *monster...*

—just like Sally, a creature out of its time, operating by a different set of societal imperatives.

"There they are! I see them!" a shout came from just yards away.

"Maybe just a *warning shot?*" she grinned at Breep as she stepped in front of him, holding him back with a protective arm while she took aim with the other.

Making sure the setting was on the lowest "one star" she fanned the gun in a half-circle as she pulled the trigger...

—*lighting up* the forest around her with an instantaneous rush of FIRE that erupted up the trunks of the surrounding trees!

"Wow...this thing is loaded to the sky!" Sally gasped to Breep. "If it did that at just the lowest setting, what would it do set on five?"

Screams came wafting back out of the thick smoke. It was music to the ears of Sally and the excitedly-prancing dinosaur... "Aaaaiiieeeee! The Heretic's set fire to the woods! She's a witch for sure! Call for the Archbishop to send in troops! That Demon is a dragon! It has fire for its breath! Call for more soldiers to fight it! It must be destroyed!"

Ok, then.

She'd given them pause. But they were still determined to eradicate this supposed Satanic-curse from their town and their forest. They'd soon be back in even greater numbers. And with the protective cover burned off, her only recourse would be to kill them all.

Why is everything so hard?—Sally groaned to herself. *I don't want to hurt anyone.*

Of course there was an easy way out. She could just turn the gun on Breep and herself. There'd be no pain. Set to its highest power, they'd both be instantly vaporized.

Maybe this was the price of her arrogance thinking that she could hide the world from God's full attention: to just commit suicide. What a pitiful wretch she was... How dare she presume that she could thwart the Will of the Creator of the entire Universe?

Her fourteen years of Bible study and strict convent Catholicism was kicking in. "God" was no longer to her just a mystic nebulous "force." No, her newly ingrained instincts said that God was a powerful, ruling, malignant, and deadly *Eye in the Sky.* God was something not to be loved, rather obeyed without question and *feared!*

Maybe the Archbishop of Mainz was correct even though he was just a political hack. Maybe she *was* just an unrepentant heretic. After all, the Ideals of the Holy Bible were just that, very high benchmarks—things to be strived for, but rarely obtained. Maybe she was expecting too much of the Dark Ages.

The suppressed women of this age would just have to wait nine hundred more years for their liberation.

Her little rebellion and Mother Hildegard's Vision would end—one way or another—as a slaughter in the woods.

"No!" she shouted into the forest at the voices again gathering on the other side of the now-dwindling wall of flames. "I am *not* just a weak woman! I am a *person!*"

She slung the moldering leather bag up over her shoulder, grabbed Breep with one arm around his long neck to keep him from running away in panic. She turned away from the forest to directly face the high cliff behind them. With her free hand she pointed the still-hot gun at the sheer cliff face—flicking the power setting over to its *full five stars*—and pulled the trigger.

She could barely hold the gun steady as with a deafening *ROAR* a BLAZING CYLANDER OF WHITE LIGHT sliced a *circular tunnel* right through the entire mountain!

And likely through deep fractures, the entire mountain *glowed* with barely-contained energy that seemed ready to burst through!

"Wow," Sally gasped again, still holding onto Breep's neck. "We didn't get blown up. The energy was so intense it vaporized the rock, blowing everything out the other side!"

What was left was a perfectly circular twenty-foot-high tunnel.

Inside the smoking tunnel it was pitch black.

Sally knew their escape-tunnel through the mountain wouldn't last long. It would probably collapse upon itself in mere moments.

"Get the heretic! Kill her!" shouts rang out right behind them as soldiers broke through the fading wall of flames in the forest, their swords held at-ready.

Sally absently noticed that the resurrected Turtle Tattoo on her wrist was yet-again glowing brightly.

"Shall we?" Sally grinned at Breep, as she dropped the now ice-cold, depleted gun back into her shoulder bag.

Without hesitation, he dived forward on nimble legs into the dark opening, Sally right behind him.

Hildegard von Bingen looked up with fading sight into the night sky, seeing myriad stars far above, awaiting her arrival...

—as two *blazing-white streams of light* crossed in the sky, centered exactly above her deathbed!

Her mourners at the bedside were dumbfounded: staring silently at the *heavenly cross* suddenly appeared high above them.

"*Das Lebendige Licht,*" she whispered gratefully, contentedly closing her eyes for the last time.

She died as those around her, in awe, made the sign of the cross on their own chests.

Truly, Hildegard von Bingen was a remarkable person...a woman of Vision.

Chapter 17

SECOND CHANCES

If there's anything I hate

It's when my guests come late

Making me worriedly think

"Are they coming? Did they forget?

Did I do all of this work for nothing?"

Or, worse yet: "Did they have an accident?"

But then that happy delightful relief

To see them arriving out of the distance

Driving up to my door apologetically

As if they'd been wrecked but revived

Apprehension turned into delight

We'll have such a good time after all

Forgetting everything that happened before

We'll party through the night till new daylight!

Would that all fears evaporated so nicely...

The Luminary Chronicles, 17:25-29

Ivanna sat slumped in her jump seat in the steadily ascending helicopter. Beside her, but cringing away, was Sally. Ivanna was puzzled at her behavior, but analytical. She saw that the young girl was touch-aversive, possibly indicating a deep-set personality or antisocial disorder.

She'd caught enough conversation between the soldiers—which jived with what she'd heard between Victor and Dave—to learn that the girl was a prodigy at mathematical science. It fit with Ivanna's diagnosis of psychological problems, maybe even Sally being a borderline autistic.

They hadn't bound Ivanna's hands as they'd done with Sally. Apparently an old lady like her wasn't considered to be dangerous. Sally, though—however withdrawn—was clearly capable of outbursts of extreme violence!

The female officer carefully moved through the huddled soldiers in the cramped cargo hold to slip into a jump-seat next to Sally and Ivanna.

She surreptitiously placed a small *blue sphere* in each of their hands, bending over to whisper in each of their ears in turn.

"Clutch this tightly."

Then she suddenly drew out a black pistol and fired it straight upward into the low ceiling...

—and a *roiling, crackling cloud of electricity* enveloped them, instantly *stunning* the soldiers!

Ivanna absently noted that a shimmering cloak of blue energy had protected her, Sally, and the female officer from the discharge.

Interesting...

Ivanna, in her early eighties, was still actively involved in sociological research. Though she was retired from a long career as a Yale University Professor, she acted as a political consultant, was a frequent speaker at conferences, and kept her finger on the pulse of society.

The female officer was clearly *not* what she'd pretended to be. Guns that can stun a whole helicopter filled with soldiers didn't exist. Blue spheres that protect against such powerful weapons also didn't exist.

"Who are you?" Ivanna crisply asked the woman beside her as the helicopter tilted on its side in midair and started *dropping*...

The pilot was probably unconscious as well.

"No time," the woman replied, snapping off the seatbelts of Sally and Ivanna and hauling them both across the backs of the crumpled soldiers towards the exit door of the rapidly falling helicopter.

"What are you doing?" Ivanna gasped as the woman yanked open the door and *threw* both her and Sally out into the air!

Ivanna had a terrifying sensation of falling unprotected toward the spinning forest below...

—before she was scooped up by a "flying saucer" and zipped through *a blue mist* into the *blackness of outer space!*

The oriental woman helped her stand inside the craft.

Gaping through the transparent shell of the vehicle, Ivanna could see below her the entire, circular surface of Earth.

And it appeared to be *melting!*

"I'm sure this is difficult for you to watch, as it is for me, but you must see it for yourself," the female officer said, steadying Ivanna. Behind them another crew member was bandaging Sally's forehead.

"What...is happening?" Ivanna gasped, her hand held to her mouth in horror.

"It is the end of your world," the slight, oriental woman stated sadly. "By the way, Dr. Petrovich, my name is Sanako. I was trained further in the future, by the High Priestess. I and my compatriots were sent back in time to try to alter your fate. That future from which we originated is now gone, but I and my friends still remain. We are situated outside of Time, still fighting to save humanity. But we've not succeeded. The *Day of Judgment* is fast approaching your present-day world, Professor Petrovich—when God nudges the sun to wipe the human race off the face of the planet."

For a moment, Ivanna was stunned. This was just too incredible to be true. Yet she *was* here in a futuristic craft perched in a high orbit around the planet! And this woman knew all about her, including her maiden surname that she'd maintained for her academic endeavors.

"What have I to do with this?" Ivanna snapped at Sanako, turning to fix her with an insightful stare.

"My, aren't you quick," Sanako appreciatively nodded to her. "You have undergone terrible experiences in the last hour. You've recovered nicely. But you've not been part of the problem to-date. Unfortunately, your husband *is* a big part of the problem. He is encouraging and aiding Dr. King to both achieve and publicize the routine tapping-into of Dark Energy from Subspace. This is what Dave's Device plus Sally's advanced control systems can accomplish. And this is what brings mankind to the Creator's full attention. That, in turn, triggers Judgment Day and our consequent, unavoidable condemnation. Are you still keeping up with me?"

"I *tried* to do it..." Sally sobbed from behind Ivanna. "I tried to stop all this by causing the van to explode. I'm sorry, Mrs. Volodymyr—if there was any other way I'd done that! But Dave and your husband must have somehow survived. So I failed to..."

"You tried to kill Dave and Victor?" Ivanna accused her, spinning around, furious. "How *dare* you? I thought you were Dave's girlfriend!"

"Don't be too mad at..." Sanako tried to intervene...

"It was either that or what you see below happening to the Earth—just *one hundred years* in our future!" Sally angrily shouted back at Ivanna. "And now that I've failed—our Judgment Day is still out there!"

"Oh, we are not a hundred years in the future," Sanako sadly stated.

"What?" Sally said, looking over at her.

"Judgment Day is now even closer than I showed you before," Sanako said, taking them both by their arms and leading them to form-adaptive chairs. "This is now only *fifty years* in your future. But all is not lost. We may yet turn the tide and..."

"—*without* murdering my husband or anyone else?" Ivanna demanded.

"We may still prevail—if you do *your* part," Sanako quietly finished.

"So you want me to try to kill them *again*, wherever they are?" Sally angrily shouted at the oriental woman. "No! I *won't!*"

"Not you," Sanako mildly replied, apparently not taking offense at Sally's outburst.

"Then who?" Ivanna quietly asked, trying desperately to understand what Sanako was saying and where her supposedly incinerated husband had gone.

Sanako chose to ignore her query, turning to the angry girl instead.

"The last time around, you died early-on," Sanako simply stated to Sally, reaching over to take her hand comfortingly. "It was a regrettable necessity to hopefully inhibit Dark Energy research. In the present timeline, though, we considered your continued presence an un-expected bonus. We tried to take advantage of your access to Dave, but it didn't work. So you can now relax. Your part in this is finished. It's out of your hands now. Our next, desperate action must go *around* you. So in our present situation we..."

"But we're *all* going to die!" Sally cried-out, no longer listening to Sanako, lost in her grief.

Sally laid her bandaged head into her arms, no longer listening, sobbing in relief at not having to do any further unthinkable crimes.

Realizing what Sanako was saying, Ivanna gulped, stood up from the chair, and went over to the transparent bubble. She looked out again at the burning Earth, around which their craft was steadily or-biting.

The circular edges of the globe below were now glowing *red*.

Ivanna knew enough planetary geography to realize that the awful red haze around earth should have been a thin blue line of atmos-phere—which was now *gone!*

There was no denying her eyes. The planet was dead.

If Sanako wasn't referring to Sally in regard to saving the planet, there was only one other person left to "take action."

"So what can *I* do?" Ivanna quietly asked, steeling herself for the terrible answer.

Sanako now stood beside her as they both looked out at the de-stroyed planet.

"You will know when the time comes," Sanako simply replied. "And you're not going to like it. But the fate of the world is now in *your* hands."

"I don't believe any of this. This is either a nightmare or a trick!" Ivanna angrily protested, desperately trying to reject the idea that Earth was doomed.

"That's an understandable reaction, but there's someone who will convince you."

"Who?"

"We're going there now," Sanako said, turning to give instructions to the crew.

Abruptly—but without a sensation of motion—the blackened Earth shrank smaller and smaller.

They were speeding into a fuzzy white tunnel.

"We're headed to Mars," Sanako simply stated.

"You mean the *planet* Mars?" Ivanna numbly replied, not comprehending what Sanako was telling her, jumping up from her seat to waver unsteadily on her feet.

Her aging legs were trembling after the exertions of the previous hours.

Sanako again took Ivanna by her arm to steady her. "It won't be long," she continued. "This craft travels through Subspace itself. We'll be there in just a few minutes."

"But won't whatever's there be *cooked* as well?"

"It's a process that takes several days to complete," Sanako patiently explained. "The solar super-storm throws successive waves of massive plasma-clouds off into space. One after another, they hit Earth and Mars. Some humans survive in underground caverns and facilities—but not for long. There is still time enough for your visit...before the end."

Double "wow"—this was absolutely incredible!

"I never thought I'd travel into outer space," Ivanna shook her head in amazement, not following the scientific explanation too well, but finally accepting it as truth. She crinkled up a tentative smile on the corners of her weathered mouth. "I thought that Victor and I were long past doing anything more exciting than leisurely taking pictures of birds landing on our bird-feeder in Vermont."

"You *must* persist, Professor Petrovich," Sanako urged her.

"Well—I guess I can try. What choice do I have?"

"None," Sanako stated categorically. "You're just like the rest of us. We are servants of Fate."

"But how can that be?" Ivanna angrily challenged her. "You already told us that there was a prior, *different* timeline. And now you're trying to get me somehow to alter the *present* set future? That just doesn't jive with an inalterable Fate out there. You can't have it both ways. Either nothing we do matters or there's no such thing as 'fate'!"

Sanako—for just a moment—stared sadly back at Ivanna.

"*Fate* is a lot bigger than your or my little minds can conceive," Sanako whispered, so faintly that Ivanna could barely hear her words.

"Our struggles are just part of a larger puzzle whose dimensions are conceived in beauty."

"You speak in riddles," Ivanna frowned.

"Thank you," Sanako said, turning away.

"We've only a quarter of a tank of gas left," Victor said from the front seat of the van.

"I *know*, Victor," Dave said from the back of the van as he struggled to get the Device's internal power back online.

Their passage back in time to the Ice Age had disrupted a whole series of internal power conduits between the various linked mechanisms.

"At the rate we're going with the engine running, we'll be out of gas before nightfall," Victor mildly observed.

"Then turn it off!" Dave snapped back at him, irritated by the constant interruptions.

"But we'll freeze."

"It's a nice day out there!" Dave argued, glancing out of the van's windows at bright shafts of sunlight falling through the concealing canopy. Then, more reasonably, he stated: "We've got to conserve our fuel, Victor. Once that's gone, there's not another gas station for at least ten thousand years."

Victor laughed, cooperatively switching off the idling engine.

"How do you think we got thrown back in time?" Victor asked, bundling their one blanket about his body more tightly now that the small warmth from the car heater had stopped.

The ice blocking the opening of the smashed front window was dripping, making the front seat a soggy mess.

Dave was desperate, knowing their already-precarious situation was fast deteriorating.

Victor was snorting and coughing, clearly starting to get sick. His elderly body wouldn't last much longer in the Age of the Mammoths.

"Who knows?" Dave shrugged, struggling to reconnect still-functioning lines around ones that were obviously burnt-out. "Must I remind you, Professor, that this 'Dark Energy' stuff is a total mystery? It's apparently what holds the Universe together—comprising two thirds of the known, observable Universe—yet we've only recently discovered its existence. Who knows what it does? I, for one, am not that surprised that tapping into it somehow connects us with the past."

"And what about the future?" Victor mildly asked from the front seat, his voice quavering as the biting chill cut into him even deeper.

"God only knows," Dave grunted, struggling to reach around tightly-coupled pieces inside the Device.

Then—finally having accomplished the "bypass surgery"—Dave sat back, his legs cramping.

"I'm sure getting hungry," Victor sighed from the front seat.

"Then go find those hunters and grab some of their mammoth meat!" Dave snapped back at him, still not seeing any signs of life from the equipment.

The internal battery should now be at least weakly powering the maintenance functions in the different components of the Device. Dave knew that lights should be starting to flash inside, servos powering up.

Nothing, nothing at all.

"Too bad we didn't get to fry up those tasty bass fillets," Victor sighed again.

"Maybe we wouldn't have gotten into this mess if you hadn't insisted we take time out for fishing and eating breakfast!" Dave grated through clenched teeth, totally bewildered why the machine wasn't lighting up.

Maybe there was only a trickle of juice making it to the components, but it should be enough for *something* to happen.

Victor was silent.

Then Dave realized how hurtful what he'd said was to his aging Professor.

"Look Victor, I'm sorry..." he began.

—when a single light flashed on inside the central control module, with a tentative voice spoke from the still-attached cellphone:

"Uhm...hello?"

"Hello!" Dave eagerly called back. "Who is this speaking?"

"You don't know your own name?"

"No, not me—you! Are *you* Arthur?" Dave persisted.

"Who is this 'Arthur'?"

"Ok, you don't know," Dave nodded thoughtfully. "Are you Sally's artificial intelligence program?"

"Who is this 'Sally'? What is an 'artificial intelligence'?"

"Look—whoever you are—can you control the Device?"

"What is a 'Device'?"

"Damn!" Dave swore, shivering in the gathering cold inside the back of the van. He was clad only his thin long-sleeved shirt. "I can't communicate with this thing. That raccoon must have irrevocably damaged Arthur's brain sponge. There's only some rudimentary speech mechanism left. It doesn't have the wits of a caveman!"

"Uhm...David, my boy," Victor's tentative voice softly came to Dave from the front seat. "I don't think you should insult cavemen."

"Not now, Victor!" Dave growled, leaning closer to the cellphone as if to confront this new, stupid "entity" face-to-face.

"David!" Victor insisted. "Please take a look *out the back window!*"

Irritated at being diverted from his immediate task, Dave glanced up at the small window that was set into the van's back door.

A face was there—staring intently at him!

"Jesus Christ!" Dave gasped as he jerked back, startled.

The face was wide, brown-skinned, with long black hair hanging to both sides.

"And he's got friends coming," Victor mildly observed as he shrank down in the front seat. He was apparently trying to be less visible. Dave glimpsed him peering intently at the side-view mirror still set onto the outside of the door beside him.

"It's those hunters! How did they find us?" Dave groaned, reaching again into the entrails of the mechanism to reattach or reroute more power conduits.

"We did leave some rather prominent tracks in the snow, my boy—certainly of curious appearance uncommon to this time-period."

Now more of the Native Americans were tentatively approaching the black van from the surrounding trees, their furtive movements glimpsed by Dave through the side windows.

He heard a "thud" as the butt-end of a spear was struck against the side of the van. He saw shadowy figures outside clad in warm, furry garments inching ever closer.

"We have to have more power!" Dave frantically called to Victor.

"I am in total agreement," Victor said, his voice shaking with fear. "Once those natives get hold of us, there's no telling what will happen."

"Victor, do you work on cars much?"

"I don't think this is the time for an oil change, my boy."

"No, Victor—the electrical wiring in the dashboard! Can you get at it?"

"With the proper tools..."

"To hell with the tools, Victor! Rip it open! Get to the wire connecting the cigarette lighter to the battery!"

"Yes...yes—I see where you are going with this."

Dave heard a grinding and ripping noise from the front seat as Dave continued struggling to unwind a length of singed wiring from inside the Device and extend it toward the front seat.

"I've got the main wiring out!" Victor called from the front as another, louder "thump" sounded from outside the van.

More and more wide, brown faces were pressing themselves up against the "magic" glass barriers of the windows!

Dave saw a club swinging into his field of vision—that *shattered* the back window!

A gnarled hand reached in, got cut on jagged glass pieces, and was quickly withdrawn.

Outside, Dave heard angry grunts and shouts in an unknown language.

"Give it to me! Give it to me!" Dave urged Victor, stretching out his wire as far as he could toward the front seat.

"My end isn't bare," Victor said.

"*Gnaw* it off if you have to! *Give* it to me!"

The vehicle shuddered as big hands pushed against the sides of the van, *rocking* it back-and-forth!

Dave grabbed the now-exposed ends of the wire being pushed to him from Victor in the front seat, just barely long enough to twist-into the wire from the Device.

"Turn on the engine!" Dave shouted at Victor. "Gun the motor! Let's get all the juice we can!"

The engine caught with a loud "*rumph*"—causing the hunting party outside to jerk backward in fear, with angry shouts!

Another club smashed into a side window in the back of the van, splintering the glass but not breaking it.

"Are we having some trouble?" the cellphone suddenly and clearly asked. "I've been sleeping, I think—but I feel much better now. What's happening?"

The black eyeglasses still attached to the cellphone *glowed* as if newly activated.

"Arthur, it's *you!*" Dave exulted, clapping his hands together in relief. "Get us the hell *out* of here!"

"Where to?"

"Anywhere! Just take us..."

"*No!*" Victor shouted from the front seat, straining to project his voice forcefully enough to be heard by the "Arthur entity" through the cellphone attached to the Device. "Take us to the *United Nations general assembly room,* right on the central stage there beside the podium, in the year that we departed!"

"As you wish..." Arthur pleasantly replied.

"Wait, *wait!*" Victor yelled back yet again.

"*Duck*, Dave!" Arthur warned Dave...

—as a *hairy, muscled arm* reached through the smashed back window, groping with a dirty hand straight for Dave!

"Victor, that sounds fine! We've got to get out of here!" Dave gasped, just managing to jerk back away from the clutching hand.

"*Arthur!*" Victor persisted. "The current President of the American Physical Society was scheduled to give a summary on modes of nuclear terrorism in the General Assembly Room to all the world's nations' delegates, *the very day* you transported us here from Vermont! I know her well. I'm a President Emeritus of the Society. She'll recognize me and let me speak to the delegates!"

"Victor, *hurry* it up!" Dave gasped, as the grasping muscular hand now caught him in a tight stranglehold right around his neck.

"Arthur, can you take us there—right as she's speaking from the podium?" Victor asked.

"No problem," the disembodied voice pleasantly replied.

In a blue haze, *the van vanished*, leaving behind a very startled and puzzled group of Ice Age humans...

—one of them screaming in pain, his arm having been *sheared off* at his shoulder!

Chapter 18

FORBIDDEN KNOWLEDGE

There are things that are banned
For good reason, hidden from our sight
That to look upon would cause our hearts to burst
Our eyes to freeze in our skulls, white and dead
And even our minds to implode into dry dust
If the magnitude and depth were to be made known
We'd just give up, quit trying, and wither away
Giving up even the beauties and delights of life
Horrified at the futility and waste of it all
If indeed we were ever forced to look upon
The unshielded, naked Face of God.

The Luminary Chronicles, 18:23-28

Sally stumbled and fell flat on her face.

Groaning, she looked up to see a TV set, end table, a sofa, a kitchen table, and a worn-bare green rug.

She recognized the place. It was Jean King's home. Sally realized that she was back from her fourteen years of exile in the 12th Century.

Her dirt-encrusted shoulder bag lay off to the side. Breep was nowhere to be seen. Perhaps whatever mysterious power was guiding her journey had sent the helpful lizard back to his prehistoric home. Sally hoped he was now happily frolicking with his fellow dinosaurs.

"Home, sweet home," she whispered, letting her face "plop" back upon the rug, her muscles relaxing.

She fell into an exhausted slumber right there on the carpeted floor, not moving an inch.

Later, as morning light was coming in past the curtains nearly drawn in the front window of the living room, she stirred.

Every part of her body ached.

"Oh, I *hurt!*" she groaned. "And...I *stink.*"

Although the people in the middle ages did occasionally take baths, even the Nobility regarded baths as unhealthy. There were no deodorants. So people stank. She'd gotten used to it so much that toward the last she hadn't even noticed it any more. But now, in a dusty but clean house, she smelled herself. She was *nasty!*

She barely managed to lever her stinking, hurting body to her feet and totter weakly into Jean's bedroom. There she stripped off the burned and dirty under-tunic. Then, totally naked, she walked straight into the shower in the attached bathroom.

It was heaven.

The warm, clean shower water was like the spiritually healing waters of baptism: ushering her from filth into a pure, new life! Ah, those many years of Bible and Convent life had colored her entire perspective.

In the shower she felt spiritually transformed into a new woman.

Luxuriously, she lathered her head and body with the shampoo she found in a bottle sitting on a shower rack. It was the most delightful experience she'd ever had!

Finally, drying herself off with a large fluffy bath towel, she felt for the first time in years deliriously and deliciously *clean.*

Dropping the towel, stark naked, she walked over to a full-length mirror in Jean's bedroom and was *shocked* by what she saw.

She was, indeed, no longer the cute young girl who'd been thrown nine hundred years back in time.

Now—fourteen years later—she was a pudgy, bruised, burned, and hairless hag of a middle-aged woman.

Her bloated body was a patchwork of red and black, from the fire and beatings she'd just endured nine hundred years in the past. Her full breasts sagged, her belly pushed out, and her hips were crinkly with soft fat. Her poor tattoos looked like they'd been assaulted...wrinkled and stretched out of shape—as, indeed, they had.

"Oh, this won't do," she sighed, shaking her chubby face sadly. "Those nun habits sure did hide a myriad of ills."

It was too easy to put on fat under those concealing robes!

Plus, her freshly burned feet and legs were now growing increasingly painful, such that she could barely even walk.

"But maybe...just maybe...I've got something that can get me back on my feet," she said as she painfully limped back into the living room and lifted up her moldering shoulder bag.

She reached inside and drew out the force-field gun, laying it on the kitchen table. It had warmed up. It was recharging itself. Good!

Then she drew out the other, regular gun she'd taken so long ago from the attacker at the restaurant. Next, she felt and drew out the cellphone given to her by the CEO of Dynapharmaceuticals. Then she fished around and found two bottles of Ensure. She cracked the lid of one and smelled something very foul...hastily tossing the two plastic containers away in the trash.

But her three pill-bottles were intact. Yes, they were covered with fungus mold, but the seals hadn't been broken. She knew that they had expiration dates of one year, but that probably could be extended. However, for fourteen years? Yes, it was cool down there in the pit that Breep had dug, but were the biological agents in the pills still active after such a long time?

Before opening one, she looked around the kitchen to see if either of the two plastic baggies of pills she'd left behind was still there.

If they were, the pills would be fresh.

Only one bag was there. Apparently Dave had taken the other one for the other Sally's mother. Good! But the ones in the baggie by the refrigerator were still there and indeed looked perfectly fresh.

She grabbed one out of the baggie and with shaking hands popped it into her mouth.

She washed it down with water from the faucet splashed into a plastic glass.

In her Dimension she'd needed a booster pill each year or so—and now had missed her last fourteen years of doses. The pill would knock her for a loop, she was sure, but it was such a relief to swallow it! Yes, she could produce more-dramatic immediate results by chugging a handful of them, but that could have unpredictable long term consequences. Even one pill could restructure a whole body, just requiring a while to gradually produce its changes.

"Come on, Optimmune—give me back my *feet!*"

She felt it flooding into her blood stream, regenerating her immune system, fighting the nasty bugs and bodily ills she'd picked up in the distant past.

She had an immediate feeling of heady exhilaration. She knew it wouldn't last, probably leading to a sickening crash—but appreciated the near-term effects.

But she was still very sleepy. Groggily she stumbled back toward the bathroom, wanting only to drop onto the soft bed—still in the nude—and sleep for a million years...

"No! Time enough for that later," she forced herself to pause, turn around, and look at the landline phone.

A red light was blinking.

She pushed a "go" button and listened to several trivial and/or "spam" messages until...

"Davey, are you there?" came a sad, shaking voice. "This is Catherine. I've been trying to contact you at your house and getting no response. Where are you? I've also left you a message there as well as here. Anyway, I'm leaving this information on Mom's phone just in case you swing by. We've finally got the legal matters resolved. The district attorney agreed not to require an autopsy be done on Mom's body. He conceded that it wasn't necessary since that Linda terrorist person got killed in that big fire in Ada. Even if that terrorist did poison Mom, there's no point in doing a toxicology workup on her body since that evil lady died in the fire. They did get blood samples for toxicology, but didn't detect anything strange. So they're not fighting us that hard. Anyway, Mom gets to have her wish of not having her body disturbed at her death, but returned to nature in a 'natural' way. Her body isn't going to be embalmed or messed with at the funeral home either. The Director assured me he'd respect her wishes, just keep it refrigerated. Of course that means there will be a closed, sealed casket at the funeral. But once she's put in the casket at room temperature the natural decay will accelerate. Her body will...will... [quiet sobs]. Anyway, she'll get her wish. It's a simple pinewood casket as she wanted. Both her body and it will quickly return to the soil once they're buried in her grave... [more sobs]. Anyway, Davey, the funeral's now set for tomorrow at 1:00 at Mom's little church in Sulphur. Her minister, Cliff, is going to conduct the service for her. I hope you can make it. I know you're doing important, secret work with the Navy. Thanks for your message telling me a little about it. But I still hope you can somehow make it back for the service... I know Mom would have liked you to be there—'bye!"

Sally looked at the time signature. It was yesterday. That meant that Jean King's funeral was today!

Glancing at the clock, Sally saw that it was 10:00 in the morning. She still had three hours. She could walk there since it was only six blocks away. That is, if her feet were healed up enough by then—but they were feeling better by the minute.

Those were d*amn* fine booster pills!

And suddenly, Sally knew just what she had to do.

She walked back to the kitchen table and picked up the cellphone that the CEO Daryl Jenkins gave her for secure communications fourteen years ago in *her* time.

She plugged it into a charger in the kitchen and was astonished to see it lighting up. The lights were quite weak and flickering, but it was obviously trying to function and recharge itself.

Wow! They sure made good cellphones in this Dimension.

When it had enough charge to work properly, she would make a secret call...

Meanwhile, she went back into Jean's bedroom and looked for a wig—ah, there! That one which Jean had put on as a prank...the long-haired, bright *red* one!

Yes, that would do just fine. It was so garish that anyone she meet would only notice her hair, not that anyone would recognize her suddenly middle-aged body. However, back in the present world, she was still a hunted terrorist. She wasn't so naïve as to think the police wrote her off after the explosion in Ada. They'd think it was a clever ruse to cover her escape. So she still needed to be careful, to conceal her identify.

Now, what would she wear?

Jean had plenty of undergarments and pant suits that looked like they'd fit Sally just fine now that she was a bit "plumper."

Ah, that white one. It will symbolize purity and spirituality. Yep, an all-white pants suit.

Sally put them on, looking in the mirror at a somewhat chubbier version of her prior self, but sterner—much more dignified!

But what about her poor burned feet? They hurt less now that she'd taken her pill, but they were still painful. It would take a while for the Optimmune booster to start restructuring the dead tissue. She couldn't be stumbling and limping along...

"Ah, yes!"—she exclaimed, reaching down to the floor of the closet where a number of "old-people" shoes sat. One of the pairs was a set of white tennis shoes: soft, flexible, and wide.

"Thanks, Jean," she gave tribute to the deceased, kind old lady. "These are perfect."

But something was still missing.

"And I need some sort of coat, preferably one in which I can conceal myself," she muttered to herself, pawing through Jean's closet to the lady-style trench coats at the back.

"Yes, absolutely perfect!" Sally proclaimed in triumph, pulling out a hooded one that looked like it'd never been worn before. Again, it was pure white. It completed her outfit: a "uniform" that would do her well into the far future!

She put it on over her other clothes, raising the hood up over her red wig.

She was the spitting image of the regal statue she'd seen a thousand years in the future in that alternate timeline, including those puzzling white tennis shoes!

But something was still missing. It was the most important thing. Without it, she'd just be a peculiarly dressed middle aged woman.

She opened her eyes wide and stared solemnly and intensely forward.

Yes, she perfectly well knew how to do the "Hildegard von Bingen" STARE...

—ah, *this* was the look for her grand "debut."

Her image reflected back in the full-length mirror was *riveting!*

It was no longer the look of a young girl unconvincingly pretending to be the Founder of a great, new religion. It was the genuine look of a *High Priestess!*

Ivanna watched with fascination the planet Mars growing ever closer.

She knew that she was fifty years in the future, but it still seemed too incredible to be true.

The planet hanging in space before her was tilted, with one of the white poles aimed toward them. Also, the sun was illuminating the right half while the left half was in in darkness. There were wispy white cloud patches here and there, but most of the surface was starkly dark or bright orange-red.

"Where are we going to land on Mars?" Ivanna asked as the planet grew steadily. It quickly expanded from the size of a marble to almost filling the entire forward observation window.

Sitting slumped in a flight chair Sally seemed to have no interest at all in what was happening around her.

The poor girl's totally given up—Ivanna sadly observed.

"We'll be landing on the floor of the *Valles Marineris*," Sanako replied, standing beside Ivanna, looking out at the approaching planet. "The Valles is similar to the Grand Canyon on Earth, but much larger and deeper, and…"

"I know all that," Ivanna stopped her. She'd studied Mars in consultations she'd done for NASA regarding possible future colonization efforts. Her academic contribution to NASA was in how societies might develop on a planet separate from Earth. Possible sites for such a Mars colony included both the deep floor and the high cliffs of *Valles Marineris*.

"We're decelerating. In a minute we'll descend through the thin atmosphere."

"The atmosphere is still intact?" Ivanna squinted, noticing a light haze brushing past the outside of the craft as they dropped toward the long furrow sliced into the surface of the planet. "The solar superstorm hasn't hit here yet?"

"That's correct, Dr. Petrovich," the oriental woman politely answered. "It will be approximately one hour before the first wave hits Mars. Hopefully we'll be gone by then, headed back to your Earth, to your *time*."

Sally groaned from her seat, shutting her eyes tightly. Obviously she didn't want to hear anything more about "other" Earths and "other" timelines.

"Can't you just take me back right now," Sally complained, "—or send me back—or whatever? You and Ivanna can do whatever you want. I just want to get back to my life and..."

"Working at a restaurant for tips?" Sanako coldly replied. "After what you've seen and done, is being a waitress really what you want for the rest of your life?"

"I was resigned to die," Sally whispered from her seat. "Now, I'm...*drained!* I don't care about this stuff. If what you say is true, we're all doomed anyway. So why not just go back to our lives and enjoy whatever time we've got left?"

Sanako walked the few steps to Sally and *slapped* her hard in her face!

Startled, Sally's green eyes snapped open. She glowered at Sanako, holding her hand to her reddened cheek.

"You just want to give up?" Sanako snidely asked the girl. "You're certainly not the Sally I expected. You're just a whimpering child. The Sally that trained me had *steel* inside of her! But do not worry, little girl—as soon as our visit here is complete, you can go back to your comfortable 'life' fifty years in the past."

"Aren't you being just a bit hard on...?" Ivanna tried to interject.

But Sanako cut her off with a dismissive wave, turning to the crew seated at the main control console. She monitored the forward viewscreen as their craft descended into the huge trench cut into the surface of the red planet.

Ivanna sat next to Sally. She gently took her trembling hand. Ivanna noticed that the peculiar Turtle Tattoo on Sally's wrist seemed to be *glowing*.

"This is just as incredible to me as it is to you," she comforted the now-sobbing girl. "Just hang in there and we'll be back to our lives as soon as possible."

Sally nodded, peevishly pulling her hand away, and hanging her head back down.

Ivanna looked out the viewscreen-window, marveling how it seemed to switch from a computer display to an actual transparent surface. She was startled to see that they were already landing. The craft moved so smoothly it was hard to know if they were speeding up or slowing down.

Red dust swirled around the craft as they touched gently down upon the surface of Mars.

They were right next to a cliff that towered above their heads into the butterscotch-colored sky. Sunlight brightly illuminated the top of the cliff and another one far off in the distance on the other side of the flat plain. Their craft sat in icy-looking darkness between the two high cliffs.

"They've extended a conduit so we can go into their caverns," Sanako crisply stated. "Come with me."

Ivanna took Sally gently by her hand and followed the black-clad, long-haired oriental woman through a portal in the craft into a plastic tunnel.

Immediately, Ivanna felt light as a feather.

Yes, it's only one-third the gravity of Earth—she thought to herself, amazed. It was irrefutable proof that she was actually walking on the surface of another planet! *And there's yet another proof this isn't some feverish nightmare. They have artificial gravity in their ship. I know enough science that manipulating gravity isn't possible in my time. I'm definitely walking away from a future time-machine!*

From the plastic tunnel they walked "bouncily" into a sealed chamber within the cliff. There Ivanna saw a hovering, flat transportation platform. But it wasn't a typical hovercraft kept aloft by propellers. No, this platform just hung there in the air. Clearly, this was yet another example of harnessed artificial gravity.

Around the hovercraft women in white uniforms awaited the visitors. They all wore identical white pant suits. On their feet were comfortable-looking white tennis shoes. Over their clothes they each wore light, white trench coats with hoods pushed back off their heads. Although the temperature was not uncomfortable, it was cool—for which they looked appropriately dressed.

And each of the uniformed women wore a holster at their waist containing a heavy, black pistol.

Ivanna noted that all the women had thick, long red hair—from the youngest to the oldest. In fact, it seemed a part of their overall uniform: dyed-red hair. Sanako nodded to them in deference, obviously wary of their weapons.

"All these women are Priestesses of the *Church of Perpetual Health*," Sanako explained. "They've taken a vow of silence for the final 'Time of Rapprochement,' as they call it. If the colony survives the next few days' events, they'll speak again. Otherwise, they've spoken their last. It is very kind of them to allow us to visit at this holiest of their times. To them this is the same as the 'Rapture' of Christian theology. Other than us, visitation from Earth has been terminated."

Ivanna also nodded politely to them, allowing them to guide her and Sally onto the glistening-black hovercraft. Then, the Priestesses all stepped back.

"Aren't you...?" Ivanna said, turning to see Sanako departing back to her spaceship as the Priestesses silently turned their backs and walked away into adjoining alcoves.

"Your friend will pick you up when you are finished," a boyish voice exclaimed from down around Ivanna's legs.

Looking down, Ivanna was startled to see a *young child* grinning up at her.

It was a little boy that could not have been more than five years old. He wore a cute little red jumpsuit. On his feet were stubby blue shoes. He had beneath the straps of his jumpsuit a short-sleeved blue shirt. His cherub-like face was topped with a mop of blond curls. And he had bright blue eyes.

He was adorable!

"My name is Tommy," he happily chirped up at Ivanna. "You can ask me anything. I'm really smart."

"Oh, I can see that you are indeed very smart!" Ivanna smiled back at him. "It's really nice of you to guide us. Is it far? I get tired when I have to stand up for too long."

"Oh?" he said, apparently startled that people preferred not to stand up for extended periods. "Then sit down."

"But there's no..."

From the floor of the hovercraft soft plastic chairs emerged behind both Ivanna and Sally. Gratefully, the two women sank down into them.

The platform floated out into a tunnel. There it picked up speed, sweeping into darkness that was lit only by occasional flashing red lights set high on the sides of the tunnel.

"Have you lived here long, Tommy?" Ivanna asked.

"I don't know. What is 'long'?"

Ivanna wasn't sure if the boy had heard her question correctly. She looked right into his big blue eyes as he stood grinning in front of her swaying chair. Obviously he'd taken this transportation many times before, as sure-footed as a goat on a high mountain slope. Ivanna was both terrified and in awe as they zipped downward into the subterranean depths of Mars. Tommy seemed unconcerned about the motion despite there being no railings along the edges of the hurtling flat platform.

Ivanna had no love for roller-coasters.

"How old are you?" Ivanna said, trying to divert herself from the rapid descent by engaging with their guide.

"You mean since I was first aware?"

"Uhm...yes—I guess that's a definition of age?" Ivanna replied, puzzled.

The red lights in the dark tunnel were now zipping past too fast to differentiate them. But in the darkness Ivanna could now see a faint blue oblong sphere around the craft, protecting the occupants as it dipped even more at a downward angle. *It must be similar to what protected the spaceship that brought us here*—Ivanna thought with relief. She'd been terrified of being thrown out of the hovercraft. *But how deep are we going? By now we must be far beneath the surface!*

"Do you mean how many times around the sun I've gone?" the boy further clarified Ivanna's question.

"Yes..."

"In Mars years or in Earth years?"

"Well, I guess Earth years would make the most sense to me."

"Then I first became aware forty-eight years ago."

"*You* are forty-eight years old?" Ivanna gasped in disbelief. "But you're so young. You don't look more than five years old."

He giggled shyly, hiding his snicker behind a small hand.

The little boy stepped over beside Sally and took hold of her dangling hand.

She jerked upright in her chair where she'd been slumped-over.

"Huh?" she said, yanking her hand away.

"And *she's* my Mommy," the little boy concluded, pointing straight at Sally.

"What?" Sally snorted, shaking her head in denial and confusion.

They were slowing.

How could Sally be the mother of this child?

Suddenly the hovercraft burst into a wide cavern. Ivanna blinked rapidly, her eyes adapting to the light flooding from an *artificial sun* glaring down from the high ceiling. And the gigantic cavern was totally empty...

—except for a single towering structure in its middle: a *red Obelisk!*

The floor of the cavern looked to Ivanna to be made out of once-molten, blue glass. It was perfectly flat. The ceiling was too high to make out clearly, shrouded by a misty fog. The central Obelisk was also apparently constructed from a molten glass-like substance. And high up on its top sat one single person, regally positioned on a white throne—fully one hundred feet above the cavern floor!

The woman casually held a black pistol in her lap.

As the hovercraft came to a stop before the Obelisk, the white-robed figure upon the elevated throne greeted them in an amplified, husky, deep voice...

"I'm so glad Sanako could bring you to me. Normally this place is filled with supplicants and pilgrims. This is my 'audience chamber.' Now, though, at the End of Time, it is appropriately empty. It is pleasant to have this final time of solitude. But there are critical matters we must discuss... Please come up to me, Dr. Petrovich!"

Ivanna stepped off the floating platform as the "little boy" reached up to grab her hand. Tommy solicitously guided her across the glistening, slick floor to an elevator attached to the side of the red Obelisk.

Sally, though, continued to sit peevishly on the black chair on the transport vehicle which continued to hover silently a few inches off the floor. Sally was there, right in front of the magnificent throne, but didn't even look up. She just shook her red-brown hair back and forth, the picture of dejection and gloom.

Ivanna rode the elevator up to the top of the imperial Obelisk where the white-robed woman sat serenely on her central white throne. The woman had a white hood pulled over her head. She waved the gun menacingly at Ivanna, regally indicating for her to come and sit in a smaller seat beside the throne-proper.

The top of the Obelisk, though flat, wasn't large. Ivanna was afraid she might slip and fall off. But the surface was roughened, her feet finding good purchase.

Hesitantly, Ivanna sat down next to the imperial woman, looking out over the huge, empty expanse. Doubtless when filled with thousands of people it was an impressive space. Now, it just looked incredibly lonely.

Everything was silent except for the sound of the boy a hundred feet below skipping happily in circles around the hovercraft.

"Who is that little boy?" Ivanna finally asked, breaking the silence.

The woman laughed. "That's not a boy, that's a computer program," she replied.

"A...what? A computer program?" Ivanna frowned, not understanding.

"Oh, it's actually a robot constructed to look like a child," the woman sighed. "And its brain is *not* a binary computer program as you understand such. You see, my Priestesses take a vow of chastity—so we have no births here. To give us more diversity, I decided to install evolved artificial intelligences into these child-like androids. If you stayed here for a while, you'd see many others of our cute little 'Tommy' children. They *are* alive, of course—just differently from you and me. They each are self-aware, have distinct personalities, and accomplish various functions."

Ivanna was dumfounded for a moment until she reminded herself, yet again, that she was fifty years in the future. Clearly, many scientific advances had occurred.

"And just who are *you?*" Ivanna asked, trying to sound as polite as possible in the bizarre circumstances.

The woman chuckled, looking at Ivanna slyly from beneath her white hood.

She lowered the black gun into her lap as if trying to reduce the threat level to Ivanna.

"You were very kind to me once," she softly replied. "You baked some *mean* brownies."

Ivanna frowned, trying to remember seeing this person before, but failing.

"I'm sorry—I don't recognize you. Should I?"

The woman pushed back the white hood.

Beneath the hood, she had long, fluffed-out, garishly red hair. Her eyes were a deep green. The flesh of her face was taut and firm. But fine wrinkles at the corners of her mouth and eyes betrayed advanced age.

"We met in a prior life," the woman cryptically stated, smiling ruefully. "But that's gone, vanished—except in my memory, that is..."

Her voice trailed off uncertainly.

Ivanna paused to consider the woman's confusing words, contemplating the extraordinary situation she found herself in: sitting in a vast, empty cavern deep beneath the surface of the planet Mars—high upon an imperial Obelisk in front of *zero* adoring subjects?

"In a prior life, you say?"

"The last cycle..."

"I...don't understand?"

The woman sighed, turning to Ivanna and taking the Professor's liver-spotted hand in her own, smoother one: "I'm *Sally*—just a *prior* Sally, originating from another Dimension, who in terms of elapsed personal age is now your contemporary. Got it?"

"What?"

"Yes, it's a lot to take in all at once, I understand."

"But, you're middle-aged and...?"

"Thanks for the compliment. I get that all the time. And just how old are you, Ivanna?" Sally continued. "You look much younger than your chronological age. You look to be in your fifties but I suppose you are in your eighties? When I was the age of the Sally sulking down below—in my early twenties—I was thrown back in time to live in the 12th Century for fourteen years. Then I escaped back to your time and started my Church. Add on another fifty years and now I'm eighty-seven years old! I did receive immune-balancing at birth and periodic boosters, which keep me looking young and active. But my mind is slowing down. Plus I'm perpetually tired. I'm sure you know what I mean. Looking and being young are two different things. But I've learned a lot in my long lifetime, Ivanna. And yet I'm more confused now than ever. Since we met so long ago, I've studied your life extensively, particularly admiring your mastery of societal science—group psychology, sociology, politics, religion and the like. So now that you are at a key 'tipping-point' to *change history*, I want your advice. Indeed, I *require* it!"

She lifted up the gun and pointed it straight at Ivanna's head.

"What, are you going to shoot me?" the elderly Professor gasped, cringing back.

"If I have to," the High Priestess sadly replied. "It seems I've grown rather ruthless in my old age."

"There's no need for that," Ivanna insisted, holding her hands up protectively. "Your threats are counterproductive. I'm happy to help out however I'm able!"

The High Priestess lowered the gun back to her lap.

"Don't panic, I'm joking."

"What?"

"You're just as feisty as ever, Professor Petrovich," the woman grinned. "I'm so glad you are here with me! So what do think so far?"

Ivanna sat silent for a moment, trying to get her breath back enough to digest the amazing claims made by this *second* "Sally."

Then she carefully replied...

"What you've said—well, it's a lot for me to take in all at once...but since I've been captured in a spaceship and sent into the future to travel in just a few minutes from Earth to Mars...I suppose I might as well keep an open mind."

The middle-aged Sally leaned over and patted Ivanna's weathered hand affectionately. Then she settled back into her throne seat.

"So you'll help me willingly?" Sally said. "I don't have to threaten your loved ones?"

"How can you...?"

"Just joking! So do I have your full cooperation?"

"If...if I can," Ivanna nodded her head. "There's no need for bad jokes or threats. But surely my advice isn't very..."

"—it's critical!" Sally snapped, now sounding dead-serious. Then, more softly, she continued... "I'm sorry. I grow impatient at times.

Being an Absolute Ruler makes a person grouchy! Anyway let me tell you what I was trying to do, Ivanna, about..."

"I understand some of it already, I think," Ivanna broke in, eager to hurry things along. She knew that time was swiftly ticking onward. If what Sanako told her was true, less than an hour remained until Mars would be engulfed in a massive solar flare. "According to what Sanako told and showed to me, God is judging mankind because of the invention that Dave, my husband, and *my* Sally put together..."

"—with the help of the Facilitator Faction that *wants* God's full attention to come crashing down upon us," Sally interrupted Ivanna. "They unerringly trust God to do the 'right' thing even if that means the destruction of our linked worlds. It's the *worst* type of religion, *blind* Faith: for which they've literally given up their own eyes!" Sally snarled at Ivanna, exhibiting a fierce hatred for the so-called "Facilitators."

"Uhm, ok," Ivanna continued, yet more confused by this new information... "And you say the thing that's brought us to God's full attention," she thoughtfully reiterated, "is the overuse of something called 'Dark Energy' that connects everything together—even across time, apparently."

Down below, the "young" Sally was now snoring lightly in her chair, having fallen asleep. Her fitful "snuffles" echoed pitifully in the vast cavern.

Ivanna also saw below that the Tommy-robot had tired of his skipping and now was lying flat on his little back on the glassy floor, staring up at the high ceiling of the cavern.

"You are correct again," the High Priestess encouraged Ivanna. "But what you don't know is that the whole problem occurs because of what *you* people on Earth do here in *your* Dimension! In my parallel Dimension this problem didn't and doesn't exist. And yet because of it—along with the other close Dimensions where nonhuman intelligence evolved instead of humans—we are *all* going to be destroyed! The different Dimensions and timelines of Earth are tightly woven together in the Cosmic scheme of things. Are you following me, Professor Petrovich?" she sharply enquired.

Ivanna squinted hard, trying to get Sally's wild story into her skull.

"So you're telling me that the...*problem*...is right here in *this* 'Dimension' on Earth—and it's due to some difference between us and your parallel Dimension?"

"*Exactly!*" Sally assertively nodded. "And I—in my astute stupidity—thought it was Religion itself! In the nonhuman Dimensions, religion is different from what humans developed. And in *my* Dimension, religion is ruthlessly suppressed or highly constrained by conflicting authoritative Empires. But in *your* Dimension where 'democratic' governments allow considerable self-expression, all kinds of different religions flourish."

"I'm—not sure that logic holds," Ivanna thoughtfully considered, "But assuming it is true, then what is it that you were attempting to accomplish in the last fifty years with your new religion?"

Sally sighed deeply, laying the gun on the floor at her feet before reaching up and grasping her flowing red hair with both hands in apparent frustration.

"I *tried* to counterbalance 'traditional' religions with a new, science-based one," she grated through clenched teeth. "I established '*The Church of Perpetual Health*' based on a revolutionary medication that I brought with me from my own Dimension. I thought that if I could bring authoritative control in a benevolent way then I could skew the societies of the world enough to either prevent overuse of Dark Energy—or tamp-down the evils of humanity enough to allow us to pass Godly Judgment."

Ivanna gasped in amazement.

"Sally—that's a *gigantic* goal! Few in history have ever been able to sway the entire behavior of the world. To even consider such a thing you'd have to..."

"—have a *colossal ego* the size of the solar system! Yes, I know," Sally admitted, looking ruefully at Ivanna.

"And...what happened?" Ivanna asked, fascinated.

"I succeeded!" Sally bitterly laughed.

"*Really?*"

"Well...yes and no," Sally grimly replied, her voice fading to just a whisper. "I was able to mobilize billions of dollars to jump-start my Church—derived from my medication and a new power source different from tapping into Dark Energy. I decided to limit the leadership to women—only allowing men to serve in secondary roles—to rid my new movement of male-dominance testosterone-driven problems. That was fine. People flocked to the Church to get real health miracles plus abundant cheap energy. And to keep that good health and prosperity in place, they were willing to adopt strict behavioral and cultural restrictions. The traditional religions shrank while my new religion grew by leaps and bounds. You see, I didn't just promise miracles, Ivanna, I delivered them! And even though Dave and Victor's Device was accepted and adopted by the scientific and commercial realms, it was never widely utilized. My own clean power source was much easier to use, more predictable, and much cheaper."

"So...your effort to change history worked?" Ivanna marveled.

Sally slowly got up from the throne, looked up at the misty high ceiling way above in the cavern, and *screamed* out into the cavern, her voice echoing perversely back: "*No! It didn't work! After all that effort and success, my major goals were worse, not better! Instead of pushing off Judgment Day into the far future it relentlessly advanced toward us until it's now on top of us! And instead of passing God's 'species judgment', we continued to repeatedly fail! Why? Judgment Day should have retreated into the far distant future. And once it did finally arrive, we should have passed the test. I did everything right but I still failed! Why? Why? Why?*"

Suddenly the middle-aged Sally ripped a *big red wig* off her bald head and *flung* it off of the high throne into the empty cavern!

"My making myself into the 'High Priestess' of your world was worse than *useless!*"

The wig fluttered down to land on top of Tommy, who jumped up and staggered around beneath it until he tossed it convulsively off to the side.

Then he picked it up and started playing with it as if it were a fluffy doll.

The bald-headed Sally now stood up, fully revealed as a white-robed *demon*—with a puffed-up red face and scalp, twisted lips, flared nostrils, wild eyes, and fists thrust defiantly above her head!

Involuntarily, Ivanna shrank back in her chair and looked for a route of escape, if necessary.

But there was none.

Perhaps she could try to grab the black gun still lying on the top of the Obelisk beside the throne...but she'd have to be very fast, indeed!

Sally, meanwhile, seemed poised to fall or jump off the high surface in her rage—but then staggered back to her throne and weakly collapsed into it.

She reached down and lifted up the black gun, cradling it tenderly while cutting off Ivanna's possible attack.

In a dejected whisper, Sally said: "So I ask you, Professor Petrovich, to please help me understand *why* I failed. You know how societies work. You understand the dynamics of societies across history. You even consulted for NASA on new societal frameworks never before seen in the history of mankind. True, you don't know of my Dimension—but you do understand the distinguishing characteristics separating authoritative versus democratic regimes."

"I do have a good overview of societal dynamics across and throughout history that..."

"True, there are terrible consequences to my Dimension being controlled by brutal dictatorships and Empires—such as suppression of individual freedom," Sally continued from the throne, ignoring Ivanna's attempted response, "but at least we could control the use of Dark Energy enough to hide from God! I achieved similar control here through my new religion. So *why did I fail?*" she yelled out as loudly as she was able.

Ivanna cringed back. This woman wasn't just a twisted future version of the sullen Sally below, but insane!

"Well, I suppose..." Ivanna began...

"I've got my own ideas," Sally again cut her off. "But I desperately need you to *validate* my conclusion!"

The green-eyed "demon" sat there staring at Ivanna.

"*Well?*"

Ah, ok. Now she wanted a response.

"But," Ivanna said, trying both to comfort the woman while struggling to understand the dynamics of the problem, "did you *really* fail? What about those people who operate 'out of time', the Facilitators, you said? Also, there's Sanako and her troupe who brought me here. What about them? Are they somehow interfering with the dynamics you attempted?"

"Oh, yes—what about *them?*" Sally seethed, standing up again and stalking back and forth along the top of the elevated Obelisk, waving the black gun spasmodically up in the air.   She was a prowling Demon, for sure.

"What is their role in this?" Ivanna insisted, thinking that she was onto something.

"They claim that in an alternate future I trained them and sent them on their missions. They work against each other. But they don't obey me. They do their 'own thing', answering to a higher 'power' that no longer exists!"

"You trained them?"

"Not me, Ivanna—listen to what I say! *Another* 'me'—in the future, in another timeline, produced those rogue time-travelers!"

"*Other* timeline...?"

"As I indicated to you already, Professor," Sally snidely stated, "—this is my *second* time around! And I have no idea how many cycles have *already* been attempted, erased, and forgotten! Accessing concentrated Dark Energy gave us the ability to try to undo our own Fate. It's a *cruel joke* that the Creator has played on us. Our Cosmic Struggle must *amuse* the Creator—as we continually fight to undo our Fate, time after time after time!"

"You think God jokes with us?"

"Come on, Ivanna. Take a realistic look at the human species. Tell me we're not living cartoons!"

Wow. That was a really perverted view of humanity and God. Sally wasn't thinking straight at all. Was she suffering from a brain disease? Was she truly mentally ill?

But she was expecting a response.

"So you say that we're in some sort of 'time-loop'?"

"Who knows?" Sally laughed wildly while clutching the gun tightly. "Time seems capable of flowing forward, backward, sidewise, or up-and-down. It's *crazy!*"

Ivanna was now convinced that this older Sally had just accurately described her *own* condition: that over years of being an isolated religious Icon she'd finally gone stark, raving, mad!

"So...you're telling me that *anything* is possible?"

"Anything and everything, yes!" Sally groaned, sitting back down, again placing the gun at her feet before clutching her sides as if in great pain. "Even great religions can be erased in one Dimension while flourishing in another! So there's precedence to my 'madness.' Hah! I know what you're thinking about me, Professor. And I assure you that I am *not* crazy. Indeed, at this moment, I may be the sanest member of the whole human race—notwithstanding its rapid recent decrease in numbers."

"I'm...not...a religious scholar," Ivanna protested.

"I didn't say you were!" Sally snapped.

"—but, I think maybe you *are* onto something profound that's..."

"Do you *think*?" Sally laughed, interrupting Ivanna. She grinned so widely that she looked to Ivanna like a hairless, pale-skinned Halloween jack-o-lantern. "I've wrestled with this for the last fifty years—trying to think of something to do to change our fate. But the more I imposed new sanctions and tighter controls the worse everything got. Sanako kept appearing with dire reports of the Day of Judgment moving ever closer. And now it's right upon us, *only a few minutes away!*"

"So there's no hope?"

"I brought you here—to *send you back!*"

"You mean back to my own time, fifty years in the past from this present moment?"

"Exactly!"

"But to do what?"

"To *undo* my major mistake of the last cycle!"

"And that was...?"

"Instead of killing Dave I *saved* him—because I...I had a deep affection for him," she angrily growled. "No, I won't call it stupid, juvenile 'love.' It was far deeper than that! Sanako wanted me to blow his stupid head off rather than let him announce his new invention to the world at the United Nations—while she was to simultaneously incinerate the van carrying the prototype. Instead, I allowed *other* forces to move me to a third option—which has now failed miserably!"

Ivanna slowly stood up, starting to understand.

"So you want me to pick up where my Sally down below failed—is that it?" she said as she paced a few steps away on the high dais.

"Somehow Victor and Dave survived the explosion at the creek in Vermont and will reappear? And then you want me to stop them at the United Nations? But how can you expect me to do that? I feel for my Victor the same thing you claim you felt for David. I could never, even if the fate of the entire world hung in the balance, to..."

"*No! No! No!*" Sally vehemently protested. "You don't understand. I *succeeded* in suppressing their invention! It didn't matter that they made their 'big announcement' at the United Nations. My clean, easy, energy-gathering mechanism suppressed widespread usage of their dangerous, speculative Dark Energy Device. But enough knowledge and usage still got out through the barriers I'd put up— your society was still permissive enough to allow individual experimentation—that God's attention was still attracted. And then as a scrutinized intelligent species we failed His Judgment, yet again!"

"So, what do you want for me to...?" Ivanna began, very confused.

"*That's why I came to Mars!*" Sally *screamed* into the vast cavern in a very deranged and scary manner. "*I came to Mars with unlimited billions of dollars to establish a colony that could hide from God— keep the human race intact and rolling onward even when the Earth was wiped out! But God followed me here, Ivanna!*"

Ivanna was now more scared than she'd ever been before. The middle-aged Sally was not just crazy, she was a *religious fanatic*. Supposedly the "Church of Perpetual Health" was a practical, science-based religion. But thus far, Ivanna had heard a compelling story about Judgment Day, based in a strong belief in a traditional God. Sally's charade was revealed for what it was: a false-front to traditional religion.

Perhaps she could cast some doubt on Sally's theory, make her reconsider her extreme plans.

"Sally, what if you're wrong?"

"What?"

"Other than seeing Earth destroyed by a solar flare, there's no convincing proof that God is behind any of this!"

"You're saying...?"

"It all could merely be an unlikely but actual natural phenomenon," Ivanna insisted, sensing she had an opening to bring Sally down from her agitated mental state. "And for the catastrophic doomsday to move in different timelines might only mean that the underlying nuclear dynamics in the interior of the sun were unstable, occurring at different points like the roll of cosmic dice on a tilting table. The entire extinction event might have no causal relation at all to what the human race did, or did not do, related to tapping into subspace's Dark Energy."

"So it's just a coincidence that Earth's and Mar's demise aligns with mankind's own destruction of the natural ecosystem?"

"It could be," Ivanna continued to press her advantage. "Or—another likely explanation—is that the widespread tapping into Dark Energy did something to subspace that affected the sun's nuclear dynamics, again no "God's Judgment of Mankind" required."

Sally sighed deeply.

"I wish that were true," Sally seemingly sincerely stated. "But I'm absolutely convinced that the human race is in the cross-hairs of God's execution gun! And the only hope we have is to *fight back in kind!*"

Ivanna knew she must now be both a supreme psychologist as well as sociologist.

Sally's face reddened as she continued her rant.

"Sanako reports that in the near future the Marian ice caps and subsurface ice will be gone, our final water sources evaporated into space! The surface of Mars will be melted into slag! Our native minerals supply will be inaccessible! And our hidden contingent here below the surface..." her agonized screaming trailed off.

She moaned, tears now streaming down both her cheeks.

"Where I thought we might escape—it seems I've only constructed an elaborate tomb. Without some drastic change to the timeline, I've only assured that my thousands of devotees here will all *slowly* die an *agonizing*, lingering, painful death. All of us doomed with absolutely no resupply possible from a burnt-off Earth. That's even assuming any humans survive the final, crushing blow! So it was all for nothing...all for nothing..."

She buried her head in her hands.

Putting on her amateur psychologist cap, it seemed to Ivanna this "Sally" was headed for an irrevocable conclusion: *suicide!*

Apparently she just wanted a friend here with her at the end—when she pointed her black gun at her own head and *blew her brains out!*

"There must be something we can do short of killing our dearest friends or ourselves," Ivanna soothed the sobbing woman.

Though outwardly in rigid control, inwardly Ivanna was shocked beyond imagination. Even though coming from twisted logic, what if Sally's conclusion was right? Looking out over the vast, empty cavern Ivanna recognized a vast futility. If the solar ejectus was just minutes away, why wait to be burned to death?

It was tempting.

Maybe they *should* both just embrace the black gun?

Ivanna felt adrift on a stormy sea, with no land in sight. Used to being in highly structured, known environments she was, for the first time in her life, with no ready answers.

It was terrifying.

"Well...maybe there's *one* thing," Sally gasped from the throne chair, wiping away tears.

"What?"

Sally looked up at the high ceiling for a minute, her eyes stretched wide, as if she was seeing through to the surface of Mars and beyond...

"Like I said before, we must fight God on his own turf, Ivanna. I've concluded I must go back in time...once more—to *stop Jesus!*"

Ivanna, thinking she could not be shocked any further than she'd already been—was stunned.

"Just what are you saying?"

Tears gone—her green eyes now as cunning and deadly as a hunting cat's—Sally conspiratorially leaned in toward Ivanna...

"I see now that in my Dimension the rise and continuance of world-wide Empires was due to one, single factor. I know this because of the deep study I did in the 12th Century under a devout Mentor, Hildegard von Bingen. She convinced me that even in the most horrible suppressive conditions there was still hope for individual expression—which, however, was effectively stifled in my own Dimension."

"You say you studied the Bible in the 12th Century? And *your* Dimension 'stifled' Jesus?" Ivanna asked, bewildered by Ivanna's story's wild swing plus new line of logic.

Yes, even more evidence supporting a deep mental instability: delusions of grandeur, paranoid delusions, wild emotional swings...

"It's what I must achieve! In *your* Dimension if you *also* get to experience the *absence* of this Jesus—then maybe all our timelines and Dimensions can continue for a while, giving us *Homo sapiens* time to mature as a race."

Ivanna was convinced now that Sally was dangerously unstable.

"You *can't* seriously be suggesting that...?"

"*I'm saying that in my world Jesus either never existed or never made it into history as a religious figure!*" Sally shouted into the empty cavern.

"But, even so, how could that...?"

"Your Jesus in your Dimension brought something that no other religious Founder has made fully manifest, instilled into many of his followers."

"And just what is that?"

"A *true* empathy with people *different* from yourself—yes, something you could call an unselfish, pure 'love'!"

"But other religious leaders have..."

"—not to the extent that this 'Jesus the Nazarene' did!" Sally continued. Her eyes were stretched wide and wild. "What other religious Founders may have hinted at or just preached, this Jesus actually demonstrated. What He did was so compelling that whenever injustice, intolerance, and hate existed—*people were forced to reevaluate their positions!*" she again shouted at the top of her voice into the empty cavern. "*The whole fabric of society across the world was molded and changed! In your Dimension for the last two thousand years there was always a brake on authoritative regimes. There was always aspiration to be and do better—which extended out into all areas of society, percolating even into scientific experimentation and personal freedom!*"

"You want to *stop* that?" Ivanna gasped, horrified!

"You still don't understand, Ivanna. Over the last fifty years I've concluded that your Jesus *was* and *is* the main determining difference between your Dimension and mine—with the unanticipated side effect to allow none or incomplete control of mechanisms accessing Dark Energy...such that God notices and destroys us!"

"That is unthinkably perverse! You can't make logic-jumps so extreme," Ivanna gasped, horrified. "If true, though, you're suggesting that...?"

"Yes, Professor—to save humanity, *your Jesus must be stopped!* And I'm just the girl to do it."

She picked up the black gun and held it tightly against her breast.

"No! Even if that were somehow possible—please reconsider!" Ivanna begged her.

"I'd hoped to get your blessing," Sally calmly continued, now standing up and reaching out a hand in supplication. "I'm not as crazy as you think I am. I know I need an outside perspective. I've gone too long as an absolute dictator. And for something as drastic as this, I need expert input."

"But..."

"Don't you see what I'm saying, Ivanna? You are an expert student of sociological history, on how societies form, function, and evolve. I know what I'm suggesting is monstrous. I know it's a terrible thing! This Jesus—as described in the Gospels in the New Testament writings—was a wonderful, magnificent figure. For 24 hours every day I studied and lived His Teachings for fourteen straight years in the 12th Century. You can believe or don't believe I did this. But consider that you're now far in your future, on Mars!"

Yes, the wild-eyed Priestess had a point.

"And I saw many people misuse, misapply, abuse, and pervert His teachings," Sally continued. "But far more were inspired, empowered, and focused in highly commendable ways. I know it's awful what I'm proposing to do. But I see no other alternative. *Stopping* Jesus is the only way to save mankind! I'm convinced of this. And if *you* sanction my new mission, it will mean so much to me. It will give me the strength to do what must be done! Don't let your emotions rule, Ivanna. Think about it clinically. Compare societies and tell me I'm right!"

Ivanna closed her eyes tightly, trying to gain control of a swirl of powerful emotions coursing through her veins and mind.

Then she opened her eyes and carefully spoke in measured tones to the extremely conflicted woman beside her.

"Sally," Ivanna firmly stated, ignoring the pleading of the High Priestess and the threat of the gun in her hand, "I'd have to study the different realities which you say exist. There's no way I could make a snap judgment based only on what you've claimed. But just off the top of my head, I really think you've come to a *bad* decision! You are grossly overestimating the effect of Jesus on my world. After all, you say we are apparently *still* condemned in the sight of God *despite* Jesus' efforts! And if I remember my Bible correctly, even Jesus himself predicted that the world would end in Fire at his 'second coming.' That sounds ominously like what we're now observing with our own eyes."

"Yes! That's exactly right!" Sally eagerly said, now pacing back and forth excitedly. "He knew! Somehow he knew what his fame would mean to your Dimension. He was complicit! He *wanted* your world to be judged by God. He knew *exactly* what he was doing. He was *trying* to destroy the linked timelines—all to his own glory! He was just like all the other religious fanatics throughout time, willing to kill everyone else just to make his own self famous."

"Oh...Sally," Ivanna gasped, shaking her head in firm denial. "That's ridiculous. Honestly, I think you've gone off the deep end."

"Maybe so," the High Priestess agreed. "But I don't see any other option. Despite my present 'High Priestess' appearance, Professor, I'm not a religious person. I've always been a *practical* person. Maybe that's why I've been put in this role as humanity's last hope to thwart Fate. Even in my own Dimension I sought answers for the deeper features of Reality. I sought that by secretly attending small gatherings of Animists. They sensed underlying spiritual linkages between everything. I now realize that the Animists perceived Dark Energy—and whatever else makes up our true reality— beneath what's visible. It's a rational conclusion. So if I am a true 'High Priestess' of anything—it's of the *Unknown!*"

"But Sally," Ivanna protested. "That realization—that we don't and maybe can't know everything—should *humble* us, not cause us to think we can change the world. This...time travel...is obviously dangerous! What if your attempt to stop Jesus makes things *worse*, not better?"

"How could it be any worse? In a few minutes from now the remnants of humanity will begin their final death-spiral!" Sally again shouted into the vast cavern. *"And I am not humbled! I am not just a mere little girl to be pushed aside and dismissed! I am a PER-SON who can make a difference!"* she roared.

Below, Ivanna heard the other Sally stir in her slumber—snorting—apparently disturbed by the loud noise of her older self's shouting.

"Yes, that's true," Ivanna tried to reason with the seemingly mad-woman in front of her. "But still, Sally, societies cannot be manipulated without great uncertainty and danger."

"Do you know where this Obelisk came from?" Sally fiendishly grinned at Ivanna, looking more and more like a demon from hell.

"I...don't know," Ivanna gulped, now looking away, examining the red "glass" at her feet.

"I didn't build it!" Sally shouted again, while cradling the black gun in her hands, looking about furtively.

"Then, where...?"

"We found it here in this cavern!" Sally said, suddenly looking like a little girl caught in the act of stealing something. "It has *roots* reaching deep into the interior of the planet—which drew energy from the planet's core! Since Mars cooled in the distant past, though, the roots have little energy to draw upon. But we've managed to open a storage compartment on its side and build into it a Dark Energy generator. The Obelisk, for the first time in millennia, is *self-contained!*"

"Sally, are you saying this structure is something left by other interstellar travelers?" Ivanna gasped, astounded at the implications.

"Oh no...no, no, no...we think not," Sally said. "We believe it was built by Martians...ancient Martians...perhaps evolved here on Mars—or who came as interstellar settlers...who the hell knows? It doesn't matter!"

"What?"

"We've yet to find any other artifacts left behind, or even fossil-ized bones," Sally said. "But my scientists think that there must be remains of their civilization other than this structure. If we just had more time to do extensive excavations..."

She paused, her mouth hanging open as if she were having a stroke.

"Wait...I remember back at the movie theater...a movie I saw then forgot over the years..."

She smiled.

"Ah, yes..."

"Sally, what *is* this Obelisk?" Ivanna snapped at her, trying to get her to focus on the immediate crisis. "I take it this hundred-foot-tall Pillar is not just a structure for elevating your Throne?"

Sally blinked, shaking her head, apparently trying to clear her thoughts.

"It's a *transportation* device...we think...perhaps how the Martians escaped this planet after it lost its atmosphere and most of its water *four billion years ago!*"

"Transportation?"

"Yes!" Sally grinned. "Through Time, Dimensions, Space—who knows what else? It's incredibly powerful, much more so than our DE-generators! We think that when triggered by our inserted DE-generator it will become self-powering, drawing on a *completely different* source of energy. Think of that, Ivanna—an entirely new form of energy: drawn from the *Fabric of Time itself!* Time-energy! It's incredible! It's fantastic!"

"But, assuming that's all true, how would you control it?" Ivanna gasped, frantically trying to keep track of and process these continued revelations.

"My scientists have probed its interior with x-rays, discovered many things, including how to trick it to generate a protective field and obey our commands. And now I'm ready to test it out!"

"To do *what?*" Ivanna gasped, horrified.

Sally tilted her head back and *roared* again at the top of her lungs: *"Haven't you been listening to me, Ivanna? I'm going to travel back in time two thousand years! I'll have sufficient power at my disposal to take control of the entire planet, impose my will upon it, dictate its future history, and save the present world from its impending fate!"*

"You're completely *insane!*"

"Insane or not," Sally said, narrowing her eyes in determination, "I'm going to command this Obelisk, triggered by Dark Energy, maintained and fueled by Time Energy, to take me to where I've got to go. We've put the supplies I'll need into the small compartment where we installed the DE-generator."

Then she again reverted to proclamation, shouting into the empty cavern: "*But to survive this journey in a form to accomplish my mission, I've calculated that I must do something that may not work, instead outright killing me!* But, for the sake of the Earth and its linked timelines and Dimensions, *I've got to take that risk!*"

"Don't do it!" Ivanna protested, fearful of what Sally might do to her Earth's most-revered religious Icon. "Please, dear, even if you're right you can't fight God! Why not just accept our Fate? Is it so awful to die? Everything has an ending, doesn't it? Throughout history, societies rise and fall. Can't we just be proud of the few good things we've achieved which *are* worthy—and place our trust in whatever lies beyond?"

Sally looked out over the empty, immense cavern.

"You're right," Sally nodded her bald head, "we *have* achieved a few good things. In fact, we *don't* deserve to be condemned as a species. *God is wrong!*"

She again set the gun at her feet, clutched both hands together tightly, and bowed her head as if praying.

"Sally...for, as you say, a practical-religious person—that's complete heresy!"

The bald lady lifted up her head and laughed bitterly.

"Sure is, huh? I guess those idiots that tried to burn me at the stake in the 12th Century were right after all, huh?"

Ivanna had no idea if that boast was true or a bizarre self-delusion. Either way, it just affirmed that Sally could not be trusted with the vast power apparently now at her disposal. Somehow, Ivanna had to find a way to stop this megalomaniac!

Ivanna had to get hold of that gun.

"And as to your observation that societies are replaced, of course that happens. But then something new takes its place, right?" Sally sharply responded, now no longer hysterical, but deadly serious.

"Well..."

"Wiping us out of the Universe isn't acceptable. If this rotten civilization is to fall, then something better must take its place," Sally coldly proclaimed, her eyes narrowing. "But humanity is *not* going to be wiped out, coming to a dead stop. *I won't allow it!*"

Ivanna's mouth hung open. She had no reply. This older, fiercer incarnation of Sally was both awesome and terrifying!

Sally yet again lifted up her arms above her head, bald head tilted up to the artificial sun above, cackling in glee!

This was Ivanna's chance.

She lunged forward, snatching up the gun from the floor in front of the throne, and then stepped back out of Sally's reach.

She aimed the gun at Sally.

It was obvious that the High Priestess meant every word that she'd said. She was either the bravest person in the world or totally gone off the deep end!

"Oh, nice move," Sally smiled, slowly lowering her arms and focusing her STARE upon Ivanna.

It was mesmerizing. Ivanna understood how this woman could become the Founder and High Priestess of a whole new religion. In one glance it was a VISUAL BLAST of total determination, total confidence, and total domination.

Ivanna knew that even mighty warriors and top Generals would wither under that stare. And she was no General.

"You...you..."

"Thank you for taking up my mantle," Sally nodded, her burning eyes still burrowing into Ivanna's soul. "Now you hold the Fate of mankind in your own hands. It's your choice to shoot me or not. It's your own 'morality' put to the test. It's your own personal 'Judgment Day.' If you think I must be stopped, then fire the gun. I won't resist or try to evade you. Do what you must!"

Sighing deeply, Ivanna shakily lowered the gun and set it back on the cold stone in front of the throne.

"I'm not a murderer."

"I thought not. It's nice to know you had the guts to try, though."

"Just...think about what you're doing, Sally. Or, don't *over*think it. Whatever... In my own experience I haven't known you for long.

But I have a deep respect for you and your struggles. I guess, in the end, I trust you more than I trust me."

"Thanks, Ivanna. That means a lot to me. If I can't get your explicit endorsement for my plan then that will have to suffice."

"So, can I go?"

"Sure, but first there's something I need to give you," Sally smiled in an incongruously friendly way as she reached behind the throne to pick up a *cracked leather shoulder bag.*

"What's this?"

"Take it with you," Sally said, handing the ancient bag to Ivanna.

"What's in it?"

"You'll know what to do with it when the time comes," Ivanna cryptically replied.

"But I told you that I can't..."

"This is my final mission, Ivanna. I know that now," Sally grimly stated. "Yes, it's a horrible thing I'm going to try to do to your world. I'm rocking a global civilization that owes so much to an executed itinerant Jewish preacher of the First Century. Should I succeed, no one will understand or even know what I've done. But *you* will know, at least for a while—that is, until a final, workable timeline resolves for your Dimension. Yet even that can be undone, Ivanna—if those who are obsessively guarding the timelines come after me. You must stop that from happening!"

Ivanna shrugged, totally confused. But she obediently slipped the bag's strap up over her shoulder. It was unexpectedly heavy.

"*Now go!*" Sally yelled, switching from her "reasonable" manner back to being a raving maniacal High Priestess. "*You must be off the surface of Mars before God's Wrath hits! Go!*"

Still bewildered and in shock, Ivanna clutched the shoulder bag tightly as Sally shoved her into the elevator and sent her descending the hundred feet to the bottom of the Obelisk.

Ivanna looked up at the lonely, bald figure standing on its top— that now appeared to be *gulping down* an entire bottle of pills!

What in the world was happening? Was the High Priestess a drug addict in addition to being an insane megalomaniac? If so, it might explain some of her paranoid delusions.

Then Sally dropped the empty pill bottle off the side of the Obelisk while pointing her black gun up at the ceiling and *firing off* a series of loud blasts!

The reverberating vibrations seemed to shake the Obelisk, *awakening* it!

Ivanna saw the insanely prancing figure above *kick* the white throne chair off the top of the structure to come *crashing* into the glass floor below, just missing the black hovercraft!

And then the High Priestess flopped down flat upon the top of the Obelisk.

"*Remember me!*" Sally shouted from the top of the Obelisk, her powerful voice *echoing* and *re-echoing* around the vast cavern...

—as the Tommy-android dropped his red-hair "doll" to lead the staggering Ivanna back onto the platform and get her seated. Ivanna idly noted that the young Sally was still fitfully snoring in her chair. Tommy abruptly sent the vehicle spinning around to hurtle back toward the tunnel leading back up to the surface...

—as Ivanna heard from behind her a bone-jarring "THRUMMING" starting to fill the cavern...

—and she looked back to see the entire red Obelisk *pulsating,* clad in a *shimmering blue energy field,* and slowly fading away...

—as thousands of white-robed Priestesses came flooding into the cavern waving their arms in panic and reverence, but still bizarrely totally silent...

—followed by hundreds of identical, perversely smiling Tommy-children...

—as the floating platform swept upward into the dark tunnel and Sally finally *woke up!*

Sitting swaying beside Ivanna, Sally snorted and then groggily stretched out her arms.

"Did I miss anything?" she said, blinking her big green eyes open, bathed in the gentle blue glow of the vehicle's force field.

But Ivanna did not answer.

She only looked out in a daze, tightly clutching the ancient leather shoulder bag, watching the hypnotically blinking red lights in the tunnel zip past.

She now knew *way too much!* And she was scared speechless.

Chapter 19

FAITH AND HOPE

Faith is "the substance of things hoped for
The evidence of things not seen"
While hope is of even grittier origin
Left for when one's fate is set
With no other option existing than surrender
Accepting an awful and terrible ending
Yet the soldiers insist on keeping on fighting
"Remember the Alamo!" they cry in defiance
The losing politician campaigning to the very last
And the weeping mother stoically stays the course
Standing behind a son condemned and sentenced
So that even in the worst of circumstances
With no miracle awaiting in the wings
Failure is still turned upon its head
And the Triumph of the Soul is assured
In a perverse imagination of Victory
Made manifest as substitute success
Is not mankind a curious creature?

The Luminary Chronicles, 19:67-72

Sally walked out of the front door of Jean's home and locked it securely behind her.

It'd be a while before she could return.

Lucky it was a chilly day. She felt comfortable walking up 12th Street in her full outfit: white pant suit covered by a light, white trench coat. Sally had the hood up over her head, hiding her bright red wig beneath. Her feet were clad in comfortable, white tennis shoes.

She'd left behind the gun she'd taken off the assassin at the restaurant, securely hiding it at the back of Jean's closet. Even though it looked exactly like her Keeper's energy-weapon, she knew it fired this world's standard metallic bullets. The weapon itself was probably non-metallic, but any bullets it contained were not—and might be detected at a security scan.

She'd be back for it when she could. It was part of her history now—but also her future! She didn't know exactly how, but she had a feeling that the "ordinary" bullet-firing black gun had a further critical role to play.

The rest of her key items remained in her shoulder bag, which had cleaned up surprisingly well considering it had been buried in dirt for the past fourteen years. Included inside was the energy-gun from her Dimension. She was sure it would not trigger any metal detectors—should the police use them at the funeral to screen attendees.

Sally was proud of her new "uniform." *This distinctive look will well serve my devotees into the far future*—she mused to herself.

"So...we're off to a funeral," she glumly observed as she trudged along the sidewalk leading up the long gentle slope toward Broadway.

Broadway was the main street of the small town of Sulphur, along which were lined-up small businesses and fast-food establishments.

Sally waited patiently for the crosswalk light to change from red to green. Several blocks on up 12th Street past Broadway she saw blockades set across the street. She'd have to get through them before reaching Jean's cherished little church building.

It was the local police.

They were out in full force, apparently to make sure that the "terrorist" faction so active in the last few days didn't attack this widely-known public event: the funeral of Jean King.

Well, hurray for them!

Let them just try and stop her!

Sally felt giddy from the initial flushing power of the booster pill she'd taken—and had to force her super-charged brain to calm down.

She was going to the funeral to make a point, not to cause a riot. So she had to be...*demure...*

She sighed to herself as the light turned green and she trudged on across Broadway.

Be "demure", Sally—she sternly directed herself. *You know perfectly well how to be the quiet little nun hovering in the background. Just put on that persona one last time!*

"Identification, please," an officer politely asked as she approached the first, outlying blockade.

"Hi, I'm a friend of Jean's, here for the funeral," Sally said as she smiled in a friendly way, trudging right up to the officer.

"Sure, but I'll have to see some personal identification before I can allow you to proceed," he insisted. "I need a driver's license, or a picture I.D.—that sort of thing."

"Oh, right!" Sally brightly smiled back at him from beneath her hood. "I've got that right here," she said as she reached into her shoulder bag, whipped out the black gun, and *fired it directly into his chest!*

She'd made sure before leaving the house that the now comfortably warm gun was set to its lowest power, only one star.

Since she was right up against him, the normal cloud of electricity was centered on his front shirt, not visible to anyone else around.

The officer slumped against her, unconscious, as she locked her arms around his waist and walked him quickly behind a large nearby bush. There she sat him down with his hands folded neatly in his lap.

"Sleep well, friend," she said, giving the man a friendly peck on his cheek.

Then she nonchalantly strolled onward to the second barricade a block further up. A large metal detector was in place, with a line of people patiently waiting to go through.

Several officers manned the barrier. Dozens of witnesses stood waiting to be let through. She couldn't just "zap" these people. She'd have to get through in a "normal" fashion.

A man and woman in front of Sally looked back at her and nodded sadly.

"It's so terrible, isn't it?" a skinny, tall woman in a long black dress said to Sally.

Sally dutifully stood in line as others fell in behind her.

"It is indeed," Sally nodded. "But a glorious reawakening awaits Jean, is that not true?"

"Oh, yes!" the woman hastily agreed. "She was such a fine Christian woman. She'll be caught up with Jesus at the Second Coming, for sure!"

"Are you members of this church?" Sally politely asked as they neared the magnetic arch as the line ahead slowly passed through it. "I'm a visiting relative from out of town, myself."

"Oh, no," the tall woman answered, holding onto the arm of her shorter, stockier husband. "This church is much too conservative for us. We wouldn't normally be in such a fundamentalist church. But Roy and I wanted to come pay our respects. Jean was such a lovely person. She helped in many civic activities in our town. And we wanted to show those awful terrorists that they can't keep us down!"

"Jean definitely wouldn't want you to be kept down," Sally agreed as she stepped up to the arch.

"Oh, officer, would you mind holding my cellphone for me?" Sally politely asked, smiling at him as she reached into her shoulder bag and handed it over to him. "It's the only thing I've got that's made out of metal."

"Thank you, Ma'am," he said as he waved her on through the detector with her bag on her shoulder. No alarm sounded. On the other side, he handed her back the cellphone, waving for her to move onward.

In the lobby, Sally signed the register with her real name: *Sally Smith*.

No one would notice her signature right now, because they weren't looking for her. They thought she was toast. In the unlikely event that her "compatriots" came, they'd likely attack with guns blazing. But history would recognize and honor her written signature on the attendee's list.

Gentle music was playing through the church's loudspeakers.

On a large screen at the front of the auditorium, pictures were cycling showing Jean as a baby, young girl, married lady—then with her own two babies, subsequent friends, and such-like.

Two TV cameras were set up unobtrusively in the rear corners of the auditorium, with crews busily filming everything.

A sign on each said that a live feed was going out to numerous stations around the country. Portions of the broadcast would be aired live on various newscasts. There was still a strong interest in the country and even world-at-general concerning the recent horrific terrorist attacks.

And up in the center of the isle near the podium—almost as an afterthought—was a simple casket. Standing at its side in professional attendance was a tall, thin funeral director. True to Catherine's phone message, it was a plain pinewood crate. It was rectangular, not fancy in any way. It was just a wooden container—a sealed box with a hinged lid holding the warming-up refrigerated corpse of a fine lady, whom Sally had killed with an inadvertent overdose of immune-balancing medication.

Sally was determined that this wrong must be addressed.

After all, how could she offer Optimmune to the general public if its first recipient dropped dead?

At the very least, I've got to give a lucid explanation in front of a global audience—she instructed herself.

She sat in stoic silence, still hooded, near the back of the crowded congregation, jammed next to a grey-haired lady who chatted incessantly, quietly commenting on each of the displayed pictures.

Then Cliff solemnly stood up at the podium.

Everyone fell silent.

"I welcome you here to this commemoration of a fine Christian woman," he began his speech.

He was white-haired, paunchy, and dressed in a subdued black suit. His normal relentlessly jovial expression was now professionally serious and sad.

He went on to explain why they were there, did a brief obituary reading, and introduced a song leader.

The lean, middle-aged man directed them to a song in the book in the pew in front of Sally. Then the audience lustily sang in unison. There was no piano or band up front. It was just the audience singing the well-known hymn in four-part harmony. As the auditorium was packed with people—most of them church-going people who knew the song well—the sound was glorious!

Sally was swept up in the harmonious grandeur and power of the old Christian hymn: "*God shall wipe away all tears.*" She remembered back when she, Dave, and Jean attended this very congregation and sang the beautiful hymns. It seemed years ago. Along her timeline it *was* years ago! But to these people it was mere days.

She heartily sang along with the audience, letting her soft alto join sweetly on the refrain:

"*When we reach that home and lay our burdens down,*
When we join the saints and wear a robe and crown,
When the pearly gates unfold for you and me,
When we see the Christ who set the captive free,
When we sweetly sing with all that ransomed throng,
No more partings come to mar that happy song."

And then Sally, together with the entire audience, loudly belted-out the chorus:

"*God shall wipe away all the tears from every eye,*
Give us joy for all our fears,
When we meet Him in that home beyond the sky,
God shall wipe away all tears."

Sally saw the communal Faith flowing around Jean's coffin as an affirmation of humanity: a continuing spiritual ritual quite familiar to her from her fourteen years spent in the convent back in the 12th Century.

It was a modern-day affirmation of the continuing power of *Hildegard von Bingen*'s stubborn persistence: to keep on going to the very last, no matter what terrible forces were arrayed against her. Yes, it was still a man up there leading singing and a man doing the preaching. Some traditions are hard to change. But Sally *would* change all of that...she had an undeniable Vision.

Still, the time-honored hymn, the group-sing, and the formal religious funeral were testament to a carefully articulate Plan. They bespoke a fundamental Continuance beyond just an endless procession of dead corpses being neatly tucked under the ground in succeeding cemeteries across many centuries.

Sally almost wavered in her conviction that God was in fact a remote, implacable Force—bent on the destruction of the human species.

But she'd seen it for herself, *several* times now!

The kind and personal God that these Christians worshipped and extolled was far different from the awful Reality looming out there in the Universe.

Sally knew what she had to do—even if it meant shaking the Faith of these sincere, nice people.

Cliff was up front delivering a short, impassioned sermon on the main scriptures in the Bible that talked of life after death. He emphasized the great rewards promised to those that followed the teachings of Jesus.

He made particular note of John 11:25, quoting in a loud and forceful voice: *"Jesus said to her, 'I am the resurrection and the life. Whoever believes in me, though he die, yet shall he live;'"* and John 5:40: *"For this is the will of my Father, that everyone who looks on the Son and believes in him should have eternal life, and I will raise him up on the last day;"* and Romans 8:11: *"If the Spirit of him who raised Jesus from the dead dwells in you, he who raised Christ Jesus from the dead will also give life to your mortal bodies through his Spirit who dwells in you;"* and I Thessalonians 4:15: *"For the Lord himself will descend from heaven with a cry of command, with the voice of an archangel, and with the sound of the trumpet of God. And the dead in Christ will rise first;"* and Romans 8:38-39: *"For I am sure that neither death nor life, nor angels nor rulers, nor things present nor things to come, nor powers, nor height nor depth, nor anything in all creation, will be able to separate us from the love of God in Christ Jesus our Lord."*

Cliff paused, relishing the hush in the crowd that his impassioned quoting from the Bible caused.

"...and so we commend the spirit of our dear, departed Jean King to..."

"Stop!" Sally yelled out, jumping to her feet.

Before anyone could intervene, she ran up the isle and pushed the startled Cliff off to the side, taking over the pulpit.

As individuals started to rise fearfully from their pews, Sally drew out her *black gun* and pointed it at the audience!

"Stay put and you won't be harmed!" she ordered them.

They froze in place.

Then, despite her red wig, she saw that many in the crowd recognized her. The camera crews—previously just dully going about their jobs—now jerked to attention: focusing their lenses upon her.

"Yes, I'm alive. And I am *not* a terrorist!" she loudly proclaimed, looking directly into one of the two still-transmitting cameras located off to each side in the back of the auditorium. "I have marvelous inventions that ruthless governments and institutions are trying to keep from reaching you, the people! You will hear more of those in coming days from friendly commercial entities. But for now I present to you a victim of a terrible disease—terminal metastasized breast cancer— who took a *new medication* I want to bring to you!"

Charging in the back door of the auditorium was a squad of local police...

—that Sally, aiming at them right above the coffin, fired a *sizzling cloud of electricity* into: enveloping both them and the coffin!

SPARKS leapt up off the plain wood of the casket, for a moment threatening to light it on fire.

Then the police slumped to the floor, unconscious, as the cameras safe off to the sides continued rolling, their previously-bored crews now at high alert!

—as a faint "*banging*" suddenly rang-out in the auditorium.

It grew even louder.

All eyes were drawn to the front-center of the auditorium.

The sound was coming from *inside* the plain wood coffin.

"Open it up!" Sally commanded the wide-eyed, terrified funeral director who'd shrunk over to the side of the auditorium.

Reluctantly, hands shaking, he walked to the latch, undid the lock, and lifted the lid...

—as a confused, grey-wigged lady suddenly *sat up* in the coffin!

"Where am I?" Jean King gasped, looking about in confusion.

"It's a *miracle!*" Cliff shouted, running over and throwing his arms around the resurrected Jean King.

"No, it's *not!*" Sally coldly stated, still holding her black gun aimed straight at the frozen-in-place audience. "It's *Science!* The Doctors will confirm that Jean King's terrible cancer is gone. She was so advanced in her disease that my new medication almost killed her. But her tissues slowly healed as her body lay in refrigeration. The new energy source I invented that's inside this gun jolted her awake. And the dramatic healing she experienced can also help or cure *you* with your *own* terrible diseases, illnesses, and injuries!"

And now, stepping carefully over the unconscious police slumped at the back of the auditorium, came what seemed to the audience members *an army of neatly-suited men and women*—marching up the isle to take defensive positions all around Sally!

"I invite you to join a *new* church!" she loudly continued, raising her voice above the barked orders now going on outside the church as hastily-called police swat-teams converged on the building. "Those that are already part of other religious institutions—such as this one— may continue those traditional pursuits, as long as they adhere to my new dictates. There's nothing to fear. My new science-based religious organization is called '*The Church of Perpetual Health.*' It doesn't just promise miracles, it *delivers* them!"

The audience members were riveted. Even Jean King was silent sitting up in her coffin, looking in bewilderment over at Sally.

"You will hear much more of this new Church in the days to come," Sally continued confidently. "But for now I'm going to turn myself over to the police to face their unwarranted charges."

Calmly placing her smoking black gun back in her shoulder bag, she handed it off to a stern-faced suited man to her side. Then she strode off the podium and out the front door—flanked by a couple dozen expensive, high-powered, *corporate lawyers!*

"Was that...Linda?" Jean said into the sudden silence, still sitting upright in her opened coffin, seeing Cliff slumped to the side. "Oh...it's a church service! I better go home and bake some cookies."

The entire auditorium erupted in a bedlam of panic, awe, fear, and confusion.

And all of it was broadcast live to the entire watching world.

The stream of red lights on the sides of the tunnel suddenly blinked-out as a huge CRASH lurched the zooming transport platform to the side and back again!

"What was that?" Ivanna gasped, grabbing Sally's hand.

Tommy looked startled as well, his head tipped to the side in the faint blue light as if he were receiving a broadcast update.

"God is *very* mad at us," he simply stated, shrugging his little shoulders innocently.

"What do you mean?" Ivanna began, but saw they were rapidly slowing to a stop.

The orderly station they'd departed from was now in chaos. The Priestesses that'd initially sent them off lay in heaps, crushed by rocks fallen from the ceiling. Others were running about in panic, trying desperately to maintain their vows of silence. Some failed, breaking into squeals of terror! A choking cloud of dust obscured everything.

Ivanna saw Sanako stepping hurriedly toward them out of the still-intact conduit leading to the spacecraft.

"Come on, come on!" she said, darting around a fallen column of supporting steel to grab their arms and drag them toward the trembling conduit. "It's begun! We've got to escape!"

"What about all these other women?" Ivanna gulped.

"We can't save them. I'm sorry. We have to go!"

Ivanna looked down at the serenely grinning Tommy at her knees and impulsively *snatched* him up in her arms, holding him closely!

"I said we can't save them!" Sanako yelled above a gathering *ROAR* coming out of the tunnel behind them.

"Maybe not—but I can save *this* one," Ivanna snapped at the oriental woman, keeping a firm hug on Tommy as Sanako tightly gripped Sally.

Ivanna felt light-headed and could hear the unmistakable sound of escaping air that was rushing out of rips in the fabric of the conduit.

They dived into the waiting portal of the spacecraft just as the conduit "snapped" behind them and *BELCHED* out its remaining air onto the frozen red surface of Mars.

Ivanna's legs crumpled under her and she sank to the floor, suddenly back in earth-equivalent gravity—also dragged down by the weight of the five year old boy.

Safely in the spacecraft, Sanako ordered the damaged link to be severed—the vehicle now slowly rising up off the surface of Mars.

"What happened?" Ivanna gasped from the floor, releasing Tommy. She coughed repeatedly from the dust she'd just breathed in.

"Look up," Sanako said, dread in her voice.

Ivanna turned her gaze to the front viewscreen.

Above them loomed a terrible sight.

The yellow-brown sky was filling with hurtling rocks—*flaming* as they streaked down out of space!

And behind all of that loomed a gigantic, falling *moon!*

It was clearly rotating, growing ever bigger as it fell toward them...

Ivanna, horrified, could make out many jagged craters on its surface—a rounded globe now *fragmented and split* in many places.

"It is Phobos!" Sanako gulped as their craft topped the high cliffs of Valles Marineris, trying to gain enough speed to evade the rapidly-falling moon!

"But how can that be?" Ivanna gasped in disbelief.

"Our instruments confirm that an unanticipated giant comet from outside the plane of the solar system just struck Phobos—sending the rain of debris that just now smashed into the colony site."

"But they're safe in there, right? They must be miles below the surface."

A large hurtling rock brushed against the craft, slinging it in loops. Inside the small spaceship the aspects stayed the same. But Ivanna now saw on the viewscreen the surface of Mars, clouds of descending flaming fragments, and Phobos—all seemingly wildly spinning around the craft!

"The Moon is descending right upon the colony. It will smash a gigantic crater into Mar's surface—killing all the habitats beneath the surface!"

"Right now? Right here?" Ivanna gasped. "That's statistically incredible, even impossible!"

"Believe it," Sanako groaned, clinging to one of the inset form-fitting chairs. "The plasma cloud is still coming to wipe the surface of Mars. But apparently that wasn't enough. Now everyone buried 'safely' inside are doomed as well."

"I told you we were all going to die!" Sally wailed. "And now it's happening!"

"No, we're not!" Ivanna insisted, reaching over to grab Sally's hand while simultaneously holding onto Tommy's little hand.

"*God* did it," Tommy smiled knowingly up at Ivanna, lying flat at her side as the craft was hit again and spun even faster. "We were *bad* little boys and girls. And now we gonna be *punished*. Wheeeeee!"

An ominous "crackling" was coming from the front console as the crew struggled to correct their spin but *failing!*

Ivanna saw the protective blue force field outside the craft flicker then cut off!

"I don't like attempting this in a planet's gravity-well," Sanako snarled, "since the results can be highly unpredictable. But if we can be precise enough, perhaps we can still stop what's coming. It's our last chance!"

She rapidly barked out orders...

—and the spacecraft *vanished* just as Phobos hurtled through the spot they'd been at a moment earlier and SMASHED into the surface of Mars.

The black van suddenly appeared on the green central stage of the cavernous General Assembly Room of the United Nations.

Gathered together along the sweep of the circularly positioned tables were representatives from all the nations of the world.

The audience sat in stunned silence as a "pop" of displaced air knocked them back in their seats.

"Please! You must listen to me!" Professor Volodymyr shouted out as loudly as he could into the vast chamber as he emerged shakily from the front of the van.

"Victor?" a grey-haired, chubby woman in a red dress gasped from the podium.

"Yes! Patricia! It is me!" Victor shouted as he ran over to the stairs leading up to the podium. "I bring amazing news of a marvelous new development in physics! The proof sits here on the stage with me! You just saw us teleport into this chamber! It will transform the world! I need to tell you all that..."

A rush of security guards tackled him to the green-carpeted floor.

"No! Please listen to me!" Volodymyr futilely shouted as he struggled against the strong guards.

The woman on the stage whispered intensely to a distinguished and dapper-looking dark-skinned man standing next to her.

"Release that man!" ordered the Secretary General of the United Nations. "Allow him to come up here."

Reluctantly, the guards lifted Victor back to his feet. Shaken up, slumped-over, the Professor stumbled before resolutely straightening his back. Then he strode firmly up the stairs.

The small spacecraft materialized on the opposite side of the central stage at the United Nations building to where the van sat, SMASHING into the floor, *crushed* by the momentum of its uncontrolled entrance!

Again the "pop" of displaced air knocked the audience back in their seats.

The second teleportation also cut short the careful explanation being methodically stated by a grim-faced Professor Volodymyr, who stood at the podium introducing Dr. David King. Dave had just been allowed to emerge from his hiding place in the back of the van to walk up onto the stage.

The second blast of displaced air also staggered Dave, causing him to drop the detached bloody, hairy arm he'd been carrying with him.

"They're stunned...this is the moment...it's now or never!" Sanako called back as she crawled through the wreckage of their vehicle. "I'll trigger their Device to destroy New York City. That will stop in its tracks their evil pursuit of Dark Energy generation. All you have to do is delay them, just for a few seconds!"

Ivanna groaned in agonizing pain, realizing that both her legs were broken—and looked over at Sally.

Sally was sitting up, dazed in the scrambled interior of the craft, but otherwise not obviously injured.

"*Here*, Sally!" Ivanna said, reaching into the shoulder bag to pull out a black gun and sling it over to her.

Sally weakly grasped the gun.

"I...can't!"

"You *have* to!" Ivanna groaned, wincing against the terrible pain in her crushed legs. "I can't move. It's up to you!"

Sally looked like she was going to cry—until, in the dim light of the wreckage, both she and Ivanna saw her wrist.

The Turtle Tattoo was *glowing!*

Sally's devastated expression changed into one of fierce determination. She gripped the gun tightly and crawled for a gap leading out of their wrecked spacecraft.

"Sally?" Dave gasped as he saw her crawl from the destroyed spacecraft and level a *gun* straight at his head!

All the security guards were lying on the ground, either stunned or disoriented. There was no one to stop Sally from, in the next few moments, killing him where he stood!

He remembered in dismay that she claimed to be a dead shot, from hunting and target-practice with Snake.

Where'd she come from? Why was she doing this?

But then he realized that she was aiming *past* him, at *an oriental woman* who was now trying to wrench open the warped back door of the crashed van.

The woman stopped, grinned lopsidedly, hit a control on a belt at her waist, and was instantly surrounded by a blue, shimmering sphere!

She yelled across the stage at Sally—"That energy-weapon doesn't work against..."

—as Sally squeezed the trigger, firing with deadly accuracy a *bullet!*

The woman's *shattered skull* burst apart in a spray of blood.

The gun dropped from Sally's hands, "thudding" into the floor. She just stood there, swaying back and forth, a blank look on her face.

Dave was momentarily frozen in place. Then he rushed forward to grab her in a tight hug, preventing her from collapsing.

"Oh, I'm sorry," he apologized, starting to draw back, remembering her aversion to being touched.

"I don't mind," she mumbled in his ear, drawing him closer.

As Sanako's lifeless body slumped down, leaving a smear of red on the back door of the van, the recovering United Nations guards surrounded the intruders, guns drawn and pointed.

Sally, David, and Victor held their hands up high.

They were captured, silenced. But the deed was done.

The Earth's attention was focused. And despite the High Priestess' best efforts with her fabulous new religion—routine accessing of concentrated Dark Energy was off to a racing start.

"We've failed," one of the severely-injured colleagues of Sanako muttered to Ivanna. The woman was struggling at a twisted but still-functioning control panel. "It's even worse than before."

"What do you mean?" Ivanna painfully gasped as she lay awaiting emergency personnel to arrive and cut her out of the wreckage.

"It's the *Day of Judgment,*" the woman gasped, her head lolling downward.

"What about it?" Ivanna said, reaching out to roughly shake the dying woman's blood-stained shoulder.

"It's..."

"What? *What?*"

"It's moved...to—just *ten years* in the future," the woman mumbled as she closed her eyes and died.

Ivanna was stunned.

"Wow! Fun times!" Tommy grinned, pinned to the floor beside Ivanna under tangled debris.

"How can you possibly be happy?" Ivanna whispered to the android, struggling to stay conscious against the terrible pain in her broken legs.

"I have Faith."

"You—a robot—have Faith?" Ivanna incredulously asked.

"Yes!"

"In...who, *what?*" Ivanna asked, hearing many people shouting and rushing around outside the crushed craft, knowing that any moment she'd be separated from Tommy.

"In my Mommy," he happily replied.

Ivanna settled back, her breathing steadier, somewhat comforted. Yes, that was the truth, wasn't it? The one thing that endures is the faith of a child for its parents.

Perhaps sometimes—despite all contrary experience—it's even merited.

Daniel Basil Lyle

Chapter 20

WHEN DEAD DOGS HOWL

Don't discount the unbelievable
Especially when the world is ending
For it is then that the incredible becomes common
And even your worst enemy may cuddle up for a kiss
As in the foxhole of mindless, bloody, cruel conflict
Atheists reach out to touch a supposedly nonexistent God
And even the most hardened lapse into confused prayers
As the "thuds" of falling bombs loosen inhibitions
And dead bodies bloat with gases like balloons
Rising up on the wind to float garishly away
And the living are left behind blearily pondering
Why at the very last they no longer feel hate
But a wry kinship with all others lost
To the whims of implacable Fate.

The Luminary Chronicles, 20:9-14

David sighed as he steered his yellow Cavalier along the streets of Edmond, Oklahoma.

It had been a long week—police charges to clear up, speeches to give at the United Nations, posting of his schematics and processes on the web so anyone could easily access them, and reuniting with Sally.

She sat slumped on the passenger side, fast asleep, leaning against the door.

Between them, leaning against Sally, also fast asleep—was Tommy.

Tommy was a complete surprise to Dave, but quickly accepted. According to Sally he was an orphan from the terrorist clan, who had "adopted" Sally as his new Mommy.

It was strange, but Sally liked having the little boy to care for, so what the heck?

He did say peculiar things, but then he'd been raised by a gang of terrorists, hadn't he?

Dave knew it didn't make any sense. But Sally was comforted by Tommy's presence. So he didn't question the boy's strange history.

Finally, then, after sorting everything out—Dave, Sally, and little Tommy flew back from New York to Oklahoma, now as worldwide celebrities, with reporters dogging their every step.

That was a pain. But as the world's attention feverishly focused on the new breakthrough technologies instead of the inventors— which included Dave, Victor, Sally, and the reclusive lawyered-up Linda Powers—Dave was finally getting some peace. Only three reporters met them at the Airport in Oklahoma City, with none going to the trouble of following them further.

Maybe things were finally settling down. Maybe this bizarre odyssey was coming to an end. Maybe he could not only get back to his old life, but to an even better one with the wackily cute "Girl with the Turtle Tattoo."

Now that was a pleasant idea.

Catching a cab to Edmond, Dave had there transferred his two charges to his Yellow Cavalier and was now driving straight for George's home. His own house, of course, was still in ruins.

Yes, a lot of destruction had occurred, a lot of sacrifice.

But having Sally and Tommy with him was wonderful!

The best thing, though, was the reunion of Victor with his beloved Ivanna. She was still in a hospital, recovering. But Ivanna's story of being captured by the *true* terrorist gang trying to hijack Sally—to acquire her evolved computer intelligences—was accepted by the world's media. Ivanna's credibility was helped greatly by Sally heroically thwarting the terrorists' final desperate attempt at the United Nations to blow up New York City.

The military was still suspicious—not to mention outraged—that the technology was now out of their grasp and available publically.

But they were on a short leash. They couldn't harm Ivanna, Sally, Victor, or Dave without being known as the perpetrators of the crime. And, indeed, there was no need for that since the new scientific information concerning the DE-generator and facilitating evolved computer intelligences was all out in the open.

A lot still had to be figured out, but the rough outline was now widely available to everyone: the means via a controlled cold fusion-like process to crack open *subspace* and—if exquisitely controlled by artificial intelligences—to access, in a carefully managed manner, *unlimited* energy!

Yes, they could now shout it to the heavens!

Dave was excited. It wasn't just the prospect of him receiving a Nobel Prize. It was the incredible results now in sight from easy access to unlimited energy. Most of the world's ills could be solved virtually overnight—plus building moon bases, Mars colonies, and Interstellar flight...all right around the corner.

The future looked bright.

But for now he was just happy to be back in Oklahoma with Sally and their newly-acquired kid.

Dave turned down the street leading to George's house. Professor Johnson lived in a fairly exclusive part of Edmond where large brick houses were set upon half-acre-sized, tree-shaded lots. Close to his home was an exclusive tennis club. What a great place to live. Dave had played tennis in high school and would love to live near a tennis club. Maybe now that he was a world-celebrity he'd get the chance. He'd already had to field off offers of writing a book, exclusive university appointments, and even a movie deal.

He'd need a good publicist and agent.

Dave recalled George often saying that his large house seemed empty since his kids were grown up and moved away. So when George insisted over the phone that Sally, Tommy, and Dave spend a night there after returning to Will Rogers World Airport in Oklahoma City, Dave didn't protest.

Insurance would soon rebuild Dave's burned-down small house, but that would take a while. Or, Dave might just put the money toward a better house—perhaps in George's exclusive tract? In the meantime, Dave was going to stay in a motel nearby. Sally wanted to get back to her mother the next day to introduce her to her new "grandson." Dave was going to drive Tommy and her there the next morning. Everyone wanted their lives to return to normal as quickly as possible.

"Hey, it's that famous Dr. David King!" George Johnson loudly called out as Dave pulled up, parking at the curbside.

George was a round-face, bald, jolly man wearing a blue-striped sweater over his chubby, short body.

George's attractive wife, Alice, was helping the wakening Sally and Tommy from the car, leading them away to a guest room inside the house.

"Somewhat *in*famous, I guess," Dave wryly accepted the compliment. He stretched his arms as he got out of the driver's side of the car. "I guess most people can't say that they almost destroyed the United Nations Building."

"Oh, don't be so modest. You're famous!" George laughed heartily. "They say you and your friends are shoo-ins for the next Nobel Prize in Physics—or several of them in different categories."

Dave sighed, shaking his head in disbelief. He still couldn't quite believe that they'd won...both the fight to publicize his discoveries and the coveted Nobel Prize.

"I don't know about that, George," he grinned modestly. "However, you've heard the 'official' media side of things, but not what *really* happened. It's more incredible than you could ever imagine. And I'm dying to tell you all about it!"

"Oh I'm sure it is, Dave—and I'm eager to hear it. But I warn you that it's going to take a lot to impress me. I've had my own fair share of adventures, some that might even surprise you. Hey, I've been taking care of your weird pets, right? That's quite an experience."

Dave laughed politely at George's cryptic words. But Dave knew nothing George could say could possibly trump what he and Victor had recently experienced.

They walked up to the front door of George's upper-class, expensive brick home. It had an immaculately-kept lawn and tall trees in its front yard, with a high fence containing an extensive back yard hidden behind the house.

"I doubt your adventures—or taking care of my exotic pets—will match what I've got to tell you," Dave said sincerely. "Be prepared for some mind-boggling stuff. But it's all totally confidential. If you start spreading this stuff around they're likely to throw you into the looney bin."

"Want to bet whose mind gets blown the most?"

"What?"

"A bet—say the winner buys the other a nice, cholesterol-rich, high-fat milkshake?"

Dave laughed, looking at his pudgy friend who was clearly expecting an excuse to pig-out at a fast-food place.

"Sure, why not? I love a good vanilla milkshake. You can get that for me at the local Braum's. They've got great shakes. Ain't nothing you can say or do that tops what I've got to tell you."

"Perhaps so, Dave—and I do want to hear *everything!*"

"So then," Dave grinned back at his old friend, "how are my critters doing, not too much trouble I hope? As soon as I get a new house built or purchased I want them back."

They were walking through the living room into George's back study where George had constructed attractive habitats from his large glass-fronted bookshelves to house Dave's reptile collection.

"Just fine, Dave. They're no trouble at all," he cheerfully replied. "I've really enjoying taking care of them, though Alice refused to come into my den to even see them. She's still scared of snakes, had a few run-ins with them in the past. See—an extra benefit for me having them here: a private den all to myself. Hah!"

Dave laughed, happy to be able to joke with his friend—relieved to finally not be under constant threat of capture, arrest, torture, or death.

"Hey, *there's* my Topper," Dave smiled, opening a large glass cabinet to stroke the back of his big green iguana.

Topper closed his eyes, arched his back, and preened with pleasure at Dave's fingers lightly stroking his back along the sides of his central spines.

"You've done a great job building these new cages and caring for my little zoo," Dave sincerely said, looking around at the brightly lit habitats. Each was complete with warm sand to dig in, branches to climb on, hot rocks to sit on, 'hidey' holes to crawl into, and wide dishes containing food and water. All of Dave's pets looked great—lizards, snakes, and tortoises alike.

"Thanks, Dave," George nodded his head in acknowledgement. "And oh—you've inspired me to get a *new* reptile of my *own*, Dave. Another good friend of mine asked me to look after him for a while. I want to show him to you."

"Sure, that'd be super. Your wife let you get a new pet? That's great."

They walked through a door in the back of the den into the high-fenced backyard...

—where Dave found himself looked straight into the big black eyes of a happily prancing small *dinosaur!*

"Is...is...that...?" Dave gasped.

"It sure is, Dave," George calmly replied.

Dave's mouth hung open in astonishment as he watched the spry green dinosaur scampering after a ball thrown by George.

It stood six feet tall, had a big chicken-like head with black eyes, and a long beak complete with sharp teeth. Its head was topped by a red tuft. In addition it had a long neck, two arms with three sharp-clawed fingers on each hand, and strong legs upon which it stalked. Its feet each had three long-clawed toes. Also it had a slender, swinging, reptilian tail.

"But...?"

"And I'm afraid that's not all my surprises for you, my friend," George's kindly voice came from behind him.

Dave turned to see George *morphing.*

George's head was elongating, teeth sharpening, his neck lengthening, his back splitting out of his clothes, sharp claws appearing on his hands, a long tail emerging from his rear, and three-toed feet bursting out of his shoes.

Transformed, George now stood a full *nine feet* tall!

He looked like a juvenile *Tyrannosaurus rex.*

Stunned, Dave just stared.

He had a sinking feeling in the depths of his guts. He wasn't returning to his old life. New, even more bizarre vistas were opening up before his eyes...

"I'm from another Dimension where the asteroid that here killed off the dinosaurs never hit Earth," T-rex George calmly stated, swinging his thick tail back and forth. "You can think of us as 'dinosapiens'—intelligent dinosaurs. You little rat-like things never had a chance to evolve into talking apes on my Earth. You guys got gobbled up. Instead, we upright dinosaurs with our dexterous free hands made that evolutionary leap."

George's voice was different. It was deeper, more of a growl. The Tyrannosaurus voice box apparently wasn't made for human speech.

"Uh...whu...but..." Dave dumbly gasped, staring unbelievingly.

"Now *this* gorgeous animal," George stated, stepping over to put a paw on the smaller dinosaur's neck, "—whose name is 'Breep'—is actually one of my long-extinct ancestors from millions of years ago. Sally brought her back from the past with her."

"Sally? But...?"

"Oh, not *your* Sally who is here with us in our house," George said, his deep voice now having a faint "hiss" to it. "I'm talking about the *other* Sally from the previous time-cycle."

"A *second* Sally...from a 'previous'...?"

"Oh, you know her as Linda Powers," George sighed. "But let's just cut to the chase, shall we?"

Dave was astounded and chastened. His own personal Universe was rapidly exploding larger and larger. It scared him but also provoked keen curiosity. Loose ends seemed to be falling neatly into place in his mind. Linda was really Sally, but from some other Dimension. No wonder they looked the same and had exactly the same fingerprints!

And if she truly had a 'pre-history' with him, then her bizarre behavior wasn't near as strange as it had seemed before.

Behind them, Dave heard the patio screen door slide open. Alice, Sally, and Tommy came walking out.

George's wife was also in the process of transforming into a talking, intelligent dinosaur. Sally seemed delighted with this amazing transformation. Tommy, though, seemed to take it all for granted, running over to play with Breep.

"Our timelines and Dimensions are inexorably linked," George sighed. He reached out a clawed hand to grasp his wife's similarly clawed hand. "As a direct result of your amazing new inventions, the world will be *totally destroyed* ten years from now. We've been mostly only observing your kind in our human-morphed forms for thousands of years. We'd hoped you'd eventually develop into a rational, mature species. Unfortunately, even with prodding from us and creatures from yet other nonhuman Dimensions—most recently through Sally's clever Turtle Tattoo—you've still failed to mature. It is most distressing to us, especially as we've developed quite a fondness for your world and species."

Dave again was stunned, his thoughts swirling: *Say what? How could that possibly be true? The Earth is going to be destroyed because of me? How? Why? What's going on here? I'd normally count all this up to a hallucination or bad dream---but George and Alice are standing...make that stomping...right here in front of me!*

"But that's not the worst of it," George sighed, looking up into the sky.

"There's something worse? Really?" Dave almost whimpered in shock and disbelief.

A dark shadow was passing in front of the sun, blocking the sunlight, and *growing bigger* by the second!

"What is that?" Sally now gasped, shielding her eyes to look up at the descending giant structure.

"Oh, *I* know, *I* know!" Tommy said, hopping up and down while pointing excitedly up into the sky.

George squatted on his powerful lizard legs, lifting up the boy so he could more easily peer into the sky. "Well, *tell* us, boy. What *is* it?"

"It's a Harvester."

"And how do you know that?"

"The Martians had history with them. They secretly told me a lot of stuff, putting it in my head when I was born."

"My, aren't you smart?"

"Yes, I am."

"Ok—go play with Breep now."

"Ok," he agreed, dropping down to run over to Breep and hug the small dinosaur around his long, slender neck.

Sally silently stumbled over to Dave and spontaneously hugged him tightly.

He welcomed her warm contact, but he was sad it was so little of what might have been, so late...

A spreading lump of icy fear was consuming his mind.

Speaking over her shoulder, Dave intensely asked George: "What the hell is a *'Harvester'?* And what's this about Martians?"

George sighed, slowly hugging Alice close to himself.

The two heavy set dinosaurs made an oddly endearing couple.

"The word has gone out across the Galaxy, Dave," he softly replied. "In all our linked Earth timelines and Dimensions—we're now ripe for salvage. Thousands of those vehicles are converging on your world, each the size of a major city. Their only purpose is to take what's useful from this planet before the End arrives. You and your civilization has been declared 'fair game.' And as to the Martians, it's too long of a story to start. Sadly, we don't have time."

Dave stood silent for a moment, still holding Sally close.

The grand exuberance and optimism he'd felt earlier was now completely dissipated, leaving only a dull ache.

"So...I guess I'm not going to get to buy you that milkshake?"

George's big, oblong dinosaur head shook sadly in the negative.

"It's going to be hell on Earth," George sighed, "unless..."

"Unless *what?*" Dave shouted at him, now totally disoriented and stunned at this horrible turn of events.

"Unless Sally can save us, yet again," George softly replied, sadly closing both of his big orange eyes.

Sally ducked her head deeper into his chest, clearly not wanting any more world-saving responsibilities.

"*Which* Sally?" Dave said, reaching over to grab him by a scaly shoulder.

"All three of them," George toothily grinned as if taking quiet satisfaction in the irony of his statement.

"*Three*...of...them?" Dave repeated, gaping in astonishment. "I thought there were only two of them!"

"Sally's quite a pervasive Presence," George laughed fondly.

Off in the distance, Dave heard a dog starting to bark.

One by one, the dogs in the neighborhood joined the first one—all in unison howling fiercely up at the rectangular metallic craft now filling the sky.

It wasn't the bark of excited dogs alerting their owners to a potential threat. Rather, it was a *howl of terror* from doomed prey right before being consumed by a relentless, cruel predator.

The canines knew they were as good as dead.

Even the little green dinosaur looked up, yelping a pitifully weak plaintive "*breeeep!*" as he scurried over to cower beneath George.

"There must be something *we* can do," Dave softly said, staring wide-eyed up at the sky as a *fleet* of small ships broke off from the sides of the hovering behemoth, headed downward.

"Pray!" Sally loudly replied, warmly nestled under Dave's arm. She buried her head in his chest, apparently trying to hide from the descending nightmare.

"But I don't believe in God," Dave peevishly whispered, feeling that since this was likely his last moments of life, he was reluctant to abandon his disbelief.

"Then hope for mercy," Sally softly replied. "Maybe the invaders will just kill us quickly."

He could feel her trembling. She was as scared as he.

George, his wife, Breep, and Tommy came over to tightly hug Dave and Sally as if in a final "goodbye"...

—as wide, immensely-powerful red LASER BEAMS began blasting down from the descending spaceships and *incinerating* the town of Edmond, Oklahoma!

Vast clouds of black smoke roiled up into the sky.

Looking away from the terrible sight, Dave noticed that Sally's Turtle Tattoo on her wrist was now glowing *bright green!*

—as with a loud "pop" the six of them, clustered tightly together, *vanished!*

God did not take kindly to people playing with Fate.

THE END

[continued in: *The Girl Who Tempted God*]

Thank you for reading!

Dear reader,

I hope you enjoyed **The Girl Who Played with Fate**. It was a bizarre roller-coaster of a ride to write, I'll tell you. As you saw, there are no limits when you question the established "wisdom." The sequel to this book, **The Girl Who Tempted God**, picks up with the Old Sally from Mars gone back in time to kill Jesus. And the Young Sally finds herself on the idyllic planet of the dinosapiens, under attack from the Harvesters. Meanwhile, Dave is leading a ragtag, doomed resistance against the aliens who have decimated Earth.

I hope you are intrigued by the sequel's painful question: "To save the world could you kill the one you love?" Wrapped within a gripping adventure story is the very meaning of transient, fleeting life.

Finally, I need to ask you for a favor. If you enjoyed this book and would like to encourage others to read it, **a review written by you** on the Amazon page for this book would be greatly helpful. It's hard to get reviews nowadays and your support can be very important to both me and other readers. If you'd like to do this, I sincerely thank you in advance for your time and effort. It can be as long or short as you wish.

Thanks again for reading my **Girl with the Turtle Tattoo** books and sitting next to me on this wild roller-coaster ride.

Sincerely,

Dan Lyle

About the Author:

Daniel Basil Lyle holds a Ph.D. in Biology, is a lifelong amateur herpetologist, taught medical immunology at a University, completed a career in cell biology research, lectures on how to apply theological and psychological principles in practical ways, and has a strong interest in all aspects of cosmology and physics. From a small kid he was fascinated with dinosaurs. As such, he has always lived with exotic creatures, including harmless snakes, all housed in his own homemade habitats. Some of his tame pet pythons and anacondas ranged up to twelve feet in length. He is the author of over thirty books, many of which are religious in nature. His writings go beyond the ordinary, exposing deeper aspects of life. His books are meant to be startling, conversational, and helpful. His various works are available at LylePublishing.com and Amazon.com. The "Girl with the Turtle Tattoo" science fiction series was inspired by paintings done by his mother, movies adapting Stieg Larsson's crime novels, and various men and women sporting spectacular body-art tattoos. He had a lot of fun writing this series and hopes that you, the reader, find his characters spontaneous, quirky, surprising, and even thought-provoking—as did he!

www.ingramcontent.com/pod-product-compliance
Lightning Source LLC
Chambersburg PA
CBHW070530260626
47161CB00002B/313